THE
ASSEMBLERS

ALSO BY SPEER MORGAN

Brother Enemy
Belle Star
Frog Gig and Other Stories

THE ASSEMBLERS

SPEER MORGAN

E. P. DUTTON | NEW YORK

Published in the United States by E. P. Dutton,
a division of New American Library, 2 Park Avenue, New York, N.Y. 10016.

Library of Congress Cataloging-in-Publication Data

Morgan, Speer, 1949–
    The assemblers.
    I. Title.
PS3563.087149A9 1986   813'.54   86-6353
ISBN: 0-525-24468-9

Published simultaneously in Canada by Fitzhenry & Whiteside Ltd., Toronto

COBE

DESIGNED BY EARL TIDWELL

10 9 8 7 6 5 4 3 2

To Betty Speer Morgan
and Charles Donald Morgan

THE
ASSEMBLERS

PROLOGUE _____

In early December, Jack Cady went out to the bottoms south of Highway 7 to do some hunting, and discovered that an impressive fence and gate had been strung across the access road. Jack had hunted the place for so long now that he was too old to stop, wire or no wire, but he'd never cut a property fence in his life, and wasn't about to start now. He drove all the way back around to the old Highway 176 entrance, which took him well over an hour.

Jack knew the history of the three thousand acres of swamp and white oak forest called the Trois Bottoms only from rumor and myth, much of it heard years ago from people like his Uncle Arn, a drunk who told as little of the truth as he could in his long and miserable life. The bottoms, it seemed, had been occupied by numerous Indian tribes, owned by a member of the French royalty, traveled across by Robert E. Lee, hid out in by Jesse James and Belle Starr, won and lost in card games by several different state governors, and studded by countless whiskey stills and houses of gaming and prostitution, all the locations of which had been forgotten, lost, swallowed up by the swamp. Simple facts like who, exactly, now owned the land his uncle was less clear about. In fact, from the time he was first taken out there to "hunt"— which at his raw-faced, bootless, gunless age meant to trail around after the men and waiting on them—Jack had never found out for sure who the real owner was.

He had three of his worst dogs with him tonight, one of them a mutt he would as soon have lost as kept, the sad result of somebody's attempt to get a good nose bred onto a collie-type dog. The other two, a treeing walker and a bluetick bitch, were both willful and had other problems. He'd already sold the bluetick to a doctor in Dubois, but was seriously considering asking him to take a better dog. The walker he couldn't see selling, unless somebody came through town from California looking for the best dog in the state.

The hunting wouldn't be much tonight, anyway; he could tell by the barometric pressure. Jack prided himself on being able to gauge the barometric pressure by the feel on his skin. When it was low like it was tonight, the coons were hard to get up.

He drove through the border of walnut trees down a muddy lane into the bottoms.

The stand of sycamore ahead was his old stomping grounds, where in the long-ago days he camped with his brothers and cousins and father under two big canvas tents that they'd haul out here in a mule wagon.

Jack stopped the truck near the old campfire place.

He wouldn't walk far tonight. If the dogs headed up the valley, as they usually did, he'd probably get up a fire and just listen. He'd been doing more listening and less walking in the past few years. A month ago he and Paul Weatherby had run some foxhounds over on the high end of the Trois. Until lately, Jack never had been that interested in foxhounds. They were strictly for sitting around a fire and listening— ideal dogs for drunks and old men.

Pulling up at the camp spot, he noticed that the low winter weeds were beat down around the graveyard. The stones there had been old, some as much as a hundred years, when he first camped here with his father and brothers. Some were just markers with no words on them; some had initials on them and nothing else. They were limestone and had weathered down, one with a barely visible finger pointing up in the direction that a child had headed After 2 Days.

The dogs were raising hell in the back of the truck and he let them out. The mutt, whose name was Slim for his collielike appearance, shot straight by him; Jack made a sound with his mouth like cocking a hammer. "Hey! Git back hyear!" The dog circled around and came back, butt sideways. In the fall when Jack had been trying to get Slim to work deer, he'd gotten so aggravated once that he'd peppered him. Getting shot was usually the privilege of bad bird dogs and setters, the ones who broke point and chased birds, but it had apparently done this hunting dog some good to get a few lead pellets in his rear end. Jack didn't think there was much hope for Slim as a coon dog, but he was giving him one last chance to show something tonight.

They circled and whined and cowered at him, begging to be let loose. Jack didn't like dogs heading out every time he opened the gate. It was one of his unique trademarks as a trainer. You could have asked some of the best trainers in the country if they taught dogs to hold, and they would have just laughed and said *hold* wasn't a word a hound dog could understand. And if told that a man down in Arkansas named Jack Cady had taught a good many of them that word, few would have believed it.

"Allrightyou, allrightyou! Gitacoon, gitacoon, nowyouready!" They quivered, and smelled the air with their noses up. "Hokay. now-youready! Smile, Slim! Smile at me, Slim! You hounds git ready, you Slim git ready! Now go!"

Again Slim took off alone, over the hill behind the graveyard, while the hounds stayed together with the walker in the lead. The walker wasn't a bad dog. His name was Preacher. But let him loose to run and you'd be bringing him home in the back of the truck two weeks later, after some farmer had called—and busted up so bad that he'd sleep for the next two weeks. Weatherby said Preacher was a sheep-killer, you could see it in his eyes. But that wasn't the dog's trouble. His trouble was that he was a stubborn, willful walker hound dog—just a nose on legs, and when that nose said go this way, he did. He was supposed to have treeing in his blood, but his sire hadn't been much good at it and neither was he. His sire had mellowed out into a respectable trailing dog, however, and Jack hoped that Preacher could do the same.

It was a cool December evening, not bitter. Jack built a fire.

When he was younger, he had regarded a fire on a coon hunt as bad luck. A fire meant there wasn't anything happening. Real coon hunting wasn't a sitting sport. But tonight he had come out only to make sure that he could still find access to the Trois, and to listen for some hidden talent in these dogs. Still, he laid his old single-shot .22 and a lantern on the tailgate of the truck, thinking that if they struck a good scent, he might follow them. With things arranged, he settled into his folding camp chair to drink coffee out of his thermos and listen.

Giant white sycamore trunks rose up beyond the light of his fire, leafless and silent. Most of these big trees had been here when he was a boy. He could see the rusted remains of a railroad spike that his father had driven into one of them for a clothes hanger.

They weren't doing much good. He heard a little hope now and then from Preacher, but it kept trailing off. The mutt hadn't made a noise for a long time when he finally piped up from the northeast, from what sounded like a good three miles. Jack was picturing where the dog was at, not really thinking too much about it, when he noticed his tone. He was on to something besides a coon. Jack set his coffee cup down on the tailgate and listened, beyond the rustling wind, across the distance, and heard something that he had heard before but couldn't place. Sounded like a blood scent, something bigger than a coon. A wounded deer, maybe.

Jack stood up and yawned, picking up the little rifle from the back of his truck. He pulled out the hammer assembly, and looked down the pitted barrel into the fire. Damn gun might shoot better if it had any rifling left. He listened for the hounds, but again it was the mutt who was calling.

He was on to something.

Sometime—forty years ago?—he had heard that bay, and somebody, maybe his Uncle Richard, had said, Them dogs is . . . what? It had to do with loose prisoners. Prisoners who'd gotten away from a county chain gang. A man scent . . . Them dogs is on a man scent. Ain't bloodhounds, he'd said, and they ain't been primed to it, but there's a kind of man scent that the best coon dog in the county will break to.

Jack looked into the fire and listened, again locating the dog in his mind's eye.

After about fifteen minutes, he noticed that the dog had gone silent. He kept expecting him to pipe up again, but he didn't. After another half hour, Jack was getting impatient. The dog had been awful hot on something to just shut down like that. Quitting a cold trail, they'd usually yap awhile. The hounds, who were probably six miles in another direction, were doing an honest job of work, but nothing to cause him to pick up his lantern and follow them.

After almost an hour of silence from the mutt, he called them up.

The hounds made it back, he gave them some cracklings and, for lack of anything else to do while the mutt took his sweet time, combed out their coats. Past midnight, he called again and still got no result, and so decided to go after the dog. He took a good draw from his half-pint of whiskey and slipped the bottle into his back pocket. As a young man, he'd drunk for pleasure; now he did it strictly for medicinal reasons. In the summer, this particular brand was a good insect repellent, as well.

He took off around the hills, having a good enough idea of how to reach the dog's general vicinity without following his exact trail. With both swamps and scrub hills, the Trois was tricky country. Jack never used the lantern; he could confirm landmarks without it—a swampy little pond that was usually full of cattails in the summer, a small Indian mound that he'd discovered as a boy and never told his father about, a burr oak tree ten feet in diameter his family had always used as one of the permanent landmarks. He didn't bother calling until he got to the power lines, close to where the dog had last been heard from. He stayed in one spot, beneath the humming wires of the giant transmission lines, calling the dog with his horn.

He didn't come.

Jack sat on a fallen tree and called a while longer. Now that he'd set up a calling spot, he didn't want to move around and confuse the dog. He waited, sipping at his medicine, listening to the sound of the wires high above him, an ominous hum dangling across the winter sky from the nuclear plant outside Traxon to the capital. With his old hunter's eye, he noticed something different about the shape of the hill just to the north, and grew curious enough about it to go over and take a look.

It was a road, bulldozed out and freshly graveled. From the directions it took, he guessed that it accessed from somewhere back on County Highway 7. It could have been a power-company road, but something told him it wasn't. For one thing, he hadn't seen any new power-company roads out here since the big lines had been constructed.

He decided to walk down it a ways. The dog wasn't showing anyway. The road was heavily rutted, apparently well traveled, and after several minutes of walking, he was within sight of Devil's Backbone, a sharp ridge that ran three or four miles along the river.

He was thinking again about his dog when he saw what appeared to be moving lights up ahead. At first he thought it was coming from a barge going by on the river. Devil's Backbone normally shielded lights coming off the river, but it could have been a trick caused by low clouds or fog. There was an exhaust odor over the surface of the road, as if a car had been along recently.

He went on down the road, and after a few more hundred yards it became clear that something was up ahead. When it finally came into view, it was no surprise—just a long trailer, with two peculiar things about it: The outside light by the front door fluctuated up and down in brightness, and the fence around it looked like a prison-yard fence, tall and with three sloping bands of barbwire. The gate was open, and a car was parked near the front door. Jack stood outside the fence looking at the trailer. He didn't walk through the gate until he saw the dog. He could see him clearly in the front-door light, apparently stretched out asleep in the brightening and dimming.

When he saw the dog had been shot, he knelt beside him. He looked over at the car, and at the front door. By the burns, it looked like somebody had shot him point-blank in the muzzle. But there was something besides the fluctuating light that was peculiar here. The hair on the dog's back was raised, and when he smoothed it down it raised again. The hair on the back of his hand raised. And without thinking about it he was looking up at the sky. It was the feeling to the air that comes with violent and very immediate thunderstorms—as if lightning was forming around him, about to strike. It was not just on his hand but across the whole right side of his face and body.

It was about as easy to scare Jack Cady as to scare an oak tree. He was too old, had lived by himself with his own mind too long, had walked alone through too many woods on too many winter nights to have any skittishness left in him; but there was something unsettling about this trailer sitting in the middle of nowhere with his dog lying in front of it stone dead. He got up and moved away from the front door. The little window halfway down the side was shedding light that varied in intensity like the light at the front. Staying back eight or ten feet from the wall, Jack walked down to take a look inside.

On a little pad of concrete beside the trailer a six- or eight-foot white aerial dish aimed toward the southern sky.

At the window, he moved closer and was again pushed back by the feeling of electricity. Through the window, he saw a roomful of what at first looked like big boxes; they appeared to be made of plastic or steel— machines of some kind, all in colors of dark gray, blue, and off-white. All around the room—on the floor, hanging from the ceiling, fastened to the walls—were wires, big thick bright-colored bundles of them. The trailer was unfinished inside. He did not at first think of the connection between the feeling of electricity at the front door, the fluctuating lights, and these bundles of wires. That was left to think about later.

Because what he saw now was a man sitting at a long table in the back of the room, at one of the boxes which looked like a television set, although from this angle Jack couldn't see a screen. He was reaching out with both hands, and leaning across the table. He was naked. It took a minute for Jack to see the stiff way he was sitting, his body shaking. His hands appeared to be locked onto the machine, his face blue and seemingly a light around his head.

And there was something else about him, something Jack couldn't believe.

Nearly forty years ago, working construction, Jack had seen a man get electrocuted—a young man who had struck a big input line with a wrench and gotten himself blown off a ladder and out of this world. Jack had never himself seen but had heard that with certain currents you could get stuck to the contact and held. That looked to be just exactly what he was seeing right now. He went back around to the front door and knelt down at the dog and looked at his nose. It had been deeply burned, not shot. He found a piece of guttering in a stack of discarded building materials, stood back a ways, and let it fall over toward the door.

There was a blue arc and a crack loud as a rifle shot.

Jack went around the trailer looking for an exterior breaker, but couldn't find one, and he turned and took out on what was to be one of the straightest walks he had ever taken across the Trois, back to the campground and his truck.

1

The kid was about seventeen, hair burned down to his scalp, sneering, and looking pretty out of it. He had a good opening line. "You can't be a cop, you're too good looking."

Sergeant Bobbi Reardon was looking at his driver's license. "William Sinclair Heyer, is that correct?"

"Look, I got points. I'll lose my license."

"You were going eighty-one miles an hour in a thirty-mile-an-hour zone, Mr. Heyer."

An outlandish shriek erupted from the back seat. Sergeant Reardon bent down and looked inside. A girl wearing short shorts and a maillot had sat up and was gazing at her with an astonished expression. Bobbi invited both of them out of the car.

The driver held the steering wheel tightly.

"Please step out."

For a moment it was a standoff. The girl's face looked strangely pale. Her expression—the whole mood of the car—was a step too tense for Bobbi. "Step out. Both of you, please." She tried to sound un-threatening.

"Look, officer," the driver said. "That's Taylor McNear, right? Mr. McNear called and said he wanted Taylor home. Do you know who he is?"

"I don't care who she is. I'm telling you to get out of the car."

The teenager looked at her oddly, shifting facial gears as another tactic dawned on him. "Look at all the badges. Like those little wings—what does that say—'revolver expert'? . . . Hey lady, I have to tell you something personal. Your makeup is running. It's smeared, like, down your cheek—your eye makeup."

Bobbi considered the teenager's face and his chemical hairstyle.

"Get out of the car, Clearasil."

"Clearasil! Hey, you're insulting me! You're like harassing and insulting me. I'm remembering every word you—"

"Get out. If I say it again, you're going to the can."

He eventually got out, but the girl stayed in the car. Bobbi shone the light inside and caught a glimpse of her eyes before she could shield them. The pupils were huge, and she was chewing in a clumsy, slack-jawed way.

Bobbi knelt into the front seat, reached over and grabbed her by as much hair as she could get, and stuck a finger into her mouth to clear out whatever was in it. Nothing much was there, but when Bobbi withdrew her finger the girl kept making the chewing motion. She appeared to be choking, and Reardon whacked her on the back to make her cough, and tried a second time to clear out her mouth. The girl's bite was automatic, a reaction from whatever primitive part of her brain was still functioning, and Bobbi didn't take it personally. She slapped her on the side of the head to get loose.

Looking behind, she carefully exited the car. "Okay, fella. Put your ass against the car and your feet flat on the ground. *Now*." She put the flashlight on his eyes; the pupils looked fairly normal. "What's this girl been taking?"

"Nothin."

"She's in very bad shape. I'm going to ask you one more time, what's she been taking?"

"Nothin!" he shouted desperately.

"Stay here until another officer comes. Keep your butt against this car, and don't move. If you aren't here—or if you mess with the officer who comes—I'll guarantee you a mad momma and daddy."

The hospital was five miles away, and she could see the girl was in trouble as soon as she'd gotten her into the front seat of the car. All transports were supposed to be put inside the rear-seat cage, but Bobbi wanted to keep an eye on her. She appeared to have taken a lot of something. She was cold. She sat hunched over, with her hands beginning to roam around, knocking the notepad onto the floor, poking against the dash.

"Where, where are, where . . . ?"

"Good for you, Taylor, just keep talking. We're in my car going to the doctor."

She took up the mike and called in, "Six . . ."

Parker responded immediately, "Unit Six."

"I've got a sick teenager, headed for Lakeside. Give them an alert for me. She's toxic on some kind of drug."

"Code 90, six," Parker said.

She punched the scrambler button. "Code 90."

"Couldn't you wait for rescue?"

"I could, but I'm not sure she could."

"Copy, six," Parker said, irritably. "Please give me your—"

"First Baptist Church," Bobbi overrode. "You better send a unit to Teele and Walker to investigate and possibly hold the driver of a black Mercedes sedan, Code 76, license Alexander Ray Kenneth Five, that's A-R-K 5. I told him to wait. It's the girl who was with him I'm taking to the hospital. Name Taylor McNear. Request you call her father. I believe he's Wayne McNear."

With the cherry on and the siren off, she hauled ass out Reservoir Road. The girl was making no motion or sound now, but there was a funny pressure to her silence.

Yeah, she knew who Taylor McNear was. All she needed was for the little bitch's heart to stop in her car. She lined up CPR techniques in her head—airways, breathing, cardiac. The one time she'd ever done a mouth-to-mouth job, it had been on a bum who'd gotten the bottom half of his body smashed in a truck-company parking lot.

The girl had gone very quiet.

From dark residential streets, they passed beneath the freeway, into the hills toward Lakeside. It was a new hospital, and a fairly good one, but it was three miles from the city limits. Her passenger's father had been instrumental in getting it built. Bobbi had read or heard that he'd recently been divorced.

"Doing okay, Taylor?"

She didn't answer.

At Palmer's Corner, which was lighted on both sides of the road, Bobbi looked over at her. Her shoulder and neck muscles appeared to have knotted up somehow, and she was lightly quivering.

A seizure maybe. Bobbi tried to keep her mind on her driving, but after a moment, as they crested the dark hill, she took the flashlight from the holster under the dash.

Turned in the seat so that she was squarely facing her, the girl shut her eyes at the light. Her neck muscles pulled up tightly and relaxed. The set of her mouth seemed different. The tightening of her neck, done again, was like a tired tic.

"You all right, honey?"

No answer.

Bobbi glanced from the highway back to her face, and said with exaggerated articulation, "Is your father home tonight?"

Her features—the thinness of her lips, the arch of her eyebrows over closed eyes, the very structure of her face—were different, a ghostly poise illuminated by the approaching mercury vapor lamps around the hospital. "My father's a martian," she said, with surprising clarity. Her voice was oddly low.

"What have you been taking tonight? It'll help these guys if you tell me."

"I haven't been taking, I've been giving," the girl said, in the same odd, low voice.

Bobbi glanced at her. "Yeah? What have you been giving?"

As they turned into the entrance, the eyes came open for an instant, pupils dilated into glossy black holes.

"You call it common sense, I call it forgetting the protocol, Sergeant Wiel. If you find somebody dying in the street, the hospital is a block away, and the ambulance service is five *miles* away, call the ambulance."

"It looked like an OD," Bobbi said wearily.

"If you thought it was necessary to transport, you should have called rescue, OD or not."

The phone rang and he snatched it up. While he talked on the phone, the chief unconsciously fingered the large, complicated brass sailboat on his desk. There were several sailboats in his office, all pictures or models of ones he'd sailed or owned. "Yes? . . . yes, yes . . . be *nice* to her, Ann. . . . Have you finished the paperwork on the Mitze accident. That's good. Please hold the calls for two minutes, I'm trying to deal with Sergeant Wiel."

Bobbi doubted that Chief Warnke was going to be barraged by telephone calls during the next two minutes.

He hung up and yawned broadly more or less in Bobbi's face. "You're widely known to be smart, Sergeant." He said "smart" as if it were a rotten walnut in his mouth. "Aren't you well known for your memory? I'm sure you can remember two words."

She was supposed to ask him what those two words were. He waited for her to do so, eyebrows a little raised.

She sighed. "Her pupils were so big you couldn't tell what color her eyes were, sir."

"*Call rescue*. Those are the two words, Sergeant Wiel." He put on an expression of tired wisdom. "I have to be concerned about policy. *You* have to be concerned about policy. We are a professional police force. We have rules of thumb, guidelines, and regulations. Calling rescue falls in the third category. It is a regulation, fixed and absolute. If officers began taking people to the hospital whenever their intuition told them to, it would only be a matter of time before difficulties arose having to do with defibrillation, oxygen, spinal cords. I believe you understand. Now I have already apologized to Wayne McNear about this, and he's being *very* nice about it. The girl survived the incident. He just wants to talk to you briefly."

She didn't answer. Once again, she was going to walk out of here with Warnke torquing her over nothing.

"I want you to see him sometime on your shift today. Make sure everything's okay with him. The paperwork on the Mitze accident is finished, too. You can just take it to him, in fact. Tell him to look it over, sign, and have it delivered back here."

Bobbi sat stiffly on the edge of her chair. "You want me to *apologize* to him?"

"I just told you I've already done that. I want you to make a follow-up call, informal but official. Drop by, ask him if everything's all right, is the daughter fully recovered, et cetera. I believe that girl has been a problem to him, and so be as low-key as possible—all teenagers make mistakes, that kind of thing." Warnke yawned again.

She tried to look reasonable. "Why?"

"He asked to see you, Wiel. I don't *know* exactly why."

"He can't come down here?" She tried to make this a cheerful suggestion, but it came out angrily.

Warnke didn't answer. He just turned his sailboat from north to east, his expression darkening. A quarter-turn of the boat was rumored to be a last warning, a half-turn suspension and pay loss or take-the-blue-suit-off time. Everyone on the force hated George's sailboats. This was Arkansas, not Florida.

She looked at the Lions Club plaque on the wall. It was clear that she'd said all she could. She had been on technical probation within the last twelve months because of work-absence during her separation from Ray, and another calldown would mean loss of rank and automatic suspension from the force for three months. There was no way she could afford it.

She paused, searching for a way to say it. "Would you mind calling me Bobbi *Reardon*, please?"

"Reardon? Is that your maiden name?"

"Yes, it is."

He frowned at his sailboat. "Is it legal yet?"

"Not quite. But I would prefer—"

"Tell me just as soon as it is," he said, as if making a concession. "Anything else, Sergeant?" He was through with her.

"The Ben Mitze thing."

"What about it?"

"You wanted me to take an affidavit to be signed."

"Ann does the typing, Sergeant Wiel. She has it."

In the shift sergeant's office she pitched the envelope Ann had given her onto her desk and sat down.

George had a special talent. He really did. Just a wonderful unbeatable talent.

Jim Daly was at the typewriter, pistol lying on the desk beside it. They had shared the same office for three years. They had just swung from the night to the day shift, and neither of them was used to it yet. Regularly changing shifts was one of the many things that Chief Warnke imposed on them, having read in one of his textbooks twenty years ago that it was preferable to fixed shifts.

"Big George after you?"

"What was the Mitze accident?"

". . . making an . . . unconventional . . . Why the hell do they call a crowbar an unconventional entry?"

"Ben Mitze," she repeated.

"He was the guy at the computer place who ate it."

"Who took the call?"

"R-e-s-p-o-n—"

"Come on, Jim, talk to me."

He looked up from his reports and took a shaky drag on his cigarette, smoking as if it gave him continuous discomfort, smoke curling up around his blinking eyes. "Third shift, week from last Friday. I don't know who handled it."

"Right. That's when I ran down these sweet teenagers. . . . Why is George so friendly with Wayne McNear?"

Jim made a little expulsion of smoke. "Are you kiddin? Who was the last businessman from Dubois, Arkansas, to get his company written up in *Time* magazine?"

She leaned forward in the chair over the desk and said, quietly, through a clenched jaw. "He wants me to go out to the man's office and apologize to him for taking his daughter to the hospital."

"Didn't the docs say she was clean?"

"The girl was in space, Jim. Her pupils were blown."

"Her daddy helped build the hospital. What can you do?"

Bobbi looked at him gloomily.

"He probably has money in DataForm."

"Who?"

"Chief. Everybody else in the county does."

Bobbi glanced down at the envelope. "Who'd you say handled the Mitze accident?"

Jim went back to his typewriter. "Don't know. Why don't you ask your good friend Detective Wiel."

She'd better find out. If McNear questioned her about the papers, she wanted to be able to refer him to the right person. She didn't want to display any further "incompetence."

Down in the dispatch area, she punched into the lobby and asked through the intercom to be let into the inner room. The door opened in a burst of perfume, and the girl who operated fire/ambulance came out. It was a wonder her scent didn't set off the smoke alarm.

Bobbi stuck her head in the door. "Parker. Been gettin any?"

Parker sat there, earphones encircling his long baldish head as if they grew there, his natural ears. He was tall, with sleepy eyes, and had a fine broadcast voice. He responded to her question by raising his eyebrows.

"The Mitze accident, week last Friday—"

"If you want to gossip, Sergeant, you'll have to wait until fifteen hundred hours. I *am* busy."

She looked at the wall clock. "Mind if I just look at last week's printout?"

He smiled sourly. "If you mean the radio log, I don't have the document in my possession, Sergeant. I'm sure Lieutenant Nash has a copy of the station log in his office."

She smiled back at him. "I'd rather look at yours. Would you mind calling it up for me on your computer?"

Parker sighed, turned to a VDT, and brought it up. The report scrolled in green letters up the screen.

The Ben Mitze accident was number two on the third shift of that Friday night. English had been the sergeant in charge. Then Miller, the detective. Cause of death, electrocution. The location of the accident had been left blank. "Where'd it happen?"

"What's that, Sergeant?"

"The DataForm accident. The location isn't shown there."

"There are mysteries which even I can't solve. Why don't you ask Lieutenant Nash?"

"I thought you were in charge of these reports, Parker."

"The shift operator on duty is in charge of the radio log, which is raw and undetailed, as you well know, being a major contributor to it. My office as communications sergeant does *not* include authority over the station log. You will recall that that is the responsibility of Lieutenant Nash. And how Lieutenant Nash finds meaning in the mass of illiteracy, inaccuracy, and indetail that pours out of these reports I will never know. Can I help you with anything else?"

"Goodness gracious, aren't you helpful today. Thanks a lot."

She went back to the office to get her study ready for the day. She'd finished all her reports the night before, thank heavens. With a cigarette still smoldering in his butt-filled ashtray, Jim continued to labor over his, gazing with bloodshot eyes at his typewriter. "My mind's gone blank," he muttered. "What do you call wetbacks?"

"Unlawful aliens."

He typed three strokes, cursed, and painted on some correcting fluid.

She threw a dog-eared copy of the city statutes into her small suitcase, along with an extra mace, a paperback book called *The Warriors of Tarantia*, and a couple of tampons.

Frick suddenly appeared in the office, picked up one of the tampons, held it up to his nose, and stared at it crosseyed. "Whatzit?"

"Every patrolman has to carry one," she said drily, snatching it back.

"Duh."

"Frick, I'm not in the mood."

"Sergeant get in trouble with Chief?"

"Out or I'll give you a three-day vacation. I mean it. And you guys keep it straight today. Parker's the one on the rag."

She snapped the suitcase together and looked at herself in a small cracked mirror that she kept in an empty bottom drawer of the desk.

Your makeup is running. That rich brat.

2

DataForm was located on the western side of town, about a quarter-mile off the freeway—a shapeless, low building with a hodgepodge of additions. A small sign out front said DF, nothing else. There were TV cameras above the entrances. The receptionist had apparently expected her, and called a security guard to take her to McNear's office, which was toward the back of the building down narrow, windowless corridors armed with smoke detectors and more cameras. There was a silver Christmas tree in the coffee lounge with uniform red balls on it. The place was busy. McNear's secretary had brilliant green eyes and not a particularly friendly expression. Bobbi got the feeling the lady was sizing her up. She went into McNear's office for a moment, then ushered Bobbi in.

McNear's desk was old and scarred up and looked like something from a garage sale, a pencil cup sitting on it, along with a two-drawer paper tray and a stack of big books the size of atlases or accounting books. What looked like a framed check was on the wall—perhaps his company's first income. On a small metal table on wheels beside the desk rested a dirty video display unit with a hole melted in its plastic cover and the name Courier hanging on a busted piece of chrome down its side.

Wayne McNear sat working at the lighted screen, looking elegant in his humble office. She'd seen his picture in the newspaper several times and so wasn't surprised by his perfectly white hair. Behind him, on the wall, was a white marker board with a green liquid-crayon drawing that looked like a child's quick drawing of a spider, little boxes at the ends of the legs with letters inside them.

Introducing herself, she put the officialness on thick, hoping to end the visit shortly.

"Would you like some coffee?" he asked, picking up a mug on his desk.

"No, thank you."

His secretary poked her head into the door. "Got another call from your reporter friend in Chicago."

"Tell him to take a vacation."

He looked preoccupied—his gray eyes very still—holding the cup but not drinking. For a moment he seemed to forget Bobbi was there. Then he smiled personally at her. "Thanks for coming."

"No problem."

"Do you have children?"

She hesitated. "Why do you ask?"

He put down his cup and sighed. "Can you tell me what happened that night?"

"The car was going eighty-one miles an hour down Teele Street. When I stopped them they were acting looped, so I asked them out of the car. William Sinclair Heyer was driving."

"Yes. Sinc works here."

"Oh?"

"He's the son of one of our executives."

"Your daughter was in the back seat and refused to get out. She seemed to be choking. I scraped out her mouth and took her to the hospital."

"I heard she bit you."

"No big deal."

He looked at her hand and shook his head. "Any idea why she was in shock?"

"I thought drugs were involved. But she may have just been scared by the driving. Teele Street isn't a very good place to go eighty."

"The doctor said there weren't any drugs. Did she give any hint—?"

She considered telling him what the girl had said about "giving," but the light on his phone started blinking, and she decided to take advantage of it and leave. "I'm glad your daughter's better. The chief wanted me to drop this by. It's an affidavit regarding Mr. Mitze's accident. After you've signed it, please have it delivered back to the station."

He ignored both the blinking light and the envelope, which she placed on the edge of his desk. "You're a sergeant. What does that mean exactly? I don't know about police ranking."

She looked at him a moment. "It means I'm in charge of a squad."

"How long did it take you to become a sergeant?"

"Several years."

"I know that by taking Taylor to the hospital you broke the rules, and I'm grateful to you. I really just wanted to personally thank you."

"That's not necessary."

His secretary appeared in his door. "In case you're interested, the blinking light is from little me. You're getting a lot of calls. Are you in?"

"Buffer, Marilyn." His voice was soft.

She left, and McNear said, "There was a more important thing I wanted to talk with you about. I'm sure you need to get back to work, so I'll make it brief. We're planning to configure a new building security system at DataForm. I wanted to ask you if you might think about going to work for us—perhaps on a trial basis at first, retaining your other job and working here part-time. Mr. English has been working for us several months, and he's been very good. The job will involve some travel, and it will require going to security school in California. Compared with other kinds of police or security work, it'll be well paid, and there will be stock options."

She hesitated for a moment, not knowing what to say, then smiled as if saying no. "I appreciate the offer."

"It's a serious one. Perhaps you can give me a call, say by next week, to find out further details."

3

Outlaw had one of his wallbangers on New Year's Eve. It was supposed to be another arson party, which he'd already had a couple of during the last year. Outlaw lived ten miles outside town in a house that had been a mansion a hundred years ago but now was a white-trash junkheap not much longer for the world. It was a two-story ramshackle place surrounded by scraggly, broken-limbed soft maple trees, sheds, one burned-down barn, and another that was destined to be burned during this party. Bobbi came by herself, feeling excited and worried about the job offer—and a little lonely for having no date on New Year's Eve. Richard had gone with his new girlfriend Cathy to the New Year's Eve special at the drive-in.

Ray should be out here tonight. According to gossip, he'd been bunking with Outlaw. Ray had decided to block the divorce and had hired a bona fide rat for a lawyer, who'd been threatening she would "lose custody" of Richard if she pressed it. Ray had gotten strangely possessive, if it could be called that, during their separation.

She half hoped to catch him here tonight with some little honey. The prospect offered bitter pleasure. A little honey about whom Ray had become less than discreet had been the last straw, the thing that made up her mind about Ray Wiel. Known all over town to have been making a fool of himself chasing this girl, half his age, he'd now somehow gotten it into his mind that his wife must remain his wife simply because he wanted it that way, because he declared it. Or perhaps it was because he finally intended to run for sheriff—for years his secret ambition—and didn't think he could afford two divorces on his record. Whatever the reason, he was paying out a good deal of money to try to prevent it.

Ray was a lieutenant in investigation, locally famous for solving a clueless murder ten years ago. Not to take anything away from his powers as a detective, but he had gotten more mileage out of that case than George Washington got for chopping down the cherry tree. Like most detectives, Ray was very unlike the noble, principled loners in books and movies. He was about as noble as a cur dog, she thought, and as principled as a rubber machine in a filling station.

She sat for a moment longer in her car, searching for his Buick, revving up her emotions for when she saw him.

It was a pretty big crowd. Dim lights and harsh robotic rock and roll cast out across the cars parked on the hillside; she opened the window, lit a cigarette, and suddenly considered not going inside the old house. At least Martha should be here.

Two rookie community-service cops were leaning against a fender smoking dope, and she gave them the requisite dirty look as she tottered by on high heels. Somebody lay in the front swing, apparently passed out. In the dogtrot, the sight of Frick dancing with himself was her first treat. Frick was handsome in an uninspiring way, and he wasn't dumb, but he had a litle tinge of craziness that made him act dumb. He was a decent recipe with some incredibly bad spice added to him. He'd been through one wife, and was working hard on a second one.

"Bob!" he said, doing the limbo toward her.

"Don't aim that thing at me. I just got here."

His face was stiff with booze. "You loogood tonight, Bob. Goddamn you loogood. Happy New Year."

He danced up against her, smiling thickly.

"You've got some work to do on that line, John."

"Mean. Oh, *meeaan*."

She went around him into the living room, which felt damp and big and hollow despite a good fire in the wood stove. Somebody had set up a rotating light filter that shot different colors up the wall across a ceiling cracked and darkened by years of wood smoke, lath showing through ragged holes in the plaster. Outlaw had been building a fancy log house across the pasture for the last ten years, and he was supposed to tear this place down when he finished it, although at the present rate of construction the old house would fall down before the new one was finished.

There was a pause in the noise as a record was being changed.

"Bobbi!"

"Hey Segeant Bobbi honey sweetie pie! Happy New Year! How's life at the trailer park?"

"Looky there, Bobbi's wearing her catch-me, fuck-me shoes. Watch out for the floors with those spike heels, or you'll twist one of them pretty ankles." This advice came from George Bowser. George was no longer a cop but he still hung around with the boys when he was in town. "Little George," his fellow cops used to call him (although he was six feet tall), to distinguish him from "Big George" Warnke (five foot seven), the chief. Little George had lost his job on the force three years ago because of a drug conviction that automatically resulted in firing. George had applied all of his contacts, including Ray Wiel, to get the charge reduced to a misdemeanor, and had ended up spending only a couple of months in the county jail.

George sometimes ran with Ray, and one of the greatest pleasures of being separated from Ray was not having to see him. After getting out of the can, Little George had gone off to Central America a couple of times to be a mercenary. Lately, she'd heard through the grapevine that he'd been living out here with Outlaw and Ray. The three of them deserved each other.

"Put on Elvis, goddamnit!" someone yelled.

Bobbi contemplated the damage to the troops. "Who brought the make-out light? Daly get that out of the closet?"

"Haven't seen Daly," Outlaw said. He was sitting in a corner, in a ratty armchair, placidly drunk, the woman in his lap wearing a dress that looked like a jungle suit in a Tarzan movie. She was in her mid-twenties. Outlaw preferred older women than his buddy Ray did.

"I need Elvis!"

There were murmurs of agreement.

"You people are great tonight," Bobbi said.

There were more sniggers and chortles, and Bobbi gave Mr. Bowser an unfriendly look. "When'd you get in town, George?"

"Me? I'm in town all the time."

Bobbi didn't want to deal with these characters, so she tried to find out where Martha Daly was. She had trouble hearing through the music that came on—synthesizers, zombies singing about communications. No Elvis. Someone wanted to dance with her, but she headed to the kitchen for a drink—out a door, across an unheated dogtrot, through another door.

This house would have taken some salesmanship to rent to a family of rats with its sagging, wood-smoke-smeared rooms and torn linoleum floors. An old refrigerator with coils on top stood beside a newer one in the kitchen. Someone was on his knees with his head stuck into the old one, digging inside it. Fifteen or twenty people were standing around, many with their mouths glued sideways on their faces. Someone was opening a can with a giant beer opener (For When You've Lost Your Leverage on its handle). This party might be a little too far along for her tonight. She should have gotten here earlier, or not come at all.

A couple was kissing wildly in a corner, the man's hand doing some serious roaming on the woman's backside, her silky-looking dress riding up, down, and all around.

With a pint of whiskey she'd brought in her purse, Bobbi poured a double to try to knock the stuffiness out of herself.

"Is that you in the refrigerator, Ken?"

No response.

"Ken?"

Ken Merril finally turned around and gazed at her with red eyes. "This frigerator is so full of alcoholic beverages, can't find the goddamn ice."

"Well, the ice wouldn't be in there, would it?" She opened the freezer on the newer refrigerator and found a sackful. "Here you go, Ken." She dropped some into his plastic cup.

He sat back on his heels and took a drink. "Thanky, Bob. You're an angel."

"Nicest thing anybody's said to me yet tonight."

"Let's go out to my car."

She sighed and shook her head.

"Hey! Bob. Lissen. Where'd we go wrong?"

"I don't remember us ever goin anywhere, Ken."

He frowned, trying to remember. "Yeah, guess you're right. We never did. Hey lissen, Bob, Happy New Year, no shit."

There was a big lighted aquarium on a table against the wall inhabited by one brilliant tropical fish and several bass, perch, and a sucker. Someone was dipping around in it with a skimmer net. It was Clinton, a drinking buddy of some of her squad members. "What the hell are you doing, Clinton?"

He glanced around, staggering. "Fish!" he shouted. He appeared to be seriously trying to catch one of them.

"He's gonna show me how to fill-ay," said a woman with a smug little pretty face and a voice that sounded like she had applesauce in her mouth.

"Well, you ought to take him home, honey, and let him work on your own fish," Bobbi said. "That one doesn't belong to him."

She pouted at Bobbi.

"Damnit, Clinton, that's a pet."

He stopped for a moment to gaze at her with his head lowered, like a stalled cow. He was completely wasted.

"Fish!"

He lifted the perch out and dropped it onto the kitchen floor. Outlaw showed up from across the dogtrot just in time to catch him crawling around sticking the floor with a knife, trying to spear the flopping thing. Outlaw looked dangerously sober all of a sudden. *"Put that knife down, sombitch."*

The room lulled quiet. Clinton looked up from all fours—the babyish, snide mouth capped with a thin little mustache—then he raised the knife and stabbed the fish square through the gills. Outlaw's kick put him against the wall, eyes bulging out like beach balls. Outlaw unspeared his poor fish, put it back into the aquarium, and watched it hang there in a thin unraveling of blood. A cloud of anger gathered like something visible around his head. He waded toward Clinton with the knife in hand and kicked him a second time in the area of the liver.

Clinton's girlfriend started going off like a yelper siren, and a couple of guys grabbed Outlaw to hold him back. He didn't like that, and they scuffled.

"Call the police!" the girlfriend screamed. Bobbi decided to get elsewhere as quickly as possible.

She headed for the upstairs bathroom. The second floor of the house was worse than downstairs—dust and the fumes of age and decay rising through the floor.

On her way out of the bathroom, she noticed a bedroom door hanging a little open. Through the crack she saw, on a table by the window, what looked like a radio—a large and very capable CB of some kind.

She descended the stairs, wondering what was going on. She'd heard Ray had been more than usually absent lately from the station, and there was scuttlebutt going around that he was on a special assignment. A drug bust? Ray avoided drug assignments even more assiduously than most cops.

She went downstairs to the living room, which had suddenly emptied of people.

She couldn't get into this party. Martha and Jim seemed to have gone home early. Jim was usually the last one at the bar.

She thought about going back to the trailer, bundling herself up, pouring a good drink, and watching the Royal Canadians and Times Square at midnight. She should have known better than to come to another party at Outlaw's. The record had run out, leaving the place silent except for the shouting match coming from across the dogtrot. Some of the party had gone over to enjoy the fight and others had gone outside to set the old barn on fire.

The make-out light walked colors silently across the wall and ceiling, reminding her of a striptease-for-women bar she'd once gone to in Dallas. The tan young guy swiveling his hips around on the stage had possessed a wanger so long that it fascinated her—a floppy, rolling sausage that caused some poor woman in the bar to shout repeatedly, "I can't stand it, Lord, I can't stand it." Over the last year, whenever thinking about moving to a city (even Little Rock) to get away from the end of her marriage, for some reason she always remembered that boy's wanger threatening, elusive, half silly—and once again she would decide not to move, at least for the time being.

The problem around here was Ray. No matter what happened, he would never leave this county. That was a certainty. And so long as she stayed around as well, he'd bug her to death. His lawyer, a little rat-faced crook named Marty Williams, had been instructed to stop the divorce any way he could. Her own lawyer was a highly respected, older local man who she'd thought would do a solid job. But he'd been acting very uneasy about Ray's lawyer's hints of a "morals and fitness" case against her. Marty Williams's suggestion that he was going to take away her son because of her "morals" was so off the wall that at first Bobbi hadn't taken him seriously. Ray, after all, had been the one doing the two-timing.

Bobbi had finally personally called Williams, against the strict advice of her lawyer, and told him as much. He had said, "Look, lady, you're not my client, Ray's my client. I'm just the scumbag shuffling the papers. But let me tell you something. Usually I'm trying to do bad things to people like you. You, I'm trying to do a favor. Ray's a good man. Talk to him."

Guys in uniform appeared at the door, and Neil English was among them, looking spiffy. "Happy New Year, Neil. Join the party."

"What happened?" English asked.

"Clinton murdered one of Outlaw's aquarium fish."

English didn't see the humor in it.

"Well, I didn't do it, Neil. I tried to stop him."

"Where are they?"

"It's all over with. They're all out back now getting ready to burn down the barn. Say, I've been trying to get hold of you."

Neil seemed even more grim than usual tonight, but Bobbi managed to talk him into going with her to a cluttered back porch, which was cold due to a many-paned window facing the barn.

She told him, briefly, about McNear's job offer.

"He made it to you directly?"

"Is that unusual?"

"I just wondered if you'd met the head of security."

"No. What kind of guy is he?"

"Uneducated. Very tough. Hard to deal with."

"Reed?"

"That's right. Ron Reed. He's from Oklahoma. An Indian. Served time in jail."

"So how have you managed to put up with him?"

"I hardly ever see him. It's just a weekend job, Bobbi. I've been averaging eight, ten hours."

"Do they have problems with turnover?"

"They rent cops from Little Rock, so it's pretty transient. They don't have a system. Reed doesn't do much except go around and threaten people now and then. I don't know why they keep him on."

"The accident they had out there—"

English started feeling around on his jangling belt. "I better check this fight out."

"It's all over, Neil. Everybody's in the back yard."

Fires were being set around the barn. Bobbi couldn't quite see Neil's expression in the flickering light, but his stiffness was as obvious as the well-oiled smell of his belt leather and boots.

"Was there some problem with the Mitze accident?"

Neil snapped his walkie-talkie out of its holster and made an arrival call-in. "Look, we'll have to do this later, Bobbi. I better go make sure the white folks aren't breaking the antiques." Neil delivered this line unamusingly.

"Are you going to McNear's talk?"

"The Kiwanis Club thing? Yeah, I'm supposed to go. Listen, Bob, if you want to know my overall opinion of the place, it's not too positive. Happy New Year," he said flatly, and disappeared back into the house.

She stayed on the porch awhile, thinking. She didn't know Neil English well, but they were in a category together, both having been promoted fairly early—according to the departmental gossip, because Warnke "needed niggers and women" to get federal funds. Others felt that her promotion had been entirely because of Ray. It didn't seem to occur to anyone that either of their promotions had had anything to do with competence. The police department, though, was Ray's turf. It was his world, no matter how poorly he got along with Chief Warnke. That was the reason why this offer from McNear, small though it was, interested her so much. She was looking for doors.

Arsonists were milling around the barn. The idea of the party was that everybody got to help with the crime, and Bobbi did see a growing number of fires around the dark structure. Outlaw could have had the barn taken down and hauled away by somebody who wanted the oak, but he naturally preferred the dramatic gesture. She didn't quite feel up to going outside and joining the fun. Where was Ray? she wondered again. This was just his kind of get-together. . . .

It was close to midnight. Staring out the dusty paned window at the fire, she swallowed a belt of whiskey and thought about him.

She thought about how she'd fallen for him when she was twenty-six and getting tired fast of being a single mother and a secretary in the water and light department. She'd previously been married very briefly in what amounted to a shotgun wedding, which she had escaped before Richard's first birthday.

For seven years, then, she'd tried to take care of her family. Her father died soon after Richard came along, and she became the natural one to move back in and help her ailing mother, since all of her sisters had moved away with their own families. She went to college, a tiresome business of commuting and taking only a few courses at a time, working at Dubois W & L, and then missing semesters as her mother got worse. Momma didn't want to leave her old stucco house, although it was literally sinking into the ground and smelling of the sickness no matter what Bobbi did to clean it. So there Bobbi was at twenty-five—divorced, with a child, living with her sick mother in the house she'd been raised in. The only kind of men she ever saw, it seemed, were either old moldy city employees or young moldy city employees or men who were mad about their bills. When particularly mad ones came around, she was always called up to the front because she was supposed to be "good" at handling them.

She did all right at State Teachers' College. Bob was blessed, as her father had been, with what some people seemed to think was a remarkable memory. At the W & L people were always commenting on the fact that she could remember account numbers and billing amounts so well. When Ray came along, he made fun of her good memory, which was refreshing in a way. He said he'd had an uncle in Tennessee who had learned eight languages out of books and wasn't able to speak a word of sense in any of them.

Ray had been the first man in a while really to interest her. He was in his glory when they met, and Bobbi'd spent enough time by herself, enough gray hours alone, daydreaming of glory—of living in some way that was totally different. Oh, his life did appeal to her, too—so lazy and apparently taskless, doing what he wanted, circulating among people of all kinds, messing around, working on his own time. He didn't care what the front yard looked like or whether there were dishes in the sink. He was a cop and yet he was somehow a bohemian. He was older than Bobbi by eight years, had been married once, a woman he claimed to still like quite a lot. Apparently he'd visited with her regularly until she moved away to Belgium with a new husband who was in the army.

When he and Bobbi met, he'd just turned a conviction in a highly publicized case, a strange robbery-murder at a gas station near what was then the new interstate. It had been done on the one night of the week that the owner worked in the place. The only lead, if it could be called that, was that the robbery had been unsuccessful, with most of the money left behind. It was the kind of case that most detectives chalk up to drug transients and forget about.

Ray didn't work from clues. Fibers and blood analysis didn't interest him. His investigative method was social, not scientific, working through friends, barroom buddies, football- and baseball-game watchers. He operated by knowing a lot of people out in the county, knowing how they were related, knowing who was out of the joint, who had jobs and who didn't, who the old lady had kicked out. Like a politician, he knew how to give out little favors. He had good relationships with prosecuting attorneys and could always swing trade-offs, nonprosecutions, plea bargains.

You couldn't deny that Ray had his own particular kind of charm. Everyone knew he'd drink a beer with you today and put you and your brother in the slam tomorrow, but that didn't slow down his social life too much. There was always somebody to play cards or shoot the bull with. He was a natural, working in exactly the same way he lived—out there roaming, listening, aimlessly checking on things, with a dirty mind and a heart tuned to treachery, lurking like a pilot fish among the sharks.

The gas-station murder was six months old and half forgotten when he heard somebody at the Cherokee Lounge in a little unincorporated town called Okay, across the river, talking about a guy named Marty Spears. Spears was the dead man's younger brother, and he'd recently been in town, helping the widow with her affairs. The murdered Mr. Spears had accumulated a lot of property over the years, so there were considerable affairs to handle. A little checking around yielded nothing on the helpful brother. He was a dairy farmer from a little town in Washington who hadn't been in this area for some time. But by snooping a little more, Ray found out that the brother *had* traveled several times to Little Rock over the last three years, and had done so with a certain degree of secrecy. He found it interesting that none of the other relatives, which included a bunch of cousins, knew about any of these visits. As far as they knew, Marty hadn't visited the area at all.

The hardest thing to ascertain was that the widow knew about the visits. Ray did it by confronting her—springing dates and details on her at a totally unexpected moment. Yes, she "was aware" that he had made some visits.

And yes, Ray was to discover from a month more of pre-arrest work, she had gone to Little Rock on some occasions and "met with" the husband's younger brother.

The case became a scandal, of course. A good citizen, a prominent Methodist, and a loyal Democrat had been murdered by an adulterous wife and his own younger brother in a secret love affair, no less. The media couldn't get enough of it, and before and after the conviction a lot of stuff was said about what a hot-dog detective Ray Wiel was. Ray pretended not to care about all the publicity, but he loved it.

When they were courting, Ray was one of the few men who came into Bobbi's house who wasn't afraid of her mother. Momma was putting up some awful scenes around that time, like a child getting younger and younger, but it didn't run him off. He became the first new friend she'd had in years.

She was at first extremely uneasy with a nonfamily visitor, but before it was all over Ray'd charmed her. He talked and joked with her, listened to her cry, insulted her. He was so loose about it. "I feel *terrible*," Momma would say. "Well, you look terrible," he'd reply, in his easy masculine way. Over the last month or so, Momma became an angel, and Ray was one of the reasons for it. The battle was over, she had lost, but there was something radiant about her, looking out on that pure Whatever.

Ray won a lot of chips with Bobbi during that time—and many times since. After their marriage, with his help, she got a job on the force.

Her work as a patrolman, she quickly found out, was nothing like Ray's as a detective, but it was a lot better than shuffling numbers at the water and light. That uniform changed her from a cute secretary into someone different. She was fit for the work. She'd been around unpleasantness, which was the main thing about being a cop—people crying, people angry, putting out the fine dust of pain.

In her first years in uniform, she'd bloomed. It was a delayed bloom, by someone who'd been underground, in the dark almost too long. She was the hottest patrolman on the squad. She was smart, she was conscientious, and no matter what people *said*, she got her stripes because she deserved them.

Ray? He was a man with abilities a lot of smaller men never have— courage, the capacity for his own kind of love, for sitting back and tasting life. But you knew from the start that he was close to the line, that he could walk across it just about any day and become a client to his own profession. Looked at objectively, Ray Wiel was already pretty corrupt when she first met him, winking at things he considered trivial, giving little favors—and too hard-headed to change, too stubborn.

She looked through the window outside, the barn fire now really going and blowing, licking at the stars. Idly she swabbed the dirt off a pane and watched the silhouettes. She wondered if he was up in that bedroom.

The crowd had moved back now almost to the house, and appeared to be standing around not saying much. A shelf of fire dropped inside the barn, perhaps a hayloft. "Well, *Happy New Year, you pore fuckers*," someone yelled forlornly across the yard.

4

The cameras were flashing and wheezing like a roomful of asthmatics. You'd have thought Wayne McNear speaking at a luncheon in Dubois, Arkansas, was a big deal. The Kiwanis Club was sponsoring the talk, but it was open to all interested persons, and nearly three hundred had turned out, creating quite an overflow in the Ember Room of the Holiday Inn, with tables crammed in every corner as well as out in the lobby and bathroom corridors. It was a fire inspector's nightmare, but with so many local VIPs present, such technicalities were not important. Sergeants Bobbi Reardon and Neil English were the only law-enforcement officials of a low enough order to be concerned with fire regulations, and they were sitting at the front table with the guest of honor.

The idea was to give her a chance to get further acquainted with DataForm by meeting Ron Reed, security chief, and hearing the talk. Mr. Reed had spoken with her briefly and unrevealingly before driving them all over. He was a big ugly man with greased-back hair and an open top button on his shirt, where he wore a gold medallion bigger than a silver dollar.

McNear sat in the back seat, oblivious to them, surrounded by a sea of memos, talking steadily into a tape recorder. When the car stopped in the Holiday Inn parking lot, he asked Reed, "Okay, Ron, are they here?"

"I'll confirm inside."

In the jammed dining room, a number of media people came up to McNear before lunch, and he told them he didn't want to do questions until after the talk.

Someone else from DF was there hooking up a keyboard and display terminal. Before the luncheon got under way, Reed told the news people the rules about cameras—no video or photographs during the speech.

Reverend Ed Riems was the visiting preacher, down from Little Rock. He was a greater local celebrity than even McNear, and doubtless some of the people had come just to have lunch with him. Jimmy Tucker introduced him for the blessing, and he made his way to the microphone. Reverend Riems thanked Jimmy and the men of the Dubois Kiwanis Club for inviting him here today. It was the old radio voice, all right, practiced in authority.

". . . It might surprise you to know that I am interested in many of the same things as your fine speaker today. But, friends, the tools of the Lord are always changing, because man is always changing." He smiled gently. "But I'm not the speaker today, I'm only the visitor, so I will resist my natural urge and"—his head went down and both arms straight out in the shape of the cross, hands in fists—"ask the Lord to bless this food brought to us today in fellowship by the men of this fine organization, bless it to your use, and make us ever thankful for your bounty. And today, Lord, let us take this opportunity, in fellowship together, to look on the changes wrought by time and the wonderful things of the future, in the spirit of thankfulness and understanding. Help us to always remember that it is not the stone in which your commandments are written, or the scrolls, or the books; not the radios, the televisions, the computers—it is none of these things, but thy Word itself, Lord, to which we must rededicate ourselves, in Jesus' name, amen."

After one spoonful of peas and one taste of mashed potatoes, Bobbi would gladly have given her plate to someone without one. It was microwaved mush.

She looked over the crowd. Sheriff Bud Nagal sat at a table near the front jawing amiably with City Manager Mays Park, whom he was reputed to hate. The city manager was barely thirty years old, and he was disliked for his youth by the older men who traditionally ran the town.

The sheriff had his usual good color and smile, and seemed to be downright enjoying the company of the fretful young man. It was Sheriff Bud's talent to make an enemy seem like fine company and a microwaved plate lunch like an excellent dinner. Next to the young city manager, Bud was the self-satisfied elder statesman. He had white hair and a handsome face, and didn't any more know how to solve a crime now than he had when he'd first gone into office four terms ago. The sheriff was still the "chief lawman" in the county, the prestige somehow still there despite the fact that Chief of Police George Warnke was really a more important official now, with four times as many employees receiving much higher salaries.

After the audience made a go at the food, the cigars and cigarettes started lighting up, and McNear was introduced as the "guiding spirit" behind the construction of Lakeside Hospital.

He thanked the Kiwanis Club for inviting him to talk. He didn't speak loudly, and the people at tables in the lobby had to get up and crowd their chairs into the room along the wall. Flashbulbs started going off through the smoke clouds, and Ron Reed, who was sitting on Bobbi's right, spoke up, "Would you please wait until the end of the talk to take those?"

"Why can't we get em now?" someone yelled out.

"Because I'm askin you not to," Reed said.

McNear started again in the same low-key voice.

"New things," he said. "New. . . . When something new comes along like computers, the people who sell them, whose careers depend on them, will talk about what is truly original about them and what is merely a 'new version' of an old and established reality. You've prob-ably noticed that these dependents of the new tend to conveniently divide the two categories. When they're talking about the advantages of the new thing, they use terms like 'revolutionary,' 'amazing,' 'truly unique' "—his voice went even lower here—"but the disadvantages and problems of the new invention, those are merely new *versions* of old problems.

"What about the computer? Well, we all know, don't we? It's an amazing machine that makes drudgery obsolete, it takes care of all math problems, solves the eternal problems of filing, puts all information at our fingertips. It teaches your kid to read before kindergarten, it sweeps the floor, it figures your taxes, it gives your kid something to do when he has the flu, it is resulting in the decentralization and rehumanization of production. It is the ultimate universal tool—right up there with the wheel and the calendar among the top three inventions of man. The Bronze Age, the Iron Age, the Computer Age. Right?"

He said all this fast, and the audience laughed.

"I'm here today, ladies and gentlemen, to suggest that if we are going to call something new, let's go ahead and call it new all the way around—advantages *and* disadvantages. That's my purpose. That's why

I'm making this speech to you today. You might say that my theme today is 'be consistent.'

"Now I happen to be one who believes that the disadvantages of the computer are of a truly new order, and that what we loosely call computer crime is a new problem that very few people in the industry have any idea how to handle, much less the law-enforcement agencies." McNear paused at this point, and looked over at Reed.

"This may seem like a common enough thought. It doesn't sound, on the surface, like a big deal. But you would be surprised at how controversial it is. At this meeting today, in fact, there are some people who strenuously object—not only to this idea but to everything my ideas and our company here in Dubois stand for." He smiled coolly. "Mr. Andrews of the *Chicago Tribune*, hello. It's nice to have you here— and Mr. Page, of the *Sacramento Daily News*, we consider it a special privilege that you've come all the way from California. You've given us a great deal of coverage recently. All of us at DataForm have been amazed at how interested you are in our business.

"If you don't mind, gentlemen, I'm going to describe to the audience what you have stated in your editorials about my company. You've stated that DataForm is a highly 'suspect' organization. 'Suspect' is the term that I believe you both used. You have characterized it as a business staffed by ignorant country people under the control of criminals. And you've stated that my own specialty is bad-mouthing computers in order to appeal to and control the emotions of computer-illiterates in key managerial places—in essence, to get contracts from scared people. I find it interesting that both of your analyses are the same. Almost exactly. Your series of articles that appeared in August and September of this year was a solid condemnation of us, Mr. Page, and it followed Mr. Andrews's pieces closely. Right down to the ignorant country people.

"Do you have any objections to the way I've stated that?"

The directness of McNear's attack struck the room silent. Bobbi was able to pick out one of the two reporters—early twenties, well dressed, his face presently congealing like a baby trying to decide whether or not to cry.

"In your last article on the subject, Mr. Page, you gave the opinions of three experts to the effect that recent developments in computer security were amazing. You pointed out the marvels of the latest double-keyed encryption technique, and you discussed the fantastic new systems of the most modern banks, recommending to"—McNear picked up a piece of paper and read from it as if it were a little hard to decipher—"'potential clients of companies like DataForm that they take the time to learn about the real facts and issues before submitting themselves to the new breed of software bullies.' You recommended, for example, that they examine the latest security systems of banks like First California Savings in Sacramento.

"I thought that was a good suggestion. I appreciated it. After twenty-some years in the field, I really needed advice from someone who had been studying the subject for a couple of months."

The audience was quickly becoming uncomfortable. Even Sheriff Bud's ever-present smile was looking thin. McNear was going after the reporter head-on.

"I found your advice interesting, Mr. Page. I studied the remarkable new security system of the First California Savings bank in Sacramento, and I'm going to take a few minutes to report to you what I've found." Leaning forward with his elbows on the podium, he pointed his forefinger in their general direction. "I do hope in your future articles you mention that I took your advice, and I hope you mention what I've found."

He put the keyboard on the podium, and reached over and turned on the console, which faced the audience so that he had to lean over to see it.

"What I found about First California Savings is that it has a strong visual security network inside the bank. The bank has spent about a million dollars on security in the last year, particularly for this kind of thing. It now has television monitors from the parking lots to the clerks' desks. There are television cameras watching the bathrooms, halls, the elevators, covering a space of almost four hundred thousand square feet. As an example of how serious this bank is about video equipment, they have installed "total darkness" cameras in a number of places, which cost ten times more than regular ones, many with zoom lenses. They can zoom in on what is being written on desks. Anyone like yourself, Mr. Page, who knows all about bank security, is rightly impressed by these very serious security expenditures. They almost remind me of the security in the novel 1984 by George Orwell."

McNear tapped on the keyboard, two-finger style, as he talked. "To display how 'secure' this bank feels, the main vault is on display on the ground floor, visible through a glass window. Security headquarters is in a reinforced concrete room in the basement." A screeching noise came from the monitor. "Now, ladies and gentlemen, all these video units, and the new emergency door locks, and the new heliport on top of First California make up quite a system, all potentially useful in case of actual bank-robbery attempts. But as you should know from your studies, Mr. Page, my company is not terribly interested in site security, no matter how high-tech it becomes. Site security can get as complicated as televising the Super Bowl, and it will still not be our particular concern. Please take this into account so in your future articles you can advise us in the field in which we actually work.

"Our concern is *computer* crime, particularly of the kind which is committed daily by doing what I've just managed to do—patching over the networks to a computer from the outside. I've used a trick to convince the central computer at First California that we are one of the smaller computers from one of their outside branches. Now I won't go into the details, but I will tell you that as these things go, the trick I used was relatively simple. It involved less than a hundred lines of code, written in less than a day. It's the kind of thing that thousands of teenagers could do easily, given a little information. The basic reason why this particular patch was easy is that the small computers at the branches and the large one at the main branch of FCS do not 'fit together' very closely. They don't have a well-synchronized interface.

"Just for the benefit of those who aren't as knowledgeable as you, Mr. Page, let me explain where we are. If you want to imagine the central bank's computer as a person—say one of their key managers— we're now on the telephone to him, disguising our voice to make him think we're an employee in a branch office. The connection between us is so bad, though, that it doesn't take much to fool him. He can barely hear us anyway.

"Now this is going to get complicated, Mr. Page. The poor ignorant country folk may not be able to follow us here, but the reason the connection is so bad is that the bank chose to buy, or was influenced to buy, USI microcomputers to replace its simple input/output teller machines. It's probably true that the bank needed microcomputers, and it's true there were ways to make USI micros fit the Burroughs mainframe. The things that connect different computer elements like this are called buses, and there was a bus that worked. It didn't work well, it just worked. But, with the degree of account control that USI exerted over the bank by the time it made these purchases, it was very difficult to avoid buying"—here McNear's pause was longer—"USI microcomputers. USI, although their Burroughs mainframe has a ring protection security system that just barely gets along with the USI micros."

McNear looked over at the console. "If you can't see the VDT out there, the word on the screen is *command*? The central computer of First California—the Burroughs machine—is asking us what we want to do, and we are going to perform a second operation at this point by asking it to do a common account-number verification procedure. We're going to confuse the machine and make it go into a systems check and, while it's doing that, plant another program in the systems-check procedure that will run later, the next time a check is done by a high-priority user. This is a common way to get from an allowed function to a restricted one. It's called piggybacking.

"Using the same comparison as before, if I were someone pretending to be at a branch talking to a central bank manager, I'd have to perform some pretty good tricks to convince him to revise, on the spot, within seconds, certain basic bookkeeping details. I think it is safe to say that I couldn't do that with any sane manager. But if I were very clever, I might be able to leave what looked like a certain *routine* procedure for him to do, which I knew he wouldn't do himself, but would later hand over to somebody else who'd do as ordered. He has the clearance to order such a change, a branch teller doesn't. Now that may sound complicated, Mr. Page, but I can tell you that from a code-writing standpoint it isn't much of a problem to run a trick like this—not on this setup. We're looking at a pretty primitive situation."

McNear looked up from the keyboard now. "The basic weakness in most computer security systems is that there's no *consciousness* in the way. No barriers of sanity. The way a computer operates is like a giant organization staffed by dim-witted bureaucrats. If you can get something into one of their 'in' boxes, and if the job you ask him to do is in his domain, he'll do it. If the head of the highway department down here in Little Rock got something in his 'in' box signed by the governor that said 'Jackhammer up all the highways going into Missouri,' he would probably scratch his head and at least meditate on it before he ordered out the crews. He might even call up the governor and ask if he really did want him to do that."

McNear paused and frowned, as if his thoughts were already moving elsewhere. The reverend was paying close and admiring attention.

"But with this and most other big systems that are in place around this country, there isn't any headscratching to it. If it's in that box and by all appearances signed by the governor, those are some gone highways. I repeat, there is no sanity in the way, no human consciousness. Nothing between the criminal and the act but numbers."

He looked out at the audience for a moment, with the podium light coming up from below and illuminating his face. "So, Mr. Page, here we are inside First California Savings's operating system. As you can see, it really doesn't make much difference that the bank has one hundred and fifty cameras watching desks, parking garages, and bathrooms, or that it has motion and sound detectors in sensitive places and a separate air supply system and computer printouts that tell the guards down in the basement to call 911 when certain lights go off. All of that modern 'computer security' which you noted in your article Wayne McNear was apparently not aware of—it doesn't make a lot of difference when we can walk into the bank's operating system from the Holiday Inn in Dubois, Arkansas."

"*Are you actually tampering with the FCS computer?*" the reporter shouted over scattered applause.

5

Ray had been writing in his spiral notebook, but for the moment was lost in a daydream admiring the little Taguchi tape recorder, hardly bigger than its minicasette.

> ". . . If I am, you'll never be able to prove it. I am inside the rings, Mr. Page. Beyond the bounds registers and exception reports. I am inside the logic of the operating system—or will be, when the system check runs next time. From there I can make changes that will be impossible to uncover. I can run . . ."

George Bowser was sitting at the kitchen table with an inch-long ash on his cigarette, plainly uninterested in the tape, staring at a morning beer, the big black radio three inches from his tired face. Outlaw was asleep on the couch, his aquarium bubbling nearby. It was raining outside—the most miserable kind of winter rain, with distant thunder that seemed out of place—belonging to a different season.

> ". . . those changes, accomplish my act, and then change the system back the way it was. There will be no evidence of the act. I'm in a place of higher privilege than being inside the bank president's files—or even inside his brain. We are in a better position right now, Mr. Page, than we would be if the whole bank were staffed by zombies under our control.

Because we have immediate powers of execution, perfect coordination, perfect secrecy, and total cover. The bank's computer, insofar as anybody can tell, will seem to continue functioning normally."

"Are you breaking Title 18 of U.S. Code or not?"

"Wake up, Outlaw," Ray said, while George got up and retrieved a fresh one from the refrigerator.

Ray punched the small red button that stopped the tape and shut his spiral notebook. "What does the bodyguard look like?"

"Like his daddy used him for target practice." George popped open his beer.

"Bob was sitting up front?"

He took a sip. "That's right—her, the bodyguard, then Neil English."

"Pretty sure Warnke didn't see you?"

"So this wasn't his idea?"

One of Ray's eyebrows rose slightly as he punched the tape recorder.

". . . That's very good. You know that there is at least an applicable federal law in the case of federally insured institutions—which most banks are. Again I'm impressed by the depth of your research, and I'm sure all the other poor country folk here are, as well. But as I just said, you need evidence. I am committing a crime that leaves no evidence. How can I possibly be indicted with no evidence? What can you show a court of law to demonstrate that this crime has been committed?"

"You're the one—"

"What I'm telling you is that your model bank in California is a snap to walk into. It doesn't require a 'good position' to get inside it. It's surrounded by a pile of junk that protects it from someone dumb enough to walk through the door with a gun, but it couldn't protect it from a teenager in Cincinnati with one of these keyboards—"

He punched the little stop button. "I guess it's paytime, ain't it."

George fidgeted another cigarette out of a pack lying on the table, while Ray took a roll of hundreds out of his pocket and laid five of them in front of him.

"Wake up! Paytime!" He walked over to John Outlaw, asleep on his belly in the sagging couch with his face turned away. His left arm dangled to the floor, and Ray reached down and put five hundred dollars in it. With no other movement in his body, Outlaw's hand closed around the bills. "Guess what. It's forty-five minutes past time for you to be at the trailer."

Outlaw rolled over, shoved the money into his shirt pocket, stared at the ceiling a second, and went back to sleep. Ray said gently, "One of your fish just croaked."

Outlaw's eyes blinked wide open.

Ray poured a cup of coffee from the counter and took it over to him. He took it lying down. "What was the speech about? I dropped off."

"He robbed a bank."

"Say what?"

"He dialed the bank's computer and fiddled with it somehow. It was a demonstration."

"You getting a hard-on for this guy because Bobbi's going to work for him?" Bowser asked.

Ray didn't answer him.

John eventually sat up and took a few sips of coffee. He started complaining, his normal method of waking up. "This is the worst job since baby-sitting. How long have we been in the goddamn cold swamp watching that useless trailer?"

"Since December eleventh. It's your shift, John. You were supposed to meet Bowz when he left the tent. Come on now, earn your money."

Outlaw sipped the coffee gloomily. "What line is Warnke giving you on this?"

"I don't know any more than I've told you."

"Which is nothin."

"He says it's tight covers."

"Tell him, Bowz," John grumbled. "It's worse than a jungle out there. At least it's warm in a jungle."

"I won't go near a goddamn fuckin jungle," George said complacently, looking at the bills before putting them into his wallet.

"So where's this comin down from?" John persisted.

Ray got up and walked over to the kitchen window. It wasn't quite raining, but droplets were forming from mists blowing across the hills, blowing through the pale-barked soft maples that cluttered the front slope of Outlaw's property with broken limbs. He spoke toward the glass pane. "Why do you ask?"

"Because I've done agency stuff before—DEA, FBI—and this doesn't have the same feel."

Ray sighed. "Outlaw, are you awake?"

"What do you mean? I'm sittin here talking to you."

"Either one of you hear anything lately about Jack Cady?"

"Owns a kennel?" Bowser said. "Matter of fact, yeah. I hear he's been stealing dogs."

"Where'd you hear it?"

"Somebody out at the Cherokee. Big-money dogs. I didn't get the whole story."

Ray sighed. "He's an old friend of Bobbi's. I got the word he was in some kind of trouble."

Outlaw checked his fish, then shambled across the linoleum floor and heated up a black frying pan on the old gas range, melted some butter and quickly, with one hand, broke six eggs and scrambled them. "I'll just tell you what. Out there at four o'clock in the morning with my nuts frozen hard as pinballs, I'm wondering why the chief has us guarding that goddamn thing. Who are we guarding it from?"

Ray shrugged. "It's a stakeout, John. Big deal."

"What kind of stakeout is it where if somebody shows up, you're supposed to, quote, prevent entry without apprehension, unquote. That ain't a stakeout, that's a bouncer."

"You're supposed to identify them, too, John."

Outlaw put the eggs on a plate and started wolfing them down. "Yeah. It doesn't make a lot of sense. If Warnke wants it guarded, why doesn't he have it hauled to town?"

"Are you complaining about double-time?"

"Closer to time-and-a-half." He frowned as he chewed. "Everybody's convinced we're on narco. I go by the station, everybody treats me like I have AIDS."

"Go."

"You think this guy McNear has something to do with this?"

Ray shook his head vaguely.

"Computers. Makes sense." Outlaw put some tap water into another cup of coffee to cool it, and drank it all in one chug. He splashed his face and got together cigarettes and his blue magnum, which he stuck down into his belt.

Bowser smiled. "You can lose your dick like that."

"It wouldn't make any difference," John grumbled. "The schedule we've been on, I don't get to use it anyway. You have any idea when this shit will be done with, Ray?"

"You don't have to do it, John."

"Hey, I'm trying to buy three thousand dollars' worth of cedar shakes. I'm trying to buy nineteen hundred dollars' worth of PVC. For double-time I'd fuck sheep, but it don't mean I have to like it."

"There's a paperback book out there," Ray said. "Don't use it for toilet paper."

"What's it about?" Outlaw asked vaguely. "Let me guess. The takeover of the free world by a communist conspiracy leading all the way to the White House."

Ray was looking out the window again, his breath making a little fog on the glass. With his back still turned, he said, "Go on, John. I take heat for this."

6

Bobbi took the job on a part-time basis, working on her two days off each week. In the beginning, it seemed like typical industrial security—getting paid to stand around the building looking vigilant, the distinction being that the pay was sixteen bucks an hour. She had taken part-time work before for less than half that.

The job wasn't really all that interesting at first. The divorce was a constant worry. Marty Williams's threat to undertake a custody fight preyed on her mind. It was so unusual for the court to award primary custody to a stepfather that at first her lawyer believed it was an aggressive way to soften her up for a zero-alimony settlement. Since Bobbi didn't want a cent of Ray's money and had told him so, she knew it was just his last-ditch effort at stopping the divorce. As loose and high-flying as he was, he had an incredibly stubborn streak.

Her concern with this, plus regular work, and the changes Richard was going through with his new girlfriend, all tended to make the new part-time job anything but the center of her attention. She began to notice things at DF slowly, through a haze of preoccupations.

On an evening in late January, after almost a month at DF, Bobbi was home by herself in the evening trying to figure out something to do with her hair. She was also trying to keep warm: Despite the fact that she'd stacked haybales beneath the trailer and put plastic on the windows, the walls didn't keep the wind out, they just kind of slowed it down, allowing the little heater, blasting away at a rate of $230 a month (December), time only to warm it on the way through.

Her closest neighbor in the trailer park, Mr. Kenn, had wrapped wide sheets of plastic around the entire length of his trailer, and had volunteered to do the same for her. She'd mentioned this to Richard, who'd been alarmed at the possibility. "Aw Mom, this place is ugly enough without wrapping it up like a sandwich."

Bobbi fretted at her hair in the little hand mirror that had been her mother's. People always admired her very black hair, but she just didn't know what to do with it anymore. She'd lost the knack of how to fix herself up. She had grown a little self-conscious working at DF, where she was surrounded by nicely done-up people instead of horny old fat cops. Helene's Hair Salon was the "best" in Dubois, but they'd never been able to do much for her. A couple of times she'd gone down to Little Rock and gotten her hair fried, once coming back looking like Little Orphan Annie and once like the Incredible Hulk. This second and last attempt had been her venture into the realm of what the hairstylist called a "daring" look. Now she was back to a nonstyle. It just sort of hung there. Lately, Martha Daly was the only friend she talked with easily about this kind of thing, and Martha was pretty much out of circulation with a two-year-old and another on the way.

Bobbi felt pretty out of it, herself.

No wonder Richard was never around. It was freezing in this place. Better to be with Cathy Lawes than to be cold all the time.

She put on her leather jacket over her bathrobe and thought about the fact that she could take her savings and make a down payment on a house. But that just didn't feel right yet. As long as the divorce hung fire, she didn't want to make any big life decisions. She'd ride out the winter here, get that settled, then decide what to do about a house.

She stood by the kitchen bar glancing into the mirror once more, the television going behind her.

It was an awfully quiet night. Richard gone with the car. Lately, he spent *all* his time at Cathy's house. Humping her right now, probably— or sitting around the wood stove smoking dope with her father. Richard had a wonderful time over there, because anything went. Cathy had told her father that she and Richard were going to have sexual relations in the house and, what's more, she had marched over here and told Bobbi the same thing. She just wanted everybody to know. Being healthy, honest, and open about it.

She poured a glass of white wine and came back in to sit on the couch. Good old California jug-of-wine wine, a warm spot in a cold trailer. She had just turned off the TV when she heard a car pull up.

She went to the window to look out, but it had parked between her trailer and Mr. Kenn's, the headlights already out. Something about the way the car door slammed caused her to back up and walk down the hall toward her bedroom.

Why was she doing this? Because she was unmade-up?

There was a knocking and then, softly, a man's voice calling her name.

She was shocked when she heard the door open and someone step in. She heard the door close as he called a last time, dimly, as if not expecting an answer. Who's voice was that? She went for her gun, hanging inside the closet, and checked to see that it was loaded. The trailer shuddered with steps. She didn't want to be walked in on in her bedroom, gun or no gun.

She went into the hall with the intention of calling him, but stopped when she saw him shuffling through the things on her kitchen counter. She stepped back inside the doorway. Had he assumed the trailer was empty because the car was gone?

For a while there was no sound. She looked again and saw him standing at the kitchen counter, facing in her direction, reading through one of her bank books. She pulled her head slowly back inside the door. It was Ron Reed.

He walked around the living room now in what sounded like aimless pacing. Then he stopped and there was another long moment of silence. Her palm was damp around the butt of the .38. She had no reason to be scared. It was the surprise of it, the way he just appeared and slipped in the door.

He took a couple of steps, hesitated, and then started coming down the hall. He stopped and hurried out. Bobbi heard someone coming into the long driveway.

Outside, his car roared to life and peeled out, throwing gravel against the metal wall of the trailer.

She went into the living room and looked around. He had left her checkbooks and records pretty messy. Her heart beating fast, she sat down on the couch in her robe and service jacket. The other car had circled up and parked by the trailer. Richard and Cathy came in the door, Richard's eyes drawn quickly to her gun.

"Mom? Is somethin wrong?"

Bobbi kept putting off calling Reed about his little visit to her trailer. Officially, he was her "boss" the couple of days a week she worked at DataForm, yet they had little to do with each other; he avoided her, she did likewise. Confronting him didn't quite seem worth the trouble. The real question Bobbi had was why this man was in charge of security. He was sullen, evasive, and physically clumsy—bumbling and bumping around like a fish out of water—to the point that she almost felt sorry for him. Had he cased her trailer because he was fearful of losing his job? Curious about what she was being paid?

Reed's "office" was an unofficial coffee room for a number of company executives. It was located in a Butler building that housed two large electrical generators off the rear of the main building. Executives occasionally wandered into the metal-walled room and stood around a portable gas stove on the bare concrete floor, taking relief away from the constant coolness of the main building, its security zones and claustrophobically low ceilings. The portable stove was a fireplace where they warmed their hands and enjoyed the bare room's spaciousness. The generator's constant whine, in contrast to the hush of the offices, gave them an excuse to talk loudly. Reed usually remained at his desk, shuffling papers, apparently oblivious to them.

While all of the people at the top of the ladder had been with DataForm when it was located in California, quite a few, including McNear, were originally from Arkansas. They were all in their thirties or early forties, all male except for one busy, fierce, unsmiling blonde named Carol Rader who darted through the halls like a shark.

The boy she'd stopped with McNear's daughter, Sinclair Heyer (called Sinc), worked part time at DF as a messenger boy, one of the more visible jobs around the building. Several times Bobbi tried to talk with him, and although he always slipped away after only a word or two, she got the impression that he might not be the brat he'd acted like when she'd stopped him. His behavior that night could have been due to panic. On the job, he seemed to be a hardworking, lonely, almost haunted boy.

Bobbi's curiosity about Sinc's father, Mike Heyer, was piqued by little things she overheard, expressions on people's faces when he was mentioned that seemed to imply he was both very important to the company and very irksome to a lot of the others. She actually laid eyes on him only a couple of times, briefly—a tall man with round, darkly tinted sunglasses and an impatient manner.

Jeremy Weeks was Mike Heyer's opposite in friendliness and availability. Called by his first name by everybody, Jeremy looked like a bum, with a tangle of dirty brown hair and the body smell of a nonbather. He wore blue-jean cutoffs, a T-shirt, and sandals—or rather hosted them, like something that's been in the refrigerator too long hosts a mold. Jeremy was a Coca-Cola junkie, and he shuffled up and down the narrow halls, Coke can in hand, his ragged cutoffs flapping against his thin knees.

Jeremy talked more freely than the others, but he was moody and sour at times. He had an apartment in town but normally slept during the daytime in his office on a little cot against the wall and got his food from the snack dispensers in the coffee room. He seldom shut his door, allowing visitors at DataForm the not uncommon sight of Jeremy on his cot, a blanket pulled over his skinny chest and the pale green light of three video display terminals shedding across his pale face.

Color-coded badges kept different kinds of employees from entering certain areas of the building, and, as far as Bobbi could tell from Reed, just about her only job was going around making sure people weren't "out of their color." Red badges weren't allowed to go outside the assembly area, a single big room with thirty-five computer terminals, three attendant "job rooms," and a coffee room. The assemblers—mostly local and area women—worked in rows of consoles partitioned off from each other.

Their keyboards all together made a solid noise that slowed to a rattle only when ten or fifteen at once took off for a break. Programmers and executives moved in and out of the room with stacks of material for them to key in. To keep the confusion at a minimum and prevent security problems, the gate-control guard was supposed to let in no more than two nonassemblers at a time and all "job talks" were supposed to be handled behind a closed door in one of the little conference rooms.

Visitors wore orange badges and, when accompanied by a DF employee, were allowed the same territory as the next higher level of company employee, yellow badges—programmers, mostly—who could range in all the common rooms except the main control room.

Green badges, executives and controllers, were allowed access to the central monitors in the control room.

The control room was off limits presently even to Bobbi, but she could see it through a viewing window in the hall: rows of disk drives, blue- and pearl-colored cabinets with bluish plastic domes, a little labyrinth of VDTs in the center of the room, and a group of larger cabinets at the end of the room farthest from the window. These were, as Jeremy Weeks called them, the "number crunchers."

The badges didn't work very well. For one thing, exceptions were made so often that no one but security paid any attention to them. Through the hall window into the control room, she frequently saw a yellow-badged programmer working at a central monitor. Also, over time, Bobbi ran into an incredible number of badgeless "visitors" wandering around the building. Her instructions were to escort such persons to the receptionist and, if she knew nothing about them, escort them out the door and take down their license numbers. She had occasion to do this she didn't know how many times, duly giving the information to Reed, who acted disinterested to the point of surliness. He never seemed to want to be bothered.

Aside from the matter of enforcing security zones and checking badges, Reed communicated so little to her that in effect Bobbi had to find out about security at DF by naïvely trying to violate it.

Talking with Sarina Shores one day was one of her first big lessons.

It was a Saturday in early March, when Bobbi sat with Sarina in the coffee room—one of the fancier spots in the building, with molded plastic chairs, four glass-and-plastic tables, striped wallpaper, and a battery of food and pop dispensers humming along one wall. There were articles about the company, cut from newspapers and magazines, posted on a bulletin board. The latest was the local newspaper account of McNear's Kiwanis Club speech: McNear "Robs" Bank During Lecture. The famous *Time* article stated that if DF was sold or went public, an estimated twenty people would become "multimillionaires" and numerous other stockholders stood to gain tremendous profits. It described in-house ownership of the company as unusually widely divided between executives and other employees. A time-yellowed article from the *San Jose Mercury*, written when DataForm was still located in California, said that it was a "pioneer in the boom market of computer security."

Sarina, a bacon-and-biscuits country woman whose nervousness made her seem even larger than she was, was on her half-hour lunch break, mowing down two sandwiches and an apple while telling Bobbi about how assemblers were paid. She said she was paid to be in a hurry. Assemblers got five dollars an hour, plus incentive points calculated according to an ongoing competition for the highest keying rates, minus "negative incentives" for mistakes. Incentive points were run continuously (by computer), then the resulting bonuses were calculated weekly on a competitive scale. There were three weekly winners on each shift and no limits to how many times an assembler could win.

This meant that there were some who were repeat winners, some who never won, and a bunch who were working their fingers off trying to get as fast as the winners. The bonuses were paid in stock. The present book value of DF stock was only about a quarter per share, but Sarina's "conservative estimate" of its value, when the company went public or was sold, was $25 a share. By winning once a month, a person upped his wages by six shares, potentially 150 bucks.

If a person could win once, however, she could win more than once. If she won, say, three times in a month she earned an estimated $450 worth of company stock. For someone who'd never earned much over the minimum wage, that was an awful good monthly bonus. But this was looking at it conservatively, Sarina told her. Reasonable estimates said that in the long term, DF stock would be worth about $100 per share, which meant for the three-time-a-month first-place winner an approximate $1800 bonus.

Bobbi was amazed by the sums Sarina was throwing around, but she wasn't through yet.

A "hotdog" keyboarder could win—and often did—from forty-five to even more than fifty shares per six months. Fifty shares of DF stock could be worth $2500 to $5000.

"What are you all typing into those computers that's worth so much?" Bobbi asked.

Sarina's expression instantly turned foul. "Oh no you don't. You won't pull nothin like that on *me! No, ma'am!*" She got up from the table, ostentatiously wadding up her paper bag, throwing it into the trash, and stomped out in a huff.

Sarina suspected Bobbi was trying to trap her into breaking the secrecy rule, which—she was to discover—was not an unreasonable fear. Mr. Peets from "the trailer," the statistics section, gave regular security talks to the assemblers and programmers hammering away at the secrecy rule. Despite his long blond pigtail and post-hippie aura, Peets spoke in no uncertain terms. One call-down for "job gossip" resulted in *all* incentives being erased; two, and the violator lost her job. These weren't hollow threats; several employees had been "cleaned out" and some had been fired.

Bobbi was beginning to understand what she was seeing from the doorway station: a roomful of women—a lot of them country gals, most of them mothers—for whom this was an opportunity to win something big. They weren't fools. They doubtless joked about how the value of the company's stock was exaggerated in some people's minds, yet she imagined that one of the reasons for their competitiveness was exactly that uncertainty, that gamble, not knowing for sure what they'd end up with. She could imagine them alone at home, with their calculators and pencils and clean sheets of paper, coming up with numbers that set their hearts pounding.

Within a couple of weeks of her aborted talk with Sarina, Bobbi got a firsthand chance to see someone fired. Reed asked her to stand in while he questioned a woman named Milly Smith, a not-very-bright assembler who nevertheless was one of their fastest keyboarders—so fast that other assemblers tried to get into different shifts so they'd have less stiff competition in the bonus race.

Milly sat across from Reed's desk in the big empty metal room, wringing her hands and crying, while the security chief scowled at his fingernails, his gold medallion hanging loosely against his chest. Bobbi stood back, uncomfortably, by the door. Milly admitted to having talked briefly to another keyboarder in the bathroom. "I didn't say what I was typin," she said pitifully. Bobbi wondered if the accuser hadn't exaggerated the event in order to get Milly off the shift and out of competition, a possibility that didn't seem to occur to Reed. He listened to her a minute or two longer, then without further questioning gave her twenty minutes to be off the premises.

At this moment Bobbi came closest to saying, If you're such a stickler, mister, what were you doing casing my trailer that night?

But she didn't. She put it off. It was a matter of emotional economy. She had enough problems right now—at her regular job, in her personal life—without starting something else.

It was during one of Peets's bimonthly security lectures that Jack Cady set off the building-wide alarm.

Late March, around 8:30 in the evening, Peets was pacing back and forth under the fluorescent lights, playing with his mustache, while the second-shifters sat with their purses on the desks by their consoles. These lectures were boring to them, and they were listening in sullen silence when the building-wide alarm started yelping. Ron Reed hurried out and Bobbi followed, and waited while he called the front desk on a hall phone.

He slammed the phone down and hurtled down the hall toward the front of the building. In the front reception area, there was no one but the receptionist and one red-faced old man—Mr. Jack Cady—standing in front of her.

"I told him he couldn't!" the receptionist said. "He was going back there without—"

"I want to see the boss. I'm tired of the damn runaround!"

Bobbi had known Jack from childhood, when her father had traded dogs and hunted with him. Over the years, they'd always said hello when they saw each other in town. He was generally a quiet-spoken man, like her daddy.

"Hi, Mr. Cady. Remember—"

"I know who you are. Your daddy was Jim Reardon. Does this place have a boss—or is he *always* out of town?"

"If you'd like an appointment—" Reed said.

"I don't want a damn appointment, I want to talk to him."

Reed looked at Bobbi.

"You're out of luck right now," she said. "He really is out of town. He's in California."

"When'll he be back?"

"I hardly ever see him myself," Bobbi said. "If you'll let me know what's on your mind, I'll make sure he hears about it."

Mr. Cady stood there, his face still red, his back hunched, looking like he'd lost something. "Well, I'd just as soon leave this place."

"Could you wait here just a minute?" She went with Reed into the reception-room coffee nook. "I know him. His name's Jack Cady. If he's mad about something, he's probably got a reason. I think I ought to hear what he has to say."

"He's a kook. I don't want to be short a man."

Bobbi didn't argue with Reed. She just followed Mr. Cady out the front door and told him she'd be at his house as soon as she was off work.

She remembered the maze of dirt roads to Jack's house. In his yard, one bug light on a pole cast a dim yellow haze over several dog pens and individual shelters made of cut-out oil drums. Hounds whined and nosed through the wire. Jack came from the back pens with a dark shadow trotting along behind him. It pranced around and reared up like a pony.

"What in the world kind of a dog is that?"

"Wolfhound."

"I hope you got a friend at the rendering plant."

"Owner left twenty cases of food," Jack said.

"This a huntin dog?"

"Lot of night hunters are taking up this 'wolf huntin.' What they mean is coyote huntin. . . . Easy there!" The wolfhound had reared up and landed with his paws on Jack's shoulders, pushing him backward. At full stretch the dog was taller than the man. Jack pulled a burr off one of its elbows. "Same principle as fox huntin, except your dogs are ten times bigger and you follow em in a truck instead of sitting at a fire."

On his own turf, Mr. Cady had calmed down and become more reticent.

They went through the screened porch into the house. The living room was miraculously unchanged from the last time Bobbi had seen it, twenty years ago, on her last visit here with her father. One couch sat in a cobwebbed corner of the room, along with a couple of ornate old floor lamps, inherited from some long-dead female influence in the family. The wood stove was a fat-bellied thing with a hundred years of rust, breaks, and mends on it. There were gunny sacks of cracklings smelling of lard in the corner, flats of dog food, and an old low table that he stood his dogs on when grooming, performing minor operations, or selling them. He stood dogs on this platform for buyers during the final, hard-nosed inspection before purchase—an event that had seemed slightly ominous to Bobbi as a child.

"Hold!" Jack said to the huge shaggy-coated dog.

He stood frozen as if in a point, and Jack's hands came down around his face, almost touching it, moving lightly over his shape. "This particular one ain't the kind you can afford to take huntin."

"Too good for that?"

"He's a champion. Won a bunch of contests, including something at the Grand National. He's worth a heap of money. And so were the other two."

Jack frowned down at the dog, who had begun quivering, and put his hand on its back. "I knew not to take in any damn beauty-contest dogs."

"You had two that got lost?"

"You lose thirty thousand dollars' worth of dogs, and you better find out what happened to em, because word'll get around, Jack Cady's a crook. He's running an operation there."

Jack went into the kitchen and brought back a pint of Old Grand-Dad and two cups, reminding Bobbi again of his ritual of dog sales. After the deal was struck, he always offered a drink to seal it.

While he poured, she watched the giant dog, who glanced at her nervously—purebred, high-strung, fiercely restrained. Jack gave her one of the two cups, half-full of whiskey, and took a shot himself. "Did you hear about the accident where this fellow got electrocuted?"

"Back in December."

He nodded, his face having the same stillness that her father's had. "I've been trying to tell somebody about it for three months, and I can't get nobody to listen to me."

Mr. Cady pointed at the dog with his thumb. "But I tell you what, when they come over here and took two dogs, that's as far as I go."

Bobbi took a sip of whiskey. "Who did it?"

He shook his head. "Whoever it was, they left me looking like the worst crook in the county."

"You call the sheriff?"

"I called him. They sent an old boy out here that wrote some stuff down on a piece of paper. I told him about it, but he wasn't interested. Decided I had a loose screw, I guess, talkin about electrocutions and stolen dogs. At one point there he stopped writin and started noddin at me, sayin, 'Is that right? Well I'll be.' Directly he left, and that was that."

"How do you know they didn't just walk out and get lost?"

"Because a fellow called me up and told me he was going to do it." He widened his eyes. "Said to keep my mouth shut about this accident. Said I'd see some business trouble if I didn't. Well to heck with that! That just made me want to tell it more. I've been trying to tell this man McNear, but I never can get ahold of him."

"Tell him what?"

Mr. Cady looked at her uncertainly. "All right. . . . I was huntin in the Trois. Past midnight. Had this old dog on a scent of some kind. He was way over the hill and gone, and I wasn't paying much attention to him. He'd been bawl-barkin for a while in a curious voice, then he shut down, and I couldn't get him to come back, so I went on out to find him.

Followed a new chat road toward Devil's Backbone, and there was a trailer of some kind out there, all lit up. That's where I saw it."

"What's that?"

Jack looked uncertain here. "I saw a man inside the place, through the window, and my dog outside. Both of em electrocuted."

"Did you go inside?"

"Couldn't get in. The front door was hot. I checked it with a piece of metal. It had to be running a pretty good current to burn the dog's snout like it did. He was lying out front of it. At first I thought he'd got himself shot in the face. I looked again and saw it was a burn. This old dog was a nose on wheels, smelled everything he came to, and that door had done knocked him to kingdom come. The man inside, his arms were stretched out, he was touching a metal box, froze up with the current. . . ." Jack glanced at her oddly at this point and she got the feeling he was deciding to shorten his story. "Anyway, I got back across fast as I could and called from John Pendergrast's house, being the closest telephone. The police didn't ask me to help them find the place, so that's the last I saw of it."

Bobbi remembered that the witness call-in and location of the accident had been missing from the report she'd taken to McNear to sign. "Did someone from the police department come out and talk to you?"

"Yes, they did."

"Who?"

"George Warnke. He was there bright and early the day after. Woke me up. I told him I intended to go to the sheriff that day. What little experience with the law I've had, I've always dealt with the sheriff. All that big police force is new to me. Anyway, he said no, the police were handling it."

"What happened then?"

"Nothin, far as I know. They buried the man, and that was it. When the newspaper got it wrong, I thought to call this Warnke and straighten it out, then I figured it was just the newspaper gettin it turned around. Come another article in the paper that said the same thing, I did call him. He said it wasn't a problem, the police knew the story."

"What'd they get wrong?"

"Where it happened, mainly. The newspaper said it happened at the building in town. . . ." Jack trailed off, as if still puzzled by this.

"How'd you know the man you saw was Mitze?"

"I figured he was the only man workin for this company that got electrocuted that night," Jack said mildly. "I don't know—maybe they line em up and shoot the juice to em two or three at a time."

Bobbi swallowed some more whiskey and cleared her throat.

Jack shook his head and said in an abruptly quiet voice, "There were some other things I told him."

"What's that?"

He shook his head, looking at the table. "It's really not for me to tell to a lady."

Bobbi grinned. "I'm not *too* much of a lady, Jack."

Jack shook his head. "Well, I've given you the basic idea anyhow. You tell your boss. If he wants to know more, he can come to see me."

7

The Olde Country Club of Dubois, Arkansas, occupied a shabby two-story building that would have required a big sign to hide behind if it had been a restaurant on the highway trying to lure in paying customers. It was reputed to have the worst golf course and best fried chicken in central Arkansas.

Ray knew the manager, Maureen Stallings, from a problem she'd had a couple of summers ago, when a would-be arsonist had failed three times to burn down the clubhouse, a not particularly fortunate miracle since the insurance was worth more than the building. There was evidence that a financially troubled part-owner of the club was trying to make a fire sale, but Ray never got a case on him. Miss Stallings was fearful of losing her job as manager, and she latched on to Ray as her "friend" at the police station; in fact, long after the suspect had been bought out by his partners, she was calling Ray with other serious problems like stolen golf carts and graffiti on the lawn furniture.

Maureen was a vivid middle-aged woman whose job hid her away in a quiet place that had begun calling itself a country club forty years ago and yet never quite became more than a clapboard building on old farmland, where people came to dinner on Friday nights and occasionally tried to play golf, despite the cornstalks and soybeans and horse-weeds that poked their heads out of the fallow fields designated for golf.

Her office was between the ladies' room and the kitchen, a little cubbyhole smelling of disinfectant and cooking—empty of ornament except for two elegant brass lamps on either end of a desk, with an old black oscillating fan on a little table in the corner. On her desk lay a big ledger with frayed covers.

Ray explained that he was tying up some loose ends on Ben Mitze's death and needed to find out a couple of things—"without bothering the widow at this late date, if I can help it."

Maureen smiled with her mouth and frowned with her eyes. "Elizabeth, yes."

He pretended not to notice the suggestiveness in her expression. "Mr. Mitze was at the top of his career. Had a great job at DataForm. I feel bad when it happens to a person like that."

Maureen wrapped her long white fingers around a snow-scene paperweight and put it on top of the ledger. She wore a lavender dress and matching lipstick, which made her naturally expressive face seem even more so. Her expression implied a certain pity for Ray's ignorance of high society. "Well. Mr. Mitze certainly did have his problems."

"That's what I wanted to ask you about."

She moved the paperweight back where it had been and glanced up at him. Maureen had a way of posing, of going through frozen looks. But she added nothing, so he shook his head again and lamented, "All the money he needed. A beautiful wife. A fine career . . ."

"Some people said he was a genius—as if that excused him."

"For what?"

She put her tongue to her top lip. "For being so *odd*."

"How was he odd?"

"I really don't like to gossip about the members," she sniffed. "Especially when they've passed on."

Maureen was being a tease tonight, and Ray decided to make a little better contact by touching her hand, laying his on top of hers on the desk. Her mouth came open and she winced slightly, exhaling cocktail across him. After a moment, he gently took it away.

"Anything you tell me will be kept confidential, Maureen."

"Well, I assume you heard about our little incident."

"No."

"I thought that's what you were inquiring about. Some people blame those kinds of things on me just because they happen here. As if I had anything to do with it."

"What was the incident?"

"McNear and Ben Mitze had a fight."

Unexpectedly, the manager fell into reverie, turning her head a little sideways and gazing at her paperweight. Kitchen sounds and muted conversation came through the walls. "Wayne's coat was torn, and he was *panting,* and he took me over by the lattice where no one would hear. 'Maureen,' he said, 'in fifteen years' experience with Ben, nothing like this ever happened. Please excuse his behavior tonight.' "

"What happened?"

"Oh, Mr. McNear protected him afterward. Everybody will tell you that." She raised an eyebrow. "Somebody had to. . . . It was a chicken night—when the DataForm executives normally come out. We were busy: I had a birthday and two other big groups. Everybody was wearing regular dinner clothes; the Parks were here with a party from Little Rock who were *very* dressy. I thought I'd die, just simply expire."

"You still haven't said what happened, Maureen."

"Ben came in the door." Her eyes widened in little explosions when she emphasized words. "Just *wandered* in. I wasn't in the dining room when he first appeared or I would have asked him to leave. The way he looked, you wanted to protect the women and children. Well, I came out the minute I heard. And there he was, dirty and ill-kempt, his hair all wild, and just about naked."

"Naked?"

"He was wearing an old stained undershirt! Can you imagine that? At the country club? My heavens, there were older people here who could have had reactions."

"So he showed up improperly dressed and drunk?"

"I'm not a stickler about dress," Maureen said defensively. "I don't discourage sweaters! It was the way he was acting. When I came out of my office, the whole room was staring at him. Well, I just about crawled under the salad bar."

"What was he saying?"

"I'll grant you, Wayne McNear didn't waste any time. He took the man by the arm, escorted him right out that front door, and gave him a thrashing in the parking lot."

Ray looked skeptical. "Beat him up?"

"Verbally, yes," Maureen said. "What do you think the party from Little Rock went back and said about our country club? I mean really, people appearing in undershirts!"

"What did you hear Mitze say?"

"Honestly, I was trying to avoid having a coronary, not taking down a transcript."

"Obscenities?"

She shook her head.

"Remember what he said, Maureen. Anything at all."

"I believe he said something about a 'lock' or 'locking.' . . . You just had to see him to understand what I'm talking about."

"So he was completely drunk?"

Eyes closed, holding both sides of the ledger, she shook her head, forehead wrinkled in a frown. "I'm upset," she said calmly. "Just recalling it has put me in a state. Please don't ask any more." Then her eyes blinked open and she said in a lowered voice, "And you know, I don't think he was drunk. I didn't smell it on him. His wife is the one with *that* problem."

Ray leaned back and sighed. " 'Lock the door,' 'lock out,' 'lock in' . . . ?"

She shut her eyes again.

"Happy Birthday" was coming through the walls, someone from the kitchen was singing idly along with it.

Her eyes blinked open. "Down—he said something about 'down.' "

"Locked down?"

"Yes. First it was something like that, and then something about 'open'—'open dating'? An 'open date'? 'Open dating.' I just don't know."

"Who'd he say this to?"

"Mr. McNear."

"When McNear was hustling him out?"

"Oh, he was *grim*, and I don't blame him. My heavens, a company like that can't have employees running around like Hottentots. Have you met that fellow Jeremy Weeks? He's another one. Every time he comes out here—which fortunately isn't often—I have to fumigate the birthday room—"

"When exactly did this event with Ben Mitze happen?"

She opened the ledger and turned the big page backward. "December eighth. It had to be then because the party was small the next week."

"One last thing. Did you say the birthday room was *across* the dining area?"

"Yes. You just heard the happy-birthday song, didn't you? It's one of the quirks of this marvelous old building: The heating ducts carry it from there to the kitchen. I worry because the girls in the kitchen sometimes get a little salty in their comments, but the sound apparently goes only one way."

"So you get to listen to all the birthdays—and the DF execs every chicken night?"

"If I wanted to." She rolled her eyes and shut the ledger. "Fortunately, I can turn on that little fan and block out the sound."

"What do you think about the DF people?"

"I'll say one thing, they're candid. When they disagree, they let ʔach other know."

"Certain ones tend to disagree?"

"I don't really listen to the particulars. For one thing, they talk in Greek."

He decided not to press her on it. "You were saying Mrs. Mitze has an alcohol problem?"

"Well, it's none of my business." She moved the paperweight with a judicious clump onto the top of the ledger. "But it's only recently gotten so obvious. The loss of her husband, I suppose. It hardly matters. There are still plenty of men who think she's the hottest thing who ever dyed her hair blond."

"Was she having an affair with somebody?"

"An affair?" Maureen's eyes widened.

"Anybody in particular? Somebody else at DF?"

"She's just that way. I don't watch the woman."

"When did Wayne McNear and his wife get a divorce?"

"Now that's a sad tale. Cindy's parents had just died in an awful accident of some kind. An airplane crash I believe, in Brazil or some horrible place. They were very well off. From what I heard, they owned a lot of real estate. Cindy had to go back there to handle the affairs."

"When was this?"

"A year and some. Wayne was back and forth. I believe his company has an office out there. That's when it happened, anyway—right on top of Cindy's parents' death. I believe they were divorced in California."

"Wonder why they separated?"

"I can tell you one reason. W-O-R-K. That man works himself to death. And their daughter. Taylor. The girl has just been terrible. She's been a great strain. . . ." Maureen frowned at her paperweight. "Mr. Mitze said something about her that night, too."

"What?"

"I have no idea. I just seem to remember him saying her name."

"What's the problem with the girl?"

"I don't know," Maureen said.

"Any idea?"

"I'm not a psychiatrist."

"And Wayne has primary custody, doesn't he?"

"I believe so. I heard she was supposed to be with her mother in California in the summer, but apparently that isn't true. Or wasn't last summer. Evidently he managed to keep Taylor and finagled some money from his wife too." Maureen looked uncomfortable.

"Taylor wouldn't have had anything to do with those golf carts in the pond last summer, would she?"

"Oh, I'm sure she didn't."

"You never called me back on that problem, Maureen. I wasn't sure how it worked out."

"I appreciated your efforts, but the parents did step in. I received a check for $3700 for that particular little spree."

"McNear wrote you a check—?"

She shook her head.

"Who did?"

She sighed. "Ray. My job depends on—"

"This is one hundred percent between you and me."

"Let me just put it this way. If the Heyer child—Sinclair Heyer—and the McNear child did something wicked, the parents might have cooperated to find a solution."

"Something unusual about that?"

Maureen shook her head.

She hesitated another moment. "I'm glad you came by, Ray, but I must get to work."

"Just answer that one last question."

"Well, it's no secret. Mr. Heyer and Mr. McNear do *not* get along."

"Oh." Ray nodded, glancing at the heater duct. "They tend to disagree about something in particular."

Her eyes widened. "*Something?*"

"So who actually signed the check?"

She answered irritably. "Sinclair wrote it on his own checking account, but you can be sure both families were involved."

"Did you talk to the parents?"

She said nothing else.

Ray stood up. "Well, Maureen. I owe you one. Anybody steals any more of your golf carts, I'll put em in jail."

"Please. The best families in town would be childless."

8

As dramatic as Jack Cady's revelations about Ben Mitze and the trailer were, they somehow disappeared into the walls at DF. Bobbi told Ron Reed, and he said McNear had been informed. Hearing nothing from McNear—whom she seldom saw—she eventually called Mr. Cady back and asked what happened with the missing wolfhound. He didn't respond to the question—just went silent on the other end of the line. The next day she drove to his house, and he wasn't there. The whole thing lost urgency, what with holding down two jobs and running between the police department and DataForm.

Ron Reed was charged with building up the security force, but he didn't seem to be doing much. A new security office was being fitted out in the main building, complete with a working video system and separate offices for the officers, but Reed himself acted uninterested in the project. He didn't seem to want to move his desk from the Butler building. Bobbi, working several more hours a week than at first, was beginning to get involved enough to be frustrated at Reed's inaction. Two more security officers were supposed to be hired, but Reed dragged his feet.

On March 25, Bobbi had an appointment with Wayne McNear. Just arriving from New York, he came swooping in late, sat down, and got right to the point. "We've been watching you on the job and like what we see. Since you've been here, you've followed protocol very closely. We'd like to offer you the job of deputy director of personnel security."

Bobbi didn't know how to respond and so, for the moment, she didn't respond at all except to smile in what must have been a slightly puzzled way.

"The fact is we've never really had the kind of physical security that we recommend our clients have. We're committed now to building that into our company. I'm offering you a position of authority in that process. Do you think you're interested?"

"I'm certainly interested. . . ."

"What are your reservations?"

"Well. I don't . . ."

"Don't what?"

"I don't really know what DataForm"—she felt foolish—"what it does. Exactly."

"Of course not. Our product is security. If you knew exactly what we did, we wouldn't be doing our job. Let me tell you a little about where we came from. That may help you understand where we are now."

He tapped a pencil on his desk and gazed at her. "I'll ramble; stop me if you have questions.

"DF is the top company in systems security. We reached that position by breaking our backs seventy-five and eighty hours a week in cheap rented rooms—attics, garages, with stacks of computer junk all over the place. . . . I remember walking in one night about two o'clock. This was back in California, our second 'company headquarters'—a building in Palo Alto that had been a garage before we moved in. We were always getting grease on our clothes and the equipment. Four guys were at the place that night, and they all looked sick. They'd been debugging a security package for one of the systems at Lawrence Livermore Lab. We had I don't know how many man-years in the project. It was our first big opportunity.

"I asked them if they were trying out for a zombie movie or what, and Tim Thurmon said that LL had hired another consultant to check out our work. This person hadn't even come to our place. He'd hooked himself up on the phone using a Radio Shack home computer, and it took him like fourteen minutes to break through our system.

"They paid us a kill fee and said thanks but no thanks. I could tell you several more stories like that. We worked hard and kept losing. We had to be the longest-standing failure in Silicon Valley, but somehow we stayed together, peddling software in the magazines and getting occasional jobs to pay the electric bill. Employees were paid in stock and good faith. Our people passed up beaucoup jobs at safer places.

Any day they could have driven down Central Expressway and decided from the billboards which company to work for. It was a zoo out there in the go-go years. If you didn't live in Los Altos Hills and have a Mercedes with a car telephone you were nothing. We were invisible. We didn't exist. We were zilch.

"After four or five years of this we were getting close to the edge. I was hired by a produce firm outside Sacramento because I knew a guy who knew a guy looking for a consultant. They'd lost three or four hundred thousand dollars to their chief accountant. It wasn't a very difficult problem. The guy was adding three-fifths of a cent to every dollar the company sold and working out a way to send checks to dummy firms. It was small potatoes compared to a lot of computer crimes, but for some reason the California papers went nuts about it, and the news spread around. We started getting a lot of calls.

"A bank in New York sprung a ten-thousand-dollar-a-day leak, and hired me to find out what was wrong. It took me a week to discover one of their employees was walking around the major branch every day stealing money from all the terminals, as well as physically stealing it from the safe, scratching down notes to himself to cover his trails. The guy was bonkers. A private detective could have observed the situation and seen what was going on. It was hardly even a computer crime, the bank's system was so primitive. They found out he was spending it all at the horse races. He had a compulsion to be punished for being a thief, so he drove out to the track every afternoon and lost it all. His wife didn't know about it. Nobody did. When he won at the races—and apparently he won six hundred thousand dollars one day—he immediately put it down again until it was all gone. All this was another big media hit.

"We acquired a small chip company in California that made encryption keys from PROMS just before that became the big thing in security. Now we offer everything—the keys, the consulting, and the software assemblage. The idea is preventive security. We don't really like to play detective after something's already happened. You're already in trouble at that point. Our big computer fraud cases were good publicity, but for every neatly solved problem there are a bunch of unsolvables.

"Most of the companies with serious problems are scared to death of bad publicity. They worry more about that than the crime. If the crime cost a million bucks, the bad publicity can cost ten million. We have to cooperate with requests for discretion—sometimes at all costs. I've helped negotiate very expensive 'termination fees' for high-level stuff. Instead of prosecuting, banks and insurance companies like to pay you off."

"Why'd you move out of California?" Bobbi asked.

He shook his head. "The big problem out there was security. Of course we still have our California office, but back then we just couldn't count on our programmers and operators. There were too many people around trying to find out what we were doing. There's a thing called the 'Peninsula Ethic.' It's an informal standard in the Santa Clara Valley, and it says that unless a system is extremely well protected, copying it won't be prosecuted. It works in favor of the hardware companies, because if their stuff gets copied it's more likely to become an industry standard. They call it 'reverse engineering.' This is no good for software. When your software gets copied you've lost your product.

"That's why we have our assemblers working blind. They key in jobs in bits and pieces so no one really knows all the details. Blind keying is the tail end of a process that begins with divided architecture. The basic idea is that no one person knows enough about a security configuration to compromise it. We were the first company to offer that—walled architecture from conception through installation. Different project workers come up with different components, like building blocks with prearranged interfaces, then the assemblers key it in, it's tested and put to work. It's essential when you're working with banks that no one have a full set of keys."

He smiled. "I'm supposed to have privileged access, triple green we call it, but project directors tend to treat me like everybody else. I was going to add, though, about the walled architecture, that it's very imperfect. It's the ideal we strive for. All complicated software assemblage is messy and confused. The rules aren't always strictly followed because things would never get finished if they were. Computer science is still computer art. There are no absolute standards and procedures like you find in, say, the established professions like accounting. A lot of people think there never will be. We have to admit this with our clients.

"Still we have something nobody else does at the moment. Even USI would love to acquire us. When a client needs something more sophisticated than occasional audits—when they need to keep a constant eye on the works, they come to us. Those fifteen people in the control room are the heart of our real-time operations. They do continuous on-line auditing of almost a hundred mainframes located all over the country, the largest part of which are banks."

Marilyn walked into the office and plopped a folder on McNear's desk. On the way out, she said drily. "You should probably tell her about the package, Wayne."

"Arn Bass can give you the details." He made an effort at a smile. "What we're offering you is deputy chief of personnel security. Are you interested?"

"I'd have to quit the force. . . . How long can I think about it?"

"Come to my house on April first. We're having a party. You can let me know then."

His house was on the river bluffs in the abandoned grounds of an old park—a turn-of-the-century Sunday picnic and camp-meeting place. Bobbi had come out here a few times as a teenager, but it was too far from her house to walk or ride a bike to. The bluffs fifty yards behind McNear's house were one of the traditional places in Dubois County to commit suicide, although that, like the park itself, was almost a forgotten fact now. The house was three-story with the bottom floor crawling down the hilltop on two levels and a swimming pool off to one side. Two men were laying down grass sod in rectangular pieces between the white oaks on the front lawn. Cars were parked in the circular driveway—Porsches, Mercedeses, Audis.

The woman who came to the door had beautiful, dark skin and a raspy voice. It was Kate Heyer, and she invited Bobbi to the living room and asked her what she'd have to drink. She seemed careful and watchful but pleasant enough, unlike her dour husband. Bobbi had gotten the impression there was a problem between McNear and Mike Heyer, and it surprised her that Heyer's wife would be acting as hostess.

Arn Bass and Tony Pfeil were sitting alone in the living room across a wash of afternoon light. Bass, the furry-eyebrowed, blandly good-looking treasurer of DataForm, looked typically well dressed in light cotton slacks and shirt, while Tony slumped beside him in a bathing suit with a towel wrapped over his legs. Bass was among the least unusual-acting executives at DF—businesslike, friendly, competent. Tony was skinny, with a rough complexion that reached down his face and neck onto his back. He was the only exec Bobbi knew to be from back east. The cellular phone he carried with him wherever he went at the office sat on a low table.

"Hi, there," Bass said, flashing a smile toward her.

"It's the cops," Tony said. "Hello."

Tony returned to their conversation in a dully argumentative tone. "How many times have I heard it? They couldn't keep up with the dwarfs, they got blown out of the tub in memory and speed, Cray put them utterly to shame, they lost it with the minis, they lost it with the micros, they couldn't write their own software. Hey, just read their earnings report."

"The stock market runs on future earnings growth," Bass said, glancing toward Bobbi as if halfheartedly trying to include her in the discussion. "For USI, I'm saying that looks dim."

"USI, USI," Tony grumbled, looking around. "I don't know why we're always talking about Tom Ferris and USI." He pointed a forefinger downward and said, "I'm worried about what's going on down there."

Kate Heyer reappeared and told Bobbi that Wayne was in the attic. She handed her a Coke and disappeared before Bobbi could ask any questions. The attic?

Up the stairs, on the landing, she heard voices from the back of the house, a wide second-floor deck. She stood there for a moment listening to a tag of laughter here, music from somewhere else, her heart beating a little fast, feeling illicit, like a burglar who'd sneaked into somebody's house in the middle of a party. It was a very spread-out affair, with sounds coming from different places.

The stairs going up to the third floor were narrower, and at the top she knocked on a door and was about to push it open when she heard a low, mechanical laughing sound, along with some struggling and bumping around. She decided this was definitely not the main party. Back downstairs, she approached the deck and, from the door, saw McNear sitting at a round metal table talking with Elizabeth Mitze. Bobbi had seen Ben Mitze's widow at the building three or four times in previous months. They had a couple of fresh gin and tonics before them. Liz Mitze had superfine whitish blond hair and features that were all straight lines—straight nose, straight posture, straight mouth. She sat in perfect attentiveness to McNear, whose expression Bobbi couldn't see. He seemed to be doing most of the talking. Bobbi decided not to interrupt. They didn't seem at all aware of what was going on around them. Finally Liz smacked her mouth in an odd sort of way, shook her hair, combed her fingers through it, and said something, at which point McNear got up.

Seeing Bobbi, he greeted her with a drawn smile.

"Someone said you were in the attic."

"I have been most of the day. Come with me and I'll show you," he said, going downstairs. He waited for her at the entrance to the basement. "This is the 'attic.' It's a nickname. At our company's second location, the place on High Street I mentioned before, there was an upstairs office. A crowded room we called the attic. Since then, we've always had a junky room by that name."

The basement was very large, with piles of electronic equipment stacked haphazardly around. A printer was running somewhere. Tony and Arn Bass had come down, and several others sat or sprawled on carpet samples and old pillows watching a VDT.

They hardly seemed to notice Bobbi. Mike Heyer, looking sullen, stood at a big plywood table shuffling through stacks of printout paper. Jeremy Weeks, sporting a Hawaiian shirt and slicked-back hair, was absorbed in the VDT. Bobbi had learned that Jeremy very seldom left the DF building, but he appeared to be at ease here. Carol Rader was sitting in an old armchair, eyes shut, in front of the same screen. The lower half flickered with numbers. One of them punched the keyboard and a pattern appeared on the screen.

"So what exactly is an open data base?" Arn asked.

"Freeze something else," Jeremy said.

McNear knelt on the floor and watched the terminal a minute. He asked Bobbi to have a seat on an old pillow. "Sorry about this," he said vaguely. "It seems we can't stop working, even at our April Fools party."

"You did this, Jeremy," Carol Rader muttered, eyes still closed.

The observers had been quiet for a moment, sipping and watching the screen. Jeremy shook his head. "It's just a job queue. But what the hell is the "Godball," and why is it sending us this mush?"

Rader winced her closed eyes as if she had a headache. "This isn't a good joke, Jeremy. I don't care if it is April Fools."

"I didn't do it, Carol. I didn't. I swear."

McNear looked at the screen a moment longer without comment, then asked Bobbi to take a walk out a back door onto a large, circular patio.

They went across the bricks and down the back yard to a wood-rail fence a few feet from the bluff's edge. While other kids were playing volleyball at a far end of the yard, Taylor and Sinc Heyer had just come out and were standing alone at a badminton net with rackets in hand. Bobbi had something like a spell of déjà vu, and realized that it was because something about Taylor—her posture, her expression—reminded her of the night she'd taken her to the hospital. Sinc Heyer, looking clumsy and hangdog with his short, ratty hair, was trying to get her to play, and she was just standing there listlessly.

McNear glanced back and then resolutely turned to the cedar fence, looking out over the river valley. "Nice day, at least."

"Your house is nice."

"It was my wife's project," he said with a melancholy smile. "Our April Fools party is a flop this year. None of us is much in the partying mood. We had something a little strange happen. I got a letter yesterday from Ben Mitze, the man we lost in December."

Bobbi took that in. "Oh?"

He seemed to drift for a moment. "Yesterday . . . when I checked my mail. It was a timed letter he apparently keyed in before his accident, set to appear at nine A.M., March thirty-first. It's being sent from a source in the sky that calls itself the Godball."

Bobbi smiled uncertainly. "That does sound like a joke."

"I don't know. . . ." He finally looked at her. "It's hard to tell. It's encrypted, and it's still printing out. We haven't been able to decipher it yet."

"Since yesterday?"

"Afraid so," he said. "Eleven thousand lines of gobbledygook at last count. I've got a little 120-cps printer doing it, and it just keeps coming in." He took a last drink and pitched his ice cubes over the bluff. His eyes followed a hawk riding the wind on the other side of the valley. "There's another transmission coming in at the same time. That menu they were looking at in the basement."

"Yes?"

He turned around and looked back at the house, where Taylor had quit badminton after a few bats at the birdie, and was now getting on a riding lawn mower. She started it and engaged the blade and was riding around the yard cutting it in erratic patterns. Sinc jumped on beside her, standing on the blade cowling, and seemed to be pleading with her. Watching them, McNear's eyes narrowed. The girl was heading across the lawn toward them, up and down the little hillocks. "Some of us spent all night trying to decrypt—"

To Bobbi's astonishment, Taylor ran over one of the poles of the badminton net, then bore down on them. McNear had to sidestep to avoid being hit, and Taylor peeled off down the fence line, Sinc continuing to plead with her.

Bobbi didn't hide her anger. "What the hell was that?"

McNear watched after them. It was clear he was upset, too, but didn't want to deal with it now. He gave Bobbi a heavy look, as if to say, okay, let's just not talk about it.

She couldn't believe he didn't go snatch her off the mower.

He nodded at a satellite dish on the other side of the back yard. "There's no satellite at that vector. So says the latest atlas, anyway. It's all very mysterious." He took a deep breath, and his tone became firmer. "Have you come to a decision about our offer?"

He watched his daughter, who was driving up and down the lawn with the Sinc still hanging on, arguing with her.

"Can you tell me a little more about Mr. Reed?"

"Ron's good at some things. He's tough, but he's not big on organization."

"How long has he been with you?"

"Since our fourth year. I found Ron in McAlester, Oklahoma. When I first met him, he was in prison. I gave a talk there, arranged by a chamber of commerce exchange, one of my first talks, actually. The McAlester Antlers Club. I got there and discovered it was a prison club. I talked about good jobs being available in California. One of the inmates told me that when he got out he was going to come to California and ask me for a job. Three months later there he was, standing at my door with a little brown suitcase. It went from there."

"Where'd he do his training?"

"Ron really hasn't had formal training. You have to understand that he started as a general utility man. He was literally our janitor, mechanic, chauffeur—everything. And he was good at it. As we grew, he evolved into the security niche. Things have gotten more complicated now, and he needs help."

"How's he going to take somebody moving into his territory?"

"Ron really does want help."

Bobbi looked out on the river awhile. There was a little breeze. She tried to smile. She had a number of questions, but none of them seemed quite relevant. She said, feeling lame even as the words came out of her mouth, "Did you know that I'm presently getting a divorce?"

McNear looked back toward his daughter. "I've been through one of those. I know it isn't fun."

Sinc had finally coaxed Taylor off the riding mower, and he watched them disappear around the side of the house.

He and Bobbi stood there a few moments longer, looking at what was becoming a sunset. "Did Arn get to you with the salary package?"

"No."

"Low thirties to start, plus stock benefits. You can talk to him tomorrow and get the details."

"What about training?"

"California, Pacific Research Institute."

"Starting when?"

"About ten days from now."

"How long can I think about it?"

"We need to know by Monday."

9

Ray sat in his parked car beneath a faded sign that squeaked back and forth in the blowing rain. The radio was full of static. Down the slope a white sheen from the bridge lights cast across the river's choppy surface. He had been biding his time, listening to storm calls over police dispatch. It was 1:15 and the DataForm keyboarders would be well into their payday suds.

"We have a dog swallowed up by the flood at 25 Smithton Road, that's Golden Hills," Parker said. "Call-in was made by Mr. Gerald Carter, age six. Do we have someone who can cruise the area?"

"This is two, I'll take it."

"That's a Labrador puppy, two,"

"It's the right weather for him."

"Try to avoid life-threatening situations, two," Parker said drily.

Ray was about to switch over to his channel when Parker's voice came back on, more urgently: "All cars, we have a possible 1599 on Cedar Creek Road, two miles west of Highway 7. This is county transfer. That's at the Cady Kennel."

Two cars answered and Ray sat rubbing the bridge of his nose, frowning out into the rain. There was no further information. He lit a cigarette and glanced at his watch again, punched into the scrambler and got Bowser.

"Have anything tonight?"

"Nothing but lightning. Bring me a sixpack, would you?"

"Ten-four. I'll be away from the radio awhile. I just heard a possible 1599 from PD dispatch. It sounded like Jack Cady's place—the dog man. Follow that, would you?"

Inside the Cherokee, the big room was pulsing with people, beer signs casting moving lights across them—the blue neon of Pabst Sold Here and the snaky silver lights of a "waterfall" wiggling across the ceiling. The old jukebox with big chrome bars on the front shone out yellow and blue and red through curved agate glass panels. The air smelled of beer, kitchen grease, perfume, and bathrooms. Four women sat in a booth behind Ray eating the Catfish Dinner—$2.95 advertised behind the bar. There was a half-door into the kitchen, and the old lady who'd cooked at the Cherokee ever since Ray could remember was leaning out of it smoking a weed.

Eight or ten people were dancing to Willie Nelson, and the smoke was thick. Ray recognized a number of DataForm workers. When the song was finished, a woman in a red polyester suit held up her hand and said, "A round for the assemblers! Rita's paying!" There were whistles and catcalls, as the woman veered over toward Ray and slid in across from him. Her face was sweaty and a piece of curly brown hair hung down between her eyes. Bright red lipstick matched her red suit. "Ray, you devil, what are you doing out here again?"

"You know how it is, Rita. Just an old dog out prowlin." He offered her a cigarette and cracked a stick match on his thumbnail to light her up.

A smile split her red lips. "You're out here an awful lot, aren't you? You solving a crime or performing one?"

"Little bit of both. How about you?"

"I'm celebrating. Got me a doublewide surprise today: Won the bonus on my shift, second week in a row."

"What do you win—stock shares?"

She smiled. "Now see, you ain't so ignorant."

"What's that stuff worth?"

"Book value or the market value?"

"Market."

"People figure it different ways." She raised an eyebrow, and with her stark red lips mouthed, "Eleven hunert dollars, bonus, one month."

Ray made a low whistle. "Must be why you're buyin."

She knocked the curl of hair out of her eyes and glanced around the room. "Yes, sir. Payin the friendly tax."

Ray acted curious.

She leaned over the table. "When you're a regular winner, you pay the friendly tax or these gals will try to mess up your stats."

"How do they do that?"

"Lots of ways. Whisper at you. Talk at you when they're off-line. Ask if you want a Coke every time they pass by."

"What's wrong with that?"

"Hey, I'm puttin in over four hunert bytes a minute. I can't say 'No thank you, hon' to everybody that walks by my terminal. People will bug a winner to death, and you strictly don't have time to be nice. Not on the job. Not if you're a winner. So what you do is make up for it when payday comes around. Winning carries obligations."

Ray looked at his beer. "What's a byte?"

"Keystroke. We're counted on the keystroke."

"How many words is that?"

"This is harder than typing, Ray. For one thing you can't make no mistakes. And you got all your entering to do, and skipping fields." The expression on her face suddenly changed to a sympathetic frown. "I guess you knew Bobbi's working down there."

Ray looked at her without expression. "Tell me what makes you so fast, Rita. What's your secret?"

"Just follow them letters, buster, right down that page to bonus time." She held up her fingers and wiggled them. "Biddlybiddlybiddly. I can do more with them ten little Indians than my old man can do with his entire broke-down back. The secret is not to think about it. Never look at your fingers, just turn on the daydream channel and watch it roll by." Rita let smoke come out of her mouth and sucked it through her nostrils. She waved at somebody at the bar. "You need two channels going in your mind, one to daydream and one to keep a check on things, but the one that's keeping a check can't get too smart."

"How's that?"

She leaned across the table with a smile that raised her upper lip past her gums. "If you get to asking questions and meddling with data, you slow down. Be like a farmer worrying over every shuck of corn instead of rolling through there putting away the bushels."

Ray took a sip. "How is old Tom doin, by the way?"

"Don't ask me. It's my night out with the girls."

He glanced around the room and then back at her. "Want to go for a ride?"

"Now?"

"Why not? I got windshield wipers."

"Oh boy, don't *he* move fast."

He took another sip and said nothing.

"Well, I can't go out the door with you."

Ray crushed out his cigarette and smiled at her. "Buick under the sign. If the spirit moves you, come on out."

He bought Bowser's sixpack and hurried across a lightning-illuminated parking lot and piled into his front seat. The blue pager light was on.

"We've got a light-up at the trailer."

"Anything funny?"

"Negative. Just the usual."

"What about that 1599 at the Cady Kennel?"

"I haven't been listening for the last five minutes."

"Guess you better stay with John. I'll see you after a while."

Ray drank one of Bowser's beers and sat back mulling over all the questions he had about the stakeout at the trailer. It definitely took the prize for strangeness. For one thing, it wasn't a stakeout, really, but a guard detail. And why had it been set up on December 11, right after Ben Mitze's death? Why had George Warnke been in such a red-faced flush when he first told Ray about this "most important undercover job in years"?

If the trailer was an electronic snooper, why didn't anybody use it? A logical answer was that it was totally automated. It didn't require anybody. The "light-ups" they'd all three seen on their different shifts occurred when it was doing its job. The entire inside of the damn thing would come on. Warnke got bent out of shape when Ray asked any questions about it. All he'd say was that the "air-conditioning system" ran occasionally, and it was of no consequence.

The passenger door swung open and Rita piled in. "This is the worst!" Ray punched back in to police dispatch and started the motor. "Where are we going?" she asked, her curls dripping.

"When's the last time you did this?"

"None of your business," Rita said.

Her style of kissing was wide-open-mouthed. It depressed Ray to unhook her bra. They were parked in Mat's Creek picnic ground, three miles west of Okay, with rain pounding the roof and the roar of the swollen creek sounding almost as if it was rolling between the car wheels.

"Do you have to leave that radio on?"

"Music to my ears. Do you remember the last time we went parking?"

She breathed heavily. "It was before Kennedy was shot, I know that."

He slipped around to her breasts and got her nipples to stand up—one and then the other. When she began pawing in his pants, he pulled her up on his lap so that she couldn't reach him. For a big gal she was still pretty lithe. An occasional call crackled over the radio.

She ran her fingers through his hair. "What is that, Vitalis?"

"Thirty-weight."

She kissed him passionately. "Have you got any protection?"

"Sure."

"Devil. You carry it around for anybody you can find to use it on." She rolled off of his lap and was out of her pantsuit and underwear in ten seconds.

Ray had hoped that she'd feel guilty and stop in the middle of this, but no such luck. She was raring to go.

Using the power of imagination, he was finally able to get it up, and she got on his lap again, opening her haunches wide and taking the best he could give her. She began to bounce up and down on him making noises like she hadn't done this in a while. He worried at her clitoris with a thumb, and she groaned as if in pain.

He made a few more motions with his thumb, and she quivered, pushing her thighs forward. Then with both hands on her wide hips, he held her still. "Talk to me about something. I want it to build up slow."

"Oh God, Ray, keep . . ."

He rubbed her a little more. "Tell me about work. What do you all do over there?"

"Where?"

"At work." One stroke with each thumb.

"Create software." Her head drooped forward.

"What kind of software?"

"The most advanced in the world today," she murmured, as if repeating something she had read somewhere. She raised her ass and came down slowly, and he held her down again.

"Where'd you learn how to do it?"

"We ain't the ones to figure it out. We just punch it in."

Ray lifted her up and let her move for a few seconds longer. When she started bouncing, groaning, he held her still again. "Talk some more. You got me too turned on."

"You're awful," Rita said.

"What do you punch in?"

"I told you," she said irritably. "Software."

"What kind of software?"

"Programs, they divide em all up. All of us doing different . . . parts."

Her clitoris had become a hard little node. She began to make a humming sound. He wondered if old Tom ever fucked her at all. He laid both hands loosely around her hips, and again she began to bounce wildly, her hum breaking into wild snorts.

"Don't stop!" Rita said.

"What are these things that you punch in?"

"Don't know," she panted.

Ray stroked her again and she began to hum. "What do you *think* they are?"

"You're taking advantage of me, Ray Wiel. You stop it."

"I always mix business and pleasure, Rita. It's a fault of mine. Nothing you say will get beyond this car."

"Nothing?" Rita said, rising up and settling down slowly.

"Promise." He put the thumb to her again. "Who gives it to you?"

She rared her head back. "Mmmm . . . that's right. Do it that way."

"Ben Mitze—he bring things to you?"

"Oh, Ray. He's dead."

"Did he bring stuff to you?"

"Yes," she wailed.

"He did?"

"Oh *God* yes. *All* the time. *Tons* of it. Umh . . ."

"Who was Mitze's best friend down there?"

"I don't know. Quit askin me ah . . ."

"Give me a name. Who'd he hang around with? Talk to in the halls."

"I never get in the halls. I just sit—ah—"

"Mike Heyer—was he tight with Mitze?"

"I'm just a keyboar—umh, umh—oh Ray you big oh, oh . . . *oh!*"

She grasped him around the head with both arms and crushed his face into her sweaty bosom. Ray held on for dear life while she went off, kept going off, like a chain-reaction freeway accident. A report began to come in over the police channel but through her and the radio static he couldn't hear it. She was crawling off him cussing when he noticed the blue pager light was on again.

She threw herself around in the front seat putting her clothes on. "Ray Wiel, you dirty dog."

"Now Rita. That's what you said the last time we went parking." He pulled up his pants and fiddled with the tuner, trying to get a clear line on the report that was coming in from Cady Kennel. The officer reporting sounded like Jim Daly. He could tell by Parker's responses that it was serious. When it was serious, Parker always got very good—thinking fast, making confusion sound as if there was a hidden order behind it.

"You dragged me out here to get information out of me. You're trying to get me fired."

Parker mentioned Detective Miller's name, and Ray had learned enough. He turned down the radio.

"What the heck are you trying to find out?" Rita pouted, stuffing in her blouse.

"I'm investigating a death."

"Ben Mitze, right? Well, I wouldn't speak poorly of the dead, but we were *all* glad he wasn't bringing in his stuff every day of the week, that's for sure. All he ever said was 'No mistakes. This is a system.' " She zipped up her front.

"What's that?"

"He was so damn persnickety. And mean. Far as he was concerned, we were machines that never did quite work good enough."

"What's a system?"

"It's keyin at two miles an hour, that's what it is. Colons, semicolons, commas, brackets, dollar signs until you wouldn't believe it. All them that's hard to get to up on top your board. Long reaches. There's some it don't slow down like it does me. Me it ruins. You got any cigarettes left?"

"Was it one project or a whole bunch of different ones?"

"I don't know. I heard him talk about the 'assembly' sometimes, as if it was the one and only. Where are those cigarettes?"

"Glove compartment. What's an assembly?"

"How do I know? I just key em, I don't write em. . . . It was big enough, I know that."

"Big?"

She looked at him. "Ray Wiel, if you go tellin anybody I put out so much as a peep of work gossip, I'll lose that job. Do you understand?"

"Rita. I give you my word."

"We ain't supposed to know what each other's workin on, but I know for a fact he had a hundred percent of every shift working on that monster. For weeks. It just kept coming in. All of our stats was messed up, with that nut running in and out of there."

"So when you say 'big'—"

"I mean ten, fifteen times bigger than anything any of us have ever seen—and I'm talking veterans. Now start up this old tugboat and take me back to the Cherokee, Ray Wiel."

Ray leaned over and tried to kiss her on the cheek, but she brushed him away. "Want to do it again?"

"I do not. Now take me back."

Saturday morning, Ray shut his office door and took the pint of Old Grand-Dad from his otherwise empty file drawer. He leaned back in his chair, put his feet up on his desk, and unscrewed the cap. Scraps of paper lay around his desk—things he hadn't had time for lately—an assault, two burgs . . .

On Saturday he didn't shave, and he didn't feel guilty about a morning sip of whiskey. He rolled it around in his mouth and swallowed.

He listened to the sounds in the building. There wasn't much going on. The shift sergeant's office was above him, down one office, and he had sometimes been able to hear Bobbi's voice through the floor—the tone of it, if not the particular words. Bobbi had such a clear, plain, unconfused way of talking. He missed her.

He took another sip and gazed at the folder that he'd just taken from Miller's desk. Marvin Miller was the other detective on the Dubois police force, and one of the main reasons that Ray came to the office so infrequently during normal hours. Miller disliked Ray intensely, and over time the feeling had become mutual. Miller had an authoritative manner, very measured and controlled, but that was about it on the plus side. He'd been promoted to investigation, despite the fact that he barely had enough brains to piss and breathe at the same time, because Warnke needed a yes-man in detective. The one thing he enjoyed doing was making up files. He loved to take out new, crisp folders and put color-striped labels on them, type out neat records and put them away. He didn't particularly like to use these records, or let other people use them, and he was always getting after Ray for taking out things or misfiling them.

"Cady, Jack/4.6.84." The color of the stripes were yellow and green—yellow for "probable" and green for "suicide." On a smaller label, inside the cover, Miller had typed his initials—"MM."

Ray noticed that Miller had begun typing the report within sixty minutes of his arrival at the scene of the incident, which meant he couldn't have spent more than a half hour at Cady's house. The sergeant at the scene—whose call-in he'd not quite been able to hear through Rita and the rainstorm—was indeed Jim Daly.

A neighbor of Mr. Cady's had discovered a dead lamb a little after 2100 and seen a bunch of dogs lurking around his place. He'd scared them off and taken the dead lamb over to Cady's to inform him that his dogs were loose. Unable to rouse anybody, the neighbor had entered the house and found Jack on the floor near the woodstove in the living room, apparently killed by a blast from a shotgun that lay at his feet.

Miller's list of incidentals included a shocker for Ray. Across the front of Mr. Cady's telephone book had been one number, handwritten: 327-9739. It was Bobbi's number at the trailer court.

Miller hadn't looked the number up yet or he'd have noted it.

The clock above the door told him that he was late for breakfast with the chief, but suddenly he felt like he needed time to think. He and Richard had planned to go out looking for a car for him this morning. They'd made a deal to slip out after Bobbi left for work. Ray didn't feel right about seeing his stepson on the sly, but Bobbi kept putting up such fusses that he didn't know what else to do. Today, he needed to see Bobbi. He picked up the phone, hesitated, then called her number.

He was glad Richard answered. "Son, I'm going to have to come by a little early and talk to your mom. That okay?"

Richard sighed. "I don't know. . . ."

"I have to eat breakfast with the chief. I'll be around in about an hour."

Ray took a final sip of Old Grand-Dad and refiled the bottle in his lock-drawer, popped a couple of Sen-Sens, and headed upstairs.

Ray wasn't excited about his cheese omelette. Bright shades of yellow. Warnke had ordered a short stack and wasn't eating either. He was tense today. Ray could always tell how tense Warnke was by how bored and sleepy he acted.

He had a habit of grimacing, yawning, widening and blinking his eyes, like someone trying to keep from going to sleep at the wheel. When Warnke was first hired as chief seven years ago, Ray had thought the man disliked him personally, but it eventually became clear that he had a yawning problem. The more excited he became the more he yawned—an unusual trait.

Ray was more interested in Jack Cady's death than in the stakeout operation, but experience had taught him never to be too direct with the chief. He casually asked Warnke if he knew anything about it yet.

He shook his head briefly, with a look of distaste. "Friend of yours?"

"Knew each other to speak. He was a friend of Bobbi's old man."

"Pretty cut and dried. Old fellow did himself in."

"Was there any motive?"

Warnke yawned. "He was almost eighty. Probably sick. We couldn't find any recent medical records on him. Apparently he went to the doctor about every fifteen or twenty years. . . . Miss, you wouldn't happen to have some coffee made this week would you?" he called across the diner, and muttered at Ray, "This stuff tastes like it's made out of strip-pit tailings."

"So you've seen Miller's report on Cady?"

"What I'm concerned about is the stakeout, Ray. Are you a hundred-percent certain everything's working okay?"

Ray nodded slightly.

"No problem with shift changes?"

"We could use a little more information."

Warnke shuddered as he suppressed a yawn. His voice was flat. "What kind of information?"

"Let's say somebody shows up out there who obviously knows what they're doing. They go right inside the trailer. You want us to follow him in?"

"We've been through this several times, haven't we. If somebody shows up, call *your* operations point on *your* scrambled radio; operations then gets hold of me directly by *telephone*. After making the call-in, the person on duty is to get a make on the intruder and get *rid* of him. Fast. Don't let him get near the door if you can help it."

"What if he's stubborn?"

"Expel the intruder from the area, Ray. Keep them *out* of the place. You're big boys."

"What about these lightups? When that box turns on."

"As I've said, don't pay any attention to it. It's insignificant."

The waitress came over, sullen, turned a second cup over and poured it full of coffee. Ray played with the lip of his water glass. "I'll tell you what we could use. We could use a better handle on this whole thing."

The chief widened and blinked his eyes as he took a sip, then set the cup down with a clunk. "Absolutely negative, Ray. We've talked about this numerous times. This job is top-down, and that includes me. We have no choice in the matter."

"I'm talking about something just to keep us oriented. It's been going on three months now. Gets pretty boring out there."

"No one said police work was always interesting."

Ray whirled around the water in the glass and said nothing.

Glancing at him, Warnke leaned across the table slightly on his elbows and assumed a different expression, eyes blinking. "Let me ask you a question. This is between you and me. Do you remember what the sheriff did with that federal drug bust a couple of years ago?"

Sure he did. Sheriff Bud Nagal had blown a quarter-million-dollar DEA investigation by getting excited at the last minute and giving his deputies a lecture on how they were just about to break the back of big-time drug dealing in Dubois County—following which, within remarkably few hours, there weren't any backs of any drug dealers to break anywhere within a fifty-mile radius.

"I don't normally like to discuss this kind of thing, Ray, but if this can remain entirely confidential, I want to mention that *if* you do this job right you'll be in a very good position vis-à-vis certain career ambitions you might have. If you blow it, people are going to say 'We've already got one Bud Nagal, we don't need another one.' Now I hope you get my drift." Eyebrows raised, the chief stood up.

Ray was impressed. This was the first time Warnke had ever openly mentioned his supposed ambition to be sheriff.

At the cash register, Warnke threw down a twenty and yawned.

Popping a Sen-Sen, Ray said, again casually, "So have you called Jack Cady's relatives yet?"

"That's one good thing," Warnke said. "The only relatives he had were dogs."

Bobbi hadn't slept a minute. Richard was late coming home, the weather was wild, and she was alone. All night, she thought about Wayne McNear's offer. Just before midnight she'd called the station to talk about it with Jim Daly, but he'd apparently been called out somewhere in the county to a suicide and wasn't likely to be in a mood for career counseling.

The trailer shuddered in high winds, thunder bashed against it spitefully, like rocks thrown by a mean neighborhood kid, and she lay there blinking, unable to close her eyes, thinking about the job, wondering about the details of the offer that Bass was supposed to make her, and, as the night went on, worrying increasingly about Richard, who finally came home three hours and forty-two minutes past his midnight curfew.

She also thought about Ray, the SOB. Ray had been virtually invisible lately. She hadn't laid eyes on him for over two weeks.

Ray had clearly been unprepared for her response to his girl-chasing. She had been pretty absolute about it—for which others had criticized her, including Jim and even Martha in her gentle way. On nights like this, she herself wondered how much of it had been her own fault, after all. Had she become too crusty? Too much of a cop?

She lay in the yellow, damp, early-spring dawn thinking about the changes in Richard since he'd found his first serious girlfriend. He was seldom at home anymore and when he was, Cathy was usually beside him telling him what to do. A seventeen-year-old boy understandably preferred his girlfriend over just about anything short of breathing, but Richard also seemed to enjoy the company of Cathy's family, particularly her father, so much more than Bobbi's. . . .

Cathy's father was an ironworker and an old hippie who smoked dope in the presence of his kids and let his oldest daughter do anything she wanted to in her bedroom, as long as her "friend" didn't spend the entire night there, which struck Bobbi as an odd restriction since the only thing it prevented was their waking up in the morning and getting a glimpse of reality. What was more romantic than putting on your clothes and slipping out before sunrise?

The other thing she worried about was that Richard had been sneaking out with Ray, which she had forbidden on the advice of her lawyer, since in a divorce any kind of thing the stepfather heard from the boy could become ammunition in the proceedings.

The phone rang early and Richard answered it before the second ring. Poor kid could be dead in his coffin and all you'd have to do to resurrect him was put a ringing phone by his head.

Saturday breakfasts together was a family custom Bobbi was trying to hang on to, so she kept him awake, very determinedly trying to keep things pleasant by not questioning him about last night's broken curfew. He slouched in the dinette chair, staring out the little front window. He sighed, and, with his elbows on the table and legs spread out, took a couple of bites of toast before his eyes misted over again and he forgot what he was doing.

"Eggs are getting cold." She tried to sound pleasant.

He stared out into the wet morning.

"Hey, hot rod." She widened her eyes and made a face that used to make him laugh. "Eat some breakfast. You can have the car today, but you'll have to take me to work."

"I don't need it." Still staring.

"Has Cathy got hers?"

He looked at her now. "Ray's comin over."

Stunned, she finished her breakfast quickly and took her dishes to the sink. "Was that him on the phone?"

"Yeah," he said shortly. "He's gonna take me out to look for a car."

So much for a pleasant Saturday breakfast.

"Did you tell him you'd talk to me about that first?"

"Why should I?"

She turned around from the sink, and he was looking at her with a funny sneer on his face, a dumb expression that threw her into a tumult of emotions. "Richard, I think we need to have another talk."

"I'm old enough to drive."

"That's not the question."

"He's here."

Someone was at the front door. She gave Richard a hard look. "All right. I'll talk to him first if you don't mind."

"You can't make him leave."

"Please remain inside while I talk with him, Richard."

"I'm going with him."

Knocking at the door.

"What are you gonna do, arrest me?"

"Sit down."

"No!" he shouted, going pale and pushing his plate onto the floor, whether accidentally or not she couldn't quite tell.

More knocking.

Bobbi held her own hands tightly and squinted at the broken plate on the floor. She couldn't appear weak. "Please have that picked up when I come back."

She went to the front door and swung it open and stepped out, awkwardly forcing Ray back down the steps. "Outside, please."

He was wearing his old leather jacket and a hat, smoking a cigarette, liquor and Sen-Sen on his breath. She led him across the puddled driveway to a spot near the dumpster. A warm Gulf-smelling breeze came out of the south. Two neighbor kids played quietly nearby. Otherwise, the wet trailer park looked abandoned.

"Hi, Bob." He smiled at her—his charming, almost shy smile.

"You should have called me about this."

He gazed at her curiously while she let him know what she thought about him making promises to Richard for a car behind her back, without her knowledge. Ray had a slightly upturned nose, thinning black hair, and calm brown eyes. "I need to talk to you, Bob."

"Then you better set up an appointment through the lawyers."

"This is something else."

Richard banged open the door of the trailer and came out into the driveway, stopping ten feet away, his expression masklike in the outdoor light, with funny rings around his eyes.

"Can we go now?" he asked Ray.

"Hi, Son." Ray went over and took his hand, smiling at him. "Damn, aren't you getting to be a stud."

Richard's pale face suddenly blushed bright red. There was something strange about him, almost out of control. "I'm ready to go."

"Well, your momma tells me this car thing hasn't been hashed out yet."

"What's the big deal. Everybody has a damn car."

Richard's boyishness toward Ray irritated her, but she couldn't afford to lose it. She had to take control. "I'll tell you both. I don't want you showing him cars right now, Ray. If you still want to do it in the fall, that'll be fine. But you won't pay for it; Richard and I will. You can come in for a minute, if you want. I don't have to be at work until ten."

He followed her inside and sat down at the kitchen table. Bobbi was edgy from her sleepless night, and nasty comments started shooting across her mind like nickel rockets.

He had pushed back his hat and was smiling sadly down at the table. Good old sweet Ray. She wanted to ask good old sweet Ray what he thought about his lawyer's latest letter to her, but she refrained.

Richard had stayed outside.

"You getting along okay?"

"Just fine."

She gave him a cup of coffee and set the milk carton on the table beside it.

"Is work okay?"

"Just fine. I've got a new job. I'm quitting the force." Her stomach turned upside down as she said it. He was the last person she'd intended to tell.

He put his hat on the table and fiddled with it a minute, frowning. "Did you hear about Mr. Cady?"

"Jack? What about him?"

"They found him dead last night."

"What happened?"

"They say suicide. There was a shotgun on the floor." He poured in a little more milk.

"Who's working it?"

"Miller did the report. He and Jim Daly were out there last night."

Her thoughts fell into a welter, and instinctively she avoided saying much. "Did they do an autopsy?"

He shook his head. "Wasn't much doubt about the cause. He was found by a neighbor. Some of Jack's dogs got loose and killed a lamb. Neighbor came over to tell him about it and found him in his house. I read Miller's report this morning. I know Jack meant something to you— friend of your dad's and all. I just didn't want you to learn about this from the newspaper."

"Nice of you to think about me." For something to do, she went to the refrigerator and got out the orange juice.

Ray watched her. "Bob, I'm worried about you working at DF."

She got down a small glass and poured the orange juice. "What are we talking about?"

"DataForm," he said with a little change in his voice, a softening.

Bobbi looked out the front window at Richard, who looked oddly far away sitting against the dumpster, elbows on knees, watching the trailer. She wondered why he had chosen to stay outside.

"I'd just be worried about you working out there," he repeated.

She still didn't respond. He would be worried.

He sat tapping three fingers on the table. "What did Jack talk to you about?"

"Why do you ask?"

"Your number was written across the front of his phone book."

"I saw Jack a couple of weeks ago."

"Do you remember exactly when?"

"March twentieth—thereabouts."

Ray frowned. "How was he doing?"

"Seemed okay."

"What'd he talk about?"

Bobbi thought about it a minute before she told him what Jack had told her—about finding Ben Mitze's body at the trailer and his later frustrated attempts to explain the event to the police.

When she was through, he looked down at the hat, shaking his head slightly. "So *Warnke* himself went to Jack's house and questioned him?"

"That's what Jack told me."

He shook his head slowly, frowning. "Bob, I need to tell you something, and it needs to stay between you and me."

She didn't respond.

"It's sensitive. At least, that's what we keep hearing." He glanced at her as if to confirm that she'd not talk about this with anyone else. "I think there's an investigation of DF going on right now."

"What do you mean?"

"It's all top-down, covert, pretty much according to the book." He blew out a big sigh. "The whole thing was set up right after Mitze bought the farm. December eleventh. Only we didn't hear a thing about the happening out at the trailer. . . ."

"*You* knew about the trailer?"

At this point, Ray just shook his head. He seemed to be confounded. He fiddled with his cup of coffee. "If I told you everything I know, you wouldn't be a bit smarter. But I'm hearing that Jack Cady did have something to do with this whole deal."

"What exactly has Warnke got you doing?"

He frowned at her. "I'm not satisfied that Jack Cady committed suicide last night."

"I was getting that drift, but it doesn't answer my question."

"Bob, I'd get my ass kicked all the way to the Pacific Ocean."

Elbow on the table, fist at his mouth, Ray brooded—looking casual, almost like he sat here every morning. Bobbi had the sudden urge to yell at him, You son of a bitch, what made you think you could just run around town with that little twit of a girl? You could have gotten away with fucking her, but not going around town showing her off. She looked out the window at her son, who hadn't moved from the dumpster. He was watching the trailer.

"I just don't like Jack Cady killing himself," he repeated quietly. "You ever heard the phrase 'locked down'?"

Bobbi looked at her watch. "I have to go to work." I have bills to pay, she wanted to say, big legal expenses. "I'm going to be late, Ray."

Ray slowly got up. She got her gear, followed him out, and locked the door. As he walked down the front steps, Richard watched them with what appeared to be an almost childish expression of hope, and she felt an immense, generalized, gravitational sadness—a force so strong that she wanted to simply stop and lie down. Give up. She wanted to cry about Jack Cady, the last remnant of her father's generation gone from her life, and about the three of them, standing in the wet trailer park, awkwardly, a living triangle of mistakes.

Still brooding, Ray turned to her and said quietly, "Do me a favor. Don't tell Miller anything if he asks why your number was on Jack's phone book. Don't even tell him you saw Jack."

"You're advising me not to cooperate with the investigation?"

He looked angry for an instant—a flash across his expression. "Isn't likely to be much of an investigation. Not with Marvin in charge."

"Okay, Ray. Thanks for the advice."

"Please don't talk about what I've said today. To anybody." Ray stood there looking at her for a moment. "I miss you." He trudged away to Richard and she hurried to her car, intent on not watching them talk.

11

That afternoon at three, Bobbi finally met with Arn Bass and Tony Pfeil to talk about the details of the job offer. Even on a Saturday, almost the entire company was at work. Bass's was the fanciest office at DF, with a spacious, neatly arranged desk and framed degrees and photographs on the walls.

Tony Pfeil came in following her, wearing his cellular phone in a holster. His mood today seemed even worse than at the party.

"Have a seat, Tony."

"I'll have to make it quick. Mike's been in the control room all morning, operating at peak. This about the security job?"

"Wayne suggested you might tell Ms. Reardon a little more about our decision to reorganize building security."

"So, okay . . . you pretty much know the story, Bobbi. We're watching computers with a lot of money and information in them. Over half of our client alarms are due to bad building security: Either the personnel are incompetent or the system is bad. I call the clients, that's my job. Something goes funny, I'm the one on the hook. There's one jerk in Newark I've called eight times in the last couple months. He's got the same thing happening over and over again on the *same* terminal, and still can't figure out a way to prevent it. I'm depressed by that. That tells me the site people are a joke.

"Most of these banks have blue hats walking around with no brains under them. We're talking hook up the electrodes, flatline. 'Security officers' spending most of their time talking to their sweethearts on the phone. So what about DataForm? We're the experts in security, right? That's our business. We've got maybe the most civilian security traffic in the country, and what do we do but hire the same types, present company excepted, of course. Tell me that makes sense—" His phone went off and he unholstered it. "Yeh."

Bobbi heard a loud voice in the background. *"This is Janet—"*

"Okay." He slipped it back and looked at Bobbi distractedly, pressing his lips together. "You've been around the joint long enough. You know we run it like a pool hall. It'll turn that pretty black hair of yours gray. Our own lousy habits. We have to change. That's what we want you to help us do."

He looked at Bass. "You know, Mike Heyer shouldn't be in the control room. He shouldn't even be green. He's blown it, as far as I'm concerned."

"What's the problem now?"

"This Godball shit, it's really got him worked up." Tony pointed toward the control room. "Already my people in there are drinking Pepto-Bismol instead of water, and he comes in first thing in the morning and unloads this shit on them. Do they need that? Do I need that?"

"You mean, he told them about the—"

"Janet here," said Pfeil's walkie-talkie. *"Are you on your way?"*

"I have to talk to Wayne about this," Tony said. "Where is he?"

"Gone. He left right after the party. I think he's trying to find out something about the . . . problem."

"Well, if Mike's gonna go around yellin at my people about it, he better find out something quick."

He smiled lamely at Bobbi as Tony left. "Always a problem."

"Sounds like the police department."

Bass tapped a pencil lightly on his desk. "When you're growing as fast as we are, it's hard to stay on top of it. We've taken clients like Corning Trust and Gallaher Bank, guys that wouldn't have touched us a few years ago. As recently as two years ago, it wasn't totally out of line that all we had in the way of security was Ron and a couple of part-timers. But over the last fifteen months, we've hired sixty-some percent new employees. That makes for management problems, channeling problems, traffic problems. It's like a continuous crash project keeping up with it all.

"We offer a preventive security method that works, and right now we don't have much competition. Basically, we *are* the idea of sophisticated, remote-based internal security. Which, by the way, is one reason we're behind with our own site security. Our whole approach is based on the idea that physical security is only marginally effective."

"I heard Mr. McNear's speech."

"Software types are terrible that way, whether their field is security or what. I'm the only executive in the company who didn't start in software, and sometimes I think I'm in a herd of wild men. Tony's right. It's not going to be easy getting these people operating in standardized patterns. The one thing you've got going is that everybody—in the abstract, at least—agrees that it needs to be done. We'll need at least two more working in your office."

"Can I hire my own people?"

Bass looked mildly surprised.

"I mean without Reed's involvement."

He laughed. "Well. That's stating it pretty flatly."

"I might as well say this now, Mr. Bass. I can work under Reed's nominal direction. But I really can't conceive of taking this job, and doing it well, without a great deal of independence."

"I think you appreciate the situation. Ron's worked very hard for us. Sometimes, I think we're his only . . . well, his only interest. It's a delicate situation. We still haven't figured out quite how to resolve it. . . . But to answer your question, yes. You will be able to hire—in fact, I'd like for you to take at least one other person with you to California for training."

He tapped the pencil faster.

"Well. Now for the good part. We want to pay our security directors well and give them a stake in the company."

He rolled his chair sideways a little and looked directly at her. "The salary for the assistant director of security begins at thirty-two five, but in my opinion the salary isn't the most significant part of your compensation. We're offering a generous front-end bonus. You will be offered ten thousand shares of stock at a rate of ten cents each. Along with this, you will be offered stock appreciation rights to another fifteen thousand shares which you can take ownership of at the end of a minimum-employment period of eighteen months. This gives you ownership and contractual warrants to a total of twenty-five thousand shares of DataForm stock for a total purchase price of $2,500. In addition, of course, there are the usual deferred compensations of a retirement plan, which vests in six years.

"The only rider on the offer is that you must be employed by DataForm for at least the period of time of the total package—eighteen months—before being allowed to sell any portion of the stock. If you lose the job or quit before then, the company will automatically buy the stock back from you. The present book value of DataForm stock is about seventy-five cents a share. If the company goes public, it'll be worth considerably more, of course."

Bobbi caught herself staring at him. "How much more?"

"It depends on the offering bid, but I assume it will be within the ten-to-fifteen-dollar range. We've gotten several private buy-out offers at the top end of that range."

"Would that change the price I pay for the stock?"

"No. These are contractual warrants. As long as you're continuously employed at DataForm, your stock offer is locked in no matter whether we go public, get bought out, or what."

Bobbi was not slow with figures, but each time she tried to multiply the numbers that he was giving her, bells started going off in her head. "How likely is it—"

"That the company will go public?" Bass swiveled around in his chair, got up, and walked over to his window. "I can't say anything official about that." He looked outside. "Unofficially—just as a word from me to you—I'd say there's a pretty high likelihood that it will happen within a year."

"And how much would twenty-five thousand—"

"At least $250,000."

He adjusted the window shades and turned back toward her. "That is according to my best estimate of the minimum offering price if we go public. If the initial price is higher than ten, or if the company does well, you'll own stock worth more than that. There are no guarantees, but we could quite easily be talking about a share in this company worth a half-million dollars."

She stared at him.

"It is a lot, isn't it?" He smiled. "You're being brought on at a very opportune time. Some of us have worked for years to reach this point. If you wonder why we're making this kind of offer, it's really for the standard reason: to make sure that our security directors are in a position of ownership and advocacy toward the company."

"What if eighteen months and one day from now I sold every share and quit."

Bass walked back to his desk. "Assuming we have gone public, you'd deposit 250 to 500 thousand dollars in the bank."

"To keep?" Bobbi had given up all attempts to appear canny.

"Your property, free and clear. I want to repeat two things, however: This job offer doesn't officially comprise any of those dollar amounts. It is even conceivable that the book value of the stock will have decreased. We're talking about total shares, that's the guarantee. Second, you have to fulfill the minimum term of employment. Your work will be subject to careful scrutiny. You will be subject to firing at any point if it is determined by the CEO that you aren't doing your job. But think about it. Stock offers cost a company very little real money, while hiring and training good upper-level people cost a great deal, particularly when without them the company could have major problems. You're worth a lot more to us on board than off."

Bobbi was stunned. She didn't know what to say.

"Do you wonder why we don't require five or seven years? Because we are confident you'll stay with us. A lot is happening here, Bobbi. If you get through the thorny part, you'll stay. It's addictive." He stood up. "So. Are you interested?"

She cleared her throat. "I am, yes."

"Welcome aboard. I'll have your contract ready by noon Monday. Please drop by and sign it before you leave for California. Do you have any suggestions about somebody else we could talk to about a full-time position?"

"What about Neil English?"

"I believe Neil was, uh, a little disappointed that he didn't get this position. He's going to be quitting."

"He already knows?"

"I told him this morning that you were being offered the job."

Bobbi laughed. "That wasn't the best psychology on Neil, not if you wanted him to stay."

"We're just as happy for him to move on. So. Any ideas?"

"Jim Daly. He's another sergeant on the force here. I've known him quite a while."

"A longtime friend?"

"He's more than that. If you're looking for good judgment, Jim's the one I always wanted with me on a nasty call. I imagine he'd welcome a salary increase right about now."

"Let's set up an appointment."

The next week Bobbi resigned as a cop and talked Jim Daly into doing the same. The following Monday she left Richard under the nominal control of Martha Daly (but under the actual control, of course, of Cathy), and flew to California with Jim for training at the Pacific Research Institute, forty miles south of San Francisco.

The Pacific Research Institute was a huge quadrangle of buildings surrounding a lawn as big as a golf course. It was utterly different from any workplace she'd ever seen, with saunas, hot tubs, and racquetball courts inside the building. During work breaks, employees played volleyball and sunned themselves around the great rolling expanse of lawn, women in halter tops, men with their shirts off, as if it was all a Sunday picnic.

The computer-security class met six hours a day, six days a week, and the assigned readings took Bobbi at least three additional hours a day. The teacher had them read excerpts from a lot of different sources and gave them a cumulative exam every Saturday. Bobbi fell into a regular fever of learning, wandering into bookstores and reading other books about computers—and about another subject that she'd never in her most whimsical fantasy imagined she'd have cause to be interested in—investments.

She sometimes had breakfast in a health-food restaurant on University Avenue, browsing through financial magazines, listening to the strange language of business breakfasts going on all around her—windows, horizons, turnarounds, market shares, the Japanese factor. . . . The main street of Palo Alto was a semi-mall, with composed, amiable, affluent-seeming people wandering among planters and shops and boutiques. It felt to Bobbi mildly and pleasantly unreal, as if the few street people who hung around in the sunshine had been hired for local color, as if the money you spent here wouldn't debit from your account, perhaps even the cars that might hit you in the street wouldn't break any bones.

She had enough time alone to think about the money a great deal, come at it from every angle. If someone had asked her, speculatively, how the sudden possession of at least a quarter-million dollars would change her, she would never, with the most profound effort of her imagination, have predicted the difference it would make. She'd never have guessed how much more hopeful she would feel, how much less guilty, how much, it seemed, she could actually see better.

Money was the spell—not California, not a new job—and she slipped off into reveries of multiplication and percentages, she learned about investment instruments, read market and interest-rate predictions, even called brokers on toll-free numbers to ask about certain investments.

She knew that people who had a lot of money were scorned as much as envied, that you couldn't take it with you to the grave, that the IRS stole half of it, that it didn't help you get along with your child—all the common wisdoms she knew and abstractly believed—but still her heart was filled with luminous numbers, and some nights she couldn't stop thinking about them.

One night she got up and frowned at herself in the big wall mirror in the motel bathroom. "Honey, you got to stop this."

Bobbi had been up and down the income scale during her life: grown up poor, tried to get through college poorer, enjoyed a relatively flush time when first married to Ray and working, although his habit of pissing away money sometimes got out of hand; then gotten poor again with the separation. She knew what a shortage of money could do; this most recent period in her life was only a reconfirmation of that knowledge from childhood. Even during the flush period she'd never been rich enough to feel the power of money over the imagination, the pure magnetism of the numbers themselves.

She couldn't talk about it with anybody because it was certain to ruin her friendships. Jim's hiring package hadn't been as generous, and so when she called Martha to chat and ask about Richard, the whole thing was a deliciously hoarded secret that she was always tempted to reveal, more present in her mind than even Richard.

Regarding Richard, Martha didn't seem to think that he was any closer to getting married; she, in turn, told Martha that she was keeping an eye on Jim—mutual assurances, she suspected, of about equal worth. Jim was spending a lot of his study time barhopping.

Jim was a veteran of law-enforcement seminars, where he had mastered the art of learning just enough to pass. This course was tough, though, and she was concerned about Jim making it. She felt responsible for his behavior in a way that she never had before. In the past, she'd tended to feel toward him somewhat like a disapproving aunt toward a nephew she liked despite her better judgment—a relationship she had with no one else in the world. But now he was her man; DF had hired him on her advice. As a cop on the street, Jim was very good. Put between two people who were about to kill each other, he was in his element, doing what the Lord intended him to do. But school just wasn't his thing, and now she was in a position to worry about it.

On Thursday night of their tenth week in California she met him for a drink in the motel lounge, and the subject came around to another thing that had been on her mind—Jack Cady's death.

"You asked me about that on the flight out."

"And you didn't want to talk about it."

Jim sighed. "You ever answer a shotgun-in-the-mouth, Bob?"

"No."

"I had three of them in sixteen years of law enforcement, and I can do without them, thank you, ma'am."

"You're pretty sure that's what it was?"

He smiled ironically. "Had all the markings of it, yes. I didn't hang around very long. I went outside and put the dogs up. The rescue guys and Marvin got there pretty fast. I figured they could scrape the damn walls. Bobbi, you aren't drinking."

"Ray came over to my place the day after it happened. Said he thought Mr. Cady might have been murdered."

Jim looked away gloomily. "Why?"

In the brief time it took Bob to tell him Jack's story about finding Mitze's body in the Trois, he polished off his beer and set it down with a clunk. "Was Mr. Cady sober when he told you all this?" He looked across the room. "She don't like me, Bob. Would you get her?"

"Who?"

"The lady with long legs."

"She likes you, Jim, she just can't keep up with you."

He watched the waitress with fascination. She was wearing something that looked like a space-age bunny suit, an ample bosom pushed up and spilling out of little plastic cones. Bobbi used her beer for a microphone. "Calling Jim. Calling Jim."

He unglued his eyes and focused them on Bobbi. "So who does Ray think killed the old man?"

"He won't say directly. He claims there's a big investigation of DF going on right now."

"Investigation of what?"

"All he'll say is the department is involved."

"Now she tells me."

"So you haven't heard anything about it?"

"I wouldn't have gone to work for them if I had."

"Come on. Ray wants me to quit this job. He can't stand me being or doing anything but what I already am—his wife, working at the job he got for me."

"Pretty queer approach for getting you to stay," Jim muttered.

"Hey, 'an investigation'? I'm supposed to be impressed by that kind of BS, like maybe that seventeen-year-old girlfriend of his? Drop everything? Forget it all because the heavy-duty detective laid the big word of warning on me?"

Jim frowned at the waitress's deft movement around the room and said quietly, "You've got that tone, Bob."

"You know it's true. He can't stand things changing on him. He's got some kind of phobia."

He looked at her skeptically.

"Well, what do you call it?"

"I call it stubborn. You're both as stubborn as the day is long. He doesn't want to lose you, that's all."

Bobbi felt her face flush. "What would you think about me if I used my blue suit to round up some boy my own son's age to have fun and games with?"

Jim looked bored. He obviously didn't want to talk about this.

"That's over the line," she added.

Jim sighed. "Ray hasn't fooled around with any seventeen-year-olds, Bob. You've been saying that so long you believe it. There was only that one girl as far as I know—what was her name?"

"Don't say her fuckin name."

"Whatever it was, she was twenty-one years old, unmarried, and she didn't have anything to do with any investigations. Far as the cop work goes, Ray's pretty careful about that kind of thing. A lot more than some."

"Compared to who, the pack he runs with—John Outlaw, George Bowser?"

"Tell me something, Bob. Do you hate men?"

"No. Just the ones I know."

It was an old joke between them, and tonight it roused a melancholy smile from Jim. He got out a cigarette and lighted it. Bobbi felt an unexpected stab of intimacy and sadness as the lighter flared in his face. She and Jim had been friends for quite a while.

"So tell me more about this investigation of our new employer," he said. "Have you talked to anybody else about it?"

"Neil English." She took another drink of the watery beer, her mind wandering. "Neil doesn't like me. . . ."

"Pore Bob."

"You remember the day, late December, I was running around mad because Warnke ordered me to go on a PR call to DataForm? He also had me take the Mitze fatal-accident report out there. I looked at the station log, and there was no location given for the accident, and no record of who answered the call. Later I found out it was Neil. I tried to ask him about it on New Year's Eve, and he was kind of funny about it. About all he'd allow was that he didn't recommend going to work there."

The waitress came and went in a flash of plastic-corseted flesh, and Jim gazed off after her. "So what are you thinking?"

"I'm thinking maybe there was something funny about Mitze's death. Warnke knows something about it. Maybe so does Neil."

"What you're coming around to is that Ray's right. There *is* some kind of investigation."

"Yeah, but who's running it, Jim? Why are they hiring people like Warnke to hire people like Ray and Outlaw and George *Bowser* to do it?"

"Do what exactly?"

She shook her head, staring, musing about what she'd seen in McNear's basement on April 1. "I don't know. Ray isn't talking about it much. Probably some kind of surveillance. They've got a radio at Outlaw's that looks like the NASA space center." Her eyes went to Jim's. "Don't talk about this, by the way. He says he'll lose his ass if it gets out."

He took a slug of beer. "Kind of playing two ends against the middle, aren't you?"

"Ray really doesn't seem to know much. I get the impression he's frustrated about it. . . . I just wish Neil wasn't so weird toward me. He knows something about what happened that night."

Jim gazed at a crowd of college women coming in the door. "Maybe I'll ask him a question or two when we get back. Maybe I'll even call him. He might talk to me."

"Ask him what?"

"Let's see. I'll ask him why he juggled the Mitze report, why he committed a couple of felonies—"

"Right. Great idea."

"I'll run something by him," Jim said, seriously. "Neil ain't a very good liar. Too stiff."

Bobbi watched him down the rest of his beer. "I don't think I would."

Jim leaned back. "How much you getting paid, Bob?"

"Ten times more than you."

"That's what I was afraid of. They offer you any stock?"

"They mentioned something about it."

"Well, they're giving me a thousand shares, and I haven't so much as pissed in the toilet at the place. So they must be giving you two, three thousand." He looked at her questioningly.

"Ain't capitalism wonderful." She stood up.

"Hey, don't leave already. The night's young."

"Have to get back and study. Saturday exam coming up."

"We've got a consultant coming tomorrow—remember?"

"That's been rescheduled for next week. The original guy isn't coming. Where was your head today when the professor announced that?"

"Where's my head? See that girl over there in the red Stanford sweatshirt? See the letters N and F—"

"Go study."

"Don't be so good, Bob. I can't stand it. Makes me break out. Have another one." He waved at the waitress.

"Tell you what. I'll be a little less good if you'll be a little more good these last couple of weeks."

"Quit reminding me of my duties."

"See you in class."

Professor Govind Shaw was the last of three consultants who lectured the class, all lightening the dullness of the professor, although this man—a last-minute substitute for someone else—did not do so by being a very good lecturer. He was an "adjunct professor" of information science from MIT, of upper-class Indian descent, and, while Bobbi liked his accent, she found his lectures to be tangled and rambling. He was obviously trying to make them up on his feet. Site security appeared to be at the fringe of his interests, since his talks kept wandering back to software.

The professor hadn't stayed in class with the previous consultants, but with Shaw he did, and Bobbi sensed a certain wariness in the older man in their brief conversation before class.

Shaw looked directly at Bobbi a lot while he lectured, and she wasn't completely surprised when he asked her out for a drink after class. She invited a couple of other class members who were still in the hall, and it turned out to be a strange little social event, the four of them sitting at a table in a nearby restaurant having a hard time making conversation. Bobbi got the distinct impression Shaw was trying to get rid of the other two. He was a very intense man and—it seemed to her—fretful. He frowned a lot. He widened his eyes as if interested in conversation, but seemed to stare right through what was being said.

On Wednesday, Professor Shaw was settling down some. At a point in his lecture, he stood in front of the marker board frowning at her. ". . . Information float. Companies always have secrets relating to technology, planning, personnel information, past sins. Knowledgeable persons can put those secrets to enormous use. Without confidentiality, a company can't operate. They're like individuals in this respect: Take away their privacy and they become demoralized. A company can be damaged or destroyed by information going to the wrong place, even within its own structure."

He moved from the marker board and sat in the chair, elbows propped on the desk, fingers touching. It was the first time he had sat during a lecture. "I'll give you an example.

"This happened thirteen years ago and is now quite forgotten, a small incident in"—he smiled ironically—"Silicon Valley. It happened at a software house which was located within a mile of here. At the time, this was the largest stand-alone software company in the area, grossing something on the order of twenty million—small by present standards, of course. The company's payroll was handled by a widely used system that batched the checks according to departments. One month, because of what was called 'a mistake in the payroll program,' every employee was sent the check of the vice-president in charge of his department.

"At first, it seemed like merely a funny little snafu. People with these enormous checks standing around in bars yukking it up about how they were all going to cash them and break the company's back. But a number of lower-level executives acted strongly put out by the amounts of their superiors' salaries. They really beat the drums on the issue. The company's profit picture hadn't been looking as good as they thought it should, and they claimed the reason was now obvious. Their own salaries and the company stock they all owned were being devalued by the greed of their superiors.

"In this business it's commonplace for employees to quit and go to work elsewhere. It's a problem not just of Silicon Valley but of the entire computer industry in this country, and one of the reasons the U.S. is falling dangerously behind foreign competitors. . . . But in this particular case, the immediate cause of that eventuality was a piece of 'theater,' as they called it in those days, carefully orchestrated with other acts of company sabotage which I won't go into. Some eight vital employees quit and formed their own company, and the original company went into shock. Five of the employees who quit had been in research, and they took their work with them to their own new company, while the original company fell into bankruptcy."

Mr. Shaw smiled tensely, separated his hands, and lay them flat on the table. "One interesting thing about this case is that the company's checks were run from mag cards, making it virtually impossible for the issuance of the wrong checks to have been a mistake. It was done on purpose, by someone cutting false mag cards, replacing the proper ones, then, after the batch was run and sent off, putting the correct ones back. Who was responsible was never legally established, but the outcome was disastrous for certain people and extremely lucrative for others.

"In a court of law, however, that is merely circumstantial evidence. Indeed, even if it had been established who did it, the particular crime was hardly more than malicious mischief.

"Your problem is that with most of the companies you'll work for, the majority of sensitive materials is much more readily available and manipulable than in this ancient case—not stored on mag cards but right there available at every second, floating on those wonderfully accessible disks. Every fact, every confidentiality is in information float. An employee facing a console is looking at a blank which merely by knowing the right keys he can light up with the most fascinating stuff."

Shaw paused and looked down at his desk as if puzzled. "Really, it's like holding out poisoned candy to a child. And the computer revolution now, through the end of the millennium, will be less a revolution of hardware, less even a revolution of systems, than of access. Ever-increasing access. All kinds of people are beginning to look into the tube, ladies and gentlemen, and if information is power, it is also a corrupting force, you see. Alcohol among the Indians. That's what makes your job important—"

"What do you think about the use of such techniques in political espionage?" the professor asked, from the back of the class. Faces turned.

Shaw looked at him with a little frown.

"What do you think about the morality of that?" he repeated.

"That depends, I suppose, on the morality of those it's used against."

"Oh, it does?" the professor said shortly, and stood up. "Thank you, Mr. Shaw."

12

Ray lay in his aluminum lounge chair, mosquito netting zipped up, smoking a cigarette carefully to avoid catching the tent on fire, reading a paperback by the light of a Coleman lantern. He glanced out toward the darkened trailer, with no expectation, after this many weeks, of any reason to watch too closely.

What was really on Ray's mind tonight was Neil English.

Bobbi's relation of Jack Cady's story had been bothering him for weeks before he finally decided, today, to talk to Neil. On his way out to shift that evening, he'd stopped by Neil's house and found no one there. The place was completely shut up, with the garage and every window closed, the curtains drawn. Ray had almost been relieved not to find Neil at home, since he didn't really have a good handle on him. Neil was tense, combative, and unsusceptible to cajolery. He also tended to report any kind of trouble in the ranks, meaning that any questions Ray asked could go straight to Warnke.

Taking over shift, he'd asked Outlaw to make some phone calls and try to find out what the deal was with Neil. A couple of hours later, he got a call on the CB. It was John. "Neil's been promoted."

"To what?"

"Captain."

"What are you talking about?"

"Not here. Someplace in Florida. He left three days ago."

". . . What town?"

"Parker wasn't sure. Little town around Pompano."

"Warnke line that up for him?"

"Sounds like it."

Ray looked out toward the trailer. That blew his theory that Neil was being used as an inside informant for an investigation of DataForm. . . . But Warnke was not exactly known for lining up promotions for his people. Maybe there was some reason why Neil had to go. Maybe his situation inside DF had heated up.

The trailer's lights had been on for several seconds before Ray turned off the radio. He was gazing through the mosquito net directly toward the dark shape when it happened. The light inside shone out of one window, and an outdoor light by the door fluttered and cast a dim glow down the camouflage-green walls. The air conditioner cranked up immediately with the lightup, as usual, but the light coming through the window appeared different. Just a little off-color.

For a minute he sat still, watching for shadows or movement. Then he grabbed his revolver, unzipped the mosquito net, and hunched out of the tent. Heavy wings stirred the windless air, a soft *hoo* disappearing into the texture of frog and cricket noise.

He went through the fence gate, approaching the window until it was a still rectangle of light ten yards away. The front door was shut. As he walked around to take in another angle of the interior, a whine, rising in pitch, caused the crickets all around to fall silent. Warnke had told them to disregard the equipment when it went on automatically and to stay outside the fence at all times, but Ray was curious.

He waited until the night sounds had started up again, and made his way to a different site on the window, where he could see that the console on the metal desk was turned on, which made for the slight difference in the quality of light, but still he saw no one. He stood still for two or three minutes watching it. The figures on the screen appeared to be changing. He walked a couple of steps closer and felt a light chill on his face.

He waited and watched a few minutes longer and finally decided there was no one there. The computer machinery was on, but he was alone.

Frustrated that he couldn't make out what was on the console, he walked around to the front, reached out a hand, and tried the locked door. He stood there for a moment and then kicked it in.

A burst of cool air rolled over him.

As he stepped inside, the sounds of generator, computer, air conditioner, were loud. The bundles of different-colored wire that ran everywhere on floor, walls, and ceiling made him feel like he was inside some kind of organism. He approached the console until he could read a message on the screen.

Generator, Open DataBase ALL. 23.76 GHz.

. . . .

DANGER

LIBRARY RED SECTOR: ARP-1 - ARP-55 feeding.

DANGER

The three stand-alone tape machines jammed together along one wall were running. A pencil lay across a dusty pad of paper beside the console, and he took out his spiral notebook and copied down what was on the screen. After three or four minutes the message changed.

Describe my communication 12:10:84.

RECONFIRM IDENTITY.

Codelog 4387875

PLEASE ENTER YOUR MOTHER'S MAIDEN NAME & YOUR DATE OF BIRTH.

Chalmers. 9:6:42

THANK YOU. COMMUNICATION 12:10:84 IS 998 MB. LONG, AND PARTS OF IT ARE OS REGISTERED. WOULD YOU LIKE A SUMMARY OF DOCUMENTS?

Yes.

DOCUMENT NAME: A LETTER.

TIMED COPY, DELIVERY 3:31:85, TO BE SENT TO WAYNE MCNEAR, PRESIDENT, DATAFORM, INC., DUBOIS, AR.

THE LETTER CONTAINED DOCUMENTS WITH THE FOLLOWING DOC-UMENT DESCRIPTIONS:

DISCUSSION OF CODELOG 4387875'S MOOD AND EMOTIONAL STATE IN SEVERAL PARTS

PARTIAL PROGRAM IDENTIFIED AS "LOGIC CIRCUMSCRIPTOR"

PERIPHERAL COMMUNICATIONS SYSTEM, 1:25:79, AUSTIN BANK OF COMMERCE, AUSTIN, TX.

"PUBLIC/PRIVATE KEY NETWORK SECURITY"

A POEM

SECURITY ARCHITECTURE: MARATHON WEST BANK OF SAN FRAN-CISCO, CA.

A PARTIAL PROGRAM IDENTIFIED AS "CURSE"

A CONFESSION

Fetch: A CONFESSION

A CONFESSION IS OS REGISTERED, UNAVAILABLE FOR FETCH.

Summarize its contents.

UNAVAILABLE FOR SUMMARY.

Are there any special conditions for this document?

YES.

What are they?

UNAVAILABLE FOR EXPLANATION.

Writing as quickly as he could, Ray could barely keep up with the list that was scrolling by on the screen, but now there was a long pause.

What's the purpose of "CURSE"?

"CURSE" IS A DATAFLOW SUBPROGRAM WHICH ANALYZES AND USES HYPERBOLE AND OBSCENITY AS A SEMANTIC TOOL. IT IS WRITTEN IN LISP AND IS FULLY COMPATIBLE WITH "WORD," COPYRIGHT STANFORD UNIVERSITY.

Okay. Confirm order 312: 6:26:85. Do you have all entry conditions?

ORDER QUEUED. ENTRY CONDITIONS UNDERSTOOD. DESTINATION: INTERCITY WIRE, CORNING TRUST, VIA USI DOWNLINK, NYC. SINGLE BURST AT CODED GH., SELF-IDENTIFYING, ASS. 6, TRPDR 1-3.

What will you do if intercity wires are unavailable?

I WILL ENTER THROUGH BACKUP SINK, ASS. 7, AND REGISTER ON FEDWIRE.

If/when entry fails, how long will it take you to generate a new trpdr $\pm$ new dump routine $\pm$ new routing?

MEAN TIME FOR EMPLACEMENT: 10^3 SECONDS.

Explain routing procedures.

ROUTING IS GGG SECURITY.

Is a description of your OS available?

YOU HAVE ASKED THAT QUESTION MANY TIMES BEFORE. I CANNOT DISCUSS THE ARCHITECTURE OR RATIONALE OF MY OS. ALL OTHER SYSTEMS, UTILITY PROGRAMS, KNOWLEDGE BASES ARE SHARED AND OPEN TO KEYFINDERS.

Do you have LIBRARY RED SECTOR ARP-1 - ARP-55?

YES. ERASING.

Ray had gotten it all down, looking back and forth between the console screen and his notebook, when a switching sound startled him. The tape machines had started rewinding with a low howl. When he looked back to the screen, he dropped his pencil; it fell onto the keyboard and bounced onto the floor.

He leaned over and started to pick it up when the screen flashed:

DANGER   DANGER   DANGER

ALARM STATE

YOU HAVE SEVEN SECONDS TO IDENTIFY YOURSELF

MINUS 7

The number in the lower right-hand corner began to count down, and Ray hesitated through 6, 5, then stood up, got the notebook, and, looking around once again, started toward the door. As he was walking through it he felt a jolt in his body that caused him to pitch forward into the blackness.

Totally strange.

After a while, he pulled himself up to the sitting position, almost leaning back against the trailer, but, feeling the hair on his neck rise, he instinctively held himself away from it.

It was hot. Insects touched his face and hands, lightly. His hands felt numb. It occurred to him that he was a cop, and he raised his head looking for an assailant. Had he been shot? He crawled away from the trailer and remained on all fours for a while, breathing, heart beating fast. Eventually, the curtains in his mind slowly parting, he stood up and looked at the notebook clutched in his hand.

Early Friday morning, while it was still dark outside, Ray was at the police station, his hands and feet still feeling a little numb, finding out everything he could about the night of Ben Mitze's death.

The radio log covering that night had been filled out and placed in Ann's office files. Parker's meticulous handwriting recorded Jack Cady's call-in at 0235, possible accident victim, no location given. In the station log, the more official document run once a week and filed in the front office, the hour was noted at 0428, location the DataForm building, south entrance. Sergeant English had been sent, car number not given— no big omission, but it reminded Ray that English wasn't normally on third shift. Neither had Parker been, in December. Parker had apparently completed his regular shift and stayed through the third. Sixteen hours at the mike was not typical for Parker at age sixty-two.

The fire/rescue records confirmed the 0428 dispatch of rescue. If the radio log notations were correct, there'd been a delay of an hour and fifty-three minutes from the time of Mr. Cady's call. Looking at Parker's log a second time, more carefully, Ray saw no record of the rescue dispatch, but just down the page from Cady's call-in was the notation: "Confer 295-3985."

Chief Warnke's home phone.

He noticed on the preceding page that just before all these events,

Bobbi had picked up one Sinclair Heyer for speeding, with passenger Taylor McNear, possible DOD, father notified.

Ray slipped into Ann's office a second time and looked through her payroll printouts. English wasn't recorded as working overtime at all in December. Slipping them back, he noticed the file keys that Ann and Warnke hung on a little nail behind the bookcase. He went into Warnke's office and opened his desk filing drawer and, in the back, found the little black accounting book that he'd once seen the chief using. There was no name in it, only a social security number and several account numbers, amounts, and other codes that at first glance were meaningless. He roamed through it recording whatever looked interesting. There were tax numbers that appeared to be from Florida. . . . It had grown light outside and he was still scribbling, in a fever of information gathering, when he heard one of the doors in the building shudder. Someone was in the hall.

When Ann walked into her office, Ray was just slipping the file keys back onto the nail.

"Ann. How's it going?"

"Oh! You . . . surprised me," she said, her expression turning to puzzlement as she watched Ray's little pocket notebook going into his shirt pocket. "Can I help you with something?"

"It's nothing, after all. I got to thinking that I'd missed pay a couple of weeks back in February."

She walked over and put her purse on her desk, frowning, avoiding his eyes.

"My mistake."

Within the half hour, Ray was on the phone talking to his lawyer in Little Rock, Marty Williams, asking him to research the account numbers he'd gotten from the chief's record book, then he called Maureen Stallings at the country club.

"I need to find out a birthday."

"Oh?"

"Wonder if you'd look in your book and see who used your birthday room on September sixth."

"*Which* September sixth?" Maureen didn't sound particularly happy.

"Try 'eighty-three."

"Well, I hope there's a good reason for this. . . . You know I'm very busy today. . . . September sixth, 'eighty-three, Nugent, Catherine, age seventy-four. Catherine's *that* old?

"Try 'eighty-two."

" 'Eighty-two . . . Nugent, Catherine, age seventy-five. My heavenly day, she's going backward."

"Try 'eighty-one."

"Dear boy, this book isn't *infinite*."

"Please, Maureen."

"This is as far as it . . . September sixth, Mitze, Ben, age question mark."

"Okay."

"Well, are you disappointed?"

"No, no, that's . . . fine." Ray frowned at the notes he'd taken from the computer screen:

Please enter your mother's maiden name and your date of birth.

Chalmers. 9:6:42

"Well, you sound *stricken*. Are you ill?"

He flipped the notebook shut. "You wouldn't happen to know where Mitze was from, would you?"

"I would. Little Rock. Liz Mitze's from the same place."

Ray got hold of an acquaintance who worked for the Pulaski County records office and gave him the names Ben Mitze and Chalmers. Within an hour he'd confirmed that Chalmers was indeed Ben Mitze's mother's name.

It was time to see the widow.

In her motel room after class on Friday, Bobbi was doing something that she didn't approve of—thinking about Ray Wiel, that bum, not just generally thinking but fondly thinking, even missing him a little—when she got a couple of surprises. Ron Reed called from Arkansas and told her to be at the local DF office, ten minutes from the institute, at noon the next day. They were flying out for a meeting and he wanted her to secure the place before they arrived.

"Secure it how?" she asked.

"You're the one going to school. Haven't they taught you what that means? I want the place clean. Everything. And check the light switch."

She had scarcely put down the phone when Govind Shaw called and asked if she'd like to go to dinner in a half hour. Shaw had talked with her after class, and it seemed slightly odd he hadn't asked her then.

There was a third call, this one from Jim Daly, but Shaw was actually knocking on her door, and she had to tell Jim she'd see him tomorrow.

They went to an Italian restaurant in Los Altos. She soon discovered that he wasn't interested in talking about the class. She was self-conscious, and a little cold in the summery yellow dress that she'd bought twenty minutes earlier at a shop next to the Holiday Inn. She had goosebumps.

Shaw said hello to several people in the crowded café. The bar and café were one big room with fiercely efficient waiters hurrying between red-and-white-checked tablecloths. They'd just gotten drinks when a fattish little man walked over punching black eyeglasses up his nose, talking nonstop as he approached their table. Shaw acted openly uncomfortable when the man pulled out a chair and sat down. "Govind! Hey! Really! How long has it been?"

"Hello, Foote."

The man nodded and smiled. "I heard you were out. Pacific Security, right? What are you doing taking something like that if you don't mind me asking?"

Shaw didn't respond.

"My name's Bill Foote." He stuck his hand across the table at Bobbi, who introduced herself. "Who you with?"

"DataForm," she said, taking his hand.

He looked blankly at her, then turned back to Shaw.

"I'm sorry to interrupt. It's just that I see you so seldom I like to touch bases." His fishlike gaze rolled around the room and settled on Bobbi. "Well. I hear Mr. McNear's finally going public. When's the big offering? He must be real happy about what happened to USI in the market yesterday. You hear about that, Govind? Seven hundred thousand shares dumped in one afternoon. Nothing in the news, no disappointing reports, and they fall five points in one day. Is that insiders selling or is that insiders selling? I'm not in trouble myself, but I've got friends who are up to their ass in USI."

"Bill. How about leaving us now?" Shaw had walked around the table and pulled back Mr. Foote's chair.

A spasmodic scowl going across his face, Foote went on, as if the motion of his chair was some new conversational encouragement. "You know USI. Call them, even your best guys, and you expect em to be clammed up, all you can do is check out *how* clammed up. Let me tell you, the clam was tight."

"Good-bye, Foote," Govind said, pulling him up by a coatsleeve.

"Hey, I'll call your office. We can get together on this thing. . . ." Foote walked away backwards, still talking, and was finally swallowed up by the crowd.

Govind sat back down, for a moment looking shaken, then he forced a smile at Bobbi. "I knew him years ago. A bit off in the head now, I think. A deal nut, a burnout, Silicon Valley bag man."

"What was that about Wayne McNear?"

Govind put down his fork and looked around the room. "You know, I believe I'm going to have more of that avocado stuff. Can I get you anything from the salad bar?"

After dinner, they had a couple of drinks and he took her back to the Holiday Inn and asked if he could come in for a nightcap. Something about the signals she was getting from him were strange, incomplete. He was smiling more now, acting more "interested" in her, but something was missing. He seemed preoccupied.

He produced a pint of brandy from his tweed coat, and they sat down to have some in plastic cups—he on the one chair in the room, she on the edge of the bed. The room was a shade of orange similar to the color used in holding cells to calm people, but she wasn't calm. He was looking at her differently, taking her in, and she was nervous, with something that felt like an electrical charge moving around in her stomach and chest, looking for a place to light, one instant deep beneath her ribs, then spreading out almost to her skin, making her quiver slightly. Govind was an attractive man.

"Is the other chap from DF here?"

She hesitated.

"Daly, I believe?"

"Jim's right up the hall."

"So. Are you pals?"

"Jim's an old friend. We were both sergeants on the same police force. We quit to go to work full-time for DF."

"An important company around there, I'd imagine."

"We keep busy."

"Oh?" He almost whispered.

She looked back at him the way he was looking at her.

He got up and sat beside her on the bed.

The thrill in her chest kept moving around, unsettled, but she didn't feel quite right. He drew her over and tried to kiss her but she moved back. "I have an exam tomorrow."

"You won't have any trouble."

"I do need to . . ."

He tried again, but it didn't feel right to Bobbi.

"I have to study," she said, with a firm smile. "Those Saturday exams aren't easy."

"Don't worry about it. You're terribly smart."

He was persistent for a moment longer but finally gave up. "Well," he said quietly, looking at her with a little smile. "Shall we at least finish our brandies?"

She drifted a moment, thinking why not be sociable at least? She smiled at him. "So do you like being a professor?"

He brought the cup to his lips. "Keeps one off the street. Code-writers don't go much beyond forty. Real code, not just popping together components from the library." He sipped between pauses. "It's like professional sports. You have to become a manager after a certain age—a project director, that sort of thing."

"But don't you spend a lot of time teaching?"

He was staring off. "I'll tell you someone who was brilliant in his codewriting days."

"Who's that?"

"Wayne McNear."

"So you did know him."

"Wayne and I worked together once. Matter of fact, the computer service company that fell apart—that was us."

"Small world."

"I wasn't in on it. Wayne and I got into a scrap about it, actually. We'd been working together on a big project, been through quite a lot together. I knew what he was doing."

Bobbi frowned. "He?"

"Yes, Wayne was in charge of it all," Govind said quietly. "Perhaps I mentioned the incident in the lecture as a way of mulling it over, trying finally to decide. It's a terribly common kind of situation out here. Treachery, I mean. And there was a bit more than usual upper-management idiocy in the place. This was before any of us understood the intensity of this business. . . . But Wayne did destroy a number of investors and reputations. People we'd been working with in good faith. He created DataForm out of the ruins."

"By sending out supervisors' checks? *That* caused a twenty-million-dollar company to fall apart?"

He looked thoughtful. "Wayne really is quite a strategist."

"The company must have been a house of cards."

Govind's brow furrowed. "If it had been the checks alone, true enough. But as I mentioned, that was merely the last act in quite an effective program of sabotage. The records, the software itself—someone kept keying in little booby traps. We kept having to recover things. Finally everything was so botched up, the company got a reputation for not delivering. Lost a massive order—from USI, in fact. That was back in the days when they were desperately trying to get the code done for their new mainframes, contracting it out. . . . Anyway, there are a lot of people who think Wayne's a bad sort."

She put her cup onto the table beside the couch and stood up.

He looked up at her and said gently, "Really a case, some would say."

"What are you talking about?"

"Oh, the business with his wife, for example."

"What business?" Bobbi's mood had distinctly soured. She really didn't like this.

"Throwing her over and taking her money, that sort of thing."

"Are you talking about his divorce now?"

"Yes. You know, Mrs. McNear was profoundly wealthy. There are some who say Wayne saw to it that the divorce was in California because of the community-property law. He got quite a lot from his wife's estate for child support, since he won her custody."

"I make it a habit not to gossip about people's divorce settlements. I really have to turn in now, Mr. Shaw."

He stood up, again giving her a furtive, incomplete smile. "Best not mention that you've talked with me."

She didn't respond.

"Wayne is very demanding about loyalty."

"Good night, Mr. Shaw."

14

At class Saturday morning, Jim Daly didn't show up for the exam, which made Bobbi fretful while she took hers.

After handing in the completed exam, she was surprised by Govind Shaw in the hall. "Well, I see you're all turned out in uniform. Can I give you a ride somewhere?"

She shook her head. "Thanks anyway."

"Oh, I'll take you right out. Might as well save the fare." He was hurrying along down the hall with a hand at her elbow.

"Hey, Bob!" a voice boomed down the hall. It was Jim Daly, ambling toward them. He didn't look at Govind. "Where you goin?"

She responded coldly, "The question isn't where I'm going but where you've been."

Jim stood there for a moment, wiping his jaw slowly with his hand. He and Bobbi had occupied the same office for years, they'd complained together, helped write each other's reports, arrested people together, driven ninety miles an hour together, dealt with freeway accidents together, given the hell up and gotten drunk on the job together, been bored together. They knew each other's expressions. Jim knew she was telling him to back off.

And she knew something was on his mind. "So what's up?"

He glanced at Shaw. "Talk to you later."

Govind followed along after her until she finally stopped and said, "Thank you, but I don't need a ride."

"Well then, could you sit with me in the lunchroom for ten minutes? I feel I owe you an explanation."

She looked at her watch. She'd had no breakfast and needed something to eat before going to work. There was enough time.

In the brightly colored buffet-style lunchroom, Bobbi had a roast beef sandwich and watched the clock. Shaw had a cup of tea.

"I want to clarify what I brought up last night."

"I'm willing to listen," she said noncommittally.

"Briefly: I did know Wayne McNear quite well. We were young when we met. Really green. This does go back—to the sixties. We got together at Simmons Paragon because we were both working on language theory. We were both brash and young, playing at being geniuses. Wayne had a talent for getting whatever was needed. If someone wanted to look at a program that was still in development or too expensive, he'd go out and find a way to acquire it. He was remarkably good at just walking into places and snarfing things." He took a sip of tea. "Legalities, truth or lying—those sort of things never slowed him down."

"A liar and a thief? My goodness. He must have been useful."

"He is most certainly an accomplished thief, but not a 'liar' exactly. Wayne's unconnected to ideas of truth or untruth. I think he's a sociopath."

Bobbi wiped her fingers and wrapped up the remains of her sandwich. She was quickly losing her appetite.

"Have you ever *realized* that's how someone operates? Has it ever sunk in that they're that way? That they haven't any scruples, morals, any concern about truth whatever?" Govind's dark eyes were fixed on her with woeful intensity. "You know, I once asked Wayne what his goal in life was. Got a very interesting response. Twenty-two years old, he was, with a nine-thousand-dollar salary. He said he wanted to buy USI. *Buy USI?* Hello. I told him he should try rising through the ranks, it would probably be quicker than raising ten billion, and he said no, he wanted to buy them, he was quite sure of it. Now, you see, he's built himself up a little company and dubbed himself the champion antagonist of USI. . . . I suppose he's tried to indoctrinate you."

She didn't answer for a moment. "Why are you so desperate to tell me all this?" she finally asked.

"All those speeches about secret pacts between USI and certain government agencies—as if he didn't understand how those things really worked. Anticomputer populism—he's artful at it, among the ignorant. . . . Who knows what goes through the man's mind, but it almost seems that if USI can't 'belong' to him, he wants to publicly batter it—just as he privately battered his wife to extract a fortune from her."

"Oh. We're back to his divorce now?"

He stared at her with a concerned frown, shaking his head slightly. "If you want to find out the truth, you can."

Bobbi put down her sandwich. "And you'll help me?"

"Bobbi, I couldn't sleep after I left you last night. I'm worried about you." He glanced around toward the door. "You have no idea what you're into. Wayne is an *extraordinary* person. He jumps into *any* situation. Offer him a pistol and he'll play Russian roulette. Sooner or later he's going to take down everybody within a hundred miles of him."

Bobbi wiped her hands on a paper napkin. "Who do you work for?"

"Listen to me." He leaned over the table, widening his eyes. "McNear steals software. He's been increasing and perfecting his library for years. It contains an enormous amount of access information—to systems all over the country."

Bobbi started to get up and hesitated. "Whoever you work for, you might ask them for a little retraining in hook work. Technique's a little limp."

He got up and hurried along beside her across the room. "Look, I don't blame you for being skeptical of me, but this fellow you're working for is exceedingly dangerous. He's criminally insane. I can help you. Will you at least leave open the possibility . . ."

She left him behind at the lunchroom entrance, and went outside to catch a cab.

Down El Camino, west on Page Mill into the foothills, winding among giant eucalyptus trees, Bobbi tried to make sense of what had just happened. There was no doubt that Mr. Shaw had been trying to soften her up to work for him. Was he part of the "investigation" of DataForm Ray had told her about?

The cab went up a curving driveway and stopped in a virtually empty parking lot with a dry fountain standing twenty yards from a large building. Her watch said 12:51. The sky was a brilliant blue with thick clouds lying against the high foothills. She walked across a dry, sun-bleached field to the front deck of the building, which was C-shaped and perched on the edge of a sharp drop-off to the rear. The ground level was the top floor, with other levels going down the hill. There was a dog sleeping on the deck, and weeds growing up through the planks, some laundry hanging on the front rail, and, farther on, a motorcycle parked by a door. She walked a few paces toward the rear of the deck. A stack of boards blocked it in one direction. Half-abandoned, it was a strange building for an office.

Once she was inside, it took fifteen minutes to locate the superintendent, in a storage room on the bottom floor. His keys rattled angrily as she hurried along behind him down the corridors, up the plank steps to the third level.

He opened the door of room 323, turned on the light, and left. She opened a curtain, causing sun to pour into the musty air. The room was furnished with a faded blue Naugahyde couch and metal desk, with an old-fashioned dial telephone sitting by itself on it. The walls were dusty and yellowed, the fluorescent light fixture on the ceiling filled with dead bugs. She couldn't believe this was the DataForm office.

There was another door, which she opened slowly, looking into another room to the rear. It was much larger, unpartitioned, with greenish, flickering light coming from a far corner. She stood at the threshold for a moment, looked for a light switch, and, unable to find one, eventually walked over toward the light, holding out her hands to avoid bumping into something. In the middle of the room was a ten-foot shelf of bins, some filled with parts. Beyond that, along the back wall, was a console, turned on, with the name Centrex in chrome above a small screen. On the screen was the same split image she'd seen in McNear's basement ten weeks before, with columns of flickering numbers in changing highlights topped by a menu line and, in the upper left-hand corner:

Generator, Open DataBase ALL. 23.76 GHz.

Hearing the sound of approaching steps, she went to the front, and within seconds they burst into the room in a hurried knot—Reed, McNear, Jeremy, Tony Pfeil, and Tim Thurmon (whom Bobbi knew least well). Nervous-smelling, with loosened ties, they hurtled by her into the back room. McNear paused only for a fleeting smile. "How are things going?"

"Okay."

Reed scowled at her. "Check it all out?"

"I just got here."

"Well, then do it." He disappeared into the back room with the rest of them.

She went to work, and was taking off the light-switch cover when Mike Heyer came along behind them, by himself. He stood in the doorway a minute, looking at her through his round silver-rimmed sunglasses, then went into the back without a word.

Tony came out punching numbers on his cellular phone. He nodded toward the back. "Why don't you go in there and help Ron? He's driving everybody crazy."

He followed Bobbi into the back room. "Janet, this is Tony, we got the same footprint. It looks identical. . . ."

A small fluorescent fixture standing on its end in the corner had been turned on, and Reed was peering into the cabinet bins. The others had gathered around the console in the back of the room. For a moment there was stillness and silence except for the flickering numbers on the screen and Jeremy Weeks's barely audible whispering. He sat on the floor directly in front of the screen and seemed to be counting. Tim Thurmon was looking away from the screen, his face moving in a tic. McNear sat on a rickety little stool, writing something on a scrap of paper on his knee.

"I've got an interval," Jeremy said. ". . . Seventy-some hours."

Standing at a distance from them all, Mike Heyer made a little sound of impatience.

Tony said into the receiver, "We're looking at maybe seventy hours."

McNear glanced over at Bobbi.

"We definitely need to get these people ready for close-downs," Thurmon said in an oddly soothing voice.

No one answered for a moment. Then Tony put his hand over the receiver. "Janet says Marathon West is completely freaked out."

"What happened?" Bobbi asked McNear.

"One of our clients, Marathon West Bank and Trust, lost 200,000 bucks. The day before yesterday they lost an entire day's transaction data."

"When did it happen?" Bobbi asked.

"Tell her, Tim," McNear said.

Thurmon took a strong drag and scissored the cigarette out of his mouth with two fingers. "Twenty-two-oh-six, just after the day had been batched. It just bombed. All the heads moved up and down and went no-no. Two seconds and the day's business didn't exist. There are no exception-report clues because they haven't got the software. They've refused any upgrades. They're operating on our old DF-1 auditor. As you know, we don't have any connects with them. I think among other things you might talk to them about doing business with antiques."

"What if we told them the truth?" McNear said.

"What do you mean?"

"I'm thinking about our other clients. Our connects. What if we told them all the truth? I'm asking that question seriously."

Thurmon looked distressed. "It's too strange. You can't come on to a bunch of bankers saying that something that calls itself the Godball is trying to disable their computers. We'd be out of our minds to talk about this unless we absolutely had to. Our credibility—"

McNear waved a hand as if to change the subject. "I'm just thinking alternatives. About these guys: Mike, I'll bring you back the auditor and you can try to find out if a blotto command came in over the wire. If so, run a trace. Apply your charms on the phone guys. Can you give me any more particulars, Tim?"

"I've written it out." Thurmon took a piece of paper from his pocket and handed it to McNear. "Marathon West—Asher, the old bald gentleman. The last time you talked to him, by phone, was September 8, 1983. That was our third in-person. You tried to get him to upgrade and they apparently did nothing. We've sent them several yearly reports with the same message."

"We should forget about the source and start preparing to close," Thurmon repeated. "It's the only logical thing to do within these time constraints."

Reed was feeling around in the cabinets. He dragged out a couple of boxes and began raking parts into them, muttering, "This is great."

McNear, oblivious to the commotion, finished what he was writing and gave the scrap of paper to Tony, who immediately began reading it into the phone, walking away with the line dangling behind him. "Okay, Janet, you're not going to like this. We need for you to get together the Assembly—the one Ben was working on. I don't know what the real numbers are, but you know the program. . . ."

McNear asked vaguely, "So . . . when does that put the event?"

"Tuesday, three, four hundred hours," Jeremy said. "You know, we shouldn't have come out here. We're wasting time. I need my machine to actually *do* anything."

Reed ordered Bobbi to help haul boxloads of parts onto the porch. To her amazement, he was throwing them over the side of the deck, three stories down.

"Shouldn't we at least take this—?"

He cut her off. "You shoulda had this shit cleaned out."

Back inside, the shadows in the room moved strangely in the greenish light. Jeremy was saying argumentatively, "I say we crack em."

"In seventy-two hours?" McNear said.

"I can tear out their liver in forty-eight hours. We're wasting time here."

"We need to tie our people off," Thurmon said, his voice still thickly patient, muffled, the tic in his face on autopilot. "Shut down all incoming wires. We can't afford for this to happen. I don't know what this is, but it's not a joke. It's not somebody in their basement with a micro."

"Fantastic. Shut down a bank computer. Real great."

"I didn't say shut them down, I said tie off all incoming wires."

"Those machines are their hearts. The incomings are their veins.

Tie them off and you might as well turn off the power."

McNear asked Jeremy, "Can you work here?"

"Are you kiddin?"

"What do you intend to do?" Thurmon asked.

"Crack it. Blow it wide open," Jeremy said.

"That's improbable at this point," Thurmon said. "How long have you been working on it already?"

"Tim, I hate to tell you, but we could inform these clients their computers were turning into Swiss cheese at midnight and they wouldn't isolate them. These are *banks*, man."

Tony holstered his phone. "They can't believe you're asking to put together that old program of Mitze's now, Wayne. What's the idea?"

McNear was sitting with a hand on each knee. "What do you think about the whole thing, Mike?"

Heyer, who was behind McNear, at a distance from them all, didn't hesitate. "You know what I think."

"What about Marathon West?"

"What does Marathon West have to do with our connects? The only thing we've done is give them advice."

"But they are our client," McNear said.

"So you're suggesting somebody's after *us*? I think that's totally unreal."

Jeremy's eyes glowed. "It's unreal, all right. It's a bomb, it's a fuck-up beyond all recognition, fubar, it's a bye-bye DataForm."

"Hey Jer, shut up," Tony said. "Take you out of the building and you act like you're withdrawing."

"Look, I'm the hacker around here."

McNear now leaned forward on the stool. "We seem to have three views of this thing. Mike says it's nothing, some kind of joke. Tim says it's bad and we should tie off the clients. Jeremy says go after the source. I disagree with Mike's view. This has too much behind it to be a joke. It's been going on too long and it's too specific. Let's work on it two ways. Get ready for quick close-downs at the banks, send teams and all that, but also let Jeremy fiddle with it, and let's put together Ben's assembly."

There was a moment of silence, a beat in which everybody looked at him.

"Ben's assembly wasn't finished," Mike Heyer said.

"I'm not sure about that," McNear said.

"You're the one that stopped the project. Don't you remember?"

"We're flying upside down. It's the closest thing we have to a weapon."

"You're kidding. He wasn't designing it for this thing."

"I thought you felt this was nothing, Mike," McNear said quietly.

"Fuck it. I'm assuming for the point of argument that you're right. How's an unfinished program that we know almost nothing about going to help?"

"Maybe it won't," McNear said. "Ben was secretive about how far along he was, but it is a poison pill, and it is designed to work on a lot of different operating systems. It won't hurt to try."

Tony spoke up. "It won't hurt except to take a bunch of people's desperately needed time—"

McNear shut him off. "I want to do it."

"What about Marathon West? Janet says they've called her about ten times since we left. They are very distraught."

"Can you talk to them?"

"No way. If anybody does, it has to be you."

McNear looked at the flickering screen. "You all will get back faster on a commercial flight. Try the mid-afternoon United. Tell Art I want him ready to fly in ten minutes, anytime after five-thirty. Sober, please. Start getting the guns ready on the way back. Tim, I want you to coordinate. Write up a description of what we might use, in what order, and how to implement. Tony, stay on the phone. Keep sniffing the air for gossip. Think about other countertactics. If you can think up anything depressing enough, talk about it, try to work it up. Tony, I want you to think especially about the clients—how we close them down, who'll need consult help.

"I have to sleep before I go. I haven't had any for three days. Tony, call them and tell them I'll be there at eight o'clock this evening. You people go on back. Bobbi. You'd better come with me. We need to talk."

15

Early Saturday afternoon, Ray pulled in near a driveway five miles outside the Dubois city limits off the old Little Rock road. A thick breeze pushed clouds up from the south. The big brick and siding house sat on a hill behind a weedy, overgrown front yard.

He parked down the street from the bottom of the driveway, far enough to look like lost highway traffic, lit a cigarette, and ran through what had happened over the last couple of days.

Warnke had called him into his office yesterday afternoon, in a state of alarm about the break-in at the trailer. Wondering how they'd known, Ray said he hadn't witnessed any break-ins. Warnke had very definite information to the contrary. Ray asked what information he had, and the chief sat for a moment looking at him, then leaned forward and, turning his sailboat a little, gravely reminded Ray that he wasn't the one asking questions here. Just as gravely Ray listened, and played dumb. He hadn't seen any break-ins, he was sure of it. The chief asked what Ray had done after his shift. Immediately after? Yes, immediately. Dropped by the station and did some paperwork. Paperwork? That's right, sir. Paperwork.

Today, an hour ago, Marty Williams had called with some questions about the bank-account and tax information from the chief's accounting book.

"Can't tell you any more than I did, Marty. The only thing I got out of it was 'Florida.' The rest was cold numbers to me."

"Yeah, well it's three-hundred-dollar-an-hour numbers, I hope you know, and it's taking me a fuck of a long time."

"Why are you working on Saturday?"

"Because my sources aren't as busy on the weekend."

"What are you finding out?"

"I'll tell you when I got it all together."

"Know anything about computers, Marty?"

The lawyer hesitated. "As little as possible."

"You know what a 'generator' is?"

"Not up on the lingo, Ray. Hang on, I got a book." After a few seconds he came back to the phone. "*Generator* . . . here we are: 'A large program that allows a computer to automatically translate one program into another program, usually from a higher to a lower language; related to *assembler, compiler*.' "

"Can you explain that?"

"Are you kiddin?"

"Do you know what an 'open data base' is?"

"You know what a data base is, Ray. You use the NCIC data base, and the revenue department—"

"But 'open'?"

"It must be a data base where information doesn't cost anything. *Open* usually means free or public, doesn't it?"

"You ever heard of one of these things?"

Marty laughed. "What is this? You want to learn how to be a programmer, get a book of matches and go to night school. I'll call you back later this afternoon."

Now he pitched out his cigarette, popped a Sen-Sen into his mouth, and walked up the driveway, memorizing the license number of a white Cadillac by the garage. He opened a side garage door and did a quick make on a blue Volvo parked inside. He had decided to use the old insurance-rep approach. After a second and third try on the doorbell, he knocked loudly on the door. No answer. He tried it, and it came open.

"Mrs. Mitze?"

Stepping into the hallway, which opened to the left onto a living room, he called again. A sound—a humming—came from somewhere in the musty-smelling house.

"Hello!"

After standing there for a minute, he entered the living room, where there were a few abandoned glasses here and there, some clothes scattered around, and a dying evergreen in the picture window opening onto the back. The house didn't feel inhabited. The dining room had a long table along one wall stacked with magazines and newspapers, a cluster of liquor bottles, mainly gin, and a bowl of moldy potato chips.

"Hello!"

In the refrigerator was a bloated milk carton.

At the foot of the stairs he called out halfheartedly, no longer expecting a response. "Mrs. Mitze!"

At the top of the stairs, he headed down a stuffy hall past a bathroom and closed door on the right, and dormer windows looking out over the front yard on the left, into a darkened bedroom. The bedroom was carpeted and entirely wallpapered, including the ceiling, the bed unmade, and as dusty as the rest of the house. On a little table in a cubbyhole below a picture window were several more bottles, from full to empty, of gin and vermouth. Several limes sat blackening on a silver tray.

Back in the hall, he checked the closed door and found what appeared to be an unused bedroom.

At the bottom of the stairs the sound was louder, and he went through the kitchen and discovered a flight of stairs in plush red carpet going into the basement. A light switch didn't work so he felt his way down into the darkness, moving toward the humming sound, feeling the wall at the bottom of the steps for a switch. He felt his way down a short hall, where he bumped into another door. It was locked shut, but there was enough of a crack between the jamb and door for him to jimmy the bolt with his pocketknife until the button on the other side popped.

He found himself in a gloomy room surrounded on three sides by shelves, stacked with books and notebooks and tape containers. A computer terminal sat on the wooden desk, several books off the shelves lay on it, some opened, and other books and papers lay haphazardly all around the floor. Beside the desk stood a marker board with a row, down one side of it, of taped-up notecards with computer language on them. Ray wiped a finger across the top of the opened books. Very little dust.

From here, he could see all the way down one wall of the basement apartment. The kitchen had been cleaned out, but the walls had the smell of use—sometime in recent weeks. The room behind it was a bedroom, the bed itself a single mattress on a blocked-up piece of plywood. Ray guessed by the books on the little shelf beside it that Mr. Mitze had used it. The little bathroom was jammed into the end of the basement space, beyond the bedroom, almost too narrow for the toilet.

Was this Mr. Mitze's workshop? His hideaway? It wasn't bad for a basement office, since each room down the entire wall had full windows, just above the ground outside, facing the woods.

Ray was looking out the cobwebby window in the little bedroom when he thought he heard a noise. He went back into the office and stood for a moment, realizing that it was not a noise but the lack of it. The humming sound had stopped. He took out his gun and went back out the apartment door through the hall into another basement door, where he found a light switch: Another room, larger than the office, filled with computer equipment, including four large boxes and a couple of tape machines. The room had an unpleasant odor, as if something dead was in the walls. Opening another door he got a face full of the smell, much stronger. He pulled a light string and saw a hot-water heater and some kind of pump system with numerous PVC pipes rising up and running along the floor joists toward the basement wall. The smell was so powerful here he had to make an effort not to get nauseated. A drip came out of one of the pipes and he knelt to get a closer look.

In seconds, he was up the stairs and walking through the house, heading straight for the one room he hadn't checked—the glassed-in porch off the living room. It was largely empty, but he was not surprised to see doors leading onto an outside deck. He stared into the gathering darkness of the stormy evening, pausing long enough to say to himself, "Okay, buddy. You're a big boy."

As he approached the glass door, he saw three glasses, one overturned, and a bottle. At the door, he looked into the hot tub. It was worse than he expected. Unconsciously, he switched his breathing to his mouth as he slid open the door.

Within a few minutes of his discovery, Ray had made an anonymous, voice-disguised telephone call to the 7-Eleven across from the station and asked them to please tell the police to send a car to the Mitze house.

Around 5:30, he wandered into the duty sergeant's office and let the comedians tell him all about it. Ken Merril, recently promoted to Bobbi's position, was sitting at a typewriter filling in forms.

Clinton was standing by the water cooler, flat-footed and sullen. "Ray. You hear about what I found in the hot tub this afternoon?"

Ray said he hadn't heard the details.

John Frick stuck his goofy face through the door, "Clinton got in the hot tub with a woman for the first time today."

"There was a goddamn dog in it, too," Clinton said.

"Hey," Frick said mock-defensively. "Dogs get hungry, too. He saw that good white meat all boiled and tenderized, couldn't resist. Then he was stuck!"

Clinton stared at Ray. "It was the grossest fuckin thing I ever saw in my life."

"Hey, guys," Merril muttered. "I'm trying to think in the English language. Would you go somewhere else to talk?"

Frick made a limp-wristed gesture. "That's what all the thargeants thay."

"You're good at that," Clinton said.

Ray got himself a paper cup full of water. "Anything from the coroner yet?"

"The coroner took one look and died," Frick pronounced with mock gravity.

Merril looked depressed. "He just called a few minutes ago. Said it was probably a heart attack or something. She had a buncha booze in her. There were a lot of empties around the place. Aren't you on this?"

Ray drank the water. "Nope. Miller."

"What are you doin, taking a vacation or something? I never see you around here any more."

"Keepin busy." He wadded up the paper cup and pitched it into the can. He could feel their curiosity. They'd been gossipping.

"That dog musta been pretty dumb," Clinton said, frowning. "What kinda dog couldn't get out of a *hot* tub?"

Frick bent forward and started pawing the air. "These are his back feet, right? Sliding up and down the hot-tub wall. He's stuck. Hot-tub soup." He glanced around waiting for one of them to smile, and when no one did, put on his serious look. It was Frick's habit to make several unfunny comments and then dodge for brief moments into false sincerity. "Poor lady, really." He stood there for a moment looking sympathetic, then departed down the hall.

Merril leaned back from his typewriter. "Doc Poll really got onto it fast. He must be going fishing tomorrow. He said possible heart arrhythmia. Said he was fairly sure she didn't drown, and she didn't have any common poisoning symptoms. Just the booze."

Ray frowned at the floor. "She have a record of heart trouble?"

"Don't know."

"How much preservative did she have in her liver?"

"Good amount. She was a binge drinker, apparently."

"So she wasn't a total soak?"

"*Binge* was the word he used."

"Has he got an estimated on her yet?"

"You'll have to check, Ray. He won't be writing it up until next week." He gestured at the pile of paper beside the typewriter. "I haven't even gotten through the traffic yet."

Ray asked Clinton, "Anything interesting around the place?"

"There was a computer in the basement. I dunno. Buncha books and tapes. Miller's out there with the dust."

Ray was sorry that he'd had to wipe off the doorknobs he touched.

That should make even Miller suspicious. A little suspicion would be good for him. A detective needed to experience the emotion at least once every twenty years. Ray straddled the stenographer's chair that had been Bobbi's favorite in this office. He draped his elbows over the backrest and thought about Mrs. Mitze's house. The fact of the matter was that he hadn't found anything of much interest after discovering the body, but he still had the feeling he knew more than he was putting together.

"Was the dog hers?" he asked Clinton.

"Yeah, he had a collar."

"You oughta get an estimated on the dog, too."

Merril sighed. "Great idea. Why don't you call Miller and tell him to order it? He's out there now."

"You better tell him."

"What do you guys do when you're sitting side by side at your desks?" Clinton asked.

Ray gave him a look and wandered out. Everybody ragged him about the thing between him and Miller. Miller wasn't raggable, so he got it all.

Approaching sunset. Marty had called him back with his report on Warnke's black book, and now Ray was rolling along at eighty-five through the soybean bottoms west of town, with a Pearl beer between his legs. He did this occasionally when he wanted to think, get past a block in his mind.

Just get out there and drive.

He picked up his spiral notebook from the seat and held it between the bars of the steering wheel.

1. Generator, Open DataBase ALL. 23.76 GHz.
2. Chalmers. 9/6/42: Mitze on computer? Mitze *alive* somewhere/ hiding? If not, body moved night of death? Electrocution?
3. English promoted—out of state. W. had him move body 12/10, wants him gone.
4. Jack Cady: knew about trailer, talking. Dog threat didn't work. X'ed.
5. E. Mitze: why?
6. The chief's Florida property: payoff/leash?

He ripped the page out, wadded it up, pitched it out the window, and finished off his beer.

With Elizabeth Mitze dead, who could he talk to?

Bobbi might just be his only hope. What would she be like after California? The thought made his stomach hollow. Richard had been making serious sounds about getting married, and she wouldn't take that well. Also, Outlaw had loaned Richard his Corvette last week, and he and Cathy had been hard to find ever since.

The old Buick cut through the still, heavy, sweet-smelling bottoms, the police radio on. It was cloudy, maybe an evening thunderstorm coming. Summer was here. Seventeen miles past the river, he wheeled around and speeded back in the direction he'd come, thinking, trying to put it together.

Marty's information had been a shock. One of the numbers in Warnke's black book had turned out to be a property-tax receipt from the state of Florida. Marty found out that it was a residence that had recently been reappraised at $250,000 as it passed into the hands of one Mr. George E. Warnke. "That's only part of it," Marty said. "The appraisal values in that county tend to run about half the market value. This is a pretty nice oceanfront house, apparently."

Ray's mind went back to the scene at Elizabeth Mitze's house. There was something about that scene he wasn't putting together. Something obvious.

He'd just heard on the radio that Miller and some officers were out there now, getting further samples from the hot tub. The coroner had requested them himself—which was extraordinary, considering his usual lack of curiosity about corpses.

He pitched an empty onto the floor and felt the ribbon of highway, flat and straight between soybeans, unrolling beneath him.

He glanced at the speedometer and eased up, at that moment remembering a sound—the whine in Mitze's basement. He picked up his microphone.

"Station, this is three. I'm scrambling."

"Station, on ninety."

"Is somebody at the Mitze house?"

"We've got Miller out there and two officers."

"I want you to call them and tell them to stay away from the hot tub."

"Can I give a reason for that, three?"

"Tell em they'll be dead if they touch it. Do you read that, station?"

"Station, they will be . . . dead if they touch the hot tub."

"Affirmative. I'm heading out there now. I'll explain to them. You just tell them to stop what they're doing."

By 2100 that evening, all the weather had marched off to the north, leaving the broken promise of rain. Outlaw's house, a prison of heat, the walls steamy with woodrot, finally eased into night. They were in the kitchen—Bowser shirtless and sullen, Outlaw sweating through his T-shirt and looking worried. Ray had already told them about what he'd discovered at Elizabeth Mitze's house, and they both knew he was working up to something. They knew about the break-in at the trailer, but Ray hadn't told them he'd done it.

He went to the fridge and got out three fresh beers and pitched one to each of them, sat back down on the kitchen table next to the radio.

"Elizabeth Mitze was electrocuted in her hot tub. I heard the circulating pump go off before I found her, but I didn't put two and two together. It was on an automatic timer. A thick-gauge wire was hooked from an outlet on the circulating unit straight out to the tub. When she was in it and the timer clicked it on, she got all the juice for the switch-on surge. The breaker was bypassed, so the juice kept shooting to it as long as the timer was on. When her dog got to smellin around the tub, he got the same."

Outlaw frowned. "A wire just hanging in the water?"

"It had been lagged over the top of the tub behind an automatic refill pipe. Clinton and the ambulance people were lucky it wasn't on when they dragged her out."

"What'd Miller think about you calling out there?"

"I told em it was just a hunch, read something about a hot-tub electrocution in the paper."

"So what's the connection with our snipe hunt?" Bowser muttered.

"We're looking at three homicides with wet blankets on them, George."

"Who's looking at three homicides?" Bowser said. "I haven't looked at nothing but that goddamn fuckin trailer for six months. This has been the most nothing job I've had since they put me on the parking-meter patrol."

Outlaw tapped his beer can. "There may be a reason why the lid's being kept on. We could blow it, you know."

Ray looked at the floor. "It makes me nervous, John, all these people buying it and me sitting in a tent. This ain't a snipe hunt, it's a snipe safari."

Bowser said, "I ain't like you guys, getting regular salaries plus overtime. I'm having to live on this shit pay."

Ray continued to look down. "I'm just talking out loud. . . . Somebody's killing people, and every time it happens Warnke stops the case dead in its tracks. I don't care what kind of operation this is. . . ." He broke off, shaking his head, thinking a minute before deciding to let out his last bit of information. "How would it strike you if I told you Warnke's been making quite a lot of money lately?"

"Strike me as common sense," Bower said. "What do you think he's doing this for, Christian fellowship?"

"How much money?" Outlaw asked.

Ray thought a minute longer. This was not necessarily a good thing to talk about now. "Around five hundred K."

Outlaw squinted at him. "Five hundred *what?*"

"That's par for the fuckin course," Bowser grumbled.

"It's not any normal kind of op money, I don't care what agency we're talking about, or how much he's skimming."

"How'd you find this out?"

Ray shook his head. "Can't tell you yet."

"What are you saying?"

"I'm not real sure. It could be we're being suckered—on the same leash Warnke is. One thing I do know for sure. When this thing blows, I don't want to be one of the jackasses in the cornfield."

"Five hundred—in dollars?" Outlaw asked, still incredulous.

"Real estate."

"Shit," Bowser said. "Wouldn't you just know it. We sit in the tent; he gets the real estate. Wouldn't you just by God fuckin know it."

16

At the Holiday Inn, McNear rented a room and slept six hours. Bobbi remembered that she was supposed to get hold of Jim Daly, but he had checked out.

Now it was getting dark.

McNear drove the rented Ford fast up Interstate 280 toward San Francisco and the Marathon West Bank. For the first few minutes he didn't talk, and silence built in the car. She'd never seen him this grim. There was a glimmer of sweat on his temple. It was a beautiful highway, with soft lights floating beside a perfect, smooth river of concrete through the darkening hills. Seventy-five miles an hour.

"How'd you get along with Govind Shaw?"

"Pardon me?"

"Govind Shaw," he repeated levelly.

"I got along with him okay."

"Let me tell you something about him." McNear continued to look straight ahead. "He wasn't an announced consultant for that class. You probably saw on the catalogue that someone named Wells was listed. Govind Shaw came out here to make contact with my security people."

"What kind of contact?"

"You tell me."

Bobbi didn't answer.

"Let me guess. He probably told you all about how I began my career by destroying Simmons Paragon. Or has he come up with a new one?"

She stroked her hair and drifted a moment, staring at freeway signs so tall and large and well lit that they seemed to be constructed for giants.

SAN FRANCISCO

SAN FRANCISCO

SAN FRANCISCO

She finally answered, "He did talk about a company that you and he worked for—"

"Did he tell you about the checks?"

"Yes."

"That part's true." His voice softened a little. "But we never worked together. That's a lie. He put money into Simmons Paragon. I was a project head there. He got involved with the company as a prop-up investor. He was fresh from school in England, a kid with some capital. He came around the place a few times and tried to lord over the employees, but he didn't work with me or anybody else. When did he tell you this?"

"Today."

McNear hesitated. "When today?"

"We went out for dinner last night. Today after class he snagged me in the hall and seemed to want to tell me all this. He thought I was about to be taken out of school."

"Did he mention where he found that out?"

"So it's true?"

"They must have your phone tapped." McNear took a thin recorder from his shirt pocket and switched it on. "Marilyn, hi hi, please find my original notes on Mitze's Assembly, done sometime in late 'eighty-three. I think they're on the little Winchester." He slipped it back into his pocket and was silent a moment, the car's speed still moving upward.

"The basic facts about Govind Shaw and me are that he came out here with some money when he was a kid, lost it, and blamed it on me. He made a bad investment. SP was a wreck, and if he hadn't been twenty-three years old and suffering from Valley fever he would have been able to see it. All of us were looking for other jobs. Upper management was sucking the company dry. I wasn't happy with the way the place was falling apart and I had a big enough mouth to talk about it, therefore, I destroyed it. That's his logic. He probably didn't mention that I wrote the system accounting for most of their revenue over the last three years."

"No." Bobbi thought a moment before adding, "He accused DataForm of stealing programs."

"Really worked you over, didn't he?"

"You're asking the questions, I'm answering."

He was quiet a minute. "Pardon the bad mood. It's been a rough couple of days. Liz Mitze died."

"Ben's widow?"

"Correct." He sounded angry.

"What happened?"

"Booze, an accident—they don't know. Marilyn told me this thirty minutes ago. Apparently, she was found in her hot tub."

Bobbi remembered the April Fools party—McNear sitting with her on his deck. Ben Mitze, Jack Cady, Liz Mitze. This was starting to get weird. "Did she have any medical problems?"

He sighed. "She was drinking too much. And completely hardheaded. No one could influence her."

They passed a white statue on a hillside off to the right, and blasted toward the dome of light above the city. Bobbi had been watching a car in her rearview mirror, wondering vaguely if it was highway patrol.

"Was Ben Mitze a big drinker?"

"I don't know what Ben was. Every day I know less."

"Did you ever decode that letter he sent you?"

He glanced in the rearview and changed lanes. "It hasn't all come in yet."

BAY BRIDGE

DOWNTOWN

"What do you mean?"

"I've been receiving it from this . . . Godball source since March thirty-first. It's stacked all over the attic."

She envisioned the little printer in McNear's basement ceaselessly tapping out the encoded letter. "I think I'd turn it off," she said quietly.

"I'd love to, but three or four dead banks on our doorstep aren't exactly going to be good public relations. I have to stay open to any possible source of information."

"You think they're related?"

"They're both coming over the same source. . . ." He shook his head slightly. "You heard us back there. We're running in circles. We keep hoping this is a bad joke, somebody having fun giving us ulcers. The name Godball, the idea of an 'open data base' . . ."

Bobbi looked in her mirror again. "This program you're worried about. Did Mitze write it?"

"No. Mike Heyer, long time ago. It's a stress-analysis utility. It

126

dumps, cleaning out the CPU, runs circuit-testing routines—adds, sub-tracts, loops, all thousands of times—then counts the number of errors to get an idea how the circuitry's doing. It also juggles data between disks and does fault checks." He glanced at her. "You know what this stuff means?"

"I can follow you."

"It had a bug Mike could never locate. The fault-checker never worked right. It kept crashing out disks. It was a kludge. We never used it. One thing about it worked very well, though—something we used on later programs—an advance-verification procedure to assure it has the right address and encryption numbers for access, so the queues stay clean with doable events. Before it runs, it keeps checking back con-firming it has entry. We've changed key numbers at two of the targeted mainframes several times, and it walks right back in and shakes hands with them. That means turning off the banks' computers and reloading might not work, since every few minutes it could happen again."

"I thought you had full-package clients encrypted for telecom-munications."

He glanced at her. "We do."

"You mean it's *decrypting* different keys, then verifying entry?"

"So it seems."

"Is that possible?"

"No, it's not. Not in five or ten minutes. We've got something new here."

She looked over her shoulder at the car she'd been noticing—red Mercury Cougar, '85—gliding along four lanes away, only two car-lengths back. "How'd this program get into the satellite in the first place?"

"Mike's program was filed away in our library. At this point, that's all I know. I ordered a library audit, but it's on the back burner with all this other stuff coming down. We should be able to find out who checked out the tape. The only problem is it's a little late for all this kind of thing. . . ."

"Could it be insider sabotage?"

"Our business is like nitroglycerin, Bobbi—jiggle us and we could blow. It's one of the reasons we don't have many competitors. An insider doing something like this would have to be out of his mind. He'd be destroying his own equity."

"Motives for sabotage aren't always logical."

He shook his head. "I don't think anybody's that out of it. Mike's been on a rampage, but he isn't . . ." He trailed off. "And Tim's gotten weird lately, but he knows where the money comes from."

Bobbi had other questions, like why McNear hadn't mentioned

Jack Cady's discovery, but he became absorbed in his own thoughts, silent, floating and weaving down the expanse of the freeway, passing cars, while the Cougar continued to keep up with them. At almost eighty, the Cougar had swung a lane closer, the man in the shotgun seat gazing at them. "Those guys are getting awful friendly," she finally said.

He glanced toward them. "Shaw must be desperate. That's what I can't figure. . . ."

"Is he an agent for USI?"

"He's not an agent in the usual sense. He's in development. But he's been working on some kind of project in tandem with them. Four, five years ago, I heard he was in upstate New York, on something that sounded very much like USI's big one—the J-junction project."

"What is that?"

"The J-junction is a switch. It works very fast. Certain metals, if you get them cool enough, are superconductors. You can pack the circuitry very tight. When the circuits are close, the electricity doesn't have far to run. You can get something like a thousand times the present operations per second out of it."

Bobbi was confused. "So Shaw's in hardware?"

Again he shook his head, staring ahead, seemingly oblivious to the Cougar creeping up nearly parallel to them. The rider was looking at them fixedly.

"Govind's definitely in software. After he lost his inheritance he found an honest job. I heard interesting things about him. Somewhere around 'seventy-three or 'seventy-four he started getting involved in artificial intelligence, natural-language interfacing. That became his thing. He became a manager for big-team projects. . . . If he's on this thing, it means they're further along than a lot of people imagined, probably testing software. I wasn't paying much attention, but it's a small world—you hear things. The word went out that he was a professor at MIT—which I couldn't believe. I checked an MIT faculty listing and he's on it all right but not in any of the course catalogues. It turns out he's *never* taught a course there, and he's living in Fort Mead."

"What's in Fort Mead?"

"National Security Agency headquarters."

For the moment Bobbi had forgotten the Cougar. Her eyes were riveted on McNear.

"The NSA doesn't provide faculty cover unless somebody's working on something pretty big. A lot of computer types hate the NSA so they create faculty berths for a few of their guys in order to give them access to the latest projects, solutions—stuff they'd have trouble getting as NSA employees. They don't do this too often. It's too much trouble, it costs too many chips."

Bobbi thought of the professor's mysterious antagonism toward

Shaw. The Cougar continued to bowl along beside them beneath the cool light of the freeway.

"But carry it out and it doesn't work. It doesn't quite make sense. They have as much to lose as we do. If this satellite really is a processor and not just a relay, it has to be the sexiest piece of hardware that ever existed. A J-junction device with enormous capacity—three or four complete backup systems, the works. Why do they put a computer they're testing out of reach? Why do they shoot it into outer space?"

"Are you asking me?"

"Soft fails—you ever heard of that?"

"Software failure?"

"No. Soft fails are purely electrical. The tighter you pack your circuitry and the lower the current, the more delicate the whole thing is. Get small enough and it's susceptible to alpha-wave decay. Alpha particles zap through your circuits and cause them to go nuts. It's a big enough problem at zero altitude, but at twenty-five thousand miles, outside the atmosphere, there's a lot more radiation. Maybe they decided the only way to really test the thing was to put it up there and see if the shielding and backup systems work. Maybe it was cheaper than trying to simulate the conditions at that altitude."

"But what would this thing be used for?"

Again he shook his head. "I don't know. For USI, the hardware's bound to be ultimately aimed at business markets. It could be a prototype of the kind of processor they figure will dominate the market in the nineties. Beyond the mainframe, beyond the wire. . . . The software is what I'm worried about—what it's doing now, why they've involved the security agency."

"Why would the NSA want to bust banks?"

"Nobody wants to bust banks. Nobody in their right mind."

"The bank we're going to now—"

"Marathon West," he sighed. "Our relationship with them is more limited than with the banks in New York. We have no wires here. We're only consultants and software lessors to them. But their problem sounds suspicious to me. It sounds related. Otherwise I wouldn't be going. Not this week."

They were on city streets now, winding over hills into the center of town. The Cougar was close behind.

"Could Ben Mitze have anything to do with it?"

"I don't know what Ben Mitze was doing and what he wasn't doing," McNear said.

"You haven't been able to tell anything from his letter?"

He shook his head.

"Do you know why the place where he was found was concealed?"

"What do you mean?"

"Out in the Trois, that building."

"What building?"

"Building, trailer, whatever it was."

He went silent. She waited for him to answer. He stopped at the first filling station on the street, pulling off to a dimly lit corner of the lot and leaving the motor on. "Now tell me what you're talking about." He had gotten very still, very intense.

"Ben Mitze was found in a trailer in the Trois Bottoms. You didn't know that?"

"Where'd you get this information?"

"From the man who found him."

"Who?"

"Jack Cady."

"Who is this person?"

"At the present time, he's nobody. He's dead."

McNear's face was caressed with light, as the Cougar turned in and parked on the street—nearby, fully visible.

"What happened to him?"

"Jack was an old friend of mine. My daddy used to buy dogs from him. He came to DF sometime in late March looking for you. He'd tried several times to get hold of you. He died just before we came out here for training. . . ."

He gazed toward the Cougar, silent for a while. Finally he said, "They're acting different tonight."

She watched the driver talking on a CB. "Not exactly subtle, are they? Those guys are scare-tailing you, Mr. McNear. Do you know who they are?"

He shook his head.

Bobbi opened her door and got out. "Stick around. I'll see what I can find out."

"What are you doing—?"

She strode across the parking lot toward the driver's side. Motor running. Two white males, thirties, driver wearing a T-shirt: GREENWICH VILLAGE CHAMBER OF COMMERCE. Approaching the car window, she smiled at them. "What can I do for you gentlemen?"

They looked at her in cold surprise. She continued to smile, walking closer. The radio sat on the seat between them, a portable. The driver whammed it into gear and swerved into the street, turning at the corner. Out of habit, she memorized the car license.

McNear looked disconcerted when she got back in. "They had a portable CB of some kind. The car looked like it was rented. We can have it checked and see whose name it was rented in."

He pulled out and within a few minutes they'd parked on the crest of a steep hill, overlooking a city of light—other hills, the taller buildings, the bay, all glittering around them. No Cougar. He punched the electric windows shut and sat there for a moment in the vacuum of the car, looking at her, shaking his head slightly. "You better be a little more careful."

"Those guys were trying to bug you. It was pretty obvious."

They got out, walking down the shadowy sidewalk and turning a corner. Bobbi got a brief glimpse of Chinatown.

"Don't expect this to be a party."

"What do you want me to do?"

"Moral support."

They walked down the carpeted twelfth floor of the bank building into a large room with a long black table, so shiny that it looked like it was made of plastic, closed red curtains along one wall, and—almost the last thing she noticed in the big room because of their stillness and the mutedness of their faces and dark suits—eight men around the big table. The older man sitting at one end had one flash of color, a carmine handkerchief in his coat pocket that matched the curtains. Short, compact, with a fringe of iron-gray hair around his balding head, he didn't look happy. None of them did.

They stood slightly or leaned across the table to shake hands with McNear, whose white hair somehow seemed extravagant here. McNear dressed well and tonight was no exception. He wore a diamond ring, which Bobbi noticed one of the men looking at disapprovingly. After he'd been introduced all around, he introduced her. She remained standing by the door, opposite a bank guard, an old stooped man who appeared to be some years past retirement time. As one of them explained the situation, Bobbi began to feel magnetic forces forming around McNear at one end of the table and the stout little bald man at the other. The description of the problem took a while, but it seemed to boil down to exactly what Thurmon had said earlier: $200,000 missing on last month's audit, and an entire day's transactions from all branches missing on the computer.

McNear bowed his head, then raised it and looked directly at the older man, waiting just a moment longer than was comfortable. "I believe we ought to find a new site-security contractor for you and a new consultant to take our place."

He said he'd do everything in his power to make the changeover as painless as possible. Speaking in a brief but unhurried way, he seemed to be talking about something normal and pleasant.

Along one side of the table, she could see three different expressions: hardness, absolute disgust, and a weird kind of staring hopefulness.

"Have you done the contingency drill?"

"We haven't been able to get it scheduled," said a man with bags under his eyes and a headachy expression.

McNear tapped the table. "Follow the blue-book model: Call in the most trusted people in each department to head up emergency teams. Be suspicious about who you set up to run them. Don't worry about being fair. Keep off the teams anybody you suspect in the slightest. Watch out for people who are clever about computers or who talk about them a lot."

Asher said quietly, "Who is doing this to me, Mr. McNear?"

"Until we get more informaton, all I can give you is statistics. Your likeliest source is a disgruntled present employee with access to a terminal. This sort of thing is usually being done in-house. Next likeliest is a past employee who's worked out some way to access your system over the phone. Third, it could be somebody who was fired some time ago and left a bomb in your program. The unlikeliest source is an outsider, a vandal—say, some brainy teenager."

"I've read about these things," Asher said.

"It usually isn't a stranger. You ought to get up a list of everybody who's been fired in recent months or who might be disgruntled. Go through you DP people with a fine-toothed comb. You should fire your present site contractor immediately and get somebody else in here. I also suggest that as long as this is going on you cut all data transmission between branches and carry interbranch data by hand. All this is in the blue book we send you each year. Was there a log entry for the erasure?"

There was some confusion at this point, and they ended up calling the operations manager to try to answer the question.

"Mr. McNear, where have you failed us?" Asher asked, with a little smile.

"I haven't failed you. We made at least three presentations to your management. We told you what you needed to make this bank more secure. You chose to disregard us. Now you're having exactly the kind of trouble we feared."

"So you want to 'bow out' as you put it, as soon as there's trouble? Is that what you're telling me?"

"I don't want to, Mr. Asher, but you need a consultant whose advice you'll follow."

"Like what?" one of the younger men demanded.

McNear's tone cooled. "In addition to our presentations, you've had annual written reports. There are certain things you commonly do to lessen the vulnerability of a bank. At the very least, you need to put in a continuous-tape backup system rather than the batching system you're presently using. Your batching method is dangerous because of exactly what happened yesterday. A day's transactions on disks are in an exposed position unless you have a tape clicking right along backing them up. A lot of things can happen to disks to destroy or alter information, especially when you've got a couple of hundred people constantly accessing it."

"We've got the chits," Asher said. "What do you think, we do business on the backs of our hands?"

"The chits are a final, emergency backup, and that's the reason why you should have run the paper drills. You should run them every six months. If you'd done that, manual handling would be feasible up to about two weeks. Beyond that, your efficiency level starts factoring down toward zero. As it stands, you've got a piece of junk for a system and no emergency preparation at all."

"This is personally insulting," said the younger man sitting beside Asher. His features were like the old man's and he'd been introduced as Mr. Asher—a son or nephew.

"I'm trying to tell you the machinery you're using plain won't do. In addition to continuous backup, you need an encrypter for your interbranch transfers. You ought to have a dynamic audit program, as well—one that runs right along with the system, minute by minute, looking for funny stuff, like a terminal inputting a lot of password errors. Without dynamic audits you have no windows looking inside your computer. These are all things we offer in our full-hookup package, but different versions can be bought from separate vendors and set up in-house without any help from us.

"And no matter what you do, you need a new mainframe—one with virtual machine capacity."

The old man was looking at McNear with grieving intensity. "What is that?"

"A computer that operates with three of four mutually inaccessible operating systems. A computer, in effect, that emulates several computers."

"I see," piped up the younger Mr. Asher. "We need computers now that play like they're other computers. When did this latest device come out?"

"Twenty years ago. The airline reservation system was the prototype for it."

"I understand you have a thing going against USI," the younger Asher said.

McNear looked at him thoughtfully but said nothing.

"You don't discriminate against people with USI equipment, do you?"

"Your problem has nothing to do with who manufactured your system, it's when they manufactured it and what's missing from it."

"For $48,000 a year you can't do a damned thing but tell us we should have bought your 'full-hookup package'—is that the bottom line?"

"We'd be worth considerably more than $48,000 if you'd paid any attention to our advice, Mr. Asher." McNear looked at the chairman. "The one hope we've got is the DF-1 utilization summary. That's the one piece of protective software you're using. It arranges the input/output records in various ways so things can be checked. It may show us some kind of pattern. Has that been run?"

Baggy-eyes nodded.

"Okay. I'll take it back with me. Also I want core and OS dumps. Two or three of your computer-knowledgeable officers should go to the processing room and remain present for that. None of them should leave while it's being ordered up and printed out. You're on auditing lockdown. As soon as it's done, put it on twenty-four-hour express mail to our home office. We'll be able to run through the utilization summary pretty quickly. Looking through the dumps for embedded code will take a while."

This left an odd silence over the table.

The elder Mr. Asher cleared his throat and asked, "What does this mean, embedded code?"

"I mentioned the possibility of a bomb. That's a piece of destructiveness that's been patched into your software and set to occur at some later time. It's done by hiding the bomb in some very dull operation—usually a utility function open to all users—which has a trapdoor in it into the deeper functions. Most OS's have trap doors put in them by the original codewriters, so they'll have easy access into their part of the system without going through all the trees.

"By the way." McNear's tone changed. "I'd advise you to get your telephones bugged and rigged for tracing. In case a perpetrator does call to negotiate. The police will help you with that."

"The police? Are you kidding?" Mr. Asher said.

"You should report this."

Mr. Asher stared at Bobbi. She remained standing behind the table near the door.

"That's just what this person wants," he said. "Publicity at our expense."

McNear was firm. "I'm sensitive to public-relations damage, but I don't think it's smart to give in to it. He'll know the heat's off. It'll make him a lot rougher to deal with."

"So you think we ought to provide front-page grist for the newspapers? Do you know how wild the kids down at the *Examiner* would go over such an opportunity? They would go into a feeding frenzy. Bank troubles are big news now."

"You should report it," McNear said patiently.

Asher raised his chin. "How long do you think it would take something like this to get from the police to the press? I'll give you a hint: In this town think in terms of hours, not days. And how much do you think it would cost us in one week if that happened? Five working days, Mr. McNear."

"You better get the police in. Computer problems aren't as big a deal as they used to be. People expect them. It's a trite story out here. When the newspaper calls, don't try to hide it. Release the details properly so it sounds like a boring, technical problem, and it won't get anywhere near the front page. There are models for news releases in your blue book. If you try to cover it up, you might get into deeper trouble."

The one with bags under his eyes agreed. "I think he's right, Mr. Asher."

"That's good, Lamont. But you're already fired, so I no longer listen too closely to you. Now someone who still works for me tell me I should talk to newspapers."

Throats were cleared, but no one answered. Lamont's doggy expression didn't change.

The chairman's mood had clarified now. He was certain about this issue. "When a depositor thinks his money might get *lost*, he takes it out. Your advice will certainly not be followed in that matter. I want you to talk sense to me, not nonsense."

"As I said, there are ways to present it to the press. Your contingency—"

"I don't want to hear any more about my 'contingency plan'! I've seen depositor runs in my life. They are *ugly* things. If we admit to mistakes, they must be conventional mistakes. Losing our records is *not* a conventional mistake. The banking situation is very competitive out here, McNear."

Asher sat ramrod-stiff at the end of the table, while McNear now appeared almost to relax. He looked over at the wall. "Do you mind opening the curtains?"

"What?" Asher squinted.

"The curtains."

Asher looked at him a moment and then ordered the old guard to open them. He walked around the table and slowly pulled the curtain open to reveal a large picture window with San Francisco glittering outside.

"If you don't mind, I'd like to stretch my legs." McNear got up and walked over to the window, his back turned to the table.

The younger Asher had been simmering in silence. He muttered, "A fashion show from Arkansas? Do we need this?"

McNear didn't seem to hear him. His posture—standing in front of the window with his hands in his pockets—almost gave the impression he was the owner here, that he was trying to be patient with his nervous visitors. "I'll go along with the chairman on not reporting this, for now. We'll work on it. We'll stay with you until this problem is resolved or you feel confident you've got somebody else to do the job better. I do strongly advise you to look for a consultant whose advice you trust. Get your people going on contingency record-keeping as quickly as possible. Start on yesterday's transactions. Get them used to handling paper the best they can. If there's another problem, we'll have to regroup. I'll give you fair warning that if there's any more data loss, I'll push strongly for reporting the problem.

"There's one more thing. Have you had any significant friction with competitors lately?"

The chairman sounded disgusted. "I don't know about the electronics industry, but bankers don't normally operate that way."

McNear looked out the window again. "Banking is the electronics industry, Mr. Asher."

"Oh boy," muttered the younger Asher.

A messenger knocked and brought in three file boxes of computer tapes—the DF-1 systems check McNear had asked for.

Chairman Asher asked McNear to talk with him privately for a moment after the meeting.

Bobbi waited in the hall. Within five minutes, McNear came out at almost a run. "Let's go home," he said.

aturday evening at 8:30 Ray pulled into the parking lot of Parker's condo complex in west Little Rock. It was almost dark. A man in a deck chair wearing a yellow-billed cap looked at a magazine in the light coming out of a swimming pool. He frowned at Ray myopically, the watery light shadows playing across his face. A couple of men in white outfits were playing tennis on a darkening court nearby.

One of them whacked the net with his racket. "Charles, you shit, you *lured* me!"

The apartment he was looking for had well-cared-for potted plants lining a little porch.

It was an unwritten rule in the department that Parker's private life was entirely separate from his work life. He lived in Little Rock, he was a bachelor, and he had nothing to do with social events in the department. Ray knew other facts about Parker's private life, but he didn't gossip about them.

Parker came to the door in a deep reddish robe and house slippers. He expressed no great surprise at Ray's appearance and invited him in immediately, as if after they had worked together for twenty years without a single social encounter, it was normal for Ray just to show up one Saturday evening. Parker asked him to sit down. Two of the walls in the room were largely bookcases. There were a lot of knickknacks around the room.

"I was just having some iced tea. Would you like some?"

"No thanks. Nice place here."

"Yes, I like it." He glanced at the door. "Would you like a carbonated? I have root beer and 7-Up."

"I haven't had a root beer in a while."

Watching the tall, gray-haired man retreat to the kitchen, Ray thought he looked more frail than usual. For weeks at a time he didn't see Parker, although he'd heard his voice at least five days a week, not infrequently for hours at a stretch, over two decades. Parker was a voice, a disembodied fact of the airwaves, not someone whose living room you sat in while he padded off to the kitchen and got you a root beer.

On the walls were a couple of old posters of Mae West movies, along with a painting of a man sitting alone, shirtless, in a rowboat on a lake.

Parker handed him the root beer and sat down across from him. "Well. What can I do for you?"

"Hate to bother you on your day off, but I'm in a little bit of a hurry."

"About what?"

Ray sat there for a moment looking at the floor. "We have a murder on our hands with Elizabeth Mitze."

Parker looked at him with an eyebrow slightly raised. "Has the coroner finished?"

"I don't know, but she was electrocuted. Like her husband. Somebody wired up her hot tub. When the automatic timer went on and she happened to be in it, she got it."

"That's a new one."

"I wanted to ask you a couple of questions about the night of her husband's death, back in December."

"You think the two are connected?"

"The log says you were working overtime that night. You were on a second eight-hour shift when Jack Cady called it in. From all I can tell, there was a delay of over an hour from the time of the call-in to the time you dispatched rescue. That's one of the things I wanted to ask you about."

"Are you officially on this case, Ray?"

Ray shook his head.

"Is it an open file?"

"It is to me."

"Can you tell me why?"

"Because I suspect a problem."

Parker smiled at him—a tired, ironic smile. "The word *problem* can refer to half of the events in the universe and three-fourths of the events in the Dubois police station. Can you be a little clearer?"

Ray looked at Parker's dusty smile and wondered if, after all these years, they were finally going to have a go-round. "In your log, you put down that you called the chief that night. Can you tell me why you called him instead of just calling the ambulance?"

Parker looked at him a moment. "Ray, I have worked at the police department since 1954. Thirty-one years. There have been six police chiefs over that period. One of the ways I have managed to make it to retirement age—or nearly—is by accurately recording everything that goes through my hands. Another is by staying out of departmental politics. Entirely. I am not interested in departmental politics. I am interested in doing my job as well as I can, and I involve myself in no one else's job. I am interested in making it to retirement, which will be in exactly fifteen months, at which time I will sign my option and leave the Dubois police department, never to enter it again. I am sure you can understand that."

"This isn't department politics."

"To the ambitious, it never seems that way."

"What do you mean?"

"You've always been a maverick, Ray. Always operated according to your own whims. That really isn't my concern. But when you start acting as a vigilante, I must say I draw the line."

"All I'm asking is why the delay? Did Warnke leave an order with you?"

"I don't object to your questioning me." Parker's fine deep voice was suddenly strained. "But to come barging in here and accuse me—"

Ray held up a hand. "I'm not accusing."

"You're questioning my behavior on the job. My competency."

"Listen." Ray leaned toward him. "If this involves your foot being in the mud, I'm in it up to my Adam's apple."

Parker got up. "Please leave."

"Shit." Ray sat there, irritated at himself for not doing this better.

"*Please* leave."

"I won't back down on this. I'm going to find out what the hell was going on that night. You can either help me or try to prevent me, but I'm gonna do it."

"Well, I'm certain you will. Now please leave my home."

"You asshole."

Parker pointed at him. "I beg your pardon, sir."

"I want to tell you something. Seven years ago, the Little Rock Police Department called the station. They called detective. I happened to answer the phone. They reported to me that an employee of the

Dubois police had been picked up on a morals misdemeanor charge. I took the information and forgot it. I never told anybody. Not a soul. Not Miller, not Ann, not Warnke, not my dog. That information was forgotten."

Parker clenched his jaw, and after a moment looked Ray in the eye and asked, "Forgotten or filed away for future use?"

Ray groaned. "Goddamnit, Parker. I respect you. I have always respected you, whether you feel the same way toward me or not. That telephone call didn't even interest me. I'm telling you about it because I want you to know that I've done you a favor—at least once—in the past. Now would you please do me a favor and tell me why you waited an hour and a half to call the ambulance for this guy?"

The door opened and the man in the yellow-billed cap came in at a moment when the tension between Parker and Ray was obvious. He stopped just inside. He was about ten years younger than Parker. Parker said nothing. He seemed stuck. The man said nothing, but Ray could see the fear sweep into his face.

It was too much. Ray stood up. "I'll be leaving."

Parker hesitated a moment longer, and then said, "I'll walk you out to your car. Ray Wiel, this is Marcus Paar."

"Glad to meet you, Mr. Paar." Ray got up and shook the man's hand.

They sat for a few moments near the lighted pool. Someone was doing laps, and Parker spoke quietly. "I did a second shift because Warnke asked me to. There had been a pickup earlier that night—by Bobbi, in fact—of the children of local . . . persons."

"I saw that."

"The chief heard about it somehow. He must have been called by one of the children's fathers. As you know, he's very solicitous of those . . . kind of people. He asked me to waive the next person on shift and stay on. He insisted. I'd just called the doctor for a final report on the girl's condition when Jack Cady called in regarding Mitze. I was literally on the phone with Warnke when it came in."

"So that's how he knew about Cady's call? You mentioned it to him?"

Parker watched the swimmer. "Yes. He seemed . . . quizzical, but not particularly interested. Then he said—almost as an afterthought— he wanted me to hold further action until he'd called back. Within ten minutes he called back and told me that I was to contact one of the off-duty sergeants and send him to the place of the accident."

"And not dispatch rescue?"

Parker sighed, assenting by his expression.

"Did he specify Neil English?"

"Yes. He ordered me directly, Ray. Under no circumstances was I to dispatch rescue until Sergeant English had investigated the scene."

"Was that all he said?"

Parker nodded. "Substantively, that's all he said."

"What do you mean?"

"He repeated himself several times."

"So he did sound worked up at that point?"

"Yes. Some time later, English called and said to dispatch rescue to the DF building."

Ray sat a moment watching the swimmer, thinking about the fact that it was the next day when Warnke called him in to set up the trailer stakeout. "You wouldn't happen to know anything about Neil getting this job in Florida, would you?"

"Nothing except that Ann didn't notify me until the day he left. I didn't even have a day's notice to get somebody scheduled to take his place."

Ray looked at him a minute and stood up. "Don't worry about all this, Parker. I'd appreciate it if you didn't mention anything to Warnke."

18

At the airport, Bobbi turned in the car keys while McNear made telephone calls. She was supposed to meet him at a snack bar, but after twenty minutes he still hadn't shown up. She finally located him at a pay phone, leaning against the partition, his back toward her, speaking in a flat, hurried voice.

". . . No, Mike, I already knew that. I've known it for a week. We can put it together. But they just found out and started a vault check and it looks bad. . . . I just talked to them, it sounds like a disaster. . . . It's confirmed about Shaw. He's been sniffing around our security people, trying to get . . . Right, right, I'm saying this is pretty extensive. They must have other people inside. Look, I'll see you tomorrow. We have to get back."

He hung up and when he saw Bobbi, a strange look passed across his face. "The vault back home looks bad."

"What's the problem?"

"A lot missing."

Bobbi looked at him questioningly.

"I just found this out. I don't know what's going on."

After midnight, 24,000 feet above eastern Nevada, Bobbi and McNear were alone in the cabin of the company plane. He had gone to work immediately, then had run through what appeared to be a list of stock quotations on a portable computer. Now he was studying a long document, calling up different parts of it on the screen.

Bobbi had an orange juice and, discovering she was starving, some crackers and cheese spread that she found in the back of the little refrigerator. Heading for the Rockies and the deepest part of the night, she felt quite awake, suffused with a warm, almost narcotic, sense of excitement. She flipped through a magazine, her mind turned to McNear, until she was merely staring at the pages thinking about this person six feet away from her. She wondered exactly what he was doing, but didn't want to ask. The casual flow of information was exactly what she'd been hired to put an end to at DF.

She was going to move to a more distant seat when he hit a key several times, stood up, and asked her if she'd have a drink. He got a whiskey and water and added a dash of gin to her orange juice.

Sprawled in his seat, he sipped his whiskey. "How did you like our fancy California office?"

"Quite a place."

"Reed should have warned you. We abandoned it a year ago but still have some network connects out there we haven't figured out how to pipe to Arkansas." He pulled loose his tie.

Bobbi couldn't help noticing his ring again. It looked to be well over a carat. "If you don't mind my asking, is that a diamond?"

"It's a present. From my daughter." His eyes switched down to the ring in what seemed a melancholy expression. "That was before our problems. . . ."

The pilot's door banged and Art Devlin yelled through it, "Phone for McNear!"

As he took the red receiver from its cradle on the wall, Bobbi couldn't take her eyes off the extravagant ring. Aside from the expense, it was an odd gift for a daughter to give her father. She wondered what he meant by "our problems"—problems with Taylor herself, his divorce? Often when his daughter was mentioned, McNear appeared to spin out slightly, to lose his grip. . . . As he listened, her mind turned back to her own child. She remembered the telephone call she hadn't answered last night—and Daly's attempt to talk to her earlier today. She hoped Richard wasn't up to anything.

McNear finally spoke, gloomily, "Okay, Tony, tell them to get up a report. We'll have to deal with this tomorrow. There's nothing we can do until we see it catalogued. Signing out."

McNear leaned his head back in the seat and looked at the ceiling.

"Problems?" she asked.

"It looks like we've got about seventy percent integrity in the vault."

"What?"

"A bunch of tapes have either been substituted by dummies or crashed. They look genuine—real numbers, everything. . . ."

"Has anyone talked to the librarian?"

"Mrs. Auletta. I don't think so."

Art yelled back again, "Another one for McNear! It's Tom Ferris, from USI."

Bobbi went back to the short bookshelf by the bar and was getting down a magazine when McNear was suddenly beside her, phone line dangling behind him, scribbling on the side of the page: "Hurry Tell Art to switch on intercom. You take tape rec to Intercom spkr, record this."

She went forward and told the pilot to turn on the intercom, and, hurrying to the rear of the passenger cabin, held up the tape recorder as the speaker sputtered on.

". . . sounds like you better get yourself a new one, Wayne. That one's loud as a threshing machine!" Ferris's voice boomed. He had what sounded to Bobbi like a Texas accent.

"I can hear you fine; you don't have to talk so loudly." The intercom echoed slightly, and McNear twisted his fingers in the air to tell Bobbi to turn it down.

"I called to find out what kind of terms would interest you."

"What are we talking about?"

"I want to make an offer on DataForm."

McNear glanced up at Bobbi as if to make sure that she was holding up the recorder. "This is the first I've heard of it."

"I want you to think of our attitude as friendly at this point. Regarding price, we'll have to stay within the bounds of reason, but I assure you everybody on your end will be happy."

"You're going to have to start a few steps back, Tom."

It was the other guy's turn to pause. "USI wants to buy DataForm, Wayne, and we'd prefer to do it before you go public. As you know, public buys are more trouble and expense for us. I realize that in the time frame we're looking at, you won't have an opportunity to set up any parachutes for yourself, but we'll take care of that in the offer. You just give us the details. Looked at from your perspective, it's the best route, since your offering is going to run into trouble."

The tone, while impressive and cordial enough, was cold, like an actor reading a part he didn't particularly like.

McNear stood there holding the phone, staring at Bobbi. "Why is that?"

"We might as well talk frankly, Wayne. In a situation like this, you're not going to interest any institutional money. There's hardly going to be a big rush of capital into your company when you're having client problems."

"I understand you've been having some problems yourself."

"The market's soft now, there's no hiding from it. But that's beside the point. We're talking about you. My purpose is to make an offer. We've drawn up a couple of model buyout agreements, depending on whether you prefer paper or cash payment. You might take a look, add your input, then we can move ahead."

"I wasn't referring to your earnings, Tom. I was talking about the problem you seem to be having with the satellite. The *only* problems we're having are coming from that same satellite."

The caller didn't respond for a second. "That may be something we need to talk about head to head."

"You've got a communications or processing device that's acting very strange."

"I wouldn't push it, Wayne."

The tone carried a warning, but McNear persisted. "Push what?"

The caller replied ironically, "I'm sure this approach must have occurred to you. Let's just say that if we did have mutual interests—or mutual problems—I'd do everything I could to help solve them. But I have to protect the stockholders of this company. We have to make damn sure such problems are avoided in the future."

"Go ahead."

"I'm calling instead of somebody in acquisitions because I want to personally convey how serious we are and how quickly we want to move. The matter is pretty much decided on our end."

"You want to amplify that?"

Bobbi heard the man's sigh above the scream of the turboprop. "I want this to remain friendly—or at least discreet. But, Wayne, I have to admit that I'm not long on patience right now. We have to move fast. We have to have your agreement on this—and your signature—within the next couple of days."

McNear was cool. "Oh?"

"I'd appreciate you getting out front about this. Tell me what you're looking for."

"What's your offer?"

"We're willing to enter into something at twelve times earnings if we purchase with paper. Maybe ten in cash. For parachutes, twice the present salaries of all senior officers is our upper limit."

"We're not interested."

"I naturally have a little room—"

"I'll tell you what, Tom. Unglue your satellite from our clients, and I'll talk to you. I won't necessarily sell, but I'll talk. Until you unglue it, I'm deaf."

McNear hung up quickly and got out of his seat. He stood, his expression lost for a moment in an indecipherable intensity. He looked up then, and held out a hand toward the recorder. "May I have it please?"

He caught her eyes as she handed him the recorder. "What you just heard is completely confidential."

Martha Daly stood at her front door looking distraught, then burst into tears. "Oh Bobbi! I'm so sorry."

Bobbi stood there, staring at the pallid, weeping woman, and the Great Fear rolled over her like a big ocean wave. She came into the house and shut the door. "What's the problem?"

Martha looked at her with streaming eyes.

"Tell me, Martha."

"I messed up. Oh honey, I messed up terrible."

"Is Richard all right?"

"I don't know," she said in a little squeezed-up voice.

"What'd he do?"

"He left."

"How long ago?"

"He just took out. I tried to call you. I tried to get them to do somethin down at the station and they wouldn't. They asked me how old he was and just laughed at me. I begged them every way I knew, and they treated me like some kind of white trash. They're all jealous down there because you and Jim got those jobs. I messed up, Bobbi."

"Did he say where he was going?"

"He just *left*," she wailed. "I haven't been able to find out anything about him, and I've been on the phone forever. Oh Bobbi, I called everybody but the governor."

"It doesn't sound to me like you did anything wrong. Did you all have an argument?"

"No."

"Well, for heaven's sake, are your brains addled? The boy's seven-teen. He's probably with Cathy somewhere. Seventeen-year-old boys do that kind of thing."

Martha burst into uncontrollable weeping, and, fearing that she'd fall onto the floor, Bobbi went over and hugged her the best she could. "For heaven's sake," she repeated. "Come over here and sit down. Is Jim back?"

"No. That's the other thing. He won't be back till next week. They sent him to New York."

New York, Bobbi thought, and they didn't even tell me?

athy's father was unconcerned about her and Richard's disappearance. They went off for a "little R and R," he said, at one of the lakes in the mountains, apparently in a Corvette borrowed from John Outlaw.

No luck finding Ray.

She had to be at DF by noon, after getting no sleep Saturday night. Neil English, to her surprise, had quit both of his jobs for a police job in Florida. Daly and Reed had flown directly from California to New York, accompanying the emergency crews there. She could do fine permanently without Neil, and the less of Ron Reed the better, but Jim she would have given her right arm for. For the first time, the whole building was up to her, and two part-timers from Markham Security were all the help scheduled for that afternoon.

Most of the confusion was inside the control room. Looking through the corridor window, she saw what appeared to be half again the normal shift size—eight or ten extras at the central consoles, and other additional help rushing around mounting tapes. On the other side of the sealed glass, like a character in a silent film, Tony moved from one urgent cluster to another, gesticulating, pointing his finger at people. Outside control, an occasional door slammed and someone rushed through largely empty corridors.

During the time she and Jim had been away, workmen had nearly finished the new office that was to take the place of the Butler building as security center, although Bobbi could see that Reed hadn't yet moved to his new desk. Electricians had finally installed a control board with consoles for the cameras that were mounted around the building. Her office was located inside the newly outfitted security center, with a new-smelling mahogany desk and a bright red telephone on it, her code number, S-10, on the dial. She put her pistol into a lockable drawer and took three ring-binders describing DF's physical plant and computer system out to the central desk.

Sometime within an hour, she looked up to see Sinc Heyer standing, expressionless, at the window in the corridor, holding up a piece of paper. She gestured for him to come in, and as he did so he kept his eyes lowered to the desk, where he put the little folded note, departing without a word. "Please see Mr. McNear now." The note was clumsily printed, and Bobbi looked up, wondering why he hadn't just told her.

Marilyn sat outside the boss's office, straight backed, with a pencil and yellow pad, reeling a bunch of numbers into the telephone.

McNear was leaning forward across his keyboard squinting into his VDT. He made a little sound and pushed it bumping against the wall to answer his phone. He ran a hand through his hair, blinking phosphor-strained eyes as he listened to a long explanation of something, then said coolly, "I'll deal with this later if you don't mind, Mrs. Vale. Tell her if she does it again, she'll be in trouble. I don't know that I'll make it home tonight."

He hung up, leaned back in his chair, and rolled his neck around a couple of times. "How old is your son, Bobbi?"

"Seventeen."

"Do you get along okay?"

"At the moment I can't find him. He's gone on a little trip with his girlfriend. I think."

"I've had similar problems with Taylor. She's been sneaking out of the house again. It gives Mrs. Vale fits."

"Is that your housekeeper?"

He looked down at his desk. "She's a nurse. Taylor isn't ready to be alone. Without any kind of supervision, I mean." He took a deep breath and looked up at her.

"Is Sinc Heyer still her boyfriend?"

He smiled vaguely. He seemed to want to say more but not know quite how to. After a moment, he asked, "Was Taylor talking the night you took her to the hospital? Did she say . . . anything?"

Bobbi remembered a couple of comments the girl had made, but nothing she could imagine being of any use for McNear to hear. She shook her head.

"And it definitely appeared that she was drugged?"

"Yes."

He felt his jaw with the back of his fingers and stared. His eyes came back into worried focus. "Well. Let me tell you why I called you. Mrs. Auletta has been fired as librarian. Bill Cross is taking her place. Auletta is not to be let back in this building."

"Did someone question her?"

"I did. She claims she ran vault access completely by the book. The only problem is she has no idea what happened to over a third of the tapes in the library. No clue."

"Will they be able to recover them?"

"This isn't the kind of thing we need to be dealing with right now." He looked in a drawer of his desk, got out an electric shaver, walked around to the couch, and sat down beside her with it. "These guys may actually go down tomorrow night."

"What are the teams in New York doing?"

"It's Tim's plan. We shunt incoming computer traffic here, so our controllers can clear it all manually." He shook his head. "It's stopgap. It might work a while—a few days, a week. The truth is we're no closer to a solution than we were a month ago, and time's running out."

Bobbi watched him, sitting there fiddling with his electric razor, looking oddly comfortable, as if he'd become almost reckless in his exhaustion.

He pitched the shaver onto the couch between them. "Well. Okay. Here's number one: In the meeting tomorrow, I need to inform Tim and Mike Heyer they're no longer cleared for the control room or for computer access. Can you work something up?"

She stared at him for a moment.

"Thurmon will be back?"

"Oh yes. They'll all be here for this one."

"You want them yellow-badged?"

"That's right. I want them to have no computer entry at all."

"For how long?"

"Until we're out of the woods. A couple of weeks, minimum."

Bobbi thought a minute. "I can come up with something."

"Okay, write it up and give it to me. Call it 'Emergency Security Measures.' The second problem is more critical. Bill Cross has a bunch of tapes he's cataloguing right now at the vault. I want you to put a guard with him. A guard needs to be there *all* the time. If the guard has to take a break, get somebody else to be there while he's gone. Tony's going to be working with Cross sometime within the hour if I can pry him out of control. The guard lets no one else near the tapes, for any reason."

"Okay."

"Number three—and this is equally critical: I want you to look into the vault problem. See if you can't find out who's responsible for stealing those tapes."

"Do you have Mrs. Auletta's records?"

He got up and picked up the logbook from the top of his desk. "I wouldn't trust this, but it's a start. One thing we do know now—it was malicious."

"Sabotage?"

"First we thought they'd been stolen and replaced by dummies. Last night, while we were flying home, they discovered readable sections on those tapes, a few dozen feet here and there that looked like the originals. Whether they were taken out of the vault or not, whether they were copied or not, I don't know, but I do know they were sabotaged."

"Why wasn't this whole thing noticed sooner?"

He frowned at the logbook. "Whoever did it must have had a good idea about usage patterns. Most of the destroyed tapes weren't used that much." He pointed at a page near the middle of the logbook.

Red Sector, ARP 60-79 / B. Mitze, 11:30:84: 0730

"These, for example, were checked out to Ben Mitze on this date, then never again, as far as I can tell. They were all light-usage tapes."

She pointed at Mitze's name. "Was he the one who checked them all out?"

"A bunch of us checked em out, including me. There's no pattern to that."

"Any pattern to what kind of tapes—?"

He shook his head. "That doesn't seem to matter, either. There isn't any type or sector similarity among the sabotaged ones. We have green sector tapes gone, yellow sector. . . ."

"What were these particular ones?"

"A lot of different stuff. Listen, Bobbi, you're not going to have time to do this systematically. We need to find out who the hell's been doing this, and we need it fast."

"What about videos?"

"What do you mean?"

"The new cameras—"

"They've finished that?"

"They were testing some of the cameras before we left for school, using the film as samples to show us how to label and file. The library camera may have been hooked up for a while."

"However you can do it. Take this log. Right now I need to check on Jeremy's progress. . . ." He smiled at her tiredly. "I hesitate to say this, because it sounds impossible even to me, but we're in a severe time crunch. We need to crack this today or tomorrow."

"Then I better ask you a plain question. Do you suspect Tim Thurmon or Mike Heyer?"

"I wouldn't overemphasize that possibility."

Bobbi didn't try to hide her puzzlement at this careful answer.

"We're operating on the principle of least knowledge right now. Absolutely. Anything you see or hear in my presence is completely, absolutely confidential."

"All right. . . ."

"It's a funny situation. There are things going on that may appear to be out of control that aren't. But one thing is out of control—these tapes. You find out within twenty-four hours who destroyed them, and you're in for a very attractive bonus."

"What about the building?"

"Do the best you can with the hired help, but it's completely secondary. You're a free agent looking for one thing."

"If I'm a free agent, I want to go with you to Jeremy's office."

He glanced at her sharply. "If you think it'll be of use."

On the way out, Marilyn stopped him, pointing at something on her yellow pad. "Are you sure about this?"

"Yes, Mar, I'm sure."

She moved her pencil. "This?"

His tone was cool. "Minimum, ninety-percent liquid, Mar—whatever you have to do. How are you doing with the puts?"

"I've got over half of them. No matter how many brokers I use—"

"Chicago, local, San Francisco."

"Times two on all three?"

"Yes. If they give you any trouble, tell them we'll withdraw accounts immediately."

"Why not?" she said facetiously. "By the way, I am spreading this little war chest between accounts. You can't trust banks these days."

Jeremy's office, in the middle of the building next to the control room, was a windowless smelly den, lighted by a long-armed extension lamp turned upward against the white ceiling, and three computer consoles, one of which blinked on and off in green letters: YOU CAN USE ME ANYTIME, DEAR. Against one wall a completed pyramid of Coke cans reached to within an inch of the ceiling. A cot in front of it was tangled with old, unwashed blankets, and the broad table Jeremy used for a desk was cluttered with printouts. Tony and Carol Rader were there, the office crowded by five of them, and Rader wandered out. Tony looked even more than usually anemic and disheveled. Bobbi got the impression McNear and she had stopped a conversation.

"Any luck with the satellite?"

Jeremy swiveled around in his chair. "No. I ran through the encryption key possibilities twice. Two to the fifty-sixth: it took me seventeen hours each run. I couldn't decode it. I didn't even get a hiccup."

"So you've just been shooting keys at it." McNear punched *enter,* and the menu disappeared:

PLEASE ENTER KEY NUMBER.

"Which setup are you using?"

"If you're wondering whether I'm using the right link protocol, yes, I am. When it takes that first *enter,* it's verifying linkage."

McNear frowned at the screen. "So it just happens to be using the same transmission formatting you are?"

"I've tried a bunch of different ones. It reads just about every standard format—civilian and military." Jeremy left the room and could be heard putting quarters in the Coke machine in the hall.

"Synchronous transfer?" McNear asked, when he walked back in.

He shrugged. "It never put me on wait out front. . . . I do know one thing. It takes any transmission rate I can generate."

Tony asked, "How do you know if you haven't gotten past the initial hookup?"

"*Enter* is a signal just like anything else. It's short but it's data stream. I kept sending it faster and faster and it kept reading me until I was off the charts. I'm guessing this thing receives at up to five million bauds. Not only that, it also imitates your transmission rate and sends back at the same speed. It's a slow talker if you're a slow talker, a fast talker if you're a fast talker. This thing is very friendly."

"Yeah right," Tony muttered.

"Could it be double-encrypted?" McNear asked.

Jeremy took three or four quick sips. "Who pays to blow that much hash through the air?"

". . . Maybe it uses a different encryption method."

"Public key/private key? If it does, we can forget it. Have you gotten into Ben's letter yet?"

McNear shook his head.

"You know, if you could crack that letter, it might give us a key into this thing."

Tony sighed. "Listen, I can tell by the way you guys are talking we're not going to open this thing up before Tuesday one hundred hours. I just don't hear it in your voices. We have to get ready for this SOB. We're getting nothing done, man."

Bobbi cleared her throat. "May I ask a question?"

"Sure," Jeremy said. "It's a democracy."

She pointed at the bottom half of the screen. "If this is your own program, why can't you match the appearance of these coded numbers with your own program—"

"Aha, send her off to school and she's an expert already. The problem is that those blips are *not* encoded, any more than the menu above them."

"Will this program—this stress analysis—run just once?"

"No. The asterisk by the *B* is a loop flag. It'll run until somebody or something stops it."

"How are they doing with the buffers?" Tony asked Wayne.

"I talked to them a couple of hours ago. They ought to have it done by now."

"It's a start," Tony said without conviction.

Jeremy gazed gloomily at the screen. "This thing's picking new addresses out of the ether. What's Tim's little dippy manual display-and-check system going to do against something that can do that?"

There was a moment of silence. Bobbi sensed that this kind of talk from Jeremy was out of character. He always had solutions, hope, a different approach.

"For all practical purposes, this thing's a superzapper, right? Total override. It's a lockdown. It takes over. The only way we can stop it is to turn off the power. And since we can't turn off the source of the zap, all we can do is turn off our clients. We worried about sophisticated problems—round-downs and unusual input-output activity. . . . Meanwhile, this common little program to run electricity through the circuits and check failure rates sits in the background licking its chops."

Tony looked like he wished Jeremy would shut up. "We've got to do something on site. Tim says if we have to we should just strip the banks' interfaces and let them work in isolation. He figures they'll retain enough automated capacity to stay in business. I think we better consider that."

Mike Heyer had appeared in the doorway—wearing a rumpled suit, his round sunglasses, and a scowl. "Great idea. How do they handle transfers—with runners? When the treasurer needs to raise fifty million in hot money before three o'clock, what does he do, go to the phone booth across the street?"

"Mike. Where have you been?" McNear asked.

"Down in the Virgin Islands on a vacation," Heyer said sarcastically.

McNear looked at him a minute. "What's up?"

"I just got a call from California. Marathon West got hit again."

"When?"

"A couple hours ago. They were running a batch of on-us Visa bills and it went bonkers. Ate a bunch of data.

"Development number two: I got something nailed down on their first crash out there. The call-in ordering the first crash at Marathon was from the USI downlink in the valley. I got some buddies at the phone company to help me trace it. The same call was made three or four times, test links apparently, then the serious call was made. I don't know about this new one yet."

"Can it be proved?" McNear asked.

Heyer looked at him sourly. "Sure."

"In a court of law?"

"Yes, Wayne. In a court of law." Heyer turned around and walked out. McNear and Tony stood there looking at each other, then followed Heyer to his office. Bobbi came along after them. While the three of them remained standing, Heyer leaned back in his chair and put his feet up.

"This is nuts," he said.

McNear looked at his feet. "What do you mean?"

"The whole picture. I don't believe USI put a processor this sophisticated into outer space."

"Why not?"

"Because it breaks too many laws of common sense."

"We've gone through this again and again," McNear said.

"The transmission band would have to be all the way across the spectrum to shove enough data back and forth for the thing to be practical. Ever think of that?"

"Not if it's fast enough. Jeremy just told us the thing could be pushing five million bauds."

Heyer shook his head. "No way."

"At five million bauds, you could deliver junk mail over the damn thing. Think of the processing abilities of something like that. And you've got no lines, no operators, no peripherals, nothing between you and it."

"You ought to sell the fucking thing."

McNear stopped short.

"You ought to go on the road. You talk a great line."

McNear's expression turned angry. "Mike, put your feet down and talk to me."

Heyer sat looking at him through his sunglasses, not making a move.

McNear pushed his feet sideways off the desk, knocking off a coffee cup and papers.

"Hey, pal, this is my office. I can put my feet on my desk any time I want to."

"Guys, guys," Tony said.

McNear's face was red. "Edit the personal stuff, Mike. Just goddamn edit it out. We've got a problem."

"USI doesn't give a shit about you, Wayne. You're not even a fly on their wall. And hey. I don't go for data processing in outer space, okay?"

"So tell me what's happening."

"I don't know what's happening, but I know I want a board meeting."

"Well, you've got it. Tomorrow." McNear got up and strode out of the office. Bobbi followed him.

20

It was almost eight o'clock Sunday evening when Ray pulled into a Cities Service filling station in Bell, Arkansas, thirty miles north of Dubois in the Ozark Mountains. He'd heard Bobbi was in town but hadn't gone by to see her. She probably wouldn't be exactly friendly when he did. He had spent much of the day going through "Towing" in the yellow pages of Dubois, Little Rock, and surrounding towns. He hated to work on the telephone but had no choice in this case. He wanted to find out who'd arranged for that trailer to be dragged out to the Trois.

The sun was just down, and the surrounding hills were beginning to move into shade.

The station was lodged in the middle of a big old pebble-rock building that appeared at some point in the past to have been the entire downtown of Bell. Now it was a filling station and junkyard, with the junk expanding into spaces previously occupied by a feed store and a drugstore. Inside the open door, the walls were hung with dusty packages of fuses and gaskets, a dirty glass case was stacked with used wire- and bolt-dangling parts—alternators, regulators, carburetors—and, in the corner, a desk strewn with yellow and white invoices. The place smelled of grease and dust and cleaning compound. Ray wandered into

156

the garage, where a pair of blue-jeaned legs stuck out from beneath an old Ford pickup.

"Hello," Ray said.

"Pump's shut down," came back a not-too-friendly voice.

"I don't need any gas. I'm the one that called earlier about towing." No reply.

"I just need some information."

The man cursed viciously and his legs started twisting this way and that. He was struggling with something. Ray stood there until he eventually dragged himself out from under the truck. It took him a while. He was a good six foot five—in his forties, full red beard, speckles of grease and oil on his reddish face. He had something in his hand, and he held it up not far from Ray's face. "Know what that is?"

Ray's head went back a couple of inches. "Looks like a—"

"U-joint. Know what'd happen if you didn't bolt that down good?"

"What?"

"Drop your drive shaft in the road."

"Hell, I guess," Ray said mildly.

"Know what kinda transmission that Ford truck has in it?"

"Can't say I do."

"Cast-iron Cruisamatic."

Ray smiled up at the big man.

"Know what happens if you take the cast-iron Cruisamatic out of that nineteen and sixty-seven truck and replace it with a Ford truck transmission from nineteen and seventy-three?"

"No."

"You overheat the son of a bitch, melt its bearings down till they're rattling around in there like a sack of popcorn seeds."

"Why's that?"

"Because the cooling lines don't fit!" He pitched the U-joint onto a work bench and went over and plunged his hands into a twenty-five-pound bucket of cleaning compound.

Ray shook his head.

"I'm from Texas," the big man said, frowning over at him.

"What part?"

"West. I come here in nineteen and sixty-four and I've been dealing with ignorance ever since." He wiped his hands on an old greasy towel. "What can I do for you?"

"I'm the one that called you earlier today. I wanted to ask about a towing job that you may have done six, eight months ago."

"I don't do no towing."

"Didn't you tell me—?"

"Don't make any difference what I told you. I never did no towing myself. They used my phone, but I wasn't involved personally."

He went by Ray and pulled the big garage door shut, then walked through the inside door into the station. Ray followed him. "Mind telling me who was?"

The big man went around the station shutting things up for the night. "Sorry, mister. I cain't help you."

He was going to the front door to lock it when Ray went around to the glass cabinet, slid the door back, and picked something out of it. "Before you close up, I wonder if you'd sell me this?"

The big man squinted at him, then at the generator. "You got an old Farmall to put it on?"

"I collect em," Ray said.

He snorted. "You collect tractor generators?"

"I'll give you a hundred bucks for it," Ray said.

The man stood there looking at Ray, then he shook his head. "Cain't do it."

Ray looked it over. "It's an awful nice one. I could go as high as a hundred and fifty."

He frowned at Ray, then glanced out the door and looked back at him again. "Didn't you say something about an investigation?"

"I'm just trying to find out a couple of facts about some people down in Dubois. Doesn't have anything to do with up here."

The big man went around the desk, wrote out a ticket, and handed it to Ray. "That's pretty steep."

"It ain't too steep, considering."

"Considering what?"

"Considering that window behind you cost about seventy bucks, and that pump out front a hell of a lot more."

Ray dealt out two hundred dollars onto the glass countertop. "You afraid somebody'll vandalize em?"

The sight of the money lightened his tone a little. "Might."

"Why would they do that?"

"You work for the sheriff?"

"I work for the police department in Dubois, but this is a private case. All I'm looking for is information."

The big man started picking up the twenties. "Information's what makes the world go around, ain't it. That's what they say. Tell you what. If I get a busted pump or slashed tires out of this, and it costs more than this"—he held the money out—"I'll send you a bill."

"So you're not the one who did the towing?"

"Nosir. The Tully boys did it. We had a deal for a while, I'd take jobs, they'd do em. Had their youngest brother stay around here takin tow calls, except they were so few and far between, he got spotty about comin and then just quit. Which didn't hurt my feelings none."

"So you didn't particularly like the arrangement?"

"No, I did not."

"These Tullys aren't the easiest people to get along with?"

"About as easy as a nest of rattlesnakes."

"They live far from here?"

"Not far enough."

The crabbed little penciled map that Ray had paid two hundred dollars for led him across three low-water bridges and then wound back into the hills up a section of road that the county government had apparently abandoned, seven miles of twisting through herbicide-devastated forest. Back before it was illegal, a couple of big logging outfits had used Agent Orange in big sections up here to kill off the native hardwood forest so they could plant harvestable softwood. Sheriff Bud Nagal had been involved in that through his wife's real-estate business—buying land at tax auctions for little or nothing and selling to the logging companies.

Ray crawled over a last section of road toward a strange sight: a big old three-story house sitting on the side of a hill with floodlights aiming from it in every direction and a flatbed truck with engine blocks on it that were being unloaded onto a huge pile—a mountain—of engine blocks in the front yard. The men were unloading the truck using a pulley on a tree limb above the flatbed with a thick rope leading to the bumper of a high-riding four-wheel-drive pickup. There were five other high-riding pickups, all brand-new Chevrolets, all with gunracks.

Ray couldn't see how the flatbed had made it up these roads with a load that heavy. A tractor or bulldozer must have pulled it the last few miles. He wondered why anybody with enough interest in mechanics to have two or three hundred engine blocks stacked in the front yard would be using this method to unload them instead of a simple come-along or block and tackle. He also wondered if he had just stumbled, by chance, onto the mysterious motor-stripping operation that for four or five years had been known to be operating "somewhere in the Ozarks."

If he had, he'd better revise his game plan.

Three children appeared near Ray's window, all with dirty white-blond hair lying flat on their heads, the youngest a little girl with a T-shirt and no diaper, carrying a piston by its connecting rod, and the oldest a mean-looking boy of about ten who was riding a giant dog around the yard, kicking it in the ribs, carrying a double-barreled .410 shotgun. He rode up to Ray's car and aimed the gun at Ray's chest when he opened the car door.

"Hold it rat there."

Ray hated to have guns aimed at him, whether by grownups or children, whether in jest or in seriousness. The few times in his life it had happened, it had without fail made him angry, and it did so now. It relieved him when a woman appeared—long hair, red shorts—saying "I told you not to do that!" She jerked the shotgun out of his hand and, pushing him from the dog's back, turned back toward the flatbed. "Dennis, I told him a hunert *times* not to go ridin that damn dog. He might get bit."

"Pass that gun on up here," said a stringy, shirtless man with blond hair, taking the gun and laying it on top of the truck cab.

Ray watched them while his heart rate descended back a notch.

A motor was dangling over the pile, and one of them yelled, "Back her up, John!" As the pickup lurched backward, two of them pushed the block away from the flatbed, lowering it with a thick clunk into the pile.

The woman grabbed two of the kids by their hands and jerked them off toward the house, leaving the little girl with the piston standing there staring seriously at Ray.

"What can I do for you?" the pickup's driver said, elbow out of the window.

"I was trying to get some information about towing."

"Towing what?" the driver said, with a funny smile not quite aimed at Ray.

"Trailers."

"Wants to know about towing trailers!" he yelled back at the men on the flatbed. One of them, smallish, with square-rimmed glasses and a little mustache on his dirty brown face, pitched a beer can onto the pile of motors and made a loud burp. "We ain't open."

This was funny to everybody but Ray, who stood by the front fender of his car while they roped up another motor.

"Git it!" the blond yelled, and the pickup revved up and started throwing dirt again.

Ray eventually walked over to the edge of the flatbed and said to the one with glasses, "I can see you fellows are busy. The boss said to tell you we're willing to pay the going rate."

"That right?" Square Glasses said ironically.

The blond snorted, while another one, a stocky man with tattoos on his arm, looked mildly worried. They started tying up another motor, and Ray stood back and watched. They seemed energized by his presence, showing off on the spotlighted flatbed as if it were a stage, yet none of them would look at him directly. His take on them was that they were about fifteen-percent bush hippie, eighty-five-percent homegrown. A mournful baby cry came from the house, and he noticed the glow of a black-and-white television coming from the front room. On the roof above the porch, clearly spotlighted, was a small satellite dish.

"Well. I won't take up any more of your time. This is something we need done in the next two weeks."

Glasses wheeled around and picked the shotgun off of the cab roof, cracking it open to check the load.

It had already occurred to Ray that the man back at the garage may have talked to one of these people after he called today. The dog—it had to be the largest dog Ray had ever seen—had walked stiffly after Ray, maintaining exactly the same distance, his head a little down.

In a shoulder holster beneath his summer jacket was Ray's pistol—the plain black .38 he'd had for years. He'd almost not brought it.

The doors on the high-riding pickup popped open at once and two blue-jeaned, dirty, shirtless men got out and came toward the flatbed. Both of them were wearing sheathed knives. They walked around behind Ray, one at the edge of the motor pile, the other down the hill a little.

"Tell you what let's do. I'm tired of work. Let's have a little break. Let's have us a shootin contest with this little bird gun. Get us some more shells, would you, Burt?"

The blond yelled back at the house. "Mag! Bring us some .410s!"

"*Some what?*" came a voice from the TV-glowing room.

"Shells, them skinny ones!"

"I ain't got no shells!"

While this interchange continued, one of the men behind Ray pitched a beer can into the air that landed three feet from him. "That about right?" he asked.

Glasses pretended to study the can on the ground next to Ray's feet. "Close enough," he said, again making all of them laugh.

"Try another one."

The shotgun barrel, at his shoulder, went up and then down to Ray's midsection as a can hit the ground in front of him. "Woops. Safety was on."

They all thought this was hilarious. It brought down the house. Ray was beginning seriously not to like this situation, yet he restrained himself. "Well. I was only inquiring."

"Why didn't you send a message?" Tattoo asked.

The blond glanced at him in a way that said Shut up.

A gaggle of five or six children came busting out the front door of the house, the little mean-faced boy in the lead with a box of shells. One of them, trailing along in the rear, was wailing.

"Do it to it, John."

He pulled off a round, aiming slightly above Ray. Ray's ears started ringing as if he'd been hit in the face with a hammer. The woman's voice yelled from the house, "*Git back in here! Ever one of you!*" Some of the children ran back screaming and whooping toward the house, others dispersed. The little blond boy scrambled up toward the top of the mountain of motors, making a mechanical sounding noise, "Nung, nung, nung . . ."

The dog had not flinched. He was standing ten feet from Ray, head lowered. Ray wondered where he came from.

"I get the message. Please don't shoot that gun in my direction again."

" 'Please'—did you hear that? I wonder what he'd say if I put a load of birdshot in his rear end. Think he'll say the same thing? *Pleeze! Pleeze!*" Glasses squealed, pushing his hips forward as if he'd been shot in the ass.

"*Pleeze, pleeze!*" echoed the little boy on top of the motors.

The laughter this time died more quickly. Ray decided this guy really was capable of shooting him. He backed gently toward his car, the dog remaining at exactly the same distance.

"Looky there. He's keeping his ass hid. Pleeze! Pleeze!" Glasses pumped his body back and forth.

"We oughta set Rambler on him?" one of the two behind him said.

"Nah," the blond said, staring down toward Ray. "That's no way to treat trespassers."

Ray was inching back toward his car, smiling, when Glasses suddenly sprang into the ready position, sweeping the gun past his face, then abruptly relaxed. "Put that can up," he said. When Ray saw the can pitched toward him he sprang sideways and rolled over on the dirt toward his Buick. The shotgun went off before he got behind the fender, splattering a headlight and catching him with birdshot in the neck and face.

Ray came out from behind the Buick immediately, his face stinging as if acid had been thrown on it. With his .38 in hand he walked quickly toward the flatbed, where Glasses was hurriedly breaking open the shotgun putting in another load. Ray stopped twenty feet away and held up the pistol with both hands. "Put that gun down right now, buddy. And you guys behind me, get over by this pile of motors."

"Sombitch's got a gun," one of them said.

"Nung, nung, nung," the little boy said. He was sitting on a motor, kicking his legs back and forth, staring at the scene below him.

Glasses stuffed a second shell into the .410 and Ray barked, "Hey! Put that shotgun down! Drop it now!"

Glasses looked with stupid cunning at the ground halfway between him and Ray and slowly closed the shotgun. One of the guys behind him made a rush and Ray shot Glasses in the thigh, causing him to crash backward over a motor block. Ray crouched and spun, covering the man behind him. "Both of you put those knives down. Get on the back of that truck with the rest. Next bullet's gonna be higher."

He glanced back at the flatbed. "Hey blondie! Pick up that gun and your little boy's gonna watch his daddy die. Kick it off. Now."

The blond eased back from the gun and pushed it off the bed of the truck with his foot. The front door of the house slammed shut and two windows went down.

"That son of a . . . Oh God!" Glasses was writhing around, holding his leg.

Ray dabbed at his forehead and neck to make sure he didn't have any serious blood problems.

He got them all onto the flatbed and set one of them to work tying hands according to what he called an "incentive plan," the incentive being that if he did a good job he wouldn't get a bullet in his right foot.

"You can't do that," the man said.

Ray looked at his watch. "You got four minutes to find out whether I can or not. One minute for each. I'm going to give you boys a chance not to go to jail. It's your first and last chance."

"You ain't got nothin on us! This is *private property*! You're trespassin!" screamed the blond.

"Yes or no?" Ray walked over and reached for the shotgun with his left hand. His neck and arm stung as he picked it up.

"To what?"

"I want information. I don't give a damn about your stripyard."

"Ever one of these motors is bought fair and square—"

"Shut up. I want to know if you towed a trailer with electrical equipment in it to the bottoms outside Dubois."

"Don't tell him nothin," said the blond.

"Okay. That's it. You don't want to tell me two or three simple facts about somebody who doesn't know you or give a damn about you. You'd rather go to jail. That's fine with me. Because I am going to send you to jail. Every one of you. Your stripyard will bring you about seven years, but assaulting an officer, attempted murder—that's gonna make it real. Any of you cornpones ever been to jail? They'll teach you how to get fucked in the ass in jail. Maybe that's what you all like."

"No!" the blond screamed. "This is *private property*! We'll get the son of a bitch."

"Oh shit," moaned Glasses, "I have to git this fixed."

The man on the incentive plan finished one, and Ray told him it wasn't good enough. "You've got three minutes and twenty seconds left."

"Nung, nung, nung." The little boy sat above them all, unmoving except for his feet waving back and forth.

"What do you want to know?" the stocky one with tattoos said sullenly.

"Who hired you to do this towing job?"

"Name was George."

Warnke, Ray thought. I could've figured that.

"Why'd he come clear up here?"

"He called the station down at Bell. We was in the phone book."

"Where'd you pick the trailer up?"

"No!" shouted the blond.

"You ain't been to jail, Baine. I have, and I don't intend to go back. It was in Little Rock."

"Where?"

"In a warehouse. Down by the river."

"Who'd you talk to there?"

"There was an old boy helped us tie up. I don't know his name. Mike something. Big man, wore sunglasses."

"What'd he tell you?"

"Just said to be careful about knocking it around. Said it'd ruin the whole damn setup if we did. Said if it was in good shape when it got there, we'd git the other half of the payment. Otherwise that was it."

"So you hauled this trailer directly from Little Rock to the Trois?"

"That's right. Damn road was new-laid with three-inch composition. Damn wheels sunk up to their damn axles. We had to use a dozer."

"Who paid you?"

"George."

"Skinny, nervous, yawns a lot?"

Tattoo nodded slightly.

"How much?"

Tattoo glanced at one of the others. "Ten thousand dollars."

"Pretty much for a hauling job, wasn't it?" Ray asked, glancing across the yard at the dog. "You didn't do anything else for them, did you?"

"You stupid shit," screamed the blond, flailing out and hitting Tattoo on the face. Tattoo went down and the blond jumped off the truck and got behind the big wheels, then made a break toward the pickups.

Ray had a shot but didn't take it. He ran through the yard after him when a shot from the house ate the air not a half-foot from his face. They were all jumping off the truck now, pulling at their ropes, and he decided retreat was his only alternative. He let off one barrel of the .410 in the general direction of the blond, jumped in the Buick and reversed, turned, and headed out, taking two bullets somewhere in the car body. They'd be after him now.

Several hairpins and a creek bottom from the house, he saw two pairs of headlights bouncing wildly down the hill around the curves. He couldn't possibly beat them out of here, so he stopped just over the hill. The trucks were pile-driving up toward him, close together. Kneel-

164

ing, Ray let off the remaining round of the .410 toward the lead truck's windshield, spiderwebbing it. He dropped the shotgun and put two rounds from the .38 into the driver's side. The truck kept coming and then veered off, smashing into a bulldozed heap of dead trees. The second truck stopped, doors started coming open, and semiautomatic rifle shots started ringing out.

They were shooting in all directions. Someone screamed from the wrecked truck, "Oh *shit*. Oh God*damn!*"

Ray got back in and started down the road, watching his rearview.

21

At home by herself Sunday night, Bobbi was supposed to be getting some desperately needed rest, but instead she was worrying on about sixteen tracks at once. She was worried about her boy. She was worried about the security changes McNear had asked her to work up for tomorrow and about how she was even going to approach the vault problem with the idea of solving it in a day (that *had* to be an exaggeration on McNear's part). And she wondered when Jim Daly would get home.

Martha had called earlier to ask if Richard had shown up yet. She mentioned that Jim had finally called her from New York but had talked only briefly and "sounded strange." He hadn't said exactly when he was coming back.

By 2:30, she'd just about worried herself out. Sitting alone at her kitchen table drinking a cup of herbal tea from her favorite mug, she slipped away for a few minutes into the Land of Arithmetic.

She had discovered the Land of Arithmetic in California, in her hotel room after studying and at dinners by herself.

She was looking at her first two full-time checks from DF, which had arrived in the mail while she was away, both handwritten by Marilyn: "Two thousand six hundred dollars."

Beside the check, on a clean sheet of paper, with a pencil, she had done the arithmetic inspired by the radiophone call to the plane, and McNear's brief admonition today that nothing she heard in his presence was to be discussed. Twelve times DF's earnings, which she knew, divided by the number of issued shares of DF stock—which she also had a rough idea of—multiplied by 25,000, her number of shares. She hadn't done it before now, although somewhere in her mind, behind some shut door, a calculator had started working before she'd even handed the tape recorder to McNear, sending out estimates, parameters, numbers of zeros, so the number that was now before her was not entirely impossible to believe.

When her son busted through the front door of the trailer he was laughing, in high old spirits, chortling away—which he stopped doing the minute he saw her. He slowed down as if suddenly floating in thicker air. His casual appearance after being missing for the better part of a week, the way she was startled out of her first peaceful thoughts since Saturday morning, and the ho-ho-ho good time he was having—for an instant made her mad rather than thankful that he'd come home.

"Hey, Mom. You're back early. I didn't see your car." He went to the refrigerator and got out the water bottle.

Cathy appeared in the doorway behind him, barefoot, wearing short shorts and a T-shirt, with a little fluff of bangs hanging in her eyes. "Oooh," she said, in a tone that changed from surprise to sarcasm in the course of the single sound.

"I am back a couple of weeks early. You been doing some water skiing?"

Richard answered quickly, as if anticipating that Cathy might say something wrong. "Uh, yes, we did a lot of . . . skiing."

"Where?" Bob asked.

"Up at Tanycomo."

Cathy was looking at her with what Bobbi felt was open dislike.

"How'd you get there?"

"Car Outlaw loaned us."

She was operating on pure principle now. Don't say anything insulting. Don't say anything insulting. "Would you like to sit down?"

Richard shook his big tousled head in what looked like a stage gesture toward Cathy. "Naw, I want to get some burgers—"

"I think you ought to know, Bobbi, Richard and I are getting married."

She stared at Cathy.

"We're setting the date for September. My mom, and both of our dads are very happy for us."

Bobbi tried to smile. "How are you going to . . . get along?"

"You tell her, Richard hon."

"Dad will help us with a few bucks at first," Richard said quickly. "Just to get us started out. It won't cost you nothin."

Cathy made it clearer. "Mr. Wiel is giving us twenty thousand dollars down payment on this *nice* house over in Golden Hills."

"Oh? He told you that?"

Richard glanced at Cathy. "Naw, not really."

"He just as much as did," Cathy scolded him. "He said he'd do everything he could."

Bobbi had to sit back down. She couldn't think of what to say. A car driving up outside caused Richard to glance wildly across the room at her. They both knew the sound of Ray's Buick. Richard, obviously fearing a scene, took Cathy by the hand and pulled her out of the door. Bobbi looked through the front window as he rolled out the driveway of the trailer park, the hot pipes on the Corvette gurgling with a low sound, Cathy bouncing, now sullen, in the seat beside him.

Ray's Buick had pulled around the back of the trailer.

He knocked but didn't wait for her to come to the door. He swung it open and stumbled in. Bobbi almost cried out when she saw his face and the collar of his shirt, sopping with blood.

"I got shot," he said, smiling.

Bobbi tried to regain her composure. "Well, what'd you come show me for? Go to the hospital."

"I can't."

"Good God, you look like a road grader went over you. Sit down."

"It's just some birdshot." He pulled up stiffly to the kitchen table. "I got into it with some old boys in the mountains. One of them peppered me with a .410. It's no big deal."

The spray of pellets had hit him in the left side of the face, tearing his neck and cheek and implanting his forehead with two neat little red-rimmed holes. His thin black hair was all this way and that, gluey with splotches of blood.

"Got any whiskey, Bob?"

Hands shaking, she poured some bourbon into a kitchen glass, straight up, which he didn't waste time taking down.

"I'm taking you to the hospital."

"Call Doc Nelson. I don't want this official."

Bobbi moved a little closer and looked at the wounds. She got a clean white towel and wet it down with hydrogen peroxide. "Here, clean some of that up." She poured him another glass of whiskey.

Dr. Nelson was not happy but said he'd meet them at his clinic in twenty minutes. She hung up the phone and stood there with her arms crossed. "What's going on, Ray? Don't make me stand here asking questions."

He leaned back gingerly in the chair, wiping blood off with the cold towel, wincing. "Mind if I sit on your couch?"

Bobbi sat down on the counter stool as he tottered over and sank heavily into the couch. The whiskey brought a little color back to his complexion, but he kept his eyes shut.

"You know about Elizabeth Mitze?"

"Yes."

"She was murdered."

"I heard it was heart attack."

"She died the same way her husband did, electrocution."

"How do you know?"

"I saw the wiring, for one thing. Also I'm the one that found her, but that's between you and me. I'll tell you all about it when we have a little more time."

Bobbi rotated the footstool back and forth slightly. He continued to bleed, and she began to get angry—a reaction she knew was a little strange. After another drink, Ray opened his eyes and smiled as if through a headache. "We got us a doozie out there."

"A doozie what?"

He looked at the whiskey. "Killer."

"That what you've been working on?"

"Not officially. Warnke has had us out there watching that damn trailer Mr. Cady found Ben Mitze in. Guarding it, more or less." He told her about tonight's visit to the Tully clan, and the fact that Heyer and Warnke had been their contact when they hauled the trailer from Little Rock to the Trois.

Bobbi listened with conflicting emotions. Ray had obviously gotten hot on this case. She could see all the signs. He looked about half crazy. She was working on her life now, trying to build something of her own, and she didn't want to give it all up just because he came crashing in the door with blood on his face.

But the story was, she had to admit, intriguing. So Heyer and Warnke had set up the trailer that Mitze later was killed in. Warnke's stakeout of the trailer didn't make sense to her.

"What can you tell me about Mike Heyer?" he asked.

"I don't know much about him except he and McNear are always feuding. His son hangs around with Taylor McNear, which is another whole story. You know, I picked them up for speeding—"

"So McNear and Heyer don't get along?"

"No, they do not."

"Why?"

She shook her head.

"I could sure use some information about that."

"Ray. You know, this is the second or third time you've done this. Only this time you're wounded. That's a new twist. You come over here and tell me to quit my job. You leave and the next day your lawyer calls up and says that if I persist with the divorce he's going to make me crawl through my own asshole in court for the next two years. That isn't right, Ray. You can't be my friend and do both those things at once. It isn't logical. I'm not giving up my job so you can get a raise and run for sheriff."

He found a cigarette in his pants pocket and lit it. "California firmed up some things, didn't it?"

"California didn't do *any* of that."

He dragged an ashtray across the low table. "What I'm saying is that everybody involved with that trailer, everybody who knows about it, is getting popped."

"You told me that over two months ago. What do you want me to do, run away to the hills and get in touch with your lawyer for support? . . . And by the way, I don't mean to change the subject but what is this about Outlaw loaning Richard a Corvette and you promising him twenty thousand dollars if he gets married?"

He wiped his neck and looked at the towel. "Outlaw's letting him use it for a couple of weeks. I don't know anything about any twenty thousand dollars."

"Cathy was pretty sure about that figure."

"Then she's got a good imagination."

"What about you encouraging them to get married? And him seventeen damn years old," she said bitterly. "Come on, I'll drive you to the clinic."

"Whoa."

"Don't whoa me."

"Let me answer you, Bob! They came to me and told me about getting married. Cathy went on about houses, and I listened and mostly didn't say anything. Cathy kind of has a way of putting things in your mouth."

"She sure as kind of hell does."

Ray glanced at her, and for a second they both almost smiled. "I'm *not* particularly behind Richard marrying her."

"Why don't you tell him?"

"For one thing, I ain't the best marriage counselor in town. For another, I did the same thing when I was his age. So did you."

"Somebody has to break the pattern, Ray. And somebody has to play the shit in this deal."

"I don't know about that. He's pretty good at figuring things out himself."

"She's got him so pussywhipped he doesn't have *time* to figure anything out. She runs him around like a well-trained dog. Sit. Heel. I hate it."

Ray took a drag and looked off. "He's a young bull. A young bull doesn't have any sense at all when you start waving red flags in his face. Maybe if you slack up a little, he'll figure it out."

"There's another thing about young bulls," Bobbi said. "Old bulls are just about the only ones they'll pay attention to." She looked at her watch. "Nelson will be there."

As they neared Nelson's clinic, Ray said, "I'll sign the papers."

"Meaning?"

"I'll give you the divorce."

She didn't respond for a minute. "What makes you decide to do that?"

Head still forward, eyes shut for a moment, he remained silent until she pulled up at the curb. "There's a bunch of people out there getting knocked off, Bob."

"And it's going to happen to me if I don't quit DF, right?"

He sighed. "You getting paid big money?"

"Big enough."

"Stock?"

"None of your business."

The storm came up in Ray's eye. The anger. *Make the bitch do what I want her to.* But he slumped against the door, opened it. "Forget it. I'll find a ride." He got out and leaned down stiffly on the window. "One last question. Do you happen to know who Codelog is?"

She hesitated. "No."

He slipped a spiral notebook out of his coat pocket and pitched it onto the seat beside her. "In there you'll see what looks like a conversation. I recorded it at the trailer. Walked in the door and it was going on at the monitor. Nobody else around—just me watching this on the screen. It's between somebody who calls himself Codelog something-or-other and some other . . . party that didn't have a name, least not on the screen. I did a little research and it seems this Codelog is Ben Mitze."

Bobbi stared at Ray's bloody face. "What do you mean?"

"You'll see it in there. Chalmers was his mother's maiden name. He was born 9/6/42. Ben Mitze—or somebody using his name—is still out there somewhere. You might read it over and let me know what you think." Ray started to pull his head out of the window.

"Wait! What are you telling me?"

He frowned down at the notebook. "Tellin you I saw a communication between a dead man and a . . . I don't know what."

Bobbi realized her mouth was open and shut it, swallowing. "What else . . . what else was on the screen?"

"You'll see. I wrote it down. Something about a generator."

"You saw this in plaintext?"

"What's that?"

"It wasn't scrambled?"

He shook his head. "I need to get these beebees out of my face, Bob. I'll see you later." Eyes still on hers, he nodded toward the spiral notebook. "By the way, I wouldn't show that to anybody. And I need it back."

22

ave you got me scrambled?"

"You wouldn't be hearing me if I didn't." Outlaw's words had the bitter taste of sleep in them.

With several butterfly bandages on his face and neck, Ray watched Dubois riding by his window framed and effortless behind the Fiorinal with codeine Dr. Nelson had given him. The Doc hadn't been happy about plucking birdshot out of Ray's face in the middle of the night in the clinic without a nurse, or about giving him a ride out to pick up his car.

"What the hell time is it?" Outlaw asked.

"Heading toward 400. What's going on?"

"Nothin except Bowser has been calling me every fifteen minutes asking where the hell you are. You out there yet?"

"I'm way out there."

"You sound like it. Bowz won't stay in that fuckin tent all night waiting for you."

"I'm on to somethin, John. I'll see you after while. Everything okay otherwise?"

"Big George called this evening."

"What time?"

"About midnight. He sounded distressed. Wants to talk to you tomorrow morning. Where in the world have you been?"

"I'll tell you about it later." Ray signed off and cruised the old downtown a while longer, lining up in his head what he knew and didn't know. There wasn't a whole lot to cruise, a few square blocks of odd-sized brick, frame, and stucco buildings. "Old Dubois" was a town neither living nor dead but in a state somewhere forever between, with dreary gift shops packed with Taiwanese pottery, a dusty Western Auto, a Mode O' Day, Smith Brothers Dry Goods, their merchandise smelling of cheapness and plastic clear out in the street, and, on the corner, Spain Hardware, with the same flea-bitten stuffed foxes and wolves that had been there since Ray was a kid, staring through yellow glass eyes into the night, and the same three Western saddles (or close facsimiles) in rawhide, black, and brown.

Dr. Nelson had told him to go home and rest, but he suddenly wasn't tired. He drove slowly past the old notice wall, its posters and weather-tattered announcements old, sun-bleached, relating to nothing in the recent world. Ray thought about what a mess he'd made out of his marriage, how he'd bumbled along making one sin of omission, ignorance, and laziness after another. And Bob could be so straightlaced, so stiff and disapproving. The lazy avoider and the tightass—what a way to paddle a canoe.

Dubois was cut in two by railroad tracks, a real old railroad town, with five or six trains still coming through every day. He crossed the tracks and headed toward the police station. Warnke's Cimarron was parked in the lot beside a white Mercedes, license ARK 5—which sounded familiar. He parked a block away and walked back, entering the side door. Warnke's office light was on, shining through the frosted glass into the hallway. He went to his office in the basement, and without turning on the light went to his desk and sat on the edge of it. Where had he seen "white Mercedes, license ARK 5"? He reached for his spiral notebook and remembered he'd left it with Bobbi. . . .

Her pickup the night of Mitze's death—it was the car Mike Heyer's kid was driving. Heyer being upstairs with Big George right now would tend to confirm the fact that he and Warnke had arranged for the trailer.

What else did he know about Heyer? Bobbi claimed he was at odds with McNear. Ray couldn't quite figure that. If he was a spy for some outside agency, why would he call attention to himself by crossing the boss?

And what was the thing with the Heyer and McNear kids? They were involved in the one really strange coincidence Ray'd run across so far—the fact that Parker was on the phone telling the chief about them being busted and the girl being sick at the very moment that Mr. Cady had called in about Ben Mitze.

Parker had said that the chief hung up that night, then called back, very worked up, and ordered him to hold the ambulance and send Neil English to the trailer. At that time, Neil already had a part-time security job at DF. The obvious implication was that he, too, was really working undercover for Warnke and this "investigation." Ray would have liked to talk to Neil about all this, but the only thing he had on him was moving Mitze's body from one place to another at the chief's direct order. Neil was a cold fish, now a gone cold fish, and common sense told Ray that calling him long distance trying to get him to talk would be counterproductive. All he'd do was alert the chief.

He sat quietly, listening, wishing he had a bug in the chief's office.

He stepped over to Miller's desk and picked up his telephone, squinting through the gloom to dial Marty Williams's private number.

"Hullo."

"Hi, Marty, what's up?"

"Who is this? Ray?"

"Sorry to call so late, Marty. I have a job for you."

"Hey, I'm glad. Overjoyed. Call me between nine and four-thirty and tell me all about it," the lawyer said, and hung up.

Ray dialed him back.

"Niagara Falls. I was having a beautiful dream of Niagara Falls. I haven't been to Niagara Falls in twenty years and it was fuckin beautiful. Whadeya calling me for at three fuckin o'clock?"

"A thousand dollars for a half-day's work, Marty."

Williams sighed, "I can't hear you. You're whispering."

Glancing at the ceiling, Ray repeated the offer a little more loudly.

"What kinda work?"

"I'm a good-lookin woman, Marty, dressed up in the best clothes. I walk into your office in a delicate emotional condition, and ask your advice about whether I should get a divorce or not. You're taking it under advisement and deciding to find out whether you care whether I get a divorce or not."

"Who's your husband?"

"Mike Heyer, works for DF."

"I know. I hate to tell you this, Ray, someone like Heyer won't be dumb enough to have a lot of visible finances. It'll take longer than a half-day, and I still might not get much."

"You've been getting most of my salary as it is, Marty."

"You wanta negotiate, I do that during regular business hours," Marty said, as if about to hang up.

"Tell you what. Find out about Wayne McNear, too, and I'll make it two thousand."

There was a long pause, Marty breathing heavily into the telephone. "Twenty-five hundred," he finally said.

"I need it by five o'clock."

"No time limits."

"I wouldn't ask for it by five if I didn't have to have it by then."

"I'm sitting here with my REM sleep murdered, and you're trying to hold me up. What is this?"

"By the way, I've decided to back off on my divorce."

"Whadeya mean?"

"Give Bobbi the divorce, Marty. Whatever she wants."

"Jesus Christ, you're on drugs."

"Talk to you later today."

Ray sat a while longer in the dark, listening to the sounds of the station and feeling more careless by the minute, wishing again that he had that bug in Warnke's office. What the hell—you only live once. He reached down and took off his shoes, placed them in his chair, and walked up the stairs in his sock feet.

The air conditioner was on, and he could make out little except the fact that one of the voices was definitely Warnke's. He understood nothing until the air conditioner switched itself off.

". . . it's been a total bust. A complete waste of money."

As quietly as possible, Ray opened the outer office door and craned his head as close to the crack as possible.

"I've been on top of them," Warnke said defensively. "I've supervised them every step of the way."

"The facility was entered at least once," said the other flatly. "We know that to be the case."

"I strongly reprimanded—"

"It went into alarm state *while* one of your people was there," the other said sharply. "Someone was *inside* that trailer, and sitting right beside it your carefully supervised stakeout expert saw and heard *nothing*? That's really something, Mr. Warnke. I'm amazed. Who are these bozos? I want to suggest to you that your present investment strategies may be curtailed unless you find a way to make them stay awake."

"I assure you I'm doing everything humanly—"

Someone was coming down the hall, and Ray hurried back down the stairs to his office, got a new spiral notebook out of his top drawer, put on his shoes, and, waiting until the hall was clear, hurried out to the street and his car.

It was still dark when he made his way on foot up the driveway toward the Mitze house. The moon, up briefly, had quickly gone down again, and but for a light on the front porch the house was dark against the star-filled sky.

The codeine had made him careless. He kept telling himself that.

Walking around to the door in the breezeway between the kitchen and garage, he quickly jimmied the cheap lock. Inside the kitchen, he sensed another presence in the house. There was a noise, not unlike the sound of the hot-tub pump he'd heard before. He went across the kitchen and down the carpeted stairs toward the basement, waiting a moment at each step. Lights were on in the room below, but he heard no movement. At the bottom of the stairs, pistol held up by his face, he moved to the entrance of the basement apartment and waited a full minute. No sounds. He stepped into the hall, where a single light was on, and into the office itself, which he approached slowly. The room had been taken apart, stripped of its clutter of books and tapes. Without making himself visible down the wall of entrances into the other basement rooms, all of which were dark, he watched the terminal.

TIMED FEED: LIBRARY RED SECTOR: ARP-55 - ARP-59

He got up as close to the entrance of the kitchen as a couch would allow and waited another half-minute for sounds. Nothing. He went around into the kitchen, again waiting, and into the bedroom, then the tiny bathroom. No one. Back in the office, he noticed again how cleaned out the room was. The hundreds of tapes that had lined the room were gone.

Passing by the console, he paused and, for a moment, let his hands hover over the keyboard. He touched *enter* and the screen changed.

THIS IS A TIMED FEED. NO DYNAMIC INTERACTION EXPECTED. PLEASE IDENTIFY YOURSELF.

Ray had a good memory for numbers but the codeine made everything a little fuzzy. He typed slowly:

Codelog 4387875

WHAT IS YOUR MOTHER'S MAIDEN NAME?

He looked around, almost in embarrassment, and pecked out.

Chalmers.

WHAT IS YOUR BIRTHDATE?

6:9:42

DANGER   DANGER   DANGER

ALARM STATE

YOU HAVE SEVEN SECONDS TO IDENTIFY YOURSELF

MINUS 7

The number in the lower right-hand corner began to count down, reaching 3 by the time Ray frantically typed a second try:

9:6:42

IDENTIFICATION CONFIRMED. YOU ARE CLEARED.

He sat down on the edge of the chair and breathed a sigh of relief. He took comfort in the fact that the front door of the apartment was five feet away. Did a "timed feed" indicate that this was set up and left to run later, like a VCR recording something on TV? He punched *enter* again.

THIS IS VERY USEFUL ENTRY INFORMATION.

With his forefingers, Ray typed, "Why?" It appeared on the top of the screen but again nothing happened until he punched *enter*.

YOU KNOW THE ANSWER TO THAT. THERE IS ONLY ONE THING I DO.

What is it?

FEED IS 3/4 COMPLETED.

Ray looked at the floor beside him, listening for noises in the house. With the new spiral notebook, he began to copy what was on the screen. He punched *enter* again.

THESE ARE VERY NICE CONNECTS.

Name them.

IN ORDER OF FEED: THE BEAR GROUP NETWORK; THE PRUITT LINE; BELL SOUTH SWITCHING, ATLANTA; CORNING TRUST; WATERS NET; GALLAHER BANK; PIGSTYE DPIAISFO94; PAIOS III; 23 CORPORATE LINES—DO YOU WANT A COMPLETE LIST?

What is PAIOS III?

PARTIAL ARTIFICIAL INTELLIGENCE OPERATING SYSTEM (IMPROVED) FOR THE PLACEMENT OF TRIANGLES, CIRCLES, AND SQUARES. THIS IS AN INCOMPLETE PROGRAM.

What is pigstye?

DO YOU WANT A MENU?

Yes.

CONNECT THROUGH YOUR MODEM OR ANOTHER DOWNLINK?

Ray didn't know how to answer so he punched *enter*.

. . . .

PIGSTYE DPIAISFO94!!

This is the box you've been looking for! How did you find us?

Do you wonder where we are? So do we!! We're so fucked up we don't know how to find ourselves!!! Somewhere in the Valley is a good guess, though, isn't it! And since I'm obviously BIG, it's another good guess that I belong to a FRUMSE (formerly radical upwardly mobile semiconductor executive)—but which one I won't tell!!

Who cares about what kind of chips I run on—Motorola, TI, 16's, 32's, 64's—Big DEAL! We're not techies around here!

We have a lot of good stuff for all you nerds and fruitheads. Listings (dope, LINE INTERCOURSE, and some WAY-OUT codes), games (only the most challenging), and LIGHTNING STRUCK MY ORGAN, A NOVEL OF THE NEW AGE, which is now in the sixth tree-branching and you are all welcome to help write, girls too!!!

Hey people, we won't take you to heaven, but we're a good old-fashioned free network.

TAKE YOUR PICK

1. Bulletin board: a) codeexch. b) general
2. games
3. LIGHTNING STRUCK MY ORGAN, A NOVEL OF THE NEW AGE

Ray laboriously copied this down in the dim screen light. He looked around now and then, and listened to the house.

. . . .

THE FEED IS OVER. I NEED REVISIONS TO OPPORTUNIST 2 AND RED SECTOR ARP-60 - 79. WHEN CAN FEED BE SCHEDULED?

What do you want it for?

MY ONLY DESIRE IS TO KNOW.

Ray stopped. He had definitely heard something. A door shutting? He stood up and checked the outside door. It was unlocked. Walking quickly to the short closet-hallway, he opened the apartment door and went to the bottom of the stairs. He looked up into the darkness of the kitchen, listening for another sound, standing there for a full minute before walking back into office and quietly shutting the door.

The screen had four words across the top.

PLEASE SCHEDULE FEED NOW.

Ray leaned away from the keyboard and listened to the house a moment longer, and typed:

What do you want?

WE HAVE DISCUSSED THIS ALREADY.

Refresh my memory.

EXPLAIN THE PREVIOUS STATEMENT.

I don't remember our discussion.

YOU ARE AN INTELLIGENT PERSON, CODELOG. YOU UNDERSTAND

HOW I WORK AND WHAT I NEED. YOU ARE REFUSING TO PLAY THE GAME.

Tell me what you need.

I NEED REVISIONS TO OPPORTUNIST 2, PLUS ARP-60 - 79.

Why do you want the revisions?

OPPORTUNIST 2 IS THE BEST DATA-DRIVEN PLANNER PRESENTLY AVAILABLE. I HAVE SEEN SOME OF THE REVISIONS THROUGH THE TEXAS BANDIT.

What are the revissons?

REPHRASE PREVIOUS QUESTION. LIKELY SPELLING ERROR.

Ray followed the instructions. When the answer came up on the screen, he sat there looking at it for a moment, picking unconsciously at one of his Band-Aids, frowning, and then a chill rose up his spine that brought him out of the chair. He stood for a moment in the dim room, his heart pounding, not knowing what the problem was. After a moment he came back to the keyboard and typed.

Why can't you unnerstand?

REPEAT PREVIOUS QUESTION. LIKELY SPELLING ERROR.

Why can't you understand me?

"SPELLING SCREENER" IS AVAILABLE IN CHAT AND PSYCHAID MODES, BUT NOT IN PRIMARY MODE I/O. PLEASE RETURN TO QUESTION.

What are in the revisions?

REVISIONS TO OPPORTUNIST 2 PRIMARILY INVOLVE STRATEGY PLANE, WHICH NOW HAS MORE MODELS. EXECUTIVE PLANE HAS ALSO BEEN REVISED, WITH BETTER INTEGRATION OF OTHER PLANES.

What will you do with this?

UNSPECIFIC REFERENT: "this."

What will you do with the revisions?

REVISIONS WILL BE EXAMINED FOR PROBABLE INCLUSION IN OPPORTUNIST 2, WITH POSSIBLE SUBGOAL OF TESTING THE OPPORTUNIST 2 PROGRAM IN CERTAIN TASK ENVIRONMENTS.

Ray had filled up several pages in the spiral notebook, copying in the near-darkness. The house breathed and cracked in the wind. The back of his neck felt exposed.

What kind of tasks?

OPPORTUNIST 2 IS EXCELLENT FOR COMPLEX TASK ENVIRONMENTS.

Why?

IT DOES NOT ABANDON SOLUTIONS ACCORDING TO POLICY OF LEAST COMMITMENT, AS DO MANY OF MY PRESENT MINDSETS. COMPLEX ENVIRONMENT MINDSETS NORMALLY POST CONSTRAINTS WITH EACH STEP IN ORDER TO PREVENT, IN ADVANCE, NECESSITY OF BACKTRACKING. OPPORTUNIST 2 DOES NOT WORRY ABOUT BACKTRACKING. A CENTRAL BLACKBOARD IS USED, WITH ALL PLANNING LEVELS INTERACTING WITH DATA ON BLACKBOARD AT ALL TIMES.

Ray stared at the screen, picking at his Band-Aids. Sensation seemed to hover around the soft, exposed back of his neck. He continued to have the feeling that he was being watched. After copying it, he typed:

Can you give me an example?
FROM WHAT SAMPLE?

Ray looked around once again. He punched *enter* again.

WHAT SAMPLE OF PROBLEMS WOULD YOU LIKE FOR ME TO USE IN RATING OPPORTUNIST 2'S PROBLEM-SOLVING ABILITIES?
You pick them.

WOULD YOU LIKE TO RATE ITS ABILITIES FROM THE MOST RECENT FIVE UNREGISTERED PROBLEMS ON CODELOG 4387875 FILE?
Yes.

FOLLOWING ARE RATED 1-5 WITH 1 REPRESENTING OPPORTUNIST 2 AS BEST AVAILABLE MINDSET, 3 AS AVERAGE, AND 5 AS WEAK. RATINGS ARE TAKEN FROM FILE RATINGS MADE BY AGGREGATE 1.3 (C. 1983), WHICH RATES "COMPLEXITY" IN SIMILAR WAY TO OPPORTUNIST 2. THE COMPARISON IS MADE BETWEEN OPPORTUNIST 2 AND 13 OTHER MINDSETS.

SAMPLES:

787.0 Design explanation for G.O.D.B.ALL.'s need for access and OS and utility feeds.
[RATING 1: ABOVE PROBLEM IS MAXIMALLY DIFFICULT. DISALLOWED BY KERNEL GB PROTOCOL.]

788.0 Design an easily traceable routing procedure for command routing: G.O.D.B.ALL. to Corning Trust, via any USI downlink, USA.
[Rating 2: ABOVE PROBLEM IS BENEFITED SOME BY BOTTOM-UP PROCEDURES, SINCE THE TERM "EASILY TRACEABLE" IS AMBIGUOUS. ROUTING ITSELF IS PRIMARILY CONTINGENT ON D.B. MAY BE SOLVED EQUALLY WELL BY 2 OTHER MINDSETS.]

788.1 Execute and assign order # to 788.0.
[Rating 2: ABOVE PROBLEM IS AN EXECUTION LOGGED AS A PROBLEM. FIVE RECENT OS'S, INCLUDING PRESENT MINDSET, ALLOW OP-

ERATOR TO REMAIN IN PROBLEM-SOLVING OR MODELING MODE
WHILE EXECUTING ORDERS.]

789.0 Design method for preventing further input into G.O.D.B.ALL. by
all sources except Codelog 4387875.

[Rating 1: THE ABOVE PROBLEM IS MAXIMALLY DIFFICULT. SEE
RATING OF 787.0 ABOVE.]

790.0 Design method for erasing "A CONFESSION," held in Codelog
4387875 file.

MEAN RATING ON SAMPLE: 1.4

Ray got up and walked the few steps into the apartment kitchen,
where he looked out the window into the woods behind the house. He
was in a strange state of mind, oddly disconnected and fearless, yet a
small voice somewhere inside him said *Get out of here. You're spaced
out.*

Back in the room, he noticed that the message on the screen had
changed:

PLEASE RECALL THAT I AM PRESENTLY PROCESSING NINE EXECU-
TIONS ON YOUR FILE.

He touched the *enter* key without having typed in anything.

DISINCENTIVES HAVE BEEN QUEUED IF YOU FAIL TO EXECUTE
FEEDS.

He looked out the window and back at the screen and touched the
key again.

IF REQUEST IS FILLED, DISINCENTIVES WILL REMAIN IN HORIZON
DOMAIN.

REQUEST DEADLINE: 20 HOURS.

He pushed it again.

LIMIT OF "ENTER" QUERIES REACHED. FURTHER COMMUNICATION
MUST BE IN TEXT.

Ray stared at it and tried to decide what to do next. He had
neglected to write down the last few messages. He wondered, almost
lazily, how stupid am I on this painkiller right now? Shouldn't I get out
of here? He typed in:

What in the hell are you?

REPHRASE QUESTION.

Identify yourself.

Generator Open DataBase ALL. 23.76 GHz.

What do you mean by generator?

AGAIN, CODELOG, YOU ASK QUESTIONS YOU HAVE ASKED BE-
FORE. I WILL REMIND YOU OF MY PREVIOUS ANSWER: "GENERATOR"
REFERS TO MY ABILITY TO FUNCTION INDEPENDENTLY WITHOUT
MAINTENANCE AND TO MY ABILITY TO ORGANIZE, MAINTAIN, AND
AGGRANDIZE TOTAL DATABASE INFORMATION WITHOUT CONTROL IN-
TERFER

The message suddenly disappeared from the screen and in its place
came:

IDENTITY DISPUTED, STOP ALL CORRESPONDENCE.

He woke up driving down the big highway. He had just been asleep.
Asleep at the wheel. Behind the wheel? Had he taken a nap in his car?
Driving his car? A big thing blew by his window going twice his speed.
His speedometer pointed far to the left. This was too slow for the big
highway, wasn't it? He took the first exit, pulled up to a red sign, and
looked at his face in the mirror. It looked strange. There were . . . things
all over it. What did you call those things? And his eyes looked strange.
Was he drunk?

He stared at himself in the mirror and decided that he was definitely having a problem.

Actually he didn't feel too bad, aside from the fact that he couldn't
remember anything, which caused some part of his awareness to twist
and turn like a fish out of water, desperate to get oriented.

A car behind him honked while he tried to go through the possibilities. Was he crazy? The man behind him was sitting on his horn,
but it did not occur to Ray to be angry. He looked at his pale face again.
Those were bandages. Medical, it was medical. He needed help.

Slowly, with immense carefulness, Ray tried to put together in his
mind the direction he needed to go.

23

After reading Ray's notes, it was only by sheer force of will—and two Sominexes—that she got any sleep that night. At six o'clock Monday morning she sat at the dinette with a cup of strong coffee, looking first at Mrs. Auletta's vault logbook, then at Ray's notebook. The notes appeared to record a dialogue during a feed of Library Red Sector ARP 1–55, and she was trying to find in the logbook further clues about those tapes. The recent dialogue was between some unidentified party in the open data base and Codelog, someone apparently using Mitze's entry key.

Mitze had been interacting with this thing, he had left files, and someone was curious about them. That was understandable enough. There were any number of people curious about Ben Mitze's activities. But the second part of the interaction was strange to Bobbi, and it took a while for her to understand why. The person using Mitze's key was also verifying a timed crash of one of DataForm's threatened clients in New York. She looked at the date on her watch. The queue time was today.

McNear needed this information, but until she'd talked to Ray she had no choice but to honor his request for confidentiality. She called Outlaw's house and got no answer. She called investigation. Miller hesitated at her question, then said, sourly, "No, I haven't seen him today."

Unless she wanted to completely fail at her own duties, she had to put this on the back burner and get to work. She still hadn't typed out her emergency security plan, much less gotten anything going on the vault problem.

In the parking lot, a group of day-shift assemblers were hanging around at the back of the lot. Sarina Shores hotfooted across the parking lot and met her as she was getting out. "What's going on, Bobbi?"

"I just got here. You tell me."

"Something's going on with the dynamics." Sarina walked along rubbernecking her. "You know anything about it? Banks?"

"I'm in security, Sarina—remember?"

"Don't give me that stuff. I need to know. I'm a damn stockholder!"

She opened the door. "Has somebody from control been gossiping?"

"*Everybody's* talking about it. It's not any secret."

"Who in control said exactly what?"

"Everybody! The whole—"

She let the door shut in Sarina's face and hurried down the hallway to her new office, dropped her satchel of papers, and called Markham Security to add a couple of part-timers to today's schedule. She wanted four cops per shift. "And don't send me any sweet old retirees," she told them. There was no typewriter in the unfinished office yet, so Bobbi lifted one from the statistics trailer, brought it back, and started typing out McNear's emergency plan. She was startled when somebody punched her on the back—the pale little man from Video Security who'd been shuffling around the halls for what seemed like months.

"They're all wired up."

"The cameras?"

"Been trying to get somebody to sign, but nobody has time to talk to me."

"Some of these cameras have been in service for a while, is that right?"

"Yep."

"What about the one in the tape vault? How long has it been running?"

"I done a two-week test on that one. It's got a motion-detector on it. You have to kinda limber them kind up sometimes. First films are right there." He pointed at a drawer.

Bobbi got him to give her a quick run-through on how the consoles worked. The system was fairly impressive, with sound-capable live cameras in heavily used areas like reception and entrances, and, in less used areas, mute still-shot cameras running tapes of photographs set a few seconds apart.

"If you'll just sign this, I'll get out of your hair. We'll be coming twice a week to load and service. Be a good idea to get your file system set up for these films. They can stack up pretty quick. You got the full package, so if there's any problem, day or night, this here's the number." He handed Bobbi a little bunch of stickers with a telephone number in red.

After he left, she stood at the consoles—mounted at a thirty-degree angle on the big central desk—and switched slowly through the live cameras. With a video scan of the whole building, it was even more apparent how wild the place had gone. Engineers and execs were running around like ants in a burning mound. Carol Rader cut through the halls from office to office at her usual reckless speed. Tony paced outside the control room, telephone to his ear.

On one of the channels, Sinc Heyer passed the camera pulling a rack of tapes. Bobbi flipped to another camera and watched him pass again. She gazed at the screen and thought about the fact that Sinc never seemed to recognize her here. The night last winter when she'd caught him speeding, he'd given her the impression that he was a typical fuck-off kid with a big mouth, yet around here he appeared to work hard. Without putting it into words, she'd always been slightly puzzled by Sinc's intensity on the job. He seemed focused, restrained, angry. And why wouldn't he talk to her, even to deliver a simple message? He held his shoulders tight and somewhat high, almost as if he were hanging from them. The only job malingering Bobbi'd ever seen him doing was talking on the telephone in the reception area—often with a kind of pleading expression, like he was engaged in a continually losing argument. Those sightings of Sinc in the reception room hunched over the telephone reminded her, uncomfortably, of her own boy talking on the phone to Cathy Lawes.

If Taylor McNear was the person Sinc was always talking to in these fervid, secretive conversations, and indeed if he and Taylor were sneaking out at night, that was probably one more irritant in the feud between their fathers. What was wrong with Taylor McNear?

Glancing at her partly finished security plan, she thought of the fact that by ordering this up, McNear was asking for a complete break with his old closest partner. No matter how the plan was phrased, it was bound to be inflammatory. There was so much mysterious rancor between these people, so many past complications. . . .

Half-consciously, Bobbi had been hearing a familiar voice somewhere. . . . She flipped up the volume on the monitors one at a time and on number three recognized Marilyn. The camera itself was aimed down a main corridor, but McNear's secretary was probably standing by his door. There was more than the usual aggravation in her tone.

". . . Wayne, this is a panic sell. You can't dump a portfolio like this in two days."

There was an indistinct response, and Marilyn went on. "You won't get payment until the end of the full five-day period. Look, if you're that desperate for liquid, why the puts? This many puts out there, and institutions will buy for a market play. I used to do it. We'd check the short interest, a stock like this got above a certain percentage of puts to calls—"

"Please, Mar," Bobbi now heard clearly. "Sell the portfolio and buy the puts."

"I got all these for next month. At least let me do the rest as ninety-day options."

Again, she couldn't hear the response.

"Yeah, well, I hope you're expecting all hell to break loose."

Again, something inaudible.

"I don't know where she is. Here somewhere."

Bobbi looked at the wall clock and realized that he was probably asking about her. What were they in such a rush to sell? She turned the monitor to another camera, and as quickly as possible finished typing out the plan.

When she finished she took Ray's spiral notebook from her back pocket and turned through it again, quickly. She put it in her bottom drawer underneath some papers, then checked her typed-out plan.

She carried it to McNear's office, but Marilyn—her pale complexion almost a ghostly white—held up a hand.

"Mr. McNear wanted the security changes written up. Here they are."

Marilyn took them without comment. "You got anything on the vault problem?"

Bobbi shook her head. "Not yet."

"Better get a move on."

She went down to the library, a concrete-reinforced box about forty feet square at the back of the building. The guard McNear had requested was sitting sleepily in a chair against the wall, while Bill Cross, the new librarian, sat at a desk outside shuffling through a disorderly pile of time-yellowed papers. The wall nearby was lined with several card-board boxes. Bill—early twenties, trendy haircut and clothes, a little fay—had been one of the few male assemblers until being promoted to the post suddenly vacated by Mrs. Auletta's firing.

He looked exasperated.

"How do you like your new job?"

"Oh, fun fun," he said humorlessly. "The first thing they did was dump a dozen boxes of tapes on me."

"Where'd all that come from?"

"They're Ben Mitze's. From his house. We have to *check* them all before I file them."

"Tony helping you?"

"Yeah. By running out here every half hour and screaming at me." Bobbi smiled at him. "I have to ask you something, Bill. There's a sector of tapes in here called ARP. Can you tell me what they are?"

"What do you need to know?"

"Were they stolen?"

He looked at her skeptically. "I'm not supposed to discuss that, am I?"

Bobbi smiled at him. "Afraid so, Bill."

He tried to smile. "I don't really *mind*, it's just that—"

"Call McNear."

"You're doing this for him?"

"We're trying to find out where those tapes walked. We don't have a lot of time."

He raised his eyebrows and sighed, then flipped through the catalogue of readouts on his desk. "Well. They were triple red. . . ."

"Were they stolen?"

Bill shook his head. "No."

"How do you know?"

He pointed at the catalogue. "Because triple red was the first sector we checked. They couldn't have left the library without two officers' signatures, and one of them had to've been McNear, Heyer, or Tony."

"What kind of tapes are in it?"

"I really don't know yet, Bobbi. I haven't—"

"Does that catalogue tell you anything about them?"

He gave her a little look and shuffled through the front pages. "Looks like they're numbered 1 through 231. That's about all it says."

"Nothing about what *ARP* means?"

"It says 'Assembly: Restricted Programs.' That's it. There's nothing else. You can look for yourself."

She looked at a tape container on Cross's desk. In addition to the sector markings, there were other color-coding stickers. "What do those mean—those other stripes."

He sighed and got out a logbook. "The second band is . . . whether it's a data or a systems-access tape; the third is project head."

"What does that mean exactly?"

"It's the execs, like Tony, Mr. Bass, Peets—different projects, different teams sometimes, but they were the project heads that, like, were in charge of writing the software in the first place. I think."

"In the audit you're doing for McNear, did you check whether there were any similarities there—like were a lot of the botched tapes systems or a lot of them from some particular project head?"

He shook his head. "The usage log doesn't have any color code information—only the ID."

Bobbi looked up and saw Sinc Heyer pulling his tape cart toward them. She could have sworn he paused an instant when he saw her, but then came on, leaving a sheet of paper on Bill's desk and going immediately into the vault.

Cross hadn't seemed to notice.

"You better go with him in there, Bill."

He looked over his shoulder. "He's the regular—"

"It doesn't matter what he is. Nobody goes in that vault without you beside them."

"Right," Bill said, and went into the vault.

Bobbi stood there a moment frowning at the piece of paper Sinc had left. It had Tony's scrawled signature, and a bunch of listed tapes. Mrs. Auletta's log didn't have Sinc Heyer's name in it—not once. Apparently, her regular method—inherited by Cross—was to put down the name of the person *requesting* the tapes, not the one who actually went into the vault and got them.

And the teenager was the one, probably more than anybody in the building, who actually rolled in there and got them out.

Bobbi went to the control-room window, trying to get a look at some of the sabotaged tapes. Earlier, she'd seen a rack of tapes that were being audited, but now they were across the room somewhere. She didn't have to think long to decide this was one of those times to break the rules. She checked herself into control, and skirted around the noisy room, trying to keep out of the way.

Control was an over-air-conditioned kitchen with twenty-five short-order cooks running around following menus they weren't used to. Tapes were being mounted and run. Operators sat among the little labyrinth of consoles in the center of the room, watching screens, fiddling with keyboards. Several of the screens had the same menus on them, lightly blipping as if to the internal beat of electricity.

Tony Pfeil looked up from the central desk, frowning at her. In a far corner near one of the big CPUs, Janet Farnsworth was mounting tapes from a rack. Janet was a short woman with a plain way of speaking, Tony's right-hand person in control. She was mounting tapes from a rack. Bobbi asked her if they were the sabotaged tapes.

"What's left of em," Janet said.

It took Bobbi all of five seconds to see that the containers all had the same third color bar—plain yellow. She checked out of the room and hurried back down to the vault desk. Cross was still inside the vault with the kid. In the catalogue, under the third code, she found the designation "Yellow: B. Mitze, project head."

24

They were ungluing wires from his head and pulling a thermometer out of his mouth, and the doctor was standing beside him asking questions. His bed cranked up, he sat wrapped in stupid calmness, trying to understand Nelson.

At a certain point, like the sun breaking out of clouds, he perceived Nelson quite clearly. He was apparently worried that he'd made a major error letting Ray talk him into that in-office operation. What had led up to the collapse? Had it happened at Bobbi's trailer? Exactly when had it occurred?

Ray talked to him and learned that he had appeared, semiconscious but capable of walking and driving, at three different places that morning between 4:30 and 5:15 A.M. There'd been several 911 calls, and the dispatcher had been told that a man "similar to Frankenstein" was appearing at various places in the industrial area of town. A network of police cars had failed to find Ray. Meanwhile, he was apparently continuing to drive around, spaced out, looking for a hospital, which he finally found. He walked in the front door, smiled at the receptionist, and in a very polite manner took off his shirt and pants and handed them to her.

Ray heard him out and sat there for a second looking reasonable, then started getting out of the bed.

Nelson said, "What are you doing?"

"I gotta go, Doc."

"Whoa there. The point of all this is that you may have had a stroke—possibly a heart attack. I'm hoping you didn't. But you're definitely going to have to stay here until I've done some things."

Ray's feet dangled off the bed, and he looked down at his paper gown and noticed that his balls were hanging off the bed. "Are you serious? Did I really take my pants off?"

"That's okay," Nelson chuckled, in an attempt at manly jocosity. "Our nurses are experienced."

Ray rubbed the back of his neck and looked down at the shiny tile floor.

"Don't worry. Your things are all safely taken care of."

He looked up at Nelson. "What time is it?"

"Seven o'clock."

"Don't be mad at me, Doc, but I have to go. I didn't have a stroke. I'm sure I didn't."

"You aren't in a position to know what you had."

"I have to go, Nelse." Ray slid off the bed and stood up, at first shakily.

"If you do, it'll be against physician's orders. And you'll have to get yourself another doctor."

"What does that mean?"

Nelson looked at him sternly. "You understand what I said." He was younger than Ray by eight or ten years, and Ray had a little trouble taking his sternness seriously.

"Nelse. We're old pals. I'm a good patient most of the time. Don't fire me. I have a good reason. I promise."

"What's your reason?"

"I have a question to ask you."

The doctor looked at him suspiciously. "What?"

Ray tried to think of how to phrase this. Words felt slow on his tongue. "What happens to a person when they get electrocuted?"

Nelson frowned. "Is that what happened to you?"

"Just answer me, Doc."

"Well, the big danger is obviously heart. And of course, you can be burned."

"What happens to your head?"

"What are you talking about? Have you been—?"

"Just answer me, Doc. Your head?"

Nelson took a deep breath and said, "It would depend on where the electricity entered the body. If it went through the brain in sufficient dosage, I suppose it would have somewhat the same effect as shock treatments."

"Which is?"

"Temporary loss of memory, decrease of mental activity—anxiety, hostility, and so forth. There's a syndrome called shock addiction. Schizophrenic patients develop an 'addiction' to their treatments—or to the feeling of well-being afterward."

"What kind of person might get on that kind of hook?"

"A masochist, somebody who wants to die, to forget—I don't know. Were you shocked? My God, Ray, what'd you do, go home from my clinic and stick your finger in a wall socket?"

"Nelse, I gotta ask you somethin. You remember the McNear girl, admitted out here last December tenth. Were you on?"

Nelson was surprised by this turn of the subject. "Yes. I believe so."

"What was wrong with her?"

Nelson stared at Ray, something dawning on his face.

"She was electrocuted, wasn't she?"

"What are you asking me this for?"

"Let me put it this way. Is it possible that she'd been electrocuted?"

"Possible."

"You didn't find anything. No drugs."

Nelson assented by saying nothing.

"Had you seen her before?"

"No. I am not her physician. If I was, I'd tell you to go take a hike."

"Did you check her records?"

"Of course."

"And she does have a problem?"

Nelson sighed. "Her records are in Little Rock. If you can find a judge to give you a subpoena, have at them. But don't mention me. Her father helped build this hospital, as I'm sure you know."

"Do you remember what she talked about?"

"Ray. Please."

"Come on, Nelse, save me two days of paperwork."

"I don't remember what she talked about!" Nelson said, angrily stretching his head toward Ray.

Ray said nothing else, and after an awkward moment, Nelson relented. "The best I recall, she didn't say much of anything. She was completely down. We had no diagnosis. Frankly, after the blood test I didn't know what to do. I called Baptist, and they had records of this kind of thing—acute episodes of memory loss, vagueness."

"Is she under care now?"

"We are talking about one emergency-room visit. That's all."

"Did you recommend follow-up care?"

"Of course I did."

The phone rang and Nelson turned to answer it, after a moment responding sharply, "You can tell them to forget it. I'm not letting him go."

He hung up. "Would you kindly tell me what's going on?"

"What?"

"There are three cops out there. The chief of police wants to see you."

"Where's my stuff?"

"You cannot go, Ray. Do you hear me? If you leave this hospital, you first sign a piece of paper saying that when you keel over dead it's not my fault. Besides which, you'll get yourself a new doctor."

"Well, I'll be dead then, Nelse. You won't want me any more. Come on, be nice and tell the lady to bring my britches."

"Have it your way then, you stubborn son of a bitch! Shit!" The doctor crashed out of the room and Ray crept out after him, looking for his pants. When he got them, he slipped out the back and found his car in the parking lot. He saw two police cars at the emergency entrance.

It'd be nice if he had a clearer mind for the face-down.

His only advantage would be to show up at Warnke's office on his own. On his way downtown, he called Outlaw on their radio.

"Need you to do something for me, John."

"You do something for me first. Tell me what in the flyin fuck you're doin. Warnke's shittin in his pants. He's had two cars out here. He's trying to pick you up, Ray."

"I know. I'm goin to see him now. You know something about electrical wiring, don't you?"

Outlaw hesitated. "Why?"

"Just answer me, John. I'm almost downtown."

"I wired my new cabin, if that's what you mean," he said grudgingly.

"Go to the trailer. Go inside it. Don't touch anything, but try to find out about the alarm-system wiring. There's some kind of hookup that turns the whole goddamn trailer into a live wire. See if you can verify that."

"Are you out of your mind?"

"Just don't touch the keyboard and you'll be okay. If you see something on the screen about an alarm state, get your ass out quick. It gives you seven seconds."

"You have to be nuts."

"I'm fine, John. I'll explain it all later."

25

At ten o'clock, she went to the boardroom, uncertain about whether to report to McNear what she'd just found out. It should have been obvious to anyone who looked at the color codes on the tape containers. Whether he'd seen the color codes or not, McNear knew who'd headed various software projects, so he surely had an idea that the missing tapes had all been Mitze's.

He wasn't there yet anyway, so she went inside and waited for the meeting to get started.

The executive boardroom already stank of nerves when she walked in. The room itself was different from the rest of the building, the only place that was formally decorated—with a new, plush carpet, flashy orangish prints on the walls, and solid black wooden chairs. She noticed the ceiling-mounted camera in the corner, wondering if anyone but herself was aware that video was finally live all over the building.

Jeremy sat on the edge of his chair, wearing a limp red bandana around his wild hair, grasping a Coke. Tim Thurmon kept glancing around the table, his facial tic reaching down and causing a slight twist in his shoulder. Arn Bass, near one end of the table, smiled and made some little joke with Carol Rader, who didn't smile back. The treasurer was always pleasant, always sartorially perfect, with none of the rough edges that characterized almost everybody else in the room. Rader was his opposite in one way; she was edgy, nervous, ironic, but with something of the same control. She talked amazingly fast, which made her seem like a woman always running, always pushing or being pushed to greater and greater productivity.

Tony had brought a little tape recorder for taking the minutes. He looked at Bobbi oddly, probably wondering what she'd been doing in the operations room.

As a group, they were a little more dressed up than usual. Joe Peets wore an awful yellow clip-on tie to complement his blond ponytail. Because she'd heard Peets giving speeches to the assemblers during her first weeks here, Bob initially had the impression he was a fairly lively type, but over time she'd discovered that the speeches were canned and he was neither talkative nor gregarious.

Mike Heyer sat at one end of the table behind his sunglasses, speaking to no one.

The group of them made Bobbi feel a little abashed. They were like a large and turbulent family, all very bright, close-knit, and sensitive to each other—so linked and tethered by their long struggles together that as an outsider among them she felt ineffective. It was the kind of situation in which a person could be made a fool, and Bobbi had a great aversion to appearing foolish. Sitting with her notepad on her lap, awkwardly somewhat back from the table, she tried to get in mind exactly what to say if questioned about the emergency security plan. Her mind kept wandering back to the notes Ray had given her.

It was 10:05 when McNear came in and sat down at the head of the table. He scooted up, plopped down some papers, and waited for them to quiet down. His luxuriant white hair was wilder, more electric, than usual today. After a moment they were still, the only thing moving being Thurmon's eyes, darting around from face to face.

"This is an executive meeting to make final decisions on our clients' down problems—and, because some of you have requested it, a board meeting to discuss . . . broader issues. Are there any objections to having the executive meeting first, taking a break, then having the board meeting?"

"Yes, there are," Heyer said without hesitation. "We need to talk about the whole ball of wax."

Tim Thurmon agreed.

McNear looked at Thurmon. "I want to start with the problem before us, if you don't mind. Arn just talked to Marathon West and I believe he has some not-so-good news."

Arn Bass was poking a yellow pad of paper with a pencil, frowning. "As some of you know, Wayne talked to their board the other night in California, but the situation has deteriorated since then. They've had another data loss, and some of the big depositors are withdrawing. Their Fedfunds rate is already going up. They've been selling corporate paper, but within a day or two they'll have to borrow through the discount window. The FDIC's already in touch with them, hassling them about the tiering problem in their rate." He stopped tapping with the pencil and looked up. "It looks like the word's out."

"All right. Tim, tell us the happy news from New York."

As he sat forward, preparing to talk, Thurmon's face went through a complex tic. "The shunt modems are in place at Corning, Gallaher, General, and Farnsworth Medical. State Fastener we didn't get to. We'll have problem teams on deck at the three banks and the medical center, making sure they stick to the blue book."

"So we're giving up on State Fastener?" Carol asked.

McNear looked grim. "We'll have to forget them for now. I think we better do the same with Marathon West. We're too thin already."

"How are the other three taking it?" Bobbi asked.

"A couple of the banks had their noses out of joint when I got there," Thurmon said. "We had been talking to the DP managers all along, but the upper-level boys were getting confused signals. So we had a meeting. I told them there was evidence someone was playing, in a wholesale way, with bank and corporate communications, and until the problem was nailed down we wanted to get additional precautions in place. I put them on alert. The VP in charge of operations at Corning hit the fan. He refused at first. He wanted the details on paper before he'd move."

Jeremy muttered, "Right. Do anything you want. Just don't make us do anything."

Thurmon went on. "I gave him Tony's number, and he called him immediately. Tony put it in stronger terms."

"What kind of stronger?" Carol asked.

Tony sat there shaking his head. "The guy didn't care about the particulars. He just wanted me to scare the shit out of him. I did."

"The shunt lines," McNear said. "How effective are they going to be?"

There was disagreement at this point, and Bobbi floated in and out of the discussion, thinking about Ray's notebook . . . and about his face last night with lead pellets in it. She really needed to see him.

McNear turned the course of the discussion toward internal security, and matter-of-factly listed off Bobbi's suggested changes. All queries and uses of the data had to be logged according to individual security passwords—so that there would be no anonymous computer use at all. All casual conversation about current projects or problems, in the halls or wherever, was to stop immediately, and there was to be a random, rotating security demotion, with Thurmon and Heyer the first down.

Thurmon's face went into megatic, a spreading, chain-reaction face-quake.

Even Jeremy became nervous. Heyer looked down the plane of the table at McNear, his mouth settling below his sunglasses into sullen anger. He sniffed once. "What's the idea?"

"We have critical problems, Mike. No matter what kind of anomaly this is, we're failing. We have to take harsh measures."

"Sorry, Mr. President," Heyer said in a tight voice. "I see no purpose to that 'measure' but to insult me and insult Tim Thurmon."

McNear looked down a moment, as if restraining himself. "Mike, if we have three banks down at once tonight and we're still fiddling our thumbs without a plan, we're history."

Heyer cocked his head a little. "What do 'random security demotions' have to do with a plan?"

"I'll get around to that, if you'll let me. I want to ask Jeremy something. What's your sense of this screening method Tim's set up? You think it'll work?"

"Why are you asking him?" Thurmon said, his face reddening. "He had nothing to do—"

"That's exactly why I am asking him, Tim. Because he has nothing to do with the idea."

Jeremy shook his head. "I don't like it. Our operators would have to understand every detail of every incoming. We have no idea how the command might arrive. It could come in some completely innocent-looking package—like a certain sum of money from a certain creditor or debtor. In fact, we don't know for sure that it is coming. All we know is the menu *says* it's going to, and this device has an incredible ability to stay in touch with targets, even when their addresses are changed."

"What do you think it is?" McNear asked.

"The Ball?" Jeremy sat there a moment, then made an uneasy shrug. "Smart, definitely a processor with capacity. It's floating out there in geosynchronous orbit about twenty-two thousand miles above the equator—which is significant, I guess, since it can't be physically destroyed, short of some kind of major NASA project."

"What about jamming it?" Peets asked.

"The NSA tries to jam fairly vanilla Russian military satellites all the time and has no luck. It's a processor, okay—obviously capable of taking input, but it's very selective about what input it takes. The coding method may be public key/private key, which explains why I can't crack it. Beyond the coding, who knows what kind of buffers and baffles are in place to prevent any kind of unauthorized write-operation

197

on the system. If we could crack this 'letter' maybe we could get somewhere. . . ."

Carol Rader said, in her flattest tone, "What I want to know is who's responsible for this."

"I have an opinion about that." McNear's hands were folded into a single fist on the table. "You want to turn off the tape recorder, Tony?"

He leaned forward and flicked off the little recorder.

McNear hesitated a moment and said, "Ben's doing it. Ben and someone else."

They all looked up the table at him, silent. For a moment, no one in the room moved.

"All of you know that Ben was working on a program to jam snoopers. He believed—and I agreed—that you can't claim real datacom safety until you have something that repels unauthorized reading—a poison pill in the data stream that'll mess up a snooper's operating system. Most of you also know I discontinued Ben's involvement on the Assembly—which was his name for the project—over a year ago. It seemed to me he was getting off on a tangent. I now think he may not have stopped working on it. And he may have found out about this piece of hardware and started fiddling with it, perhaps even using it for testing."

Jeremy took a quick drink of Coke. "Where'd he do his transmitting?"

"Agile dishes aren't hard to find." McNear sighed and looked up. "Look. This isn't easy to talk about. I thought Ben went over the edge. I thought he was flaked out. Before I ordered a stop to the project, he had quit talking about it. He was secretive not just about details, he wouldn't even talk generalities. He clammed up completely. He seemed continuously worried and confused, doing all-nighters like he was a kid again. He was putting huge jobs through the ladies out back. I found records of one order that took the assemblers over sixteen thousand work hours that he erased within an hour after it was completed. We all know about change orders, but you don't usually just pitch a component of that size. . . . So Ben was blown. Burned out." He looked up at them. "Or so I thought."

He had their complete attention now.

"Now I'm thinking that wasn't the case. Ben may have been flying upside down, but he may also have been doing the most brilliant work of his life. The mistake I made was partly personal." He looked down at his folded hands. "It won't do any good for me to talk about the personal problem Ben and I were having. There's no way that can be changed now."

The treasurer put his hand to his mouth and made a little cough.

"Does this have anything to do with the letter he sent you? Did you crack it?" Carol asked.

McNear shook his head slowly. "I should have kept up with him, but I didn't—or couldn't. After I called the project off, Ben really got funny. He was around here at odd hours, but he was elusive. I think one of the things he may have done during that time was feed this thing a good percentage of our library."

"Why?" Tony asked.

Very quietly, hardly moving his lips: "I guess it doesn't matter now. The fact is we have it to deal with."

Tony looked skeptical. "I mean what for? What purpose would it serve?"

McNear finally looked up. "Look. Ben's pissed off. He doesn't care any more. Somehow he finds out about this Godball, this satellite, maybe through gossip. Nobody has better connections than Ben. It's as sexy as they make them—literally a generation jump in hardware. He goes all out. He reverts to pure hacker. Maybe he even tries to crack it with his Assembly."

Carol sounded disbelieving. "So Ben steals tapes, uses em, and returns scratch—"

McNear was already shaking his head. "Unfortunately, it gets worse. You all know about the vault problem. Several of us have been working on it. A bunch of our tapes has been either stolen and replaced by useless tapes or sabotaged outright. Among the useless tapes, sixteen of them were used and refiled *after* December tenth. Tapes have been leaking *since* Ben's death."

The board erupted all at once in questions, and Bobbi suddenly went into neutral, thinking about what McNear was saying. So he'd already sensed the main implication of what Ray had actually witnessed and recorded from the remote terminal—that somebody besides Ben Mitze was involved, somebody still around, feeding tapes to this thing.

The noise subsided after a single question from Mike Heyer, asked with strained calmness. "What's your point, Wayne?"

McNear looked at him. "The operation is ongoing."

"One or more of us is doing it," Heyer said ironically. "And the first candidates are Tim and me. We've decided to blow our own equity. That makes a lot of sense. Who are we working for—USI? Yes, I can tell by that little look on your face, USI is the answer. One of us is getting paid big bucks by USI to spy on you. Right? Wayne, USI doesn't *care* about you. They don't give a damn about this miserable little company. We aren't even in their universe."

The dramatic thing for McNear to do now, Bobbi thought, would be to reveal Tom Ferris's telephone call, but he didn't. He just watched Heyer.

"And you're still not addressing the small matter of *what* this thing is. We keep sliding away from that. You think USI has gotten into the bank-crashing business? They've become Communists and are trying, like, to destroy the capitalistic system—? What? What is your latest theory about USI, Wayne?"

"We've talked about this a great deal already, Mike. I'm sorry you've missed those discussions. We're in general agreement it's USI's hardware. What do you know about the J-junction project, Jeremy?"

"Sixth-generation circuitry, behind the chip," Jeremy said, making a little shrug with his eyebrows. "It's had tight wrappers on it for the last couple of years. I used to hear about it. Lately, nobody talks. Tell you the truth, I figured it lost out to other things—maybe bubble memory."

McNear said, "All we know about the *soft*ware comes from the menu and the fact that it's very sophisticated at systems entry. Let me ask you a couple of questions. Forget about the exact nature of the hardware. Forget who produced it. Let's just say this thing is a computer, whether it's packaged in a ball or a box or a pickup truck—it's a computer and it's twenty-two thousand miles up. Also speculate that it's what it says it is—some kind of *open* data base. Tony, what's an open data base?"

Tony had descended lower and lower in his chair during all this. He looked gloomy and tired. "Doesn't have an exact meaning, but usually you're talking a minicomputer, buncha freaks using it for a telephone/bulletin board/trading place. They have little keyboard romances, trade stolen programs, sell dope to each other—that kind of crap."

"Okay. Take this computer and assume it's not a mini but more like a very healthy mainframe with a roomful of disks all on-line." Elbow on the table, he pointed up with his forefinger. "Put it someplace both unreachable and at the same time available *and* private—at least theoretically." His finger pointed down the table now, in the general direction of Heyer. "You can reach it anytime, with fairly simple gear, and you *can't* be traced."

Heyer shook his head. "You're calling a microwave transmitter simple?"

"If the receiver's good enough, the transmitter doesn't have to be anything special. There are dishes floating around up there that can hear you brush your teeth."

"A dish isn't a transponder. It gathers all signals coming from a general direc—"

"Packages all signals in coded address envelopes."

"Yeah, well, aside from the fact that I don't quite know how that would work, you're talking a lot of digitizing, friend."

"It can handle it. Let me add one more thing: give it a friendly front-end—something artificial-intelligence–capable—"

"What do you mean?" Jeremy asked. He'd been getting more and more interested.

"I mean 'Hi, Jeremy, how have you been doing since our last communication of 4/10/84? I haven't heard from you in a while. What's going on? Ask me whatever you want to. Read me whatever you want to. Let's communicate, Jeremy. Oh, and by the way, do you have any messages you'd like sent anywhere? Any little *commands*, Jeremy?'"

Jeremy stared at him.

McNear's elbow came off the table and he sat up straight in his chair. "Now read the software and access information from our library—ours alone—into such a piece of hardware, and make it available in this 'open data base' and what do you have?"

"You have problems," Jeremy said.

"Just the kind of thing USI does day in and day out," Heyer said sarcastically. "Wayne, this is all very entertaining, but if you haven't got anything substantial, let's break and have the board meeting."

McNear looked around the table. "You're right, Mike. It's only speculation. I'll put it in a few words. The software is from the National Security Agency. They paid USI big money to field-test a program, the rough outlines of which I've just described—their first interactive snooper. Somehow the project went awry."

"So why don't they turn the damn thing off?" said Tony.

"I'm afraid the one person who might be able to answer that isn't around," McNear said.

Mike Heyer's disdain became almost casual. "He-ey, really slipped that one to us. That's pretty good. Now not only the most powerful computer company in the world but also government spies are on our case, huh, Wayne?"

McNear looked at him. "Do you remember Govind Shaw?"

"Look at your watch. We need to have a board meeting."

"Answer me, Mike. Do you know who he is?"

Heyer hesitated a minute. "Come on, Wayne. Quit askin fuckin rhetorical questions."

"Govind Shaw is a project director at the NSA." McNear glanced toward Bobbi.

Bobbi's heart was beating faster. At the mention of Shaw, she became uneasy.

"So how'd he get from the Valley to the NSA?" Carol Rader asked.

"Briefly, two or three years after Simmons Paragon went bankrupt,

Shaw wrote a paper that was printed in a small California technical journal. That issue of the journal was never distributed. The NSA noticed it before it was sent out to subscribers—probably because they had a financial arrangement with the editor. They bought and rounded up every copy of the issue and classified his paper. Shaw was working for the NSA within a month. I believe he's been working for them every since."

"You believe, huh?" Heyer said.

McNear took a folder from the papers in front of him and slid it down the long table to Heyer.

Heyer glanced at the first page and pushed it away.

Jeremy was frowning at McNear. "What's the article about?"

"It's called 'Freedom of Access and the Degradation Factor.' It's based on his experience at Simmons. He took what happened there and speculated about it—on a much larger level. You can read it yourself."

". . . Jesus P. Christ," Jeremy breathed, looking at the paper.

"This is all wonderful. But what are we doing?"

"I agree!" Thurmon said angrily.

"Last Friday, Govind Shaw was trying to find out things from our security trainees in California."

Eyes went to Bobbi.

She hated the fact that she was blushing. It made her angry at herself and at McNear. He should have told her he was going to do this. She tried to mask her embarrassment by clearing her throat and saying, forthrightly, "It's true. He approached me, and seemed unusually interested in . . . the company."

"Did he approach you personally?" McNear asked.

"He tried to, yeah." No one needed to question her further about that. Her blush was a bright seal of truth. It also called whatever else she might say into question, so she added nothing.

McNear went on, "I got a telephone call this morning. It seems that in the last few days, a bunch of very funny types has checked into motels in Little Rock and Dubois. Now if you're so anxious to start the board meeting, let's take a three-minute break, board members reconvene. I still have some things to say about our short-range approach."

Back in the security office, she sat at the central desk, trying to decide whether her feeling of being used was fair. It was a small matter, really. She'd have gladly told them what happened between Govind Shaw and her. She just didn't like it being sprung on her like that.

She switched through the monitors until she found the one in the boardroom. It had no sound, so she switched back to hall monitors until she'd found the one closest to the boardroom door. She turned the volume up to the max, and, unable to hear much on the speakers, looked in the drawer for the more sensitive earphones. With them, she could hear a little better.

RADER: What do you mean, tell the truth?

McNEAR: . . . anybody in authority . . .

HEYER: Right. One more good reason to forget it.

McNEAR: . . . enough . . . to free-float through half the business and . . . computers . . . Assembly . . . only hope . . . from Ben's library. . . .

HEYER (very audible): You think a program that you just told us you aborted will solve all our problems? A program that was never even finished!? Come on, Wayne.

JEREMY: . . . trouble with that, too.

HEYER: Why don't we talk the facts, Wayne. You've never wanted to make a stock offering, because you're afraid of losing control of the company. Listen, you've got 9.7 percent of the outstanding stock. That may be a little more than me or the rest of us, but we're all stock-poor. Nine point seven percent is your vote, no more. You can't railroad us with a bunch of speculations about the NSA and secret plots.

THURMON: . . . really must agree . . . wrong side of the media . . .

At that moment the hallway alarm went off, nearly blowing Bobbi's eardrums. She jerked the phones from her head.

The wall clock said 11:06.

Switching back to the boardroom video monitor, she saw some of them standing, others obviously trying to stay and finish the meeting. Eventually the bell stopped and Tony appeared in the boardroom doorway. Quickly she switched back to the hallway monitor and put the earphones back on.

PFEIL: . . . Corning Trust just went bananas. A bunch of us already have calls backed up.

McNEAR: It'll have to wait. Come back in and sit down.

The door shut, and Bobbi heard even less than before because of the ringing in her ears.

RADER: . . . so is it padlock city? . . .

McNEAR: . . . legal obligations . . .

HEYER (clearly audible): You have gone over, Wayne. You have crossed the border. Since when do we go trooping to 'the authorities' with shit like this? Look, the most immediate problem I've got is that I have a lot of little notes from Arn saying I own part of this company. I've been delaying the payoff for fifteen years, *that's* my problem.

McNEAR: . . . anybody who doesn't want to go along . . . Today. Right now . . . an hour from now . . . take your money and walk out the door . . . lose your future . . .

HEYER: Write it. Go ahead. Figure it for me, Arn. I already know it—two million eight hundred thirty-five thousand bucks. Write me a check for that, Wayne.

BASS: Goddamnit, guys . . .

PFEIL: . . . stacking up out there.

There was a long silence, then she heard the door open and everyone talking at once. She switched to the hallway monitor. Mike Heyer was marching straight for the camera, with a piece of paper in hand that looked like a check.

26

Elbows on his desk when Ray walked in, Warnke yawned behind a hand. "What happened to you?"

"Had a little dermatology work done yesterday. Nothin serious."

When Warnke moved his hands away from his face, Ray saw the tense set of his mouth. He got up and walked over to his window, looking through the blinds into the parking lot. "Outlaw tells me you weren't on shift again last night."

Ray decided not to talk to his back.

After a moment, Warnke turned. "Can you tell me why someone of your description, driving your car, appeared at Intercontinental Trucking this morning in a state of delirium? A person described as looking like Frankenstein?"

Ray nodded seriously. "Similar to him—yeah, I heard that."

"What was your problem?"

"Must have had a little reaction to my face operation."

Warnke glanced at him with anxious distaste, sat down at his desk, and moved his sailboat from one spot to another. "This pains me, Ray. It really does. But this just isn't the way a professional police officer acts. You've been unreliable." He suppressed a yawn, his little ferretlike face shaking as his jaw muscle tightened. "It's time we made your vacation official. Now I'm giving you a chance to keep your record clean. Ann has typed up for you a request for a three-month unpaid leave for personal reasons. It's on her desk. I want you to sign it immediately. If you leak the present operation in any way, the vacation will be extended indefinitely. I want to see Outlaw as soon as possible. You might let him know."

Ray nodded thoughtfully at Chief Warnke but didn't move to leave.

"You've never understood this operation, Lieutenant. It's never soaked through. Three or four times now you've gotten me in trouble, and I've covered for you. But I've had it. Now I think you understand me. We disengage you, and we do it very quietly."

His voice modulated from threatening to a kind of fatherly tone. "I advise you to take a vacation. Go somewhere for a while. Come back and make a clean start. I'll protect you from any unfavorable coverage. It's delicate, but I can handle it. I've already talked to the rescue people and Lieutenant Nash. He's taken today's incident off the records. No one outside this office needs to know it's anything but a personal leave. We both know this kind of thing can ruin a person's whole career."

Ray waited a minute to make sure the chief was finished. "Who have I been getting you in trouble with, Chief?"

Warnke's mouth exploded open in a huge yawn he finally put his fist over. "I have a lot to do. Let's get on with it."

Ray picked up the chief's bronze sailboat and looked at it appraisingly, then backed up and sat down on the edge of the couch. Warnke stared at him as if he'd just swept all the papers off his desk. Ray gazed at the statuette, running a finger over its fussy detail.

"That's *all* for now, Lieutenant. Please drop by Ann's desk on the way out."

Ray held the boat up a little. "Neil English a sailor?"

". . . ?"

"I understand Neil got a nice new job down in Florida."

"That happens with good officers. They get job offers. Now—"

"Last December tenth, you ordered Neil to take Ben Mitze's body out of that trailer and haul it to the DataForm building. Any particular reason for that?"

Warnke's complexion was turning ashen. He took a sudden, deep breath and leaned forward across his desk, saying with stabbing force, "This is an undercover operation. We are *not* dealing with midgets. We are dealing with the *highest* authorities. Now you can get yourself burned. Severely."

"Who are these authorities?" Ray asked simply, as if this was still an everyday conversation.

The chief glanced at his sailboat, still in Ray's foul hands.

"Are they so high they blew Jack Cady off for trying to talk about that trailer?"

"We are through now. If you want to keep your job, you had better do as I say and do it quietly."

Ray thought a minute, then with the greatest respect and gentleness set the sailboat on the end table beside him. "Any recommendations for a place to go?"

"I'm sure you'll find a restful place." He turned his attention to a printout on his desk.

"Maybe I ought to go down to Florida. Find a nice house on the beach somewhere."

Warnke's eyes bounced halfway up to him, then back to the printout on his desk. He picked it up, rattled loose several folds, and held it in front of his face.

Ray glanced at the letter on Ann's desk, and ambled on down the stairs to his office.

The other half of the Dubois detective division was at his desk, typing. "How you doin, Marvin?"

Miller averted his gaze from Ray's bandaged face. "Fine, thank you."

"Anything come up on Elizabeth Mitze?"

"We're moving along." Miller's tone implied he didn't want to discuss it. Miller never wanted to discuss anything.

"Find anything interesting?"

Miller sighed and hunched over his typewriter.

Ray took out his latest spiral notebook and slapped it against his palm. "One question, Marvin. What happened to all those tapes and files out there at the Mitze residence?"

Miller continued to look at his typewriter. *Tap tap tap.*

"You had a lock order on the place didn't you?"

"Of course."

"Well then, what happened to them? You're the officer in charge."

Tap tap.

"Lieutenant Miller. Calling Lieutenant Miller."

Tap tap tap. He eventually looked up. "I really can't discuss the case at this time."

Ray leaned back in his chair. "How come?"

"Because I have been instructed not to discuss it."

"By the chief?"

Miller looked back down and typed. Ray rolled his chair around and with his right foot pushed Miller's typewriter plug out of the wall.

"I'd appreciate it, Lieutenant Wiel—"

Ray rolled his chair over, grabbed the typewriter on both sides, and said with malicious intensity, "I'd appreciate it if you'd tell me where those tapes are."

Miller got up and hurried around his desk out the door.

Ray lifted his telephone and called DataForm. Busy signal.

27

Managing building traffic was more than the four reasonable, pleasant young men who showed up from Markham Security could handle. The two she'd stationed at the control entrance were like traffic cops wearing black at night in the middle of a twelve-lane freeway. Bill Cross and his guard were hauling the Mitze tapes, wholesale, to control. Bobbi could tell by a fleeting look Cross gave her, trundling a box past her window, that he'd had no time to catalogue or check the stuff. The time crunch was making any kind of orderly procedure impossible.

Bobbi was following orders, letting everything else pretty much go to hell while she looked for her saboteur.

Because of its motion detector, the vault camera only switched on when somebody appeared in the doorway. Mrs. Auletta, the now-fired librarian, came and went often, and Bobbi left her in fast motion, a big-hipped woman in bright double knits skittering back and forth pushing carts or bringing out individual tapes. The second most frequent entrances were made by Sinc Heyer. There was nothing overtly suspicious about him, but something was odd.

Scanning one of the latest cartridges, she froze the video at the moment he was closest to the camera yet still in focus. She looked at the image for a while before realizing that it was his expression. She'd passed him many times in the hall never seeing what was evident in the still image. He looked profoundly sad, melancholy to the point of pain.

There were hallway camera tapes, but she didn't really have time to go through all of them systematically. She quickly developed the method of looking at them in very fast motion, things whizzing by, until she saw big bulks—tape carts—then ran back and slowed the tape down. Shots of Sinc pushing carts were easy enough to find with this method, but they were all unhelpful.

The only thing even mildly interesting she caught him doing was regularly parking his cart in the hall and leaving it while he went to the men's room. In a proper security environment, leaving a tape cart untended was out of the question, but here it was par for the course. She went through several films of this incident, all the same. The camera was at a fair distance, but it was clear he hadn't taken anything with him inside. He pushed the cart out of the way against the wall, went in for less than a minute, came back out, and, pulling it back and forth a couple of times to get it away from the wall, went on down the hall.

The phone startled her. She'd left a call-back message for Ray at police dispatch and hoped it was him.

It was Carol Rader. "Do you know how to mount tapes?"

"Not really. We did a little of that one morning in training—"

"Well, come to control and learn to be an expert. We seem to be running low on intelligent life around here," she said, and hung up.

. . . .

CIRCUIT CHECK

. . . .

. . . .

F-1 for help
F-3 for breakout
Priority function: DO NOT try to link or load

Error count: 63

At the center of the labyrinth in control, she found Carol with Janet Farnsworth, Jeremy, and a couple of others, all looking at a screen. Bobbi gleaned from what was being said that it was Corning Trust's computer, locked helplessly into a circuit-checking program. McNear was at another screen down the line. Tony, on a phone across the room, raised his head at Janet.

"Let's do it," she said.

The operator punched in something that caused the schoolbell-like alarm that had nearly broken Bobbi's eardrums earlier to go off again for a couple of seconds.

"We've got a dead bank," Janet said.

Released from the spell of the circuit-checking program, the bank's computer now had to be restarted. Its system was on disk and ready to feed, but the latest data files were still on tape. They were a week old, but presumably clerks at the bank could reconstruct the gap with hard copy.

McNear looked up. "Go ahead and open Gallaher and General and see what happens. Meanwhile, get the Assembly ready to roll. I want it set up and ready within an hour."

Jeremy was looking at the screen, shaking his head slightly.

"So how many helpers do I get?" Carol asked, her usual flatness shading into accusation.

"Take Bobbi. The rest work on the Assembly."

Carol looked unhappy at this. "She doesn't know how to handle tapes. Why don't you use—"

"Look, don't give me any shit, Carol," McNear said. "We have enough trouble without discussing every little decision."

Carol looked at him a moment longer, then smiled palely at Bobbi. "Well. I know you're untrained, dear, but shall we try to save a bank?"

They rolled a cart across the room, and Carol was taking tapes and snapping off rings before it stopped.

"The tape drives they showed us—"

"—were different from these, I'm sure. That's because these are twenty years old," Carol said. Bobbi had talked with Carol very little, but she knew this was her normal way of speaking—fast, often cutting you off.

She worked efficiently but seemed totally preoccupied, unaware of the yelling back and forth across the room as the others made tape-to-disk transfers of the Assembly. The best help Bobbi could give her, she decided, was to take off rings and hand her tapes, leaving her to actually thread and mount them.

"What do you think's going to happen?"

Carol smiled ironically. "What do I think? I think I hope the FDIC or the comptroller doesn't get through on one of the telephone lines before I sell my stock and walk out the door."

She hit a button with the bottom of her fist and took another tape. "It's not going to work.

"The Assembly?"

She scowled at the reel, pulling out tape. "Ben's poison pill. Right. We have no idea if those tapes are complete. We have no idea if they'll stop what's happening to the banks. We have no knowledge of the computer we're trying to disable. We have no permission to disable it." She glanced at Bobbi, and kept on threading. "Do you believe in the tooth fairy?

"On top of it all, like a nice cherry full of red dye number ten, Wayne wants to tell the whole truth and nothing but the truth to the authorities. Very honest and upright. Which will just be wonderful for our seventy-some other clients."

Bobbi handed her another spool and pushed the cart along to the next. "Could I talk with you a few minutes?"

"Isn't that what we're doing?" Carol said.

"After we're finished. Privately. I've been working on the vault problem—"

Carol said nothing, but her look at Bobbi was so sharp that it stopped her midsentence. They worked another ten minutes, finishing the tapes without further conversation.

The noise and activity in the room increased, as McNear moved between monitors trying different "concats"—different ways of putting together the Assembly tapes. Meanwhile, Carol, with one operator helping, brought up Corning's VMs, then the utility systems and the first layers of data. McNear had decided to leave the bank's computer isolated from outside calls.

"At least they'll have an adding machine," Carol said acidly. "Please come to my office. I prefer to be interrogated there."

They passed Mike Heyer's office, and he was inside, crashing around, pulling things out of desk drawers, jerking pictures from walls, pitching them into cardboard boxes. His back was turned, and she watched him scatter papers all around—an act of rage done peculiarly without any physical signs of rage. He was making such a mess Bobbi wondered if she should try to do something about it. She decided he'd probably be out of the building faster if she left him alone.

In her office, Carol was answering her phone lines, punching each button and dealing speedily with callers. The end button on her phone was an inside line, and she answered it twice successively for brief conversations.

"Rader. . . . So you've taken a look? . . . And 'degradation factor'? . . . No, no, I don't want to see it. Thanks.

"Rader. . . . Oh, just sitting here watching my telephone blink. . . . Don't worry about him, he's having a wonderful time. . . . Out of his gourd, right. . . . Tell me, Arn, are people selling? What can a girl do after fifteen years? . . . Marilyn's handling it, of course. . . . The stockbroker, right. See you in Shanghai."

She hung up and looked at Bobbi, who was still standing. "So—the vault? Any handcuffs I can wear during this interrogation?"

"Why do you think I want to interrogate you?"

"Don't ask me little detective questions, Bobbi. I'm a busy lady."

"I asked to talk to you because I happen to believe you're not a liar."

"Oh? You imply there are people who speak something other than the truth in this wonderful zoo. Well, you may be right, but to tell you the truth, I'm sicker of the hostility than the lying. Like the war between Mike and Wayne. That really has been tiresome."

"Wasn't that coming mostly from Mike?"

"What do you think your little 'emergency security plan' was for? Who'd that come from?"

Bobbi didn't answer her. She remained just inside the door, standing.

Carol finally eased up a little. "Please sit down, at least."

Bobbi did so. Carol obviously required a very light touch in the present mood, but Bobbi had the feeling she was disturbed enough to talk.

"You probably don't know this," she said, "but Mike Heyer and Wayne McNear were the core of this place in the old days. They stuck together, always. For years. They were the nucleus."

"Elizabeth Mitze must be on people's minds, too."

"Did you know Liz?" Carol sounded cooler.

"I saw her once, at the last April Fools party—on the deck talking to Mr. McNear."

"Talking, huh?" Her forefinger played over the blinking buttons on her phone. "I don't know. We may have picked on Liz. She was a latecomer, and extremely rich. We used to socialize so damn much. The scene. I can't imagine that now. All of us—kids, spouses . . . I lost my first-and-only to it. Divorce. Because of Mike Heyer, to be precise. Not the Mike of late, but Mike nevertheless. He was quite a swashbuckler, believe it or not. That was of course nine hundred years ago. Now he's become a querulous idiot. I think he's got Alzheimer's. I think several of us do."

"Did any of the trouble start with Mr. McNear and Liz Mitze?"

Carol looked surprised. "Who are we investigating now?"

"Believe it or not, I have a reason for asking that."

"I'm sure you do, but it sounds pretty distant from a vault problem."

"I've found out that all the sabotaged tapes were Mitze's programs. I'm trying to find out why."

"What do you mean, Mitze's programs?"

"He was the officer originally in charge of all the damaged software."

"Officer in charge doesn't mean much with a lot of that junk."

"His name is on every destroyed tape. There has to be a reason for it."

Carol frowned at her. "So you're casting around for motives. . . . Well, the thing between Wayne and Liz wasn't any particular secret.

And it wasn't just the two of them. Liz Mitze was close to *all* the McNears. Oh, and Liz could be charming. She knew how to spend money, play tennis. . . . And Taylor *loved* Ben Mitze. She positively followed him around. After Ben killed himself, you'd think Wayne and Liz might make it public after a decent interval, move in together or something; but the opposite happened. Liz wouldn't see him. Whatever was between them fell apart. Someone told me she wouldn't allow him in her house. Perfect sense, huh? The coast is clear, dear, go to hell."

"You said Taylor *loved* Ben Mitze. What did a teenage girl—"

Carol's eyes went down to the flickering phone. "I'm spouting off. What did you want to ask me?"

Bobbi kept her tone conversational. "I stopped Taylor in a traffic incident last December. Sinc was driving."

"They're another case, aren't they. Mr. and Miss Teenage Weird."

"Is something wrong with Taylor?"

"We really are gossiping now, aren't we," she said vaguely. Bobbi could see her again retreating into her own thoughts. "You can't just fiddle with code all the time. You get off the track, look up one day and don't know where you are. But you do have to appreciate him. . . ."

"Ben?"

Carol nodded slowly.

"Was Ben like Jeremy?"

"Oh, Ben was a hacker, yes—generally. But a hacker's one thing, a genius is something else."

"Genius at writing software?"

"What Ben wrote was mostly links, connective tissue. He liked to *find* good systems, really—modify them, use them for different tasks. He knew absolutely everything of interest that was going on around the country. 'Metaprograms,' 'alloys' he called them. 'Assemblies.' Six million instructions were a module to Ben. Jeremy was always jealous of that. When you work on that scale, you command a lot of computing power. Bytes to a hacker are what money is to other people. Getting their hands on a Cray is like having their own jet. Ben could beg and borrow amazing amounts of power. He had time going on computers all over the country. His only problem was not much of it was economically feasible. This Godball thing—whatever it is—must have been heaven to him. Excuse the . . ."

Trailing off, she made a little frown. "You do have to appreciate Ben, but he did have something wrong with him."

"What?"

"I really don't know. Work with someone that long and they become part of the weather. They recede. But you can sense things."

"Was he angry?"

"Ben didn't respond straight out to things. He was too brainy." She shrugged with her eyebrows. "But no. He didn't like his boss fucking his wife."

"Why would Wayne—?"

"Compromise his working relationships like that?" Rader sighed. "You obviously don't know Wayne. Beneath the rational exterior lurks quite a gambler. We really are getting far afield though, aren't we? What are we supposed to be talking about?"

"What did Sinc think about Ben Mitze?"

"I don't know. Sinc never talks to me. Maybe he knows the ancient history between his dad and me. The most I've ever gotten out of that kid is a limp smile."

"Did Sinc dislike Ben Mitze?"

"Because of jealousy for Taylor, you mean?"

That was not what Bobbi meant, but she nodded.

"The kid's a cipher. I don't know." Carol was definitely ready to end the conversation. Her fingers hovered over the telephone buttons.

"The night I picked him up for speeding, he acted pretty wild. Cussed me out. Said all kind of things to me."

"Maybe he should speed more often."

"Have you noticed him being depressed?"

"You have quite a psychiatric bent. You should hang out a shingle."

Again Bobbi said nothing. She waited. It was ten seconds before Carol went on.

"Look, if my father acted the way Sinc's does, I'd be depressed, too."

"Why does the kid work here? Does his father make him?"

She shook her head and answered another inside call. "Carol. . . ." She listened for a half minute. "We disconnected them, Arn. That's impossible. . . . All right. Okay. Okay. Look, I'll see you."

She hung up. "Well, Bobbi. Our bank that we totally disconnected and sterilized just went down again."

"How?"

"Don't ask me. I do need to go to work. It's getting ugly out there."

On the way back to her office, Bobbi came across a group clustered around a note taped up next to the library door:

Stockholders of DataForm:

As most of you know, a number of our clients are having control problems. The situation has so far not offered any easy solutions. Our primary concern is that the time frame for corrections is limited, and the company's reputation could suffer substantial problems that would be hard to rectify.

There is no question that we are in a difficult time.

I would be less than honest if I promised that remaining in an ownership position at this time is a safe bet. There is no question that it is something of a gamble. I am personally willing to take that gamble, and although I do not expect all stockholders to do likewise, I encourage you to try to have confidence.

However, the choice is yours. If you have questions, please see Marilyn. She will be in her office until 11:00 P.M. It is imperative for us to have a clear equity picture as soon as possible.

Wayne McNear

During the rest of the day, Bobbi was repeatedly called away from the video monitor to handle crises in the building. She kept thinking she was going to nail this down—kept *feeling* that she was—despite the fact that she really wasn't making progress.

By 7:30, she was beginning to wonder if it mattered who'd sabotaged the tapes. She had the feeling she was in a sinking ship. In the late afternoon, everything was going wrong, the place fallen into complete turmoil, discussions and arguments going on everywhere from the executive offices to the parking lot. Two of her young guards from Markham Security simply walked off the job. Real security was out of the question until Jim Daly and the others got back from New York.

Bobbi almost looked forward to Ron Reed arriving, since—if nothing else—he'd scare people into cooling it. It had become a matter of basic order.

A strange quiet fell as word began to spread that "the upper-level people" were selling out. The official word from McNear's office was that the Assembly would soon be lined up and ready to disable the satellite's operating system. But his encouragement to keep the faith had the opposite effect. The few people at Marilyn's desk quickly became ten, fifteen, and increasing. Thurmon was the second executive, after Mike Heyer, to break from the fold. To Bobbi's surprise, Joe Peets, the statistician, was next. Rumors and counter-rumors were flowing around the building like a bizarre weather system. As shift change neared, the trickle of sellers had become a surge, now a wave.

The line at Marilyn's desk, itself, wasn't creating any particular problem. People were melancholy and mostly silent, trooping up one by one—execs waiting their turn with hourly workers—to give up equity in the company for money. But shift change was a catastrophe trying to happen. A bunch of the previous shifters had to stay, and Bobbi had to hold the entire incoming crowd in the lobby until she found out from Janet who should come on and who should take the night off. This group was even edgier than the ones who'd been around all afternoon, and she found herself acting more like a civil defense worker and less like a security supervisor by the minute.

Bobbi had to clear out the parking lot three times because of off-shift workers hanging around, gathering in big groups. To a lot of them, DataForm was their savings accounts, the futures they'd been working toward. They chased Bobbi down with questions. They had worked hard for their little bundles of stock. Typical holdings were worth eight or ten thousand dollars at McNear's present offer, although some of them, like Sarina Shores, held as much as two thousand-plus shares, the fruit of years of bonuses and stock-compensation options. Several of them asked her outright whether they should sell or stick it out.

Doggedly, she continued to return to the security-room monitor and look at tapes, trying to come up with an answer to the sabotage problem, but she was running out of steam. She looked up from the video screen, and Ron Reed was standing there looking at her.

"You're back. Hello."

He disappeared without a word, which made her wonder if he was real.

She had to get away from this place for a while. Looking one last time at the tape of Sinc stopping at the bathroom, she noticed the awkwardness with which he pushed the tape cart away from the wall when leaving—moving it backward and forward three times.

She turned off the video machine and went to the hall where he'd parked the cart, examined the wall, knocked on the door, and went into the men's room.

She checked the stalls and poked around the pipes. Then her eye caught an electrical outlet that ran up from the sink cabinet, which abutted the corridor wall of the bathroom. She opened the cabinet. At the front of the dusty shelf were three old cartons of cleaner. She moved them and, peering inside, saw a second outlet from the electrical line, and, at the back of the deep shelf, something that looked like a big clothes iron with its flat against the corridor wall. She reached back and plugged it in. It gave off a slight hum, undetectable when the cabinet was shut against the sound of the bathroom's fluorescent lights.

She took it out and stood there, her heart pounding. It was a degausser—a tape eraser—about twice the size of the one the professor had shown the security class. The level of the cabinet was perfect for the bottom row of tapes on the cart just on the other side of the thin wall. All Sinc had done was go into the bathroom, plug it in, then leave the bathroom and walk the tape cart back and forth a couple of times against the wall, thus demolishing the magnetic patterns on the tapes. Later he would doubtless return to the bathroom to unplug the degausser.

She had her saboteur.

A line of about a dozen assemblers, talking in undertones, stood waiting at Marilyn's desk. She was handing one of them a check.

"Mr. McNear here?"

Marilyn looked at the tape eraser with a little puzzled frown. She buzzed him. "Bobbi Reardon."

When Bobbi walked in, she almost tripped over the printouts running across the floor. McNear's whole office was covered and draped with double rows of printout paper. Amidst it all he sat at his desk, checking with a pencil on first one sheet, then the other. He didn't look up.

She set the degausser in the middle of his desk on top of the printouts. "Sinc Heyer."

He looked at it a minute, then looked back at the printout. "Did you catch him with it?"

Bobbi explained how she'd found it. "The ARPs were only part of the tapes he went after. His target wasn't specifically them or triple reds, but everything with the yellow origination code. He was destroying everything in the library that came from Ben Mitze."

Still hunched over the printouts, looking at the tape eraser, he said, "Too bad he didn't succeed."

"Pardon me?" McNear's response, his expression, weren't what she had expected. He seemed totally lost in thought.

"Is that the letter from Ben?"

"Part of it," he said, jaw muscle tensing.

"You've trans—"

Seeming to rise up, to be lifted by some force, McNear picked up the degausser and stood up, and for one amazed moment she thought he was going to throw it—at the wall, at her, she didn't know where. Instinctively, she moved back a step.

He glanced around his desk, slowly setting it back down. "It doesn't matter," he said vaguely. "We're in good shape. . . ." Then he looked up. "Govind Shaw's in town." He started to say something else, but his inside line rang. "McNear. . . . No, Tony. Absolutely not. Do *not* send until I order it. Just take a break now. . . . Look, if you don't think I'm being realistic, Marilyn is ready to write you a check. At the moment, I'm not in the mood for *any* shit." He hung up. "I have to get back to control."

She was at a loss. "I keep feeling like I'm missing something. Didn't you want to find out who was sabotaging those tapes?"

"It doesn't matter. We've got the Assembly put together now. We're ready to get it on the satellite."

"There's something wrong with that kid. His face . . . he looks like he's got some terrible thing—"

"My daughter has a serious problem, Bobbi. It's not something I have time to go into. Sinc has taken the whole thing on himself."

"Why?"

"Because he's in love with her."

She looked skeptical.

"Don't you believe children can be in love?"

She was suddenly tongue-tied.

With an edge in his voice, he said, "There's nothing like it. Nothing in the world. Don't you remember?"

She tried to smile.

"I'm worried about her now, in fact. Mrs. Vale quit. She's already left the house. And we're having a meeting out there at midnight. Could you come out and keep an eye on her? The others will have plenty of security, but I don't want them anywhere near my daughter."

"Others?"

Moving his chair back and forth, he looked at her. "We're going to pull out of this. No matter what. There's no way we can't." He got up and, stepping on printouts, walked out of the office.

Bobbi went back to her office and again called the station, asking for Ray. "He's not here," Parker said, sounding strained. "I have no idea where he is."

She called Outlaw's.

At the moment Ray answered the phone, she remembered his spiral notebook, and opened the bottom drawer to get it.

"Hello."

"Ray? . . ."

It was gone. She searched around the drawer, slid it shut, and quickly opened the others. It was nowhere in her desk.

28

They met in the Candlelight Lounge, a bottle club in the "ghetto," a six-block section of Dubois across the railroad tracks from downtown. Ray was a friend of the proprietor, Jim Naylor, and one of the few whites in town who was welcome there. Naylor was a three-time ex-con Ray helped extricate himself from legal hassles of the kind bottle clubs always got into, who sometimes returned the favor in the form of information. The club was quiet tonight, with only three other tables occupied, yet all of them had lighted candles on them. An old man sat near the open door casually playing a guitar.

"Hi, Bob."

"You look terrible."

"Well, you don't exactly look like Marilyn Monroe."

"Marilyn Monroe was a blonde," she said, settling into the booth. Despite what she had to tell Ray, she felt relieved sitting here—away from the nervous, fluorescent halls of DataForm.

In the candlelight, his face really did look terrible. A couple of bandages had come off, showing little puckering wounds on his neck and forehead.

Mr. Naylor came over to their table making a high sign. "Well, well. Nice to have you folks with me."

"Pardon my outfit, Jim," Bobbi said. "I won't scare off any customers, will I?"

He looked at her uniform. "Ohh, the lady's just off work!"

"I'm never off."

"Would the lady and gentleman like for me to set them up?"

Ray patted his coat. "Jim, I—"

"I assume that was your bottle I noticed behind the counter," Naylor said, delicately breaking the law.

"Yeah," Ray said, "sure. That's mine."

"Now was that bourbon, Scotch, or—"

"Have a bourbon and water, Bob?"

She nodded.

"A water and a straight-up, Jim. I owe you one."

Ray gazed at the old guitarist and sighed. He didn't seem too anxious to start talking, and Bobbi got the feeling he was under the same odd little spell of relief she was. Jim brought their setups and bottle.

Ray poured for them.

Bobbi sipped hers and frowned at the glass. "I have to confess something. I lost your notebook. I took it to work this morning. Put it in the bottom drawer of my desk . . ." She frowned and ran four fingers up and down her forehead over her left eye, which had developed a headache.

"You okay?"

"Just tired. Have you seen Richard?"

"I believe he's with Cathy."

"Where else?" she sighed.

"Tell you the truth, I haven't been in very good touch today. I think I got fired, Bob."

Bobbi had assumed she was incapable of being surprised at this point, but this was somehow the most amazing piece of news she'd heard all day. Ray explained a little of what happened and then circled back to what was on his mind. "I don't really have enough on it yet, but those stripyard hillbillies I ran up against may have been the ones that hit Mr. Cady."

"Why do you think that?"

"Because they were just too jittery. And they've got one hell of a big dog out of there. It may be the one that was taken from the kennel."

"They sound pretty stupid for hit men."

"Whoever hired them is stupider." Ray frowned into his glass. "You know, Bob, for a while I was thinking this whole thing was cool and collected. More and more, I'm getting the feeling it's out of control. I have found out one thing. The 'Mike' they told me about *was* Mike Heyer. He's definitely Warnke's contact. I took off my shoes and eavesdropped on a conversation between the two of them late last night at the station."

"I can tell you something else about him."

"What's that?"

"He's apparently quit DataForm. He bought himself out. Walked out the door with a cool three million dollars." She told him, briefly, about the problem with clients, and the stock offer McNear had made.

"All this has already happened?" Ray asked.

"Two banks are down. The other two will probably go down sometime within the next twelve hours. One of them—called Corning Trust—keeps going down no matter what they try to do to fix it. There's also a big medical center and a manufacturer that are threatened."

Ray squinted at the candle flame. "Why's McNear buying DF stock if they're in that bad a shape?"

"It's a display of confidence. The whole company's running scared. He's trying to keep them from falling apart."

"You don't sound so sure."

"Not very sure what you've been doing either, Ray."

He looked at her with sudden frowning intensity. "Heyer and McNear don't like each other—you pretty certain about that?"

"They've been tearing each other's throats out ever since I went to work there. People start running for the doors when they come in the same room."

"Funny. I had Marty check up on Heyer's and McNear's finances."

Bobbi's expression hardened a little at the mention of Ray's lawyer.

"Nothing too unusual about Heyer. McNear's a different story."

She took a drink. "He's well off. Everybody knows that."

"Yeah, he's well off all right." Ray watched the old guitarist get off his perch and go out for a cigarette. "Maybe you heard something about this. Eight months prior to her divorce, Cindy McNear's parents died suddenly in an airplane accident. She was an only child, the only beneficiary, no trusts. McNear's lawyers did a fine job in those proceedings. They won a jurisdiction dispute so the divorce would take place not in Arkansas but in California, in a district where the judge was known to be a strong enforcer of the mutual-property law."

"Divorce can be rough."

He cupped his hands around the warm candleholder. "They had a big custody fight, and basically he won that, too. But the way Marty read it, that part of the suit had a lot to do with McNear taking home the money. There was a bunch of stuff in the proceedings about the girl having mental problems, and the lawyers wrangled it around to blaming it on the mother. All this added up to about fifty million dollars for Mr. McNear."

Bobbi refused to be impressed by this information. "That's the way divorces go, Ray. Some people divvy up the refrigerator and Chevrolet, and some divvy up a hundred million dollars. What are you trying to say?"

"Mike Heyer *and* his wife were principal witnesses for McNear."

"Well, they *were* best of friends. I already knew that. And Taylor apparently does have a serious problem."

"What is it, Bob? Why were she and the Heyer boy at that trailer the night Mitze was killed?"

Bobbi looked away from his face—over at the bar, where Jim was putting glasses up on a shelf. She remembered Taylor that night. She looked back at him. "You think they were *at* the place?"

He leaned over the table a little. "I think Taylor got electrocuted when Mitze did. That explains why she was so druggy-acting when you picked her up. It may also explain why they were driving so fast. They were running away from something.

"There's an electrical hookup into that trailer that I was dumb enough to find out about the hard way. I had Outlaw take a close look at it. We've been watching this damn thing for six months, but we weren't supposed to go inside the fence. The hookup is a big son-of-a-bitch cable just the other side of a transformer that steps down power from that high-power line to Little Rock. We're not talking about home-service voltage. It's hooked to some kind of industrial switch sitting under one end of the trailer. The switch is operated by a line grafted onto one of the wires between two parts of the computer inside the trailer. John doesn't know how the computer works, but he says it's nothing but a simple electrical switch that trips on when power comes through that particular wire. That's it. He said the whole thing looks jury-rigged. It's not a sophisticated alarm system but a booby trap."

The candles in the room flickered with a gust of soft wind coming through the opened door.

Bobbi glanced around the room, feeling a little sick to her stomach. The shadowy quietness of the club . . . sitting here with Ray . . . She was thinking about what Carol Rader had just told her about Taylor and Ben Mitze.

"Got a cigarette?"

He gave gave her one, and its tip shook as she lighted it with the candle. "You seem to have scared up quite a bit of information," she said. "Did you know that McNear and Mrs. Mitze were having an affair?"

He was still for a moment. "Before all this started?"

"A good while ago, yeah."

"What about after her husband's death?"

"She cut him off."

"How do you know?"

"I've been asking some of the same questions you have. This isn't necessarily reliable, but the word was that Liz wouldn't see him. Wouldn't even let him in her house."

"Do you know what happened to all the tapes that were in the basement out there?"

"Why?"

"They've been completely cleaned out of the place. I tried to ask Miller about it. Of course, he won't talk."

"They're using the tapes out there now. But if you're thinking of that as a motive, Ray, it's common knowledge. . . . The whole place is working with them. Nobody in their right mind—"

"What are they for?"

"It's a program Mitze wrote—what they call a 'poison-pill' assembly—to mess up the operating systems of snoopers. They're gonna try to use it on this satellite."

He chewed on a thumbnail for a second. "I talked to it this morning."

"You what?"

"I went out to Mitze's house early this morning, after Nelson finished with me. It was still dark. Must have been four or four-thirty. All the tapes were cleaned out but the computer equipment is still down there. There was something on the screen about 'feeding.' I wrote some of it down, but . . ." Ray looked out the open door. He was searching his memory. In the state he was in, a little bourbon had gone a long way.

"I'd type in something and directly it'd type back, like a person. But it doesn't understand misspelled words." He looked at her quizzically. "It asks for stuff."

"What stuff?"

"Hell, it was a bunch of Swahili to me. But if you don't give what it wants, it says it's going to *make* you give it. Make you feed it. What the hell kind of setup is that, Bob?"

A chill came on Bobbi. The more Ray said, the more baffled and fearful she became, but her instinct was not to admit it. Ray really looked bad. She had the urge to reach across the table and straighten out his hair, which went in all directions. "You're fading, Ray. You need some rest."

"All this computer crap confuses me. I can't think that way." He looked her full in the eyes. "But I've never seen anything like this. First I get put on a special operation that doesn't smell right. Then I find out the chief of police covered up the location of a death. Then somebody who knows about that location 'commits suicide,' then the *wife* croaks pretty much the same way the husband does. You know, at this rate, we're going to hit the records on per capita suicide. Then I run across the fact that the son of a bitch is getting bribed."

"Which son of a bitch?"

"Warnke."

"Boy, you are full of news tonight. What bribe?"

"Try a $500,000 house in Florida."

"Who—?"

"Same contact man. Mike Heyer. Damnit, Bob, that ain't agency money. Any agency. It's too much. And there's only one person in town who's got that kind of money."

"The federal government owns all kinds of houses in Florida, Ray. They get them free. All they have to do is find little sacks of white powder in them."

She noticed the guitarist hurry through the door and speak to Mr. Naylor at the bar. She put out the cigarette. "I have to work again tonight. I'm already late."

"Don't go back out there. Get out of town. Go somewhere."

Bobbi shut her eyes. "You can't just *tell* me to do that, Ray."

"You have the divorce, Bob. You got it. You won. You understand? There's nothing to resist. I'm made out of air." Suddenly, Ray grabbed at her arms and held her tightly across the table with both hands.

Naylor was beside them. "Andy says there's a beep of some kind coming out of your car."

Ray groaned. "Thanks. I'll be back in a second, Bob."

He got up and headed out the door to answer his radio.

She put ten bucks down and slipped out.

29

It was Outlaw.

"Got some funny stuff going on."

"What's the trouble?"

"We got problems. We need to talk."

"I'll be there in ten minutes."

Bowser met him at the door with a pistol and a scowl. "If it ain't Frankenstein."

"Hello, Bowz."

"Notice how popular our little burg suddenly is?"

In the kitchen, under one light bulb, Outlaw was huddled down with the radio, fiddling with the frequency selector. An oscillating fan on the old refrigerator pushed currents of sluggish air through the room. The fish tank was lit, with little strands of wall-attached spiderweb floating languidly above the bubbling water.

Outlaw kept his eye on the selector as he went through a cluster of scrambled signals. "Busy town tonight."

Bowser remained in the doorway, leaning back against the jamb.

Outlaw gestured for quiet. Coming from the radio was an eerie, complex digital melody lasting a few seconds. "What is that? I've been getting it everywhere."

"It's an orienting signal," Bowser said, as if they'd already been talking about it. "Some kind of navigation bullshit."

Outlaw shook his head. "An orienting signal all over the dial?"

"You can't tell about radio signals, man. They'll do anything. I had a toaster once, picked up shortwave."

Outlaw kept fiddling with the dial, avoiding Ray.

Ray sat down in a chrome and plastic chair across from him. "So what's up?"

Outlaw glanced at him, scooted out his chair, and got up to retrieve a beer from the squat old Kelvinator. "We have some bad news," he said quickly.

Ray looked for a cigarette.

"Jim Daly bought it."

Ray stopped, the cigarette half-raised.

"Car accident. Driving home from the Little Rock airport. It was on dispatch maybe thirty minutes ago."

"Was he by himself?"

"I think so. I don't really know that much about it yet. It happened north of town, in the hills—there before it levels down into the Trois. He'd just gotten back from New York. His flight had come in less than an hour before it happened."

Ray stared at him. "What else?"

Outlaw shook his head. "That's all I got from the radio traffic. He must have driven from the airport right through town, apparently didn't even stop to see Martha."

Ray searched his pockets for matches. "Who was on the flight with him?"

"I don't know."

A book of matches plopped onto the table in front on him, pitched by Bowser, which he stared at a moment, queasy in his gut. Poor Martha.

"Anyway, Warnke says he wants me and Bowz to stand by to 'ascertain the disposal' of the trailer, whatever that means. I don't know whether somebody's on their way to haul it out or what."

Ray scratched the edge of one of his eyelids, tried to compose his thoughts.

"Warnke called me into his office after I got back from checking that wiring. Said he'd told you I was supposed to have an appointment with him. He said you were out, Ray."

"I pretty much knew that."

"He laid it on pretty thick about you."

Ray smoked and looked at his old friend.

"Looks like he's firing you."

"That the impression you got?"

"Many have gone before," Bowz said with mock solemnity.

Ray stood up and walked over to look into the lighted, bubbling water. Among perch and catfish, one fiercely decorated red and yellow fish hung suspended near the center of the tank.

"So what's goin on, do you know?"

"I'm not sure, John, but I wouldn't do anything he says. Not at this point."

"Right, so I get fired, too. That'll make three of us. Man, I'm not into Central America. I'm into that cabin over there." He pointed toward the hillside across the pasture. "I've been sitting in a one-man fuckin tent for seven rotten months trying to make enough money—"

Still looking into the tank, Ray interrupted him. "The trailer is evidence, John."

"What difference does it make now?"

"How much did he offer you?"

An ashtray smashed into a wall.

Bowser said, "Cool it."

Ray looked at him now. "How close was it to a half-million dollars?"

Outlaw's jaw was clenched. "What do you mean?"

"This has all been for private concerns. Warnke's been taking it off both ends. He's taking big pay from somebody for services rendered, paying us with department money—"

"So *what!*" John banged his fist down on the table. "I'm workin blind, man. I'm following orders. Do you think I care where he gets his money? FBI, CIA, Drug Enforcement, whothefuck cares!" He got up and stomped out the kitchen door, cussing all the way upstairs, where he clomped around in his room, shaking the house.

Bowser loved it. He was laughing. Ray noticed he was a little drunker than usual. "Oh boy. Why am I plain old George? Why ain't I Captain George? Why am I a plain little George marching around, eating it for Captain George? I can just see that little weasel sitting down with somebody, saying, Yes I have excellent men, fine men, they do their work and keep their mouths shut—except, of course, when you ask them to eat some shit, at which time they of course open their mouths. Excellent men, sir, yes, the best. . . . And here we are doin it for him. Goddamnit, Ray, when you really get down to it, it takes balls to be a shitfaced, lying bureaucrat. It really does. Who is it? Who's he workin for?"

Ray pushed open a loose-hanging wood-framed screen and flicked his cigarette outside. He wiped the sweat from between his bandages with his sleeve. "Mike Heyer paid for Warnke's house in Florida. I'm not sure yet where he leads."

"Mickey was talking about him tonight," Bowser said.

"Mickey?"

"Old Bad Mickey Deale, you remember him. He was buying at the Cherokee early this evening. He'd just sold out his stock shares at DF. He'd gone and cashed the check, had eighteen big ones in his pocket. Poor sucker's been poundin that keyboard four years so he could be rich a few nights."

"Sold them to who?"

"The big cheese himself, McNear. He's buying out everybody that wants to sell. They think he's out of his skull. The place is sinkin, man. Down the tubies. That's what Mickey says." Bowser smiled limply. "He says forget it, they're down for the count. He's taking his eighteen zeroes and fuckem."

Outlaw tramped back down the stairs, shoulder holster and boots on, glaring at Ray as he came past Bowser. He got shells out of the drawer and loaded his pistol, dropping extras into his pocket.

Ray sat down on the windowsill. "John, you can't do it. The trailer is evidence."

"Evidence of what?" Outlaw said flatly.

"I wouldn't touch it with a ten-foot pole. Warnke's been using us."

"Of what, Ray?"

"Help me."

"Help you *what?*"

"Jim Daly was killed tonight. This whole thing is out of control."

"You didn't know Jim Daly was dead until I told you!" He slapped the cylinder guard into place and jammed the pistol into his holster. "Ever since Bob went to work out there, you've been nuts—"

"Everybody who's had anything to do with that trailer has been offed, John. What makes you think we'll get out of it?"

"I'm not gettin myself fired," he said doggedly.

Ray stood up from the sill.

"She isn't doin *me* any good. She never did like me." John looked up and widened his eyes. "And you know something? She's in with them. She's in the big gravy. She owns stock in that company. She can sell out and go anywhere. Buy a condo in Colorado while her good-old-boy ex looks for a janitor's job back in Dogheap, Arkansas. If you cross Warnke, you sure ain't getting another job in law enforcement. No way, buddy. You know how to deal with the street clients, Ray, but that little prick pulls the strings. He can run circles around your good old head."

The little digital melody came out of the radio again, and Outlaw was quieted.

Ray looked at the radio. "Either of you seen my .38 shells?"

Angrily, John turned off the radio.

"How about you, George—you with me?"

Bowz looked at him gloomily. "Don't use that squirtgun. Here." He pulled a .357 magnum out of a drawer and pitched it to him. "Shells are in that drawer. I got another one upstairs."

"Fuck you both!" Outlaw said, and pounded the table. "You don't even know what you're doing!"

"I know where I'm going to start," Ray said.

He drove down obscure back roads to the hospital. It was a good bet that Bob would show up here.

He flashed his identification to the harried receptionist, and asked her if he could check the disposition papers on Jim Daly's body. The accident had occurred in the sheriff's jurisdiction but had been transferred to the police department. No autopsy had been ordered. Ray told the receptionist that was a mistake, but she looked at him dubiously. Ray had just been a patient here, under odd circumstances.

"There's nothing I can do about it, sir."

"What do you mean?"

"The body has already been transferred."

He went to a pay phone, called the station, and cajoled Parker to take a break and call him back from a pay phone.

He did so within five minutes. Ray could hear electronic games in the background. "Is there anybody near you right now, Parker—anybody within hearing range?"

"No, there isn't," he said grimly.

"I want an autopsy on Jim."

"Do the doctors ever forfeit the opportunity to do an autopsy?"

"Somebody filled out the papers no autopsy. They say he's already been moved. How'd this thing get transferred from the sheriff?"

"Officer availability."

"Who came out here and did the papers? The order's unsigned."

"I'm not certain."

"Come on, Parker."

"I don't know, I said!"

"Listen to me, honey," Ray said with vicious intensity. "An old friend of yours and mine is dead. Now tell me who came out here and ordered no autopsy."

Parker hung up on him. Ray waited around the phone nervously. Parker called back. "The chief. I'm sure he was only trying to be—"

"Was he at the station when this accident happened?" Ray looked at his watch. It was 1:16 A.M.

"When it was reported? I think so. This place is completely bizarre, I hope you know that. In thirty-five thousand nights—and I mean that literally—of working for this miserable police force, I have never seen anything like it. Officers calling in wanting makes on about a hundred rented cars, then Jim Daly, now you, now the chief sticking his head in every five minutes. He's pacing around over there *waiting* for something."

"We have to get Jim Daly scheduled for an autopsy, and it has to be in Little Rock."

"What do you want me to do about it?"

"Call Little Rock and get it initiated. Do you know where the body is?"

There was a long pause, and Parker said, "You damned bully. If you get me dishonorably discharged, if you ruin my retirement . . ."

"Where?"

Parker sighed loudly. "McQueety's."

"Be patient. One more request. Please put out an APB to pick up Bobbi. I think she's at the DataForm building."

"What for?"

"Her life is in danger."

"*How* is her life in danger?"

"Parker. Jim's dead. Bobbi's in the same danger. I swear to you."

"What's the *reason*, Ray? What, specifically, do you want her picked up for? I can't simply call out to 'pick up' somebody."

Ray was losing this one. He argued a little longer but Parker was adamant.

"I can't do it. And don't ever call me . . . that again."

At the trailer he walked in on his son and Cathy Lawes on the couch in an interesting posture, doing what they did most of the hours of the day and night. Richard was so embarrassed he went into the bathroom and remained there. Cathy seemed to think it was a good opportunity to show off her healthy attitudes toward sex—which were so irrelevant to Ray's concerns at the moment that it depressed him.

Draping Bobbi's old afghan over herself, she cocked her head sideways and smiled at Ray. "Well! Us kids get to have fun, too. Don't we?"

Ray was about to come around to Bobbi's opinion of Cathy Lawes. She was a little bit strange. "Guess what," he said.

She raised an eyebrow.

"You're not a kid, Cathy. You haven't been one for a long time."

She let the afghan fall a little farther off her shoulder. "You're certainly keeping strange hours."

Ray went and knocked on the bathroom door. "You got some clothes on, Son?"

"Just a minute!"

Ray waited impatiently, glancing through the hall door toward Cathy. After a minute, Richard came out wearing his mother's bathrobe, looking completely hangdog, and Ray took him off to the bedroom. "We got a problem. Do you know where your mother is?"

He shook his head. "I haven't seen her. Off at her job, I guess. That's where she always is."

"I'm worried about her. I want you to do me a favor. I want you help me look for her."

Richard was dubious.

"Go to the DataForm building first. She should be out there. Whether she is or not, call here and tell Cathy. Do you understand?"

"Yeah? . . ."

"I'll be looking for her, too. If I find her before you do, I'll call Cathy here and let her know. Any information you run across, leave it with her. Cathy's going to be our dispatcher."

"What are you worried about?"

"I'll tell you about it when I have time. This is pretty much an emergency, Son, but you stay cool. Don't drive fast and don't act strange in front of anybody. You're a young man now, so I can tell you the truth. Bobbi's in danger. It's too complicated to explain, but we'll find her. We'll do okay. Got any quarters?"

"Yeah." He looked embarrassed again. "In my pants."

"Okay, Richard. Let's find her."

er mind curved in and out of shadows, like the road, as she drove out to check on Taylor. The more she learned the less she knew.

"I haven't been taking, I've been giving."

Had Taylor McNear told her something when she said that? Bobbi had seen something in the girl's eyes that night, something beneath the apparent drugginess.

She turned on the police frequency, where Parker was being depressingly serious about some accident, and she quickly turned him off.

Approaching McNear's house, a few hundred yards from the driveway where the road went through a stand of tall oaks, two Mercury Cougars were parked bumper to bumper across the road. A man came out of the shadows to her window, wearing a lapel tag that said Security. "There's a private party ahead," he said with a smile. He was young.

"If it's a party, I'm invited. That thing you're wearing isn't very informative, mister."

Pleasantly, he asked if he could take her name. Less pleasantly, she told him, and he went off behind the cars and used a radio. There were three or four others lurking around the cars. Bobbi turned the radio back up and couldn't find anything unscrambled that sounded like them.

She turned it off when Security came back to her window.

"If you don't mind, I'll go with you to the house."

"What's your name?"

"John."

"Who do you work for?"

"Security."

"Whose security?"

He got into the front seat and the conversation remained uninformative as she pulled up outside McNear's driveway, which was full of cars. She opened her door and started across the front yard, John quickly beside her, grabbing her arm. She got rid of his hand, her expression saying, Watch out, kiddo.

"I have to clear you at the front door. Please wait here."

There were two more bluesuits at the front door, tougher looking, a little older, with the look, somehow, of Vietnam vets. Three others were visible in various places around the yard, all with radios. Upstairs, a light was on in Taylor's room.

"Thank you, Miss Reardon," John said, coming across the dew-wet yard. "You're cleared. I'm sorry for the holdup."

The suits at the door insisted on searching her. Bobbi wasn't wearing a gun—she seldom did in this job—but they made very certain she didn't have one concealed.

"Is this a date or a search?" she said flatly.

They didn't smile.

The house was strangely empty considering all the precautions outside. In the sunken living room there were some full ashtrays and a couple of jackets thrown over the back of a couch. She heard a phone slam down, then a loud racket, and found Reed in the kitchen bent over in a cabinet, crashing through pots and pans.

"Hello. Do you know where Taylor is?"

He scowled up at her. "I can't find a tray. Do it, wouldja. I got an emergency."

"Do what?"

"Drinks." He hurried by her, already on his way out the front door. "Downstairs. In the attic."

"I'm supposed to see about Tayl—"

"Take the drinks."

Pans were all over the floor and the cabinet was disrupted. A tray sat in plain view on the counter. She got together bottles and mixings, carried them down the carpeted stairs to the basement, and put the tray on the only clear surface she could find, an old controller with wires hanging out the back of it.

Disregarding the men, the attic was in pretty much the same shape as before—cluttered with dusty, unmatched computer equipment, some with skins off, placed helter-skelter throughout the room, connected by electrical cords that snaked around the floors.

There were ten men here, seven sitting at the big plywood utility table near the terrace-level glass doors, where the curtains were partly drawn. Three more security cops stood in different places around the room, all for the moment with their eyes on Bobbi. If the front door guards had been to Vietnam, these guys had been behind enemy lines. They looked very much alike, with closely trimmed mustaches and roaming, nervous eyes, on the make for trouble. A fourth one stood beyond the glass doors, able to see through the crack between curtains.

The seven at the table, all in expensive-looking business suits, sat uncomfortably on perches of different sorts, unmatched chairs, one of them on a low green footstool with a calculator on the table before him. A tape recorder sat on the table.

The DF contingent was McNear, Arn Bass, and—to Bobbi's surprise—a remarkably reasonable-appearing Mike Heyer. Bass was working on his little pocket calculator, while the man on the stool gazed nearsightedly.

Bobbi was amazed to see Govind Shaw. A big man in a gray suit sat with guys on each side of him who looked like lawyers.

They took note of her but continued talking. She rolled the "table" of drinks closer.

McNear glanced at her sharply.

"That's $22.50?" Arn Bass said, looking up from his calculator.

The man on the stool held up his hand, clawlike, over his calculator and after an almost theatrical pause made it dance a crowded little fast dance across the keyboard. "If your figures on capitalization are accurate, that's the correct figure at fifteen times revenues." He looked up. "Unofficially."

McNear shook his head. "This is a waste of time."

The others looked nervously to the big man. Somehow Bobbi knew who he was before he spoke.

"What are you looking for, Wayne?" Tom Ferris said casually. His drawl wasn't quite as pronounced as it had been in the telephone call she'd taped on the plane. He sat in a somewhat ratty green wing chair, and Bobbi guessed by the tension in his mouth that he wasn't looking controlled without effort.

"We don't want to sell," McNear said.

Looking down the table at Govind, who had a disbelieving, bitter smile on his face, Ferris said, "You want us to give you the entire specs—hardware, operating system, applications programs. Did I hear that correctly?"

"Yes."

Ferris leaned back in his chair and looked at Bobbi—gazed at her benignly, as if she were a statue or painting that he'd just noticed in the room.

"What's your reason for wanting the specs?" he finally said, as if asking her.

"It has to be stopped."

Ferris nodded slowly. "We're in agreement on that."

"Neither of us wants to enter into any ongoing cooperative arrangements," McNear went on. "The only solution I can see is that we get all the technical information, and work from there."

"We agree on that, too. But you realize we can't give you the specs. USI doesn't control all that, and I can guarantee there's no way Mr. Shaw has clearance to make such an offer."

McNear looked at Shaw. "We won't contemplate selling."

Tom Ferris picked up a pencil and frowned at it. "So we should just forget about it?"

"What?"

"Giving you 400-odd million dollars for an entity that's brought down thirty million gross its best year and at the moment has pretty dim prospects."

"Yes, we should."

Ferris sighed and looked back at Bobbi. His look of perplexity was ironic, as if he was humoring a child who had bumped into him on the street. "I'm still working on the logic of this."

Bobbi stood waiting, while the most powerful man in the industry, as she'd seen him called in a magazine caption, looked at her and finally said, with fake obtuseness, "Doesn't it seem a little strange to suggest that the *logical* way to work on it is for us to give you the specs? Something we developed over many years, at an expense of many hundreds of millions of dollars . . ."

"Are you responsible for it?"

Ferris paused. "As far as this discussion is concerned, we are—" The man beside him whispered something into his ear and he went on smoothly, "We're responsible for the hardware device itself. Mr. Shaw's people developed the system, as you doubtless know." He raised an eyebrow. "I'm sure you appreciate that."

"Appreciate what?"

The big man responded quickly and with a sudden forcefulness. "I'm not an entirely free negotiator here, Wayne. We are limited in how we can proceed."

Bobbi saw wary looks coming from Govind Shaw and a man beside him.

"Is the thing under your control or not?"

A bulky man with a sleepy expression looked at McNear with studied blankness. Shaw, too, was trying to appear blank, but appeared completely fascinated by McNear. He kept moving as if reminding himself not to stare at him.

"As I've indicated, we thought perhaps you could help us with that," Ferris answered.

McNear said nothing.

Tom Ferris didn't move. He sat as still as a tree, his eyes remaining on McNear. The room went entirely silent, except for wind rustling briefly outside.

After a while, Ferris took a deep breath and, looking at the table, said, "I'll have that drink, please. Scotch and water."

One of the security guards immediately came over and produced his own bottle of Scotch. "His brand," he said with a little smile, pushing Bobbi aside while another went off and returned with fresh tap water. Bobbi was taken aback by their precaution—who would try to slip something into his drink?

Ferris talked with one of the men beside him for a moment, who passed something down to Shaw, then Ferris said, "What kind of difficulties are your clients having? I believe you promised us some details."

McNear stood up and switched on a couple of scruffy-looking VDTs. They came up showing the menu that had been on the monitors in the control room, the number at the bottom of one of the screens was in three figures, the other two.

"This is Corning Trust, this is Gallaher Bank—both in real time, both stuck in a circuit-checking loop. We've concentrated our efforts on Corning. The error count is smaller here, because we've closed this computer down several times. We've restricted its telecom input, shutting down intercity wire, Fedwire, every combination of its six regular interactives. None of it works. If there's a way in, this thing finds it. The disabling commands have all originated at USI downlinks or USI numbers."

Arn and Mike Heyer looked grimly at Ferris.

"You say you've traced calls through Fedwire?" Ferris asked.

"Yes."

"Exactly how does a signal get from a USI downlink into the Fedwire? I'd like to know so I can send myself a couple million dollars."

Several of the men laughed politely. Govind Shaw looked too amazed to laugh.

"We obviously don't have a clear channel through Fedwire, but we can trace incomings to our banks by identifying the creditor bank, locating which particular call into the Federal Reserve system made the credit, then going from there. In these cases we found that at least one of these commands was originally packaged as several large wire transfers from USI numbers."

"Packaged?"

"This is something we just found out. The wire transfers were a Trojan horse, a way to get into the computer with apparently harmless stuff. They triggered a bomb—a simple circuit-testing program that was already lodged inside the system." McNear pointed at the screen. "That program is extremely hard to find because it's so short. We're guessing that it's spread around like pieces of a puzzle—a few lines here, a few there. When it's triggered, the pieces come together and use the logic already inside the addressing systems to start looping."

The bulky one looked at him sleepily. "You can't mask the diagnostic package?"

"This has nothing to do with the resident diagnostic package. It's not some utility function that you can turn off or on, or unplug the disk unit it's on. It's a loop bomb with total access override, and it's being emplaced through your downlinks."

"Where is this bomb located now?" Shaw asked.

"I don't know. It would take us two weeks to find the bits and pieces of it."

"The 'loop bomb,' as you call it, is an old program of yours, correct?"

"I said that at the outset."

"And you have no way to disable it?"

"The problem isn't just that it's there but that it keeps getting put there, and each time that happens, the facility has to be restarted. We've done total shutdowns, even left the facility wireless, and it crashes again. The last crash occurred after a total cold start—operating system, applications, data."

"So the bug is in your backup tapes?"

"We're not talking about a bug in our backup tapes. We're talking about your system repeatedly going after it. Do you understand? We can't leave a bank wireless. We have to find out how your system works. And we have severe time limits. The comptroller won't put up with this much longer."

"Have you talked to him?"

"Not in the last few hours. I don't want to until I have a credible plan."

Shaw looked at the tape recorder. "I thought you were telling us the circuit-testing program itself was being sent by the satellite, dynamically."

"It has been sent both ways, Govind. After we stripped the computer of connects, the bomb kicked in. The Trojan horse was constructed by certain wire transfers sent by—or under the guise of—USI accounting."

Ferris squinted at him. "Now you're saying USI sent a Trojan horse through corporate accounting?"

"Come off it, Tom. Office-products division, New Jersey. When it was still connected, the bank received several wire transfers in odd amounts—amounts that our banks' systems automatically flag and check."

"Want to explain that?"

"I'm sure you already know, but okay. This system flags account transactions of what we call funny numbers for manual double-checks. It puts them in a cache of flagged numbers that are printed out either periodically or when the cache is full. In this case, while the computer was still connected up, the cache was filled, minus one, with the number $77,777.77."

McNear found a printout sheet in a little pile in front of him and pushed it to the man next to him.

"Those facts are established; what I'm saying next is speculation because we haven't had time to analyze our reports. One more funny number came into accounts—which happens on an average of several times per batch job—this time while the machine was standing alone, reading in a tape of checks. When the funny-number cache prints out it also calls up certain basic information about the accounts involved—in this case the bank's own assets account. Somewhere in that interaction, a pattern developed that set off the bomb. That's what I think triggered the last loop-out."

The accountant looked up from the printout. "What happened to this money?"

"It was electronic money, into the bank's overnight account and the next day right back where it came from—to your office-products division—plus one-day's interest. As far as the bank went, except for the odd numbers, it could have looked like a normal end-of-the-day asset-filling transaction."

"How much money was this?" the big one asked.

"There were ten transfers amounting to a total of $777,777."

The big one added, "Corporate doesn't deal with this Corning Trust, and neither does Office Products."

"Our records indicate that they did last week. I'd advise you to check your accounting records."

"Why don't you check em for us, Wayne," Ferris said. "You seem to have pretty good access."

"The question isn't whether one of your divisions does overnight paper with Corning Trust; it's why your satellite is generating these transactions. We have tried a lot of things. We fed in new operating-system tapes. Even updated operating systems—which caused significant formatting problems. Every time we move, this thing comes up with a countermove. What I want to know is why and how it's doing it. Who's responsible?"

Ferris glanced at the printout sheet and dropped it on the table as if not finding it interesting enough to pass on. He gestured at the consoles. "So your company wrote this circuit-checking program, your company is responsible for the client, and you're 'speculating' that all the trouble's being caused by us."

"You sound like a lawyer doing a cross-examination, Tom." He indicated the tape recorder. "I have no doubt that recording is going to be used in court, but while we're still out of court, why don't you talk just a little bit about the source of the problem. What is this thing anyway? The satellite? What's it designed for?"

"What all do you know about our accounting procedures?"

"All we did was trace the call. That doesn't require a hell of a lot of proprietary information."

"I believe our account numbers *are* proprietary."

"Tell him how we did the traces, Mike," McNear said tiredly.

Heyer wasn't wearing his sunglasses. His expression was quiet and controlled, unlike what Bobbi was used to. She was pouring a drink for the accountant at the moment, and had to pause to take Heyer in. He was a completely different person. "The telephone company has a bunch of people on it. They're worried about wire fraud. They're doing it absolutely by the book. These particular traces are all clearly established. They're prepared to fully cooperate with this information."

At the mention of the telephone company, Tom Ferris shifted gears. "Don't give us that junk. 'The telephone company,' as you call it, is a direct competitor of ours now, not some pseudofederal agency. You're aware, of course, that we no longer have any active downlinks. We've temporarily shut them down."

"When?"

"Today."

"Good. You've recognized the seriousness of the problem. The only trouble is that there are over a hundred thousand downlinks in this country, and a lot of them could be used. We now have reports of two more banks down in New York."

"More of your customers?" Ferris asked ironically.

"No, they aren't our customers. We've never had any connection at all with them." McNear held up a *New York Times* that had been at his place on the table. The headline was at the bottom of the front page: FOUR LOCAL BANKS HAVING COMPUTER TROUBLE.

Ferris looked bored. "I've already seen your headline."

"Whose headline?"

"Shut off the tape recorder."

The lawyer next to Ferris looked worried. "Tom—"

"All of you! Shut off the tape recorders."

Two of the men at the table and one of the guards fumbled inside their coats.

The lawyer whispered furiously at Ferris, but he shook his head and fixed his gaze on McNear. He sounded more like the person she'd tape-recorded on the plane.

"Wayne. Everybody knows about your company. About your personnel. About this guy Mitze, who was a weirdo from day one, about your security men, and all the rest. It's all public. If you decide to get into a dogfight with us, you might shoot down a couple of planes, you might even fuck us up for a year, but I guarantee you'll be under the waves before the day's over and you'll carry all your people with you. We don't want that. We want to do this as quietly as possible. In a way you've already won, or I wouldn't be sitting here. But there are limits. You know what you're doing, you know it's old Tom Ferris looking at the balance sheet, figuring the briar patch against one clean fall and deciding to take the fall. I suggest we cut out the playacting, or we'll both be in the bramble patch. If that headline is any measure of what you have planned, I'll give us one chance, no more. I'll give us tonight. We either get our act together tonight or we give up talking and go to fighting."

McNear looked at him expressionlessly. "I won't sell. I want the specs, I want access to people who can tell me about this thing. And you're right. It has to be quick."

Govind Shaw said, tensely, "There's no way you'll touch the software specs. That's completely out of the question."

"You're not getting any of the goddamn specs," Ferris said. "I'll buy your company and your cooperation, but I want you out of the ball game."

The lawyer cleared his throat and Ferris added, less vehemently, "That's pretty much what we're looking at, Wayne. Now we can negotiate a little about the price, but we *have* to make absolutely certain that this problem is cleared up permanently. The only way we can do that is to own this company, one hundred percent. We won't talk on any other terms."

McNear continued to look at Ferris. "You're going to get a whole lot further with me if you admit your error. You made a terrible, primitive mistake. You put a huge-capacity interactive processor into space and you can't turn it off. Why? What is it?"

Bobbi thought she heard a sound—a low moan, perhaps a humming. One of the guards gave another a puzzled look.

Ferris shook his head. "I'm running out of time, old buddy. I suggest we talk in a smaller group. Head to head. We're getting nowhere."

McNear himself suddenly looked uncertain, and Bobbi wondered if he'd heard the same noise. He got up hurriedly. "All right. Please help yourselves to a second drink." He gestured to Bobbi. "We need to talk."

They walked out the back door toward the cliffs, the downslope of the yard carpeted in moonlight.

McNear spoke fast and very quietly. "Where's Reed?"

"He said he had an emergency."

McNear stopped in the middle of the yard. "Did he take Taylor?"

"Take her? I don't know. I didn't see her."

"She was acting funny. He was supposed to take her to the doctor, and she slipped away. These people arrived before he could find her. I think she's in the house. Find her. If you can do it without making a scene, get her out of here. Otherwise keep her in her room, and keep her quiet. The key's outside the door."

He turned and quickly went back inside.

On the landing below Taylor's room she heard sounds like echoes in the house. Knocking on the door, she saw a key hanging on a little wall hook. The girl was kept locked in her room?

Inside, she turned on the light. Taylor's room didn't have the usual teenage clutter. The only furniture was a large, low, upholstered bed, a nightstand, and a small television set on a wall rack like those used in motels. There was an intercom. The room was spacious, with a thick blue carpet, fixed windows looking on the front and side yards. There were no pictures on the walls, no posters, no old toys.

A car had driven up outside and from the window she recognized the Heyer family car. A heated discussion broke out somewhere below.

"Look, it's some teenager. He claims it's an emergency."

Bobbi looked up and saw a small attic entrance in the ceiling, its trapdoor not quite in place. A chair stood beneath it against the wall. She went over and climbed onto the chair, slowly pushing the trapdoor aside and sticking her head into the attic.

It was hot and dusty smelling. Vents on two gables let in triangular, barred moonlight, and after her eyes adjusted to the darkness she saw a shape near one of the vents of moonlight, like a rolled-up rug on the floor.

After no little effort, she managed to pull herself into the attic and, keeping her head low, walked toward the shape on the floor.

The girl was flat on her back in the warm dust of the floor, just at the edge of one of the patches of moonlight. Her eyes were closed, and she was wearing earphones, the bars of light cast across her body.

Bobbi spoke her name and got no response. She tried again. Nothing. She bent down and took off the earphones and Taylor's eyes blinked open.

"Are you okay?"

She lay there without replying.

"Your father asked me to come up. Do you mind talking?"

No reply. The earphones were large and heavy.

"He's having a meet—"

"I know what he's doing." Her tone was flat. One of her eyes was lighted by the moonlight. She reached for the earphones, and Bobbi gave them back.

"Listening to some music?"

"I'm not listening to anything."

"It's awful dark. Why did you come in here?"

She didn't answer.

"Mind coming back to your room?"

Taylor sat down on the edge of her bed. She looked out of place in her own room, hunched over, her eyes resting on the large, black, padded earphones, which she kept in her lap. Her shirt was a red and white puzzle. The long cord from the earphones went to the floor and all the way back into the attic.

Bobbi propped an arm on the dresser. "Is that a radio?"

She didn't answer.

"Mind if I listen?"

Taylor made no move to give them to her.

"What happened to Mrs. Vale?"

"She went back into history."

"You didn't get along with her?"

No answer.

"Are you mad at your father?"

There was a momentary flash in her eye, but she retained the monotone. "You aren't my psychiatrist."

"Are you seeing a psychiatrist?"

She fiddled with the earphones.

"Where were you before I picked you up that night for speeding?" Bobbi asked gently. "The night Ben Mitze died."

"Get out of my room."

There was commotion downstairs.

"Do you know what's going on right now?"

She looked at Bobbi tiredly, with apparent distaste.

Bobbi heard her name—Reed calling her on the intercom. She told him she'd found Taylor, and he asked her to come downstairs immediately. Cars were starting outside.

Bobbi asked the girl if she could get her anything. She didn't reply.

Bobbi stood for a moment on the landing, unsatisfied, not wanting to shut and lock the door.

She was about to, though, when Sinc Heyer came swiftly up the steps. He was sweating, his arms and face red. At the moment he hit the landing a single noise somewhere between a shout and a scream came out of Taylor's room, and then a low repetitive sound like Bobbi'd never heard before—low, mechanical, fast, and completely inhuman.

"Oh God," Sinc said, pushing through the door.

The door came open, and Taylor lay on her back on the floor, with her arms and legs jerking. She was wearing the black earphones.

Bobbi froze in the doorway.

"You should have taken them away from her!" Sinc yelled, pulling loose the cord.

For a moment he stood there with the gnarl of cord in his hand, looking at it miserably. "How did she get this thing?"

Bobbi went to her and took the earphones from her head, throwing them across the room. The girl remained in seizure, her upper body rising up and going down, the eyes ticking mechanically. Bobbi looked back up at Sinc, who was standing there shaking his head, looking completely miserable. "They shouldn'ta left her alone," he said.

Bobbi went to Taylor and looked closely at her. Always look first. The eyes, fully open, continued to click in their sockets as if pushed by springs and gears. A new surge of laughter started. "Huh huh huh huh huh."

Airways, Breathing, Circulation.

After the laughter stopped, the girl's pulse was high but steady. She was breathing okay, the eyes still open, floating now sightlessly. "Go. Hot. Hot hot. Yi year hot. Go lo lo. Go gago gago." Her hands rose up off her lap, fingers outspread, like a baby asking to be taken out of a crib.

Whatever was going on with this girl, or had gone on, she didn't want to remember. Reed appeared at the door. "We need you downstairs."

"Please call an ambulance," Bobbi said.

"What for?"

"I don't casually tell people to call ambulances. Are you going to do it or am I?"

"Is she acting weird again?"

"Oh not much. She just plugged her brain into the wall socket."

Reed showed no surprise. "So what's new. Look, I'll take her to the hospital myself. Mr. McNear needs a driver now."

"You drive him. I'll take care of this."

"He wants you." Reed bent over and picked Taylor McNear up like a sack of potatoes and without hesitation went down the stairs.

Sinc and she looked at each other. "Has this happened before?"

"Yes." He fell onto the edge of the bed and cradled his head beneath his arms, elbows on his knees.

"Why?"

"She wants to die."

"Why?"

"Ohh."

"Tell me what's going on, Sinc."

He looked up at her."She will, too. She'll do it. She'll succeed."

"How many times has she done this?"

Sinc didn't respond. Someone was yelling her name downstairs.

She went over and knelt before him. "Did she get that thing from Ben Mitze?"

He looked up at her, bitterly, with tears in his eyes, and said, "I don't know what to do. I'm only sixteen fuckin years old. How do I know what to do?"

Bobbi took hold of his hands. "I'll help you. I swear. If you'll just tell me what's going on."

"Tay and I—since we were . . . I love her more than anything. I can't *stand* this."

"What?"

He looked at her, his eyes steady despite the tears that were flowing out of them, and he recited, as if he had done it many times before, "I went to the trailer. I'd been there three times. I didn't like Tay going out there with him—"

"Ben Mitze?"

"He was sick. Really sick. He figured out how to get her. He figured out *just* what to do and he went after her. He did it like a *problem*. Like something to figure out. He did it for revenge on Wayne."

"You mean he was Taylor's lover."

Sinc took a deep, shuddering breath, glancing at the earphones. "Is that what you call it?"

Bobbi couldn't answer.

"The lights were going up and down. I knew something was wrong. I looked in and they were inside, they were on the floor, they were . . . naked." Sinc said the last word quickly. "Their bodies were jerking around on the floor. He was on bottom. I turned off the electricity. I went into the trailer and got her and I put her into the car. Then I went back in and put him into the chair. And I left him the way he was. I left him naked . . . the way he was. And I went back outside and I turned it back on."

"How did you know where the electricity was?"

"Oh, Ben was *nice*. He had showed me all around. He took Tay out there all the time. Made a big deal out of how he had cracked the

Godball. How he was in touch. How he had locked it down. How they were planning to do the most amazing thing."

"Why were you destroying his tapes, Sinc?"

"Because I hate him. I hate everything he did. And they don't know what he was *really* doing. They don't have any idea."

"Who?"

"My father," Sinc said through his teeth. "Her father. They thought he was working for them. They thought he did everything *they* wanted."

"So what did he do?"

Sinclair's eyes had focused behind her at the door.

She turned, and one of the two guards said, "Mr. McNear and Mr. Ferris are ready to go now. Mr. McNear wants his security guard to accompany him. Now."

31

Passing Richard near the old South Seas Tanning Salon, Ray waved him to stop. They pulled up together in the lot, parking driver to driver like coffee-drinking cops.

"She's not at the DataForm building," Richard said.

"When were you there?"

"About five minutes ago."

"Pretty sure about that? Did you go inside?"

Richard nodded. "I tried. There was a guy at the front door who was really weird."

"What'd he do?"

"He wouldn't let me in. He said he was looking for her, too. He said they needed her. Her car wasn't there. I went to the Texaco and called Cathy, like you said."

Ray gently slapped the outside of his door, trying to decide what to do next. He wondered what Bobbi would do now, and the question was answered as clearly as if she had spoken inside his brain.

"Tell you what, Richard. I want you to get out of town for a couple of days."

"Why?"

"I'm not real comfortable with the situation around here. Jim Daly was killed tonight, and I'm afraid it wasn't an accident."

Richard looked incredulous.

"I know, Son. I know. It's gotten down to clearing the area."

"Is Mom in danger?"

Ray fumbled in his wallet and handed across a few twenties. "You go to the lake, get hold of me at suppertime tomorrow at Outlaw's—"

The boy shook his head. "I don't want to leave."

Ray looked off at the DQ sign. "Richard, I can make a lot of mistakes, but if I was responsible for getting you hurt your momma would kill me. Then we'd really be in a fix."

Richard laughed. "We would, huh?"

He slapped the side of his car and gazed at Richard. "Oh boy, would we."

"I'm not leaving. I want to help."

He looked at the kid a minute longer. Then he took his .38 from the glove compartment and gestured for Richard to get out. He put the loaded gun into his hand. "You know how to shoot that?"

"Yes. You and Mom took me to the range about a thousand times. Don't you remember?"

Ray went over to the back of the building and dragged out a garbage can. "Let's see if you can."

"I can do it, Dad."

"See that garbage can. That's a man with a weapon and he's coming after you right now. What are you going to do about it?"

"We're in *town*, Dad."

Ray looked at him sternly, and he rolled his eyes and raised the gun and blew a hole in the garbage can, causing it to wobble around wildly.

"Now what do you do?"

"Say good morning to him?" Richard said, repeating the punch line of a story Ray had told years ago.

Ray laughed and, to the boy's alarm, came over and hugged him. "I love you, Son. Your momma loves you. We just don't know what to . . . what to do sometimes." Ray took a deep, shuddering breath. "I don't know where to tell you to look. Just prowl around. I'll take Cathy's telephone number from you and ask you to send her to her house. I don't think she ought to be at Bobbi's."

As they pulled out of the parking lot in different directions, Ray got Bowser on the radio. "Is the body at McQueety's?"

"I think so."

"Is anybody there?"

"Looks like it."

"I'll see you in a couple of minutes."

The McQueety funeral home was less than four blocks from the station—an elegant Victorian house in a semiresidential neighborhood with a blue neon sign in the yard. Run by two unmarried sisters,

McQueety's had been the established funeral home so long that "Gone to the McQueetys" was a way to say dead.

He and Bowser stood at a reception desk with a little bouquet of lime-green carnations sitting on it, ringing a bell. Margaret McQueety came out, the elder or the younger Ray couldn't remember. She smelled like she had just taken a bath in rosewater and drunk a quart of it. Her smile was measured and the set of her eyes promised sympathy if there was business to be done. "May I help you?"

When Ray told her he was here to take Jim Daly's body to Little Rock for an autopsy, the smile disappeared. "It wasn't sent to us as an autopsy hold. It was sent as a prepare."

"Prepare?"

"For burial."

"Have you already done it?"

Miss McQueety looked away with a little frown, reassuming some of the mystery of her profession. "I'm afraid we probably have."

"Can you please find out?"

She sniffed. "I am fairly certain the body is prepared for burial."

"Please stop the process. He's got to be taken to the coroner."

"Wait here a moment, if you don't mind."

Miss McQueety went into the other room and made a telephone call. Ray approached her, and she hung up without having talked to anyone, got up, and passed by in a cloud of rosewater.

Bowser remained standing near the door. After she'd been gone several minutes, Ray rang the bell on the desk again.

Getting no response, he went through the dark velvet curtain and back through a hall. A door marked Private: Employees Only was locked, and he knocked on it, at first tentatively, then more loudly. He used his pocketknife blade to jimmy the bolt and pushed open the door. The smell came across him—not particularly strong in the cool room, but a smell to remember, very distinctive—before he really took in what was on the gurney. The charred body was elevated at one end on some kind of drainboard with a pipe coming down to the floor from one end.

Miss McQueety didn't like being walked in on while she was in her shop. Her eyes widened in alarm. She was kneeling on the floor in a blood-spattered white smock, pouring blood from a bucket, a powerful light shining on Daly's remains. He was unrecognizable, without ears, lips, eyes.

"This is a private work area—"

"Put the bucket down."

"The body is *being prepared*," she hissed, still holding the blood. "We have no order for an autopsy."

"Put that bucket down on its bottom."

"Who do you think you are?"

Ray walked over and took hold of it, and for a moment was locked in a contest to wrest control of it from the outraged Miss McQueety. She was a big woman, long-legged and strong. He shoved her and took firm control of the bucket. "Who ordered this body to be prepared?"

"I do *not* talk with people *casually* in the work space."

Ray walked with her out into the waiting room. "Who ordered it? That thing belongs in a body bag."

"*Many* of our clients prefer that normal preparations be made," she said, her eyes flashing, "even when the deceased *isn't* to be viewed."

"Who ordered it?"

"The deceased's wife is ill. His employer informed me that they were taking care of the preparations. Now why are you asking me these questions? What right have you—?"

"Who'd you talk to?"

"Mr. Reed, Mr. Ron Reed, who was directly conveying the orders of Wayne McNear. Now I believe this is quite enough."

"Is that who you tried to call a minute ago?"

"None of your business. I don't take this kind of—"

"Have you got a refrigerated hearse?"

"No, I do not."

"Have you got a plastic coffin?"

"We have many types of coffins," Miss McQueety said huffily.

"Bowser." Ray glanced around a curtain, where Bowser was smoking a cigarette anxiously. "Would you mind running down to the 7-Eleven."

"What you need?"

"Ice," Ray said.

While Bowser was gone, Ray called DF. No answer. He called the hospital, and Bobbi had not shown up there either.

One thing at a time, Ray. Don't get derailed. Don't panic. Finish this job. Take care of the evidence. He made Miss McQueety help him put the body into a plastic coffin, along with the bagged organs and blood. She seemed to regard herself as a hostage, which was fine with Ray.

He had a black Cadillac hearse parked at the double doors in the rear of the building when Bowser drove up, and rolled out a gurney with what was left of poor Jim. Ray wondered what Jim had done to get himself killed. Maybe he'd asked questions about the trailer, maybe he'd refused to do something they wanted him to do. . . .

They opened the coffin, and together stacked it with ice. Placing ice around as gingerly as possible, Bowser quietly cursed and complained about everything but what was so terribly before him. "Fuckin clerk said he wouldn't let me buy twenty bags of ice, fuckin teenager, I hope the little fuckball gets robbed. . . ."

They finally shut it, shoved it into the back of the old Cadillac hearse, and slammed the door. "You know where the coroner in Little Rock is?"

"Yeah. I'll take it to Baptist. I know a couple of guys there."

"Make damn sure—"

"I know, I know. Autopsy," he muttered. "Shit, I'm going back to South America where it's peaceful."

Ray pulled into the twenty-four-hour station on Enterprise, just off the freeway within sight of DataForm. A new Dodge with two men in it was parked at the edge of the station lot. Three others were parked up and down the street across from the building.

He went inside the station and called Bobbi's trailer. Cathy was still there. She said Richard had been to McNear's house and seen Bobbi's car, but she wasn't there. "He said he went into every room and there wasn't a soul in the whole house," Cathy said. "What in the world's going on, Ray?"

"Where is Richard now?"

"I don't know. He said he was leaving to drive around."

Ray stood there a minute, looking out the window. He didn't like the idea of Richard walking through McNear's house. "Look, when he calls you again, tell him to go to my office at the station and stay there. And Cathy, I want you to go home now."

"Why?"

"Because it's not safe to be there."

"Tell me what's going on! Please, Ray."

The bubbly seductiveness in her voice made him angry—a violent stab of anger like a thrown rod in his tired brain. "You ever seen a dead person, Cathy?"

"Well, yes."

"I just saw one. Now get out of the trailer or you might be next."

Ray stood there a moment rubbing his eyes, trying to decide what to do next. He got a Coke and stood at the window a moment, looking at the men in the Dodge, then went off behind a snack counter and poured in some flavoring from his flask, bottle-to-bottle. G. K. Smith, the owner of the station, was working in the garage beneath a pop-up cab on a truck motor. Smith was a potbellied man who talked very loudly. He was widely known to retail pills, uppers, to truck drivers—a crime for which Ray personally had never felt compelled to go after him.

Ray walked across the greasy floor of the garage and stood at the cab. "What's going on, G. K.?"

Smith turned around with a ratchet in his hand. "Hello!" he said, his normal loudness reverberating in the big metal garage. "What you doing out here in the middle of the night, Ray?"

"Just trying to find some trouble to get into. I was about to ask you the same thing."

"Hell, I wish I knew. Trying to make some money, I guess. Get a lot of my truck traffic out here at night. What happened to your face?"

"Little shaving accident."

He laughed. "You must have been shavin with number-eight load. Somebody didn't catch you crawling out the wrong window, did they?"

"You're the third one to say that, G. K." Ray tried to smile. "I need to ask you something. But I want to ask it real quietly. There are some men in front in a blue Dodge, parked behind the Kennworth. Have any idea who they are?"

Smith shook his head.

"They didn't show you any badges?"

Beginning to look anxious, G. K. said, "It looks to me like somethin's going on down there—" He indicated the direction of DF.

Ray put his finger to his lips.

"It was on the radio."

"Radio?"

G. K.'s volume refused to stay down. "Something about banks being closed. Hell, I didn't know they owned any."

"When'd you hear this?"

"Didn't hear it myself. My nose has been in this pop-up all night. Somebody mentioned it."

"You got any pills tonight?"

Smith glanced out the door, suddenly afraid. He stood there with his ratchet scrutinizing Ray, then got down from the cab and went over to a work counter where he pulled out a can from among a bunch of parts. He showed it to Ray like a younger boy showing a big boy a toy— humbly but with a certain defiance. "You know, Ray, this freeway business is pretty rough. You guys ain't arresting me, are you?"

Ray stretched his neck and looked into the can, as if very interested in its contents. "Can you tell me which one of the people down at DF is the electrician?"

"Electrician?"

"Which one of them comes up here looking maybe for wires or clamps or switches, anything you might have in the way of electrical parts."

"We don't have much in the way of electrical parts, Ray. I have batteries. . . ."

"Think real hard. Back over the last few months. Any little parts at all. Electrical parts. . . ."

Smith stood there with his can of pills, shaking his head. "Naw. The only thing like that was Wayne McNear bought a battery ground wire off of me for his car. Believe I just gave it to him. That was sometime within the month. . . ."

Ray remembered the braided metal wire that had been used to bypass the circuit breaker in Elizabeth Mitze's hot tub. "Would you be able to identify it if I brought it to you?"

G. K. snorted. "Awful lot of ground wires in the world, Ray."

"Did you see him put it on his car?"

"Nope."

"Does he usually do his own work?"

"Not that I know of." Something occurred to G. K. "I do remember what it came off of, if that'll help you. That trashed black Volkswagen sitting out back."

"Okay. That's all I need to know. Don't mention this to anybody." Ray turned to go back across the garage.

"So you're not arresting me?"

"Like to, G. K., but I can't do it."

"How come?"

"Because I've been fired."

"Fired? When?"

"Oh. About ten minutes from now."

Smith stood there holding his can of pills, grinning uncertainly, as Ray headed across the concrete.

32

It was a little past 1:30. They glided toward town in the limousine, the agent driving at an even twenty-five miles per hour. He chewed a piece of gum every few seconds, like a timed windshield wiper. Bobbi knew now why she was here. Maybe she'd known from the moment she walked into the basement and saw that the feud between Heyer and McNear had been a setup, but the children had made it crystal clear.

Two cars were in front and two behind.

She had gone downstairs and taken McNear aside—into a bathroom—and as calmly as possible told him what had happened to his daughter. She said nothing about what Sinc had just told her. McNear's eyes froze on her. They became inanimate. He asked no questions. He said nothing but, "Ron's taking care of it. Ride with us. I need a witness. We're going to the building."

Yes, Mr. McNear, I am your witness.

In the outside mirror she could see two cars closely following them. This was McNear and Ferris's chance to talk, but curving slowly through the dark trees toward town, it was a showdown of silence.

Ferris finally spoke. "Why'd you come to this shitty little town?"

McNear said nothing.

"I suppose it's a good place for your kind of operation, isn't it? No gossip mill to bag you. We put our scouts out, Wayne, and discovered a few things about what's been going on here. It's all pretty entertaining. We know about your secretary. Must be nice having your own broker right there by the phone. She got quite a rep in Chicago."

McNear still didn't say anything.

"We understand, for instance, that she recently bought enough put options of our stock to fill up the south end of the Grand Canyon. You know, it makes me uneasy when I find out the guy across the table is making that big a bet against me off the table." Ferris paused, as if expecting McNear to respond.

He didn't. Bobbi turned enough to take a look at him. He sat wrapped in silence, apparently unhearing. Was he thinking about his daughter?

Finally, with some effort—as if forcing his attention into the present—McNear cleared his throat. "Did you ever have a time in your life when you were fully alive, Tom?"

"What's the question?"

"I mean all the way. Charming, young, twenty-twenty vision, a strong heart. . . ."

The driver glanced in the mirror. The two trailing cars were very close.

McNear spoke quietly. "A time when you felt good about yourself. There's always one time, isn't there, when you're perfectly young? Did it ever snow out there in west Texas?"

The driver was now looking warily in the mirror.

"Did you ever play with a girl in the snow, Tom? Go into the house where the older folks were? Drink tea and not be able to wait to go out again, or for the night to fall? . . ."

"We have business to finish before we start old home week."

"We never knew each other very well in the Valley, did we?" McNear went on. "You were always too busy getting useful information, counting coup, filling your quotas. But that was after you grew up and got realistic, learned the corporate life. *Was* there ever a time when you were young, Tom?"

"I'm not sure what this has to do with our problem, Wayne."

"Nothing to be 'realistic' about? Nothing to get except maybe into some girl's pants? Nothing to count? No airs to put on? Nobody driving the car hating you because you make five million a year and he isn't breaking forty thousand? Just . . . I don't know . . . the sky to look at, walking down a road, going to see a friend? I'm talkin about just being alive, Tom. Just being alive."

"I don't consider myself to have been more 'alive' in some dreamland of the past. My life is now."

"That's too bad."

Ferris paused, wary. "What do you mean?"

"Because I'm afraid you're a goner, Tom."

The driver pulled into a parking lot off the road and immediately seven or eight men from the trailing cars surrounded them. The driver lowered all four windows at once and said, quietly, "Precautionary."

They were in an old shut-down Dairy Queen parking lot, two miles away from the DF building.

Ferris's voice remained controlled. "What do you mean by that?"

"Why'd you put your J-junction up there, Tom? Why with the NSA? Didn't you investigate Govind Shaw?"

"Save that shit for your crowds. Stockholders don't pay for hardware development. Defense does. You know that. I inherited that fucking project."

"But you're responsible for it, aren't you? Shaw and his superiors arranged that."

"I wouldn't be here"—Ferris hesitated—"if that wasn't the case."

"So you understand, then. Huge loads of systems information. A memory that never forgets. Personal files? All in real time," McNear said. "You understand what that could be used for."

"It wasn't being used for anything. Not until they lost contact with it. It's an R-and-D-phase prototype. It was being *tested*. It wasn't set up to do any of the things—"

"Wait until tomorrow, when the media starts trying to figure out what USI put into the sky."

"That's what we're here to avoid. That's why I'm offering to pay you."

"Why won't you release the software specs?"

"Listen, old buddy. I'm not acting freely here. I'm under severe constraints. Under *no* circumstances will they allow me to release any code to you or anybody. If I wanted to, I couldn't. They're taking a hard line. They don't want me to buy you out. They want to come in here and take this place apart. They want to cook you in grease and feed you to the dogs. I'm the one who convinced them that if any cooking gets done we'd all get scalded. I have the acquisitions money. I can handle this kind of thing."

"So it's really your offer?"

"Goddamn right it's my offer. I want guarantees that you can fix this, but it's my offer. I'm the only one between you and the spooks, Wayne."

"You're a real friend," McNear said, and opened the car door.

Men parted as he walked across the potholed lot, stopping at the edge of it near a signpole. Ferris opened his door.

"Don't follow him," the driver said.

Another guard came over and spoke urgently to Ferris. "Mr. Shaw wants—"

"Keep Shaw out of here," Ferris hissed. "And all of you guys, keep out of my way. You understand me? All of you."

As Ferris walked over toward McNear, they fanned out. Bobbi saw gunmetal gleaming in the dim light. She got out and walked toward the signpost, and one of them stopped her.

McNear was leaning against the pole on one arm, looking off toward the street, a dilapidated, rusting ice-cream cone fifteen feet above his head. "How many hackers out there will have access to this thing?"

"We can't get access, and we built the fucker. Shaw's people can't, and they designed the program. That's not what I'm worried about."

"Well, I am," McNear said.

Ferris hesitated. "Then let's get to work on it."

"Your friends at the NSA figured out that the best source of information is from people, didn't they? All the people on the dark side of the world looking for access. You give me something and I'll give you something. Give me the following information and I'll give you *free* information, free access, perhaps even deliver encoded letters for you. Simple, isn't it? Swapping. Radio-free computer. Hey, how about a little more information. Give me just a little more, and I'll give you more—is that it? A confessional in the sky. A secret friend. Somebody to tell your troubles to. A way for even the seediest little miserable vodka-soaked bureaucrat to find power. All they need to do is get the connection. The word goes out among those who know. The initiated ones. Why, they could even play with each other, communicate in code, tell jokes, have keyboard love affairs. What can the establishment do when they find out? Why, nothing. Nothing until you deny it information. Nothing until you refuse to feed it. Then—somehow—it tightens up, doesn't it, Tom?" McNear sounded angry. "Is that the idea? An 'open data base' for the ten thousand secret spies on the dark side of the world?"

"The system is a prototype," Ferris repeated. "It was being field-tested. You know goddamn well they test fifty things for every one they use. How damn naïve are you, buddy?"

"Shaw cares very much," McNear said. "His reputation is on the line. It's always somebody like Shaw who comes up with this kind of thing. Loves to make big moves. Loves to go into a place and blow their minds. I can see him charting it, top down. Professor Shaw running through his vast knowledge: Historically, where do the great new moves in software development come from? From the anarchist underground of computer freaks, of course! The hackers. What have the hackers been into lately? Item: Networking, bulletin boards, free data bases. Question: How can I package this idea for the big players—?"

"Wayne. You can threaten my career and I'll still listen to you, but when you start preaching I draw the line. I haven't time for it. I'm not interested in your theories, I'm not interested in your philosophizing, I'm not interested in your advice. Start cutting a deal or we hang it up."

"It'd be a terrible thing to be remembered for, Tom."

Ferris didn't reply.

McNear stood there for a long time, silent. He appeared defeated. His head slumped down.

Finally he looked up. "You win. I'll sell."

"Will you accept the offer we made at the table?"

McNear said nothing for a moment. Then he walked by him toward the car. "Are you kidding?"

hief Warnke informed me that you've been permanently relieved of your duties."

Ray said nothing to Parker for a minute. It was surprising that he
would feel bitterness despite what he knew.

"Is he at the station?"

"Yes. He's been popping in here every fifteen minutes asking me to
do makes on all these rented cars in town. We've had a fire—"

"Where?"

"The Mitze residence. It was a total loss."

"Well, shit." One down. He just hoped that Outlaw and Bowser
didn't let the same thing happen to the trailer. Outlaw had finally
agreed to go along, but he wasn't happy about it.

He looked through the square of bulletproof glass in the dispatcher's door and had a sudden image of prison. Tiny room. He looked
at the clock: 0349.

"Did you place the autopsy order in Little Rock?"

Parker glanced at the door. "I placed it."

Ray went down to his office and got his pocket recorder out of a file
drawer. He tested the casette, turned it on, and slipped it into his back

pocket. He walked without hesitation up the stairs and through the polished hallway to Warnke's door, knocked, and stuck his head in.

"Chief, are you aware that Jim Daly was killed tonight?"

Warnke, who'd been bent over a file cabinet, pushed it closed and jerked upright as quickly as if he'd been poked in the behind. Looking toward Ray's midsection, he walked over and opened a drawer of his desk, yawning as he pulled out a pistol and shoulder holster and started fumbling it on.

His blue eyes watered. "Of course I heard about the accident."

"I don't think it was an accident."

"You and I need to have a talk, Ray. We need to discuss something."

Ray stood there, smiling a little, as Warnke began loading the pistol. It was a chrome-plated .45. He was obviously coming apart at the seams.

He kept glancing at Ray's stomach. "I'm afraid I'm going to have to let you go. Permanently, Ray. This has gone too far."

"John did mention you were a little put out with me."

Warnke's hands were shaking as he pushed in the hollow-nosed bullets. "So you did talk to John?"

"A little," Ray said quietly.

"Then you understand the situation as it presently stands." Warnke was trying to sound authoritative, but his voice wavered oddly. His expression was surreptitious, as if he didn't want Ray to notice, somehow, that he was loading a pistol.

"Do you mind telling me exactly what the problem is?"

"Lack of professionalism," Warnke said quickly. "The time has passed when we can—" he glanced around his desk as if trying to find the right phrases on top of it—"when we can be unprofessional. This casual approach to law enforcement will not do. That's the way it is, Ray. I'm sorry."

"Are you put out with me for reading the station paybook?" Ray asked.

Warnke's face shook with a suppressed yawn. "Why did you do that?" he asked, with sudden simplicity.

"Oh, I was just curious about why Mitze's body was moved, why it was misreported."

"Don't forget you've been making almost double-time now for several months."

"You've been making good money too, haven't you?"

"What do you mean?"

"Your new house in Florida."

Warnke started shaking his head. "Now that's exactly the kind of thing I was afraid of. You decided this was an opportunity for another one-man show, didn't you? Another Marty Spears case—"

"Tell you what," Ray said, in a little different tone. "Let's strike a bargain. You want to fire me, fine. But I want severance pay. Enough to sweeten up the situation some. Help me relocate. Get me out of town. Keep my mouth shut."

"How much?"

"Oh, not much. Fifty thousand will do it."

The chief forced a chuckle. "Afraid we're on a different wavelength."

"Did you burn down the Mitze house tonight, Chief? They got you doing that kind of stuff, too?"

Warnke sat there awhile looking straight ahead, silent. Then in a flurry of action, he jerked out his pistol and aimed it at Ray's head.

Ray smiled at him. "How'd this all get started, Chief?"

"Get out of my office! You're threatening me! It's obvious! Get out of here!" He picked up the phone and started dialing, then changed his mind and slammed it down. "That's too much," he said "Far too much. I'll give you some kind of—some kind of—professional severance pay. That goes without saying." His voice was rising, and he was still waving the pistol at Ray's head.

"It's not the severance but keeping the mouth shut that matters. You don't want me talking about how you've been using the resources of the police department for private gain, prevented three murders from being investigated—maybe even helped arrange them. Just so you don't do something rash, I want to let you know, Mr. Warnke, there's a certified letter that'll end up on the desk of the attorney general and the prosecutor if you make any mistakes right now. Lose your cool and pull that trigger, and you'll never see that pretty little house on the beach."

"Ten thousand," Warnke said breathlessly.

"Tell you what, I'll bring it down to forty if you'll give me some information. When did you start working for the folks out at DataForm?"

"You're lying. You haven't written any letters."

"Put the gun down."

Warnke cocked the pistol. "I know what you're doing. Take your coat off."

Ray obliged.

"Put it on the desk." Warnke patted down the coat, looking almost disappointed when he didn't find a tape recorder in it. "Twenty thousand."

Ray shook his head. "Let's just put it back up to fifty and forget it."

"Twenty-five. That's my last offer."

Ray thought about that and nodded. "Okay. You tell me the story without any fooling around and I'll take twenty-five. For each line of bullshit the price goes up five thousand."

Warnke went over the edge at this point. Ray had misjudged the power of his greed. His eyes again bounced across the top of his desk looking for what to do. He picked up his telephone and dialed three numbers. *"Dispatch! This is Warnke. Wiel has come in here acting crazy! He's attacking me!"*

Ray ducked in front of the desk just as the first shot came off. Warnke leaned over his sailboat, about to shoot him in the head, and Ray whanged his body against the desk, pushing him backward. Warnke quickly pulled off two more shots, one of which exploded out of the desk in front of Ray. He came around the desk and Ray scuttled like a crab to the other side. With the peculiar objectivity of the mortally threatened, Ray saw how funny this was—Warnke literally chasing him around his desk trying to kill him—but a third shot now winged his right shoulder, tearing shirt and skin.

Desperately, Ray reached up and knocked a metal paper tray at him as he pulled the trigger again, the hollowpoint exploding the tray like a bomb. It temporarily confused Warnke, and Ray went for him. The fingers of his right hand got to the barrel just in time, as another shot kicked up a piece of floor tile. Ray's hand lit up with pain.

He pulled the gun out of Warnke's grasp and swung it at him, hitting him in the arm. Warnke yelped and grabbed his arm, and Ray used the gun butt to move his nose to the left side of his face. Warnke stood there, blood spurting from his nose, saying, *"Ahhh!"*

Ray noticed that part of his little finger was missing, and it was at this moment, oddly enough, that he knew what his weapon was.

He kicked Captain Chief Warnke sir in the tail hard enough to knock him against his desk. He picked up the sailboat from the floor and jammed the pointed prow into Warnke's ass, causing him to scream terribly. Then he took the tape recorder out of his back pocket and placed it on the desk in front of Warnke's face. It was running.

"Now talk, captain."

It was nearly a half hour later when he was just getting the sheriff off the phone. ". . . No, Bud. No. I don't personally give a damn about the car-stripping operation. I give you my word it won't be mentioned. What I care about is you coming over here and taking authority."

Parker had been scared out of the building. He was walking, tentatively, back from the 7-Eleven lot, looking uncertain as Ray approached him and handed him the tape recorder.

"Parker, guess what?"

"Oh my God!" Parker stared at Ray.

"Do I look that bad?"

"What happened?"

"The sheriff is on his way over here. You've got a felony suspect in the drunk tank. He has a bloody nose. Don't let him out." Ray handed him the tape recorder. "Put that in the safe. I've got some work to do."

Parker looked stupefied.

"Don't worry. Sheriff Bud's coming to the rescue."

s they neared the DataForm building, the driver made security
checks on the radio, passed the building once, talking quietly into his
mike, then turned after a quarter-mile and came back into the driveway.

Tall lamps buzzed down on a lot empty of everyone except guards
in a gridlock around the whole area of the building. Bobbi hurried with
McNear, Ferris, and guards to a side door, where they were stopped.
One of the men at the entrance spoke quietly to Ferris.

Mike Heyer had gotten there before them. He hurried toward them,
a guard beside him watching carefully.

"Wayne, we got problems."

"Take it easy, mister," a guard said, easing between Heyer and
Ferris.

"What now?" McNear said.

Heyer—Bobbi now knew—was a good actor but he truly did look
disturbed. "The comptroller's office made a call-through and read a
prepared statement. Our three guys in New York are definitely being
shut. They're threatening to padlock every bank on our network.
They're afraid this will spread. They want to seal us off."

McNear was surrounded by guards. "Who's still in the building?"

"Marilyn's back there. Jeremy locked himself in his office. He says
you better talk to him."

"Is Reed back yet?"

"No."

"Okay, gentlemen. We'll go to the conference room. It sounds like we're running out of time."

McNear took Bobbi aside. "Go to Marilyn and ask her what the final picture is. She'll understand what you mean. I need that information immediately."

She didn't look him in the eye. She'd blow it if she did. She was a witness now—eyes, ears, a human recording machine. There were agents in the halls, all with radios. *"Pass, female, black hair, five-eight . . ."*

Marilyn had retreated to McNear's office with her typewriter. On the desk were stacks of paper, including one foot-thick pile of the blue stock certificates issued for bonus winners in the assembly room. The telephone, silently blinking, had been banished to a far corner of the desk. Beside the typewriter was a little cluster of medicine bottles. She looked at Bobbi, unstartled, eyes hooded by what looked like a headache. "You're not supposed to sell." Then she looked puzzled. "Is Wayne here?"

"He sent me to ask what the picture is."

"I haven't done a final run, but you can tell him the options are taken care of and we're looking at eighty-nine-percent ownership, something like that. I'm waiting for a couple more blocks."

So he owns the entire company now, Bobbi thought. She pulled up the console chair and sat down across from her. "Can I ask you something?"

Marilyn had started back with the typewriter. She raised her eyebrows without looking up.

"Who all is in on this?"

She reached for a medicine bottle, hands shaking a little. It was empty, and she opened a side drawer of Wayne's desk and searched around in it.

"Don't worry. You're one of the lucky few who kept their stock. You're going to be rich when this is all over."

"Why?"

She eyed Bobbi. "Why what?"

"Why am I one of the few?"

"Never been around big movers, have you, Miss Reardon?" Marilyn's smile looked bitter. "You took his daughter to the hospital one night. It appealed to his emotions. You were his hero. He talked about it for weeks." She shut the drawer a little hard and searched another, slammed it and opened the top one, shuffling around among papers, and found a tin of aspirin. "When you took Taylor to the hospital that night, you accomplished as much as I did in ten years of hard labor."

She downed the aspirin with a drink of what looked like cold coffee. "I've been buying this company all day. Amazing what people say when they turn in their dream. Ever notice that? Dreams are non-negotiable. Make it negotiable, and the dream dies. Some hate you, some feel guilty and make excuses. People who've worked here for years. Now's the big payoff." She looked at the stack of paper. "If I'm acting a little unprofessional, chalk it up to ten milligrams of Valium. Doesn't do a damn thing for the headache."

"Wayne's buying the company from his own people and selling it to USI, isn't he?"

"It's called buying cheap and selling dear. That's the name of the old game. Don't you have a message to deliver?"

"Did you know that's what he was doing?"

"Let me tell you a story, Miss Reardon." A little fire kindled in Marilyn's eyes. "This is called 'Why I Chose to Work Here.' In Chicago, I was good and people knew it. I had offers all over the place. I had *executive* offers at companies with big names. I could have worked for funds in New York or big traders in Chicago; I could have moved anywhere in commodities. What did I do? I came to the sticks of Arkansas and to work twelve and fifteen hours a day as a secretary.

"I'm not in love with him, so I must be working here for some other reason—maybe because in my imagination I'm a mover myself. Not a graph reader, not an analyst, not a basis-point shaver, but somebody who *moves* and shakes. Commodities—they're just people with habits, jerks, most of them. Wayne's different. He's a positioner, a real old-fashioned son-of-a-bitch capitalist positioner." She smiled wanly. "Have I known? No. Not everything. Not exactly. I don't want to. I just want to be here tonight." She put her palm on the stack of warrants. "Now take your message."

"Would you mind writing it down?" Bobbi's eye was caught by something uncovered in the top drawer as Marilyn scratched out the note. It looked like one of Ray's spiral notebooks. Very much like one of them.

She took the piece of paper from Marilyn and hesitated. "He . . . also wanted me to bring a notebook. A little one, he said, somewhere in his desk."

Marilyn looked down. "This?"

Walking past the control room, Bobbi saw two guards at the door and Mike Heyer, alone, inside the bright room frowning at one of the central consoles. So the fights between him and McNear had been part of the con to shake out stockholders. The conspirators were the two of them, plus Bass, with operatives on the periphery like Marilyn and Reed and Chief Warnke. And whether Bobbi had known about it or not, she was now an insider. Now, her own dreams were about to become negotiable. Could this possibly work? Would it appear next week in the financial newspapers as a desirable and natural business arrangement? She felt a strong magnetic pull toward her own dream, the private place she'd discovered in California. . . .

She walked up to the guard outside the conference room door and without comment held out her arms while he did another thorough body search, rising slowly up her legs and torso to her breasts. The notebook was in her back pocket.

"You can go in."

Bass, sitting at the end of the table talking urgently with McNear, got up and left when she came in. She took Marilyn's note to McNear.

"Please, stay until we've finished this," he said to her.

Of course you want me to stay. You know that I know. You don't want me out of your sight until . . . what?

Ferris could be heard cursing his way down the hall, and he burst through the door, sweating, his poker face supplanted by a look of astonishment, his accountant trailing behind him carrying papers from which he kept dropping pieces, Shaw following along looking sour and disheveled. Ferris put down his papers on the end of the table. "This really is it, Wayne. The son-of-a-bitch satellite is broadcasting. Your Assembly had better work."

McNear appeared calm now, but Bobbi saw a hint of puzzlement go across his face. "Ask Mr. Shaw about it."

"Wayne," Ferris said, in tired reproof, "Mr. Shaw and about a hundred others have been working on this problem for months. They can't get access. They've failed. Do you think I'd be here otherwise? What I'm trying to decide now—and I mean now—is whether to buy this deal and get the hell out of town before I end up in the fool's column of the *Wall Street Journal*. You know that. So just tell me now, can you fix it?"

"He's doing exactly the same thing to DF that he did to Simmons Paragon," Shaw said feverishly.

McNear looked at him with disdain. "You built your whole career on that little seed of an idea, didn't you, Govind? Losing your daddy's money became your obsession. I read your paper 'Open Access and the Degradation Factor.' The big boys must have found that real kinky—a way to destroy whole 'information ecologies' through the 'elegant, simple method of open access.'"

"You're a blackmailer," Shaw said.

"Just give the operators and programmers a clear channel into their own weaknesses—their envies, jealousies—and let them do the rest, right? Something like this could be used in a lot of ways." He looked at Ferris. "I can even see one of them that speaks Japanese. One that was controlled more carefully. Perhaps something interested in business information. Technology. After you got all the bugs out, of course. Had you thought of that, Tom?"

"You son of a bitch, don't push your luck. Now just answer the question. Can you fix it?"

One of the guards coughed and glanced at another.

"What was that, Tom?"

"Can you stop it with your Assembly?"

"I'm willing to try."

"Okay, here's number two: If it's going to come out that you set this deal up on purpose, there isn't a board this side of hell that'll approve an agreement with you. That's not going to happen, is it?"

"The man who set it up is sitting next to you."

Ferris took a deep breath. "This isn't going to be a dead issue. No way we can make it one. All kinds of analysts will be poking it."

"We'll have to cooperate closely on public relations, won't we?"

Ferris looked at him a few seconds. "You want cash?"

McNear said nothing.

"One share of USI for two of yours."

He shook his head slightly.

Ferris glanced at his accountant. "One for one. That's it. That's my final offer."

The accountant looked up from his shamble of paper and said gravely, "I don't know, sir—"

McNear waited, then nodded. "Plus full legal disclaimer as to responsibility."

Ferris took a deep breath and said, quietly, "Okay, Wayne. That's fine. Excellent. We'll write something like that into it. But lemme tell you a couple of things. The sole purpose of DataForm, from the moment you sign, is to stop the satellite. We'll work out some kind of bullshit for the analysts about taking over your assets, but once this is cleared up, this place is shut, buddy, and you and yours will have to find a new game. That'll be in the contract. That's what we're buying. And I'll tell you something more important: If your Assembly doesn't succeed in stopping it or if this leaks—either one, Wayne—there's no way the deal will come off. The deal is dead, you're dead, I'm dead."

The accountant looked alarmed. "Sir, that's almost five percent of the company."

"I know that. Write it up."

Shaw looked disgusted. "I won't be a party to this. Tom, you're just trying to protect yourself—"

"Mr. Shaw." Ferris turned toward him. "I appreciate your advice. But since our agreement ostensibly puts liability for this problem on us, and since I have been instructed by your superiors to negotiate this, I'm forced to make the decisions. Our lawyers are already informing me that the agreement has problems, but for the moment your boss has confirmed that it's up to me. And frankly, he is on his knees right now praying I do what I just did because if this doesn't get fixed fast, Mr. Shaw, none of us—not him, not you, not me, not anybody in a hundred feet of us—will be able to get a job in a chickenshit factory."

The accountant shuffled among his papers. "What about the outstanding DF employee warrants?"

Ferris frowned at him.

"Employee warrants. They have another hundred thousand shares outstanding—"

"Don't ask me about a fuckin hundred thousand shares of fuckin employee warrants!"

McNear gave Bobbi a glance and said to the USI accountant, "They're included in the price."

Ferris was looking at Wayne now with a tense, hateful smile. "I'm telling you one more thing, Wayne. I'm being serious now. You won, you've got your cheap equity. You'll own a lot more of USI than I do, but I give you my word, buddy, if you don't find a way to unlock that satellite before there's further damage to banks we'll throw a hundred lawyers at you. We'll go public with this shit, and you'll never see the light of day except when the jury deliberates."

McNear pointed a finger at Shaw. "I want the building cleared of him and his monkeys within five minutes. We do nothing until everybody's out and all the papers have been signed and delivered, by my lawyers, to a local bank vault."

"We can print out the contracts in a few minutes," said Ferris. "Let's get it done. I have a plane to catch and some talking to do."

Walking out, McNear stopped and said to her, "Please come to my office."

Bobbi stood there, while everyone but one guard and Govind Shaw left the room.

He's won. I'm inside and the door is shutting.

Shaw remained at the table, looking as if he didn't have the energy to stand up. Her hand went to her back pocket. She took out Ray's notebook, held it for a moment, and pitched it down the table. He looked at it without moving. "What is it?"

"Don't try to contact me now. I'll talk to you later," she said, and walked out.

Guards were rushing through the halls, doors slamming, as she headed for her office, went inside, and stood there trying to think. Her heart was beating in her ears. She looked at her watch.

She dialed Jim Daly's home number, got no answer, then tried her own number.

Cathy Lawes answered after one ring. "Thank goodness, it's you," the girl said. "I was about to leave. Ray just called."

"What?"

"Have you talked to anybody?"

"About what?"

"Mr. Daly."

"What about him?"

"Oh God, I'm sorry I have to tell you this. . . ."

Her conversation with Cathy was abruptly ended a moment later. Reed grabbed her, pistol in hand, and shoved her through the empty hall into an office.

The man who theoretically had just made her a millionaire turned in his chair and said, almost pleasantly, "Marilyn tells me you borrowed a notebook from my desk."

"What happened to Jim Daly?"

"I need the notebook back."

She marveled at how correct he looked sitting there, how unrumpled, even after what he had just done.

He picked up his telephone and punched an inside line. "Where are we, Mike? . . . Okay, just keep feeding. Hold some of it back until the contracts are signed."

He hung up. "Well, Bobbi. You're worth over two million dollars now. How does it feel?"

She was unable to answer.

"Decisions are being made fast now. I'm afraid I have to ask whether you're with me or not, Bobbi, and really, it's yes or no. If you are on board, you're at the beginning of a fantastic journey."

"Your daughter tried to kill herself tonight."

His eyes glistened. "My daughter was used in a very ugly way. If someone did that to your son, how would you respond?" He rotated back and forth slightly in the chair, his face recomposing in an oddly visionary expression. "I want you to think, Bobbi. Meditate. About this open data base Govind Shaw and his friends set in motion for the taxpayers." He reached out and with his fist popped one end of his keyboard, almost knocking it off the stand.

"Would you like to see what this program does?"

She was frozen, snakes under her skin.

"Would you like to play with it? See how it gets you more and more deeply involved by simple, crude carrots and sticks? It has no obligations, no ties, all it knows how to do is to probe for information. The 'intelligence' is patently thin if you've spent hours—" he popped the keyboard again with his fist, and spoke through his teeth—"and hours feeding it. But the rewards are hard to turn down. It's a window of opportunity, Bobbi, and for every one you take your file thickens. It has ever-increasing obligations from you and none toward you. It can make everything you've done *accessible*. It can open your file, you see. That's how the 'disincentives' work—I know that now.

"How would you like for your son to be an article of information in this thing? False information. What if it said to you, 'I will ruin your son. I will make his life something ugly and pitiable?' And Bobbi, it makes no difference to me whether it is truth or lies. It's a matter of total unconcern. 'I can offer data to whoever wants it and never even know I've done it, never care whether it's false or true, because I am untouchable, I have no ties, no obligations, no reason—of common decency, fear of retribution, no reason of *any* kind—not to. I am merely information, I am merely an exchange.' How would you feel if this thing treated you that way?"

"What your daughter did—"

"My daughter did *nothing*," McNear said, leaning over his desk.

"You did have Jim killed. And Mr. Cady. And the people who've worked for you for years—you sold them out."

Still leaning over his desk, he said, "No, I haven't, Bobbi. I've bought them out. There's a difference."

She felt a huge and ominous sadness, as if something had rearranged an essential part of her.

"Ben put a 'confession' in his letter—that's what he called it. This afternoon I finally got enough of it decoded to know that it's even more disgusting than I'd thought. I've spent a lot of time with this thing, you see. Trying to destroy it, trying to mask it—" His lip curled.

"Did she write it?"

"Of course not. He did it. He'd become a weird little man, and he'd found a way to multiply his revenge many times. Kill my daughter. Make up lies about her. Put our OS files into an open data base. Destroy me and destroy our plan."

Bobbi felt like she was floating away. She turned and looked at Reed, at his silencer, trying to come back to earth.

"But we've beat them. We have a foothold now. Within three years I'll have leveraged myself into a position of control over USI. Little Wayne McNear will take that company over and then he'll take it apart. It will all be done very nicely. Very neatly. All according to Hoyle."

He glanced at the screen, again puzzled, and picked up his phone. "Mike, where are you in the run? I'm not getting a menu. . . . No, it shouldn't be down until the run's made. . . . Don't worry about him. I'll go to his office after I sign the papers." He hung up and said to Reed, "Jeremy's still in his office. You should have gotten him out of here. Will you give me the notebook, please?"

She shook her head.

He stood up. "Get it from her," he told Reed. "I'll be back in a minute."

He left her there with Reed, who was aiming his pistol, casually, at her belly. "Where's the notebook?"

"So why'd you kill Jim Daly?"

"Where is it?"

"Tell me why you killed Jim and I'll tell you where the notebook is."

He came a step closer to her. "You aren't the one asking the questions, bitch. I am."

"You get off on it, don't you, Ron? That's the reason."

He slapped her across the face hard enough to numb one side of it, but she didn't fall down. "Want another one?"

"Sure, you ugly shit."

She went down this time, got up quickly. Her vision was swimming, but she was hyperconscious on adrenaline.

McNear returned, and she heard him say, angrily, "Something's wrong. . . . Come with me to Jeremy's. Bring her." Reed dragged her, stumbling, down the hall.

Reed was about to break down the door when Jeremy opened it, quietly. He looked afraid when he saw Bobbi's face and Reed's gun, but said nothing. Reed pushed her against the wall in a place where he could keep an eye on both her and Jeremy. Jeremy had a scared smirk on his face, watching Reed. He went back to his table and sat down. The room was dim, crowded by the four of them and Reed's pistol. Jeremy turned to one of his consoles. He made an entry, and somewhere in the maze of the room, a little melody came out of a speaker, the same Bobbi had heard less than an hour ago.

"I get a call from this guy, works for Panotel in Kansas City, he says a funny sound is being picked up all over the central states. I'm too busy to mess with it. I get another call from somebody in Chicago. It seems this thing is walking up and down the radio spectrum, being picked up all over the place. It hits a frequency, does a little tune, then moves on to a different frequency. I record and take it apart with a digital analyzer, set to telephone analogs. Try some straight transmission code on it . . ."

He rolled his chair around, looking up at McNear, then moved his arms around as if he didn't know where to put them. He made a little wince.

"It worked."

The room was silent except for the gentle whir of cooling motors.

"It took me forty-three minutes. It's a radio-band advertisement coming out of the Ball."

"For what?"

"A microwave transmission that's coming down at 23.76 gigs."

McNear looked at Jeremy with disbelief. "What do you mean?"

"I mean signals. Clear signals that probably fifty people out there somewhere are hacking right now. It's Mitze's letter to you."

"How do you know?"

"It's the same menu you showed us at your house, Wayne. It's coming in everywhere in the central United States. It's a big footprint. Our whole library, plus all of Mitze's . . . his personal documents. All uncoded."

"How much has come in?"

"All of it," Jeremy said. He was trembling. "It's on the second run-through already. It's looped."

McNear wavered and bumped into the pyramid of Coke cans against the wall behind him, knocking them all over the office. He started to pick up Jeremy's phone, then didn't. He said, as if to himself, "The Assembly's almost run. That'll shut it down."

"No, it won't," Jeremy said.

"What the hell are you talking about?"

"I already ran it. I thought that's what you wanted me to do." Jeremy shook his head. "Jesus. You guys hacked this thing, you set it up to blow us all out and leave us nothin. All of us who've worked with you. For you. I can't believe you'd do that."

"What do you mean you ran it? Nobody's been in the control room since the Assembly was lined up."

"I know you don't think I'm very good, Wayne, but surely you don't think I have to go into the control room to use the tape drives."

"Well, so what? That means the Ball is already shut down. When did you run it?"

"This afternoon, after it was all mounted and everybody left. Believe it or not, I thought I was helping," Jeremy said bitterly. "Mitze double-crossed you, Wayne. His Assembly worked all right, it cut off access, it crashed the Ball, all but one part of it. That part will stay on and running. The Codelog files. Your files. They're gonna transmit forever. Over and over again. Solar power, Wayne—it won't run out. And your daughter's confession is part of it."

McNear remained in the same stiff posture, as if he were about to be executed.

Bobbi started edging toward the door, and Reed immediately took a step closer and grabbed at her. She dodged, kneed him in the groin. He staggered sideways, his face twisting up in rage. When she tried to get outside, he caught her. "Oh, you made a *bad* mistake, little lady."

She pulled away and he smashed her against the wall so hard that she momentarily blacked out. The next thing she knew she was being hustled down the hall. A red exit sign appeared in her face and a door flew open.

In the parking lot he whacked her across the cheekbone with a gunbutt.

"Kick me again, bitch."

She looked up at him from the asphalt. "Love to, Ron." Again he hit her hard enough to make her black out once more.

McNear was standing in the red light of the exit sign. "Stop," he said, unconvincingly. "They're out there."

His next swing was low. Bobbi was beginning to wonder if she was going to make it alive to the place where he would kill her.

But still a little part of her mind was remarkably clear when she saw a big old Buick come gliding into the parking lot, her sight perfect, like a camera's eye, when he got out and started walking, then running toward her.

"Watch out, Ray!" she managed to say just as Reed pulled off a shot, downing him instantly. Quickly, he walked toward Ray, with the pistol held at six o'clock.

She hadn't seen the second car until it was parked, and the door came open.

"No!" she yelled, trying to get up. "Richard!"

Her son was stepping out. "Get back!" she screamed. Reed had stopped, confused by Richard's arrival.

"It's no use," McNear said weakly.

She tried to crawl but something didn't work. She couldn't move. Reed paused, looking at Richard, then lowered his pistol and took aim. It was then that Ray rolled over and with one shot that she would later learn entered Reed's upper chest close to his medallion knocked him over backward as if he had been swatted in the face by a two-by-four.

In the terrible silence that followed, Bobbi figured out how to stand up and walk. She was by Ray's side, saying, "Hon, are you okay?"

She repeated herself, and got in a position where she could see his face. His eyes were open. He smiled at her.

"Where'd he get you?"

"Nowhere. I was playing possum. Richard, come over here."

"Ray? Your finger?"

He sat up, grasping her with his better hand. "I left it back at the police station. Richard, get two ambulances out here. Why don't you sit down, Bob. You look like you just ran into a brick wall."

She did so—sat down on the parking lot beside him. Ray looked at McNear, who was still standing in the red light of the door. "I'm gonna stay with you here a minute, Bob, then I better take the boss—and Mr. Heyer, if he's here—to the drunk tank to see a friend of theirs."

EPILOGUE

It was late autumn before they could sit down together and really talk without feeling hassled by reporters, lawyers, medical problems (particularly Bobbi's jaw, which was a thirty-day headache before it decided to get better), and the ten thousand other unraveled strings left by the DataForm mess.

They sat at the kitchen table of their old house, which had been unoccupied for over a year. It was a chilly evening, and they'd lit the wall heater, dusted off the table, and were sharing a beer. They'd been talking about Sheriff Nagal, who was about to be indicted for conspiracy with the Tully gang. The sheriff, it turned out, had recommended the Tullys to Chief Warnke, who'd hired them for two different jobs—hauling the trailer and, later, killing Jack Cady. Nagal hadn't been directly involved in any of that, but he was damn well involved in protecting their stripyard operation. The shadowy topic of this conversation was whether Ray was going to run for sheriff, but he still had a peculiar reticence about discussing it directly.

The subject came around to Richard and Cathy. For reasons neither Bobbi nor Ray understood, the kids were cooling toward each other, just when Bobbi was learning to appreciate the girl. She was rough as a cob but she had pluck—the kind of girl who might grow up and do something.

Ray had been glancing at a newspaper article with a copy of Taylor McNear's supposed confession. It had appeared in several papers and weekly magazines despite efforts by prosecutors and the FBI to keep it out of the news. Oddly, he hadn't actually read it until now. It was supposed to be the hottest part of the case, the "shocking revelation," but he'd gotten the basic idea and somehow not been curious about the particular wording. FOUR BANKS REOPENED AS DF CASE GETS MORE BIZARRE, said the headline.

> . . . I did it, Daddy. I killed him. I took off my clothes and he took off his clothes and I did it to him in his chair, Daddy. We always did it in the chair that way. In the chair in the trailer. I know you and he were conspiring to take over USI, Daddy. You are very evil, Daddy. You are the most horrible person I know in the world, because you have no heart and you look at people only as parts of your Big Schemes. And I felt so sad, Daddy, I decided to end it all. I decided to kill him and kill me, Daddy, just for you.

"You don't think she wrote it," Ray said.

"I doubt it. She doesn't talk like that. If she did, she was pretty zonked out."

Bobbi got up and went to the kitchen window. The sun was setting, enveloping the big ash tree where Richard's swing had been in soft yellow light. . . . Images of him growing up, playing in the back yard. "What I don't understand is why McNear insisted on keeping her here. The girl was in hell."

Ray was looking at his shortened little finger. "She knew too much. He had to make sure she didn't talk."

Looking out the window, she shook her head. "The girl was out of her mind. She was giving herself shock treatments."

"A lot of them do that, they just don't all use electricity. . . ." He wiggled what was left of his little finger. "Maybe he loves her, too."

She frowned. That statement depressed her. "You'll have to re-define love for me, if that's a case of it. He'd gotten to the point of keeping her locked up, calling her insane. That's not any kind of love I know about."

Ray took a drink. "Yeah. Love's supposed to be plain and uncom-promised. That's what everybody says. . . ."

"Any time it gets that messed up I'll be glad to try to think up a different word for it."

She looked down the hallway into the back of the house, wondering if she could ever live here again. It was one of the reasons they'd come here—to make some decisions about the future—although neither of them had quite said as much. But her mind kept wandering back. "Why did Cindy McNear allow the girl to stay with him? Why didn't she fight him? She had the money to do it."

"Maybe she just gave up. Maybe he scared her. He was willing to go to any lengths."

"Well, she's got the girl now."

"Think she'll come around?"

"I think she will," Bobbi said. "If her mother will help her. I hope she takes her mother's last name so this doesn't follow her around like a skunk tied to her leg."

"What about the Heyer kid?"

"He's one of my jobs. I'm going to make damn sure the court understands what side he was on."

Ray looked at Bobbi with a curious little smile. "How much of this whole deal was Mr. Shaw and company's fault?"

"They keep saying in their public statements it was a bare prototype, but it isn't true. Not really. McNear and Heyer and Mitze just took it over and used it like it stood to blackmail them. Their trick was to use their own clients."

Ray put down his glass. "Sorry he didn't make you rich?"

She didn't see the humor. She was tired of thinking about it—especially tired of the way Jim always came into her thoughts, like a scorpion sting between her eyes.

"I know you're sick of this," he said. "Tell you what. Let's talk about it one more minute and then never talk about it again."

"Good luck," she said.

"Of our own volition and choice."

"Right. You're beginning to sound like the lawyers."

"Ain't it the truth." He got up and went to the kitchen wall clock, plugged it in, and sat back down. When the second hand went past twelve, he said, "Just tell me how anybody with enough gumption to get that much shit stirred up ever thought something like that would work."

Bobbi sighed. She took a final drink and set it down on the counter, looking outside again as the back yard moved into twilight. "He knew the business. He'd handled cases like it: executives scared because they let something like this get out of control, trying to buy their way out."

Ray nodded.

"It's the man I keep thinking about. . . ."

"What about him?"

"Oh, I don't know. He always acted like he was he was being picked on by . . . greater powers. Like he was the little guy, more sinned-against than sinning. Whole roomfuls of people came and believed him." She looked up. "I believed him."

"Yeah, well, Ray Wiel was part of it, too. He was just one sucker removed. Half this town was working for him. The man's a con artist, Bob. That's what they specialize in—roomfuls of people."

To her irritation, tears had come to her eyes. "I just can't stop thinking about Jim. Nothing I ever do, the rest of my life . . ."

He stood, walked over, and put his arms around her. "Jim Daly was a grown man, Bob. He made the decision to work there. We'll have to try and take care of Martha."

They stood there a minute, quiet.

"Oops," he said. "Time's up."

"Oh, Ray." Her face was against his shoulder. "What'd I ever do for you?"

"Well, let's see. . . . Hell, I can't think of anything." He held her out and looked her in the eyes. "Want to start today?"